OPERATION
ICE BREAKER

A Mac McDowell Mission

USS Teuthis Tracks through the Arctic

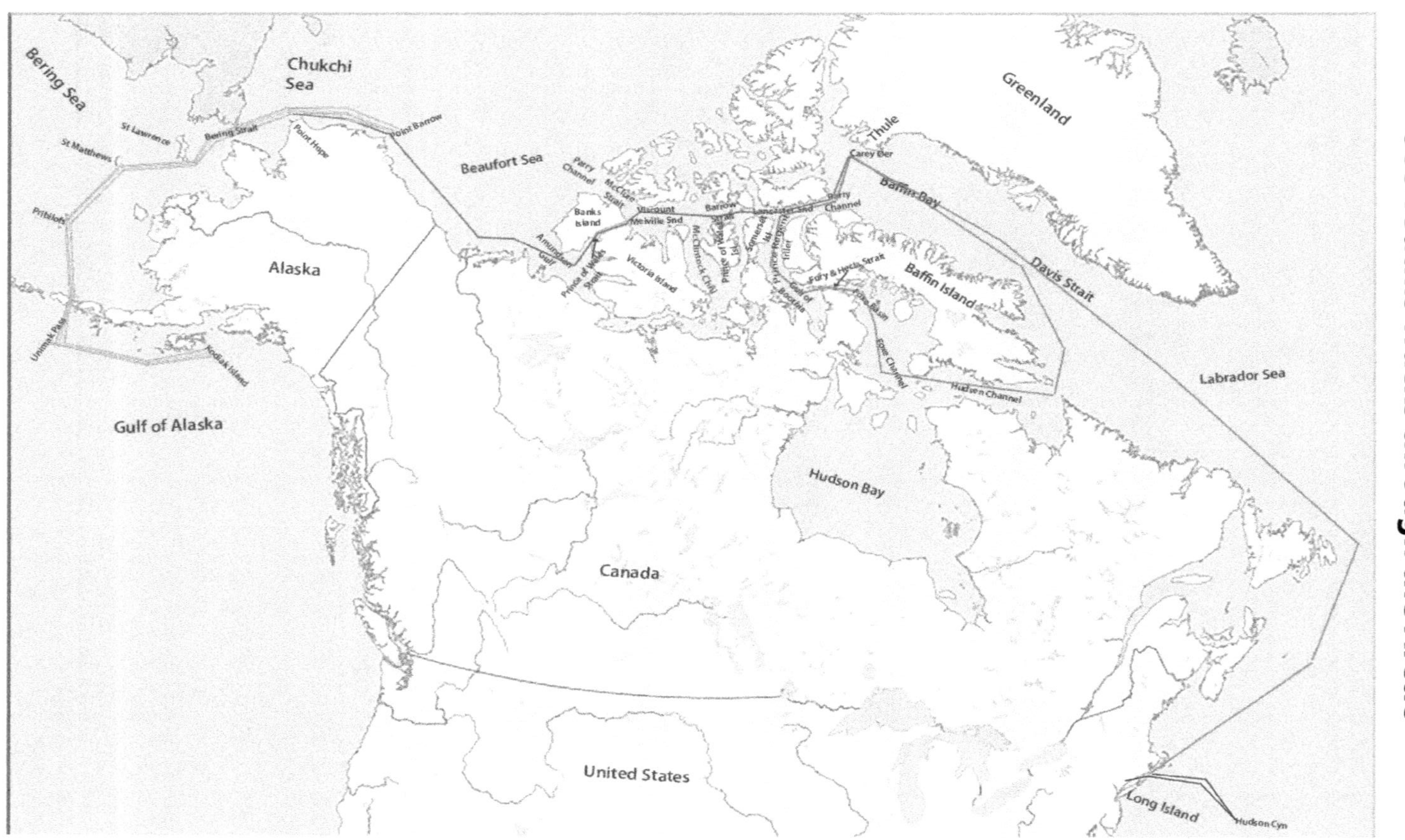

Praise for Operation Ice Breaker

Like its prequel, *Operation Ivy Bells*, *Operation Ice Breaker* shows what it's really like to live and work on a submarine deep beneath the ocean surface. During the Cold War, Lieutenant McDowell and the crew of the *USS Teuthis* secretly lay cable across the floor of the Atlantic and Arctic Oceans in order to track the movements of Soviet subs. Ultimately, the action builds to a dangerous encounter with divers from a Soviet submarine—an event with international consequences.

This is a novel about the real thing and real events, not traditional Hollywood drama. The author vividly captures what day-to-day existence was like on such a vessel, mixing long periods of boredom with perilous episodes of saturation diving and confrontations with the enemy. Especially appreciated are the humor, romance, vivid, accessible maps, and glossary of terms. The first two lighten and brighten the mood, and the last two enable the reader to follow the action more easily.

—Professor John B. Rosenman, Norfolk State University
Former Chairman of the Board, Horror Writers Association
Author of *The Inspector of the Cross Series*

Author Robert Williscroft has returned his attention to submarine thrillers in his latest adventure *Operation Ice Breaker*. The protagonist, Mac McDowell, and several of the lead characters were first introduced in *Operation Ivy Bells* (highly recommended), but this is a new stand-alone story. The *USS Teuthis* embarks on a covert mission in the far north. When she encounters Soviet subs, Mac leads his team into deadly battle. *Operation Ice Breaker* is more than a cat-and-mouse thriller with nail-biting action both above the ice sheets and in the icy depths beneath. The realism is unmatched as Williscroft draws upon his extensive experience in submarines and covert warfare.

Dave Edlund
USA Today bestselling
author of *The Peter Savage Series*

WOW!! Mac McDowell is back at it again with his team of saturation divers aboard a newly converted SSBN, specifically modified to support his intrepid divers under the Arctic Ice. Secrecy and stealth are the watchwords as they must covertly lay SOSUS arrays to close off the last remaining routes for Soviet submarines to reach open water away from NATO's prying ears. *USS Teuthis* goes up against the best subs in Russia's inventory, an *Alfa* and a *Sierra*, playing cat-and-mouse to break contact and accomplish the secret mission at all costs. Underwater knife fights with the Sierra's crew members under the ice as well as a giant squid-like creature while on sea trials spice a riveting tale of derring-do in the world's most unforgiving environment. I honestly could not put down this book once started, and dangling threads at the end entice the reader for the next saga, which can't come soon enough.

George W. Jackson, Captain USN (Ret.)
aka G. William Weatherly, author of
The Sheppard McCloud Naval Warfare Series

OPERATION ICE BREAKER

A Mac McDowell Mission

by

Robert G. Williscroft

STARMAN PRESS

Centennial, Colorado

Operation Ice Breaker: A Mac McDowell Mission
Copyright © 2025, 2020
by Robert G. Williscroft
All rights reserved

Starman Press

Email: rgw@RobertWilliscroft.com
Website: RobertWilliscroft.com

Edition 1.0 2020
Edition 2.0 2025

Cover art by Anik
Artwork by Robert G. Williscroft
Book design by Amit Dey
Covers by Stephen Geez

BISAC Subject Headings:
FIC032000 FICTION / War & Military
FIC031050 FICTION / Thrillers / Military
FIC036000 FICTION / Thrillers / Technological

Library of Congress Control Number: 2020912234

ISBN-13: 978-1-968367-22-0 Papercover
ISBN-13: 978-1-968367-21-3 Hardcover
ISBN-13: 978-1-968367-05-3 Ebooks
ISBN-13: 978-1-968367-23-7 Audiobook

Dedication

To "Kate," who inspired me.

Table of Contents

Foreword to the First Edition

by
Ed Offley

"The past is never dead. It's not even past."
—William Faulkner

In writing Operation Ice Breaker, the latest in his series featuring veteran U.S. Navy diver J.R. "Mac" McDowell, author Robert G. Williscroft on surface presents a fictional tale of Cold War submarine espionage from nearly a half-century ago. By itself, this gripping account of the Top Secret mission of the *USS Teuthis* (SSNR-2) into the frozen waters of the Canadian archipelago and its encounter with a Soviet *Alfa class* nuclear attack submarine, offers the reader a compelling sea story that—while fictional—presents a detailed, fascinating narrative of life at sea on a nuclear submarine, and the heart-stopping actions of deep-sea navy divers at work deep below on the seabed.

But it is much more than that.

A veteran of both the Submarine Service and the U.S. Navy's deep submergence systems program (translation: underwater espionage), Williscroft presents the reader a you-are-there account of the men, equipment and precise tactics that have been employed by the navy for more than six decades in some of the most daring and risky operations against Cold War adversaries like the Soviet Union, and potential foes in the unstable era that followed the collapse of the USSR in 1991. Since 1965, the U.S. Navy has operated four nuclear submarines dedicated to deploying deep-sea divers on these dangerous missions. To many Americans, the names *USS Halibut* (SSN-587), *USS Seawolf* (SSN-575), *USS Parche* (SSN-683), and *USS Jimmy Carter* (SSN-23), may mean little or nothing. To veteran sailors—and especially submariners past and present—they represent the true tip of the navy's sword.

The U.S. Navy quite understandably has remained tight-lipped about this particular chapter of its long history at sea. But a telling revelation came in the year 2000 when two prominent non-submariners attended a veterans' reunion of the *Parche* in Bremerton, Washington. Former CIA Director (and future Secretary of Defense) Robert Gates, and world-famous technothriller novelist Tom Clancy praised the submariners for their unheralded success. Clancy was effusive, saying,

"The point of the (U.S. Navy's) lance killed the (Soviet) dragon… and you were the point of the lance." Gates echoed his companion, praising the veterans for all their efforts, where "every mission (was) a life-and-death mission…. I know who you are, and I know what you did, and I am honored to be here with you tonight."

As the world struggles with a global pandemic and resulting economic distress at the mid-point of 2020, other tides are running: The revitalized Russian navy is operating with renewed aggressiveness throughout the world, even as its American counterpart continues to build and deploy modern Virginia-class attack submarines to keep the military balance. Frequent news reports tell of American submarines operating in the ever-dangerous waters of the South China Sea claimed by China as territorial waters.

The details may be different, but the basic elements of *Operation Ice Breaker* present more than a glimpse into the past; they also provide a realistic look into the present, and future, Great Game being played out at sea by American submariners.

—Ed Offley
Panama City Beach, Florida
September 2020

Ed Offley is author of Scorpion Down: Sunk by the Soviets, Buried by the Pentagon—the Untold Story of the USS Scorpion, and several books about the Battle of the Atlantic, most recently The Burning Shore: How Hitler's U-boats Brought World War II to America.

Foreword to the Second Edition

The first edition was published by Fresh Ink Group. Unfortunately, the company went out of business in April 2025, so this is a third edition, unchanged except for the publisher identification.

Robert G. Williscroft
Centennial, Colorado
April 2025

Acknowledgements

Several people contributed to the creation of this book.

My wonderful wife, Jill, pored over each chapter with her discerning engineer's eye. She kept my timeline honest and made sure that regular readers could understand fully the arcane details of nuclear submarine and saturation diving operations.

Ed Offley, who wrote the Foreword, applied his lifetime of experience writing about the Navy to edit this story.

USA Today bestselling technothriller author Dave Edlund and technothriller author and diving scientist John Clarke reviewed the manuscript from their unique perspectives, providing helpful input.

Hard science fiction author Alastair Mayer reviewed the manuscript and offered his scientific, engineering, and editorial insight, and military writer and former submarine commander George Jackson supplied his unique insight.

Others have contributed with their comments and observations, and I thank them. You know who you are.

It goes without saying that any remaining omissions, errors, and mistakes fall directly on my shoulders.

Robert G. Williscroft, PhD
Centennial, Colorado
September 2020

USS Teuthis Organizational Chart

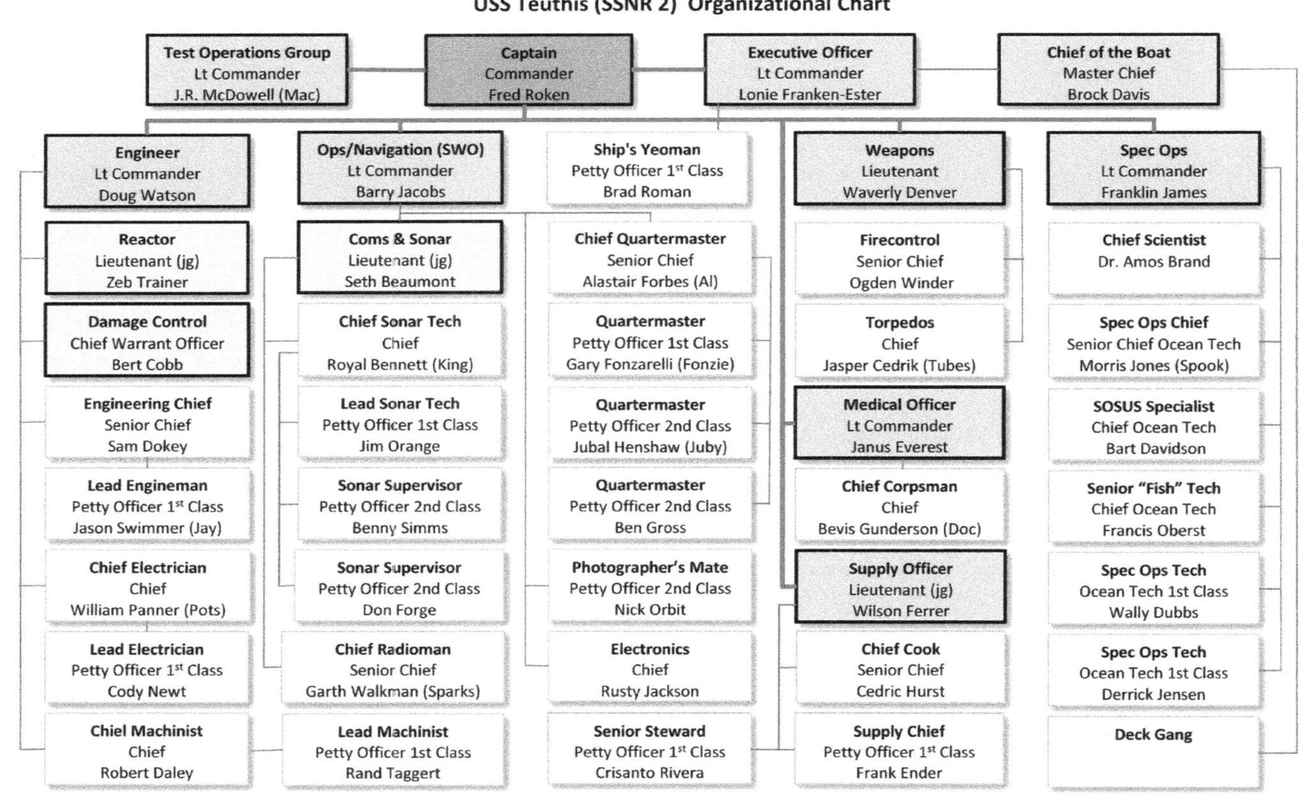

Cast of Characters

USS Teuthis
(See Organizational Chart)

Test Operations Group (TOG)
Lt. Cmdr. J.R. McDowell (Mac)—
    Officer-in-Charge (OIC) TOG (Narrator)
Master Chief Hamilton Comstock (Ham)—Master Saturation
    Diver—Came from Experimental Diving Unit and Man-in-
    the-Sea Program—Served with Ivy Bells
Chief William Fisher (Bill)—Master Saturation Diver—
    Sonar Tech— Served with Ivy Bells
Petty Officer 1st Class Harry Blackwell—Saturation Diver;
    qualified Dive Console Operator—Electronics Tech—
    Served with Ivy Bells
Petty Officer 1st Class James Tanner (Jimmy)—Saturation Div-
    er; qualified Dive Console Operator—Battlefield medic turned
    saturation diver— Served with Ivy Bells
Petty Officer 2nd Class Melvin Ford (Whitey)—Saturation Div-
    er; qualified Dive Console Operator—Quartermaster— Served
    with Ivy Bells
Petty Officer 2nd Class Wlodek Cslauski (Ski)—Saturation Diver;
    qualified Dive Console Operator—Submariner (Engineman)
    turned saturation diver—Served with Ivy Bells
Petty Officer 2nd Class Jeremy Romain (Jer)—Saturation Diver;
    qualified Dive Console Operator—Submariner (Auxiliaryman)
    turned saturation diver—Served with Ivy Bells
Petty Officer 2nd Class Jacob Palmer (Jake)—Saturation Diver;
    qualified Dive Console Operator—Submariner (Electronics
    Tech) turned saturation diver; Recent graduate of saturation dive
    class

USS Teuthis **Medical**
Dr. Janus Everest
Unnamed Corpsman

USS Teuthis **Deck Gang**

Seaman Joe Spanker (Spanky)—Topside Watch,
    Lookout / Helmsman / Planesman
Seaman Fred Jackson (Jack)—Topside Watch,
    Lookout / Helmsman / Planesman
Seaman Jake Boller—Topside Watch,
    Lookout / Helmsman / Planesman
Seaman Jeremiah Walker (Jerry)—Topside Watch,
    Lookout / Helmsman / Planesman
Seaman Todd Bennett—Topside Watch,
    Lookout / Helmsman / Planesman
Seaman Steve Decker—Topside Watch,
    Lookout / Helmsman / Planesman
Seaman Josh Raker—Topside Watch,
    Lookout / Helmsman / Planesman
Seaman Julius Hoppenstein (Hoppy)—Topside Watch,
    Lookout / Helmsman / Planesman
Seaman Fritz Able—Topside Watch,
    Lookout / Planesman
Seaman Greg Patterson—Topside Watch,
    Lookout / Planesman
Seaman Billy-Bob Yokum—Topside Watch,
    Lookout / Planesman
Seaman Randolph Zimmerman (Zimm)—Topside Watch,
    Lookout / Planesman

DIA Team

Wyatt Cook—Senior DIA *Alfa* specialist—In charge of DIA team
Matthias Hart—DIA Soviet sonar specialist
Gilbert Edwards—DIA Soviet submarine reactor specialist
Kendrick Long—DIA Soviet submarine hull specialist
Sergyi Andreev—Soviet defector; saturation diver

Submarine Development Group One (SubDevGruOne)

Captain Dan Richardson—Commander, Submarine Development
    Group One

Mystic **(DSRV 2)**
Lt. Robert Taggert—Chief Pilot
Lt. James Deckhart—Second Pilot
Senior Chief Sonar Tech Gaspard Abelé—*Mystic* technician
Electronics Technician 1st Class Parker Flanger—
    Mystic technician

Soviet *Alfa* Submarine
Unknown Soviet Officer—Commanding Officer

Soviet Submarine *Carp*
Leonid Volkov—Captured diver

Kodiak, Alaska
Master Pilot Sven Jakobsen—Woman's Bay channel pilot
Master Mariner Jack Petrikoff—Kodiak fishing boat skipper
Katherine Perry (Kate)—Widow of CG Lt.j.g. Josh Perry,
    killed in rescue of Petrikoff

***Teuthis* Watch Sections**

Section One—0600 to 1200
Deck—Lt. Cmdr. J.R. McDowell (Mac)
JOOD—Lt.j.g. Zeb Trainer
Dive—Chief Jasper Cedrik (Tubes)
COW—Senior Chief Sam Dokey
Nav—Senior Chief Alastair Forbes (Al)
Fairwater/Helm—Seaman Joe Spanker (Spanky)
Stern/Lookout—Seaman Fred Jackson (Jack)
Stern/Lookout—Seaman Fritz Abelé
Sonar—Chief Royal Bennett (King)

Section Two—1200 to 1800
Deck—Chief Warrant Officer Bert Cobb
JOOD—Lt.j.g. Seth Beaumont
Dive—Chief Ocean Tech Bart Davidson

COW—Senior Chief Ogden Winder (Oggy)
Nav—Petty Officer 1st Class Gary Fonzarelli (Fonzie)
Fairwater/Helm—Seaman Jake Boller
Stern/Lookout—Seaman Jeremiah Walker (Jerry)
Stern/Lookout—Seaman Greg Patterson
Sonar—Petty Officer 1st Class Jim Orange

Section Three—1800-2400
Deck—Lt. Cmdr. Barry Jacobs (Nav)
JOOD—Lt. Waverly Denver (Weps)
Dive—Chief Ocean Tech Francis Oberst
COW—Chief William Panner (Pots)
Nav—Petty Officer 2nd Class Ben Gross
Fairwater/Helm—Seaman Todd Bennett
Stern/Lookout—Seaman Steve Decker
Stern/Lookout—Seaman Billy-Bob Yokum
Sonar—Petty Officer 2nd Class Benny Simms

Section Four—2400-0600
Deck—Lt. Cmdr. Doug Watson (Eng)
JOOD—Lt. Cmdr. Franklin James
Dive—Chief Rusty Jackson
COW—Senior Chief Garth Walkman (Sparks)
Nav—Petty Officer 2nd Class Jubal Henshaw (Juby)
Fairwater/Helm –Seaman Josh Raker
Stern/Lookout—Seaman Julius Hoppenstein (Hoppy)
Stern/Lookout—Seaman Randolph Zimmerman (Zimm)
Sonar—Petty Officer 2nd Class Don Forge

USS Teuthis—Cross Section

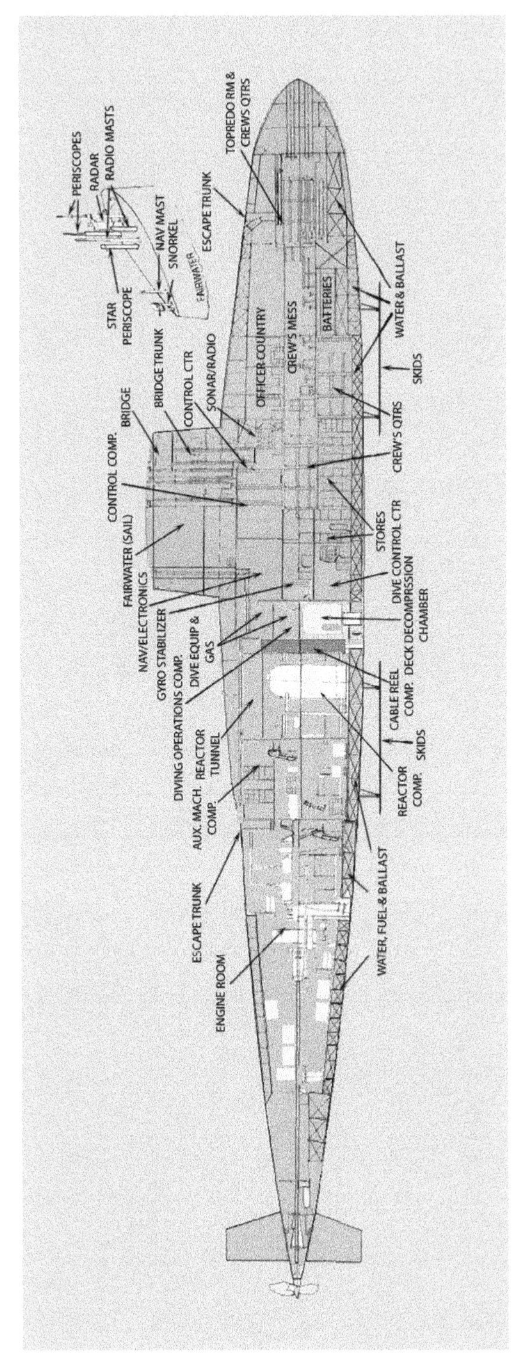

USS Teuthis—Cutaway

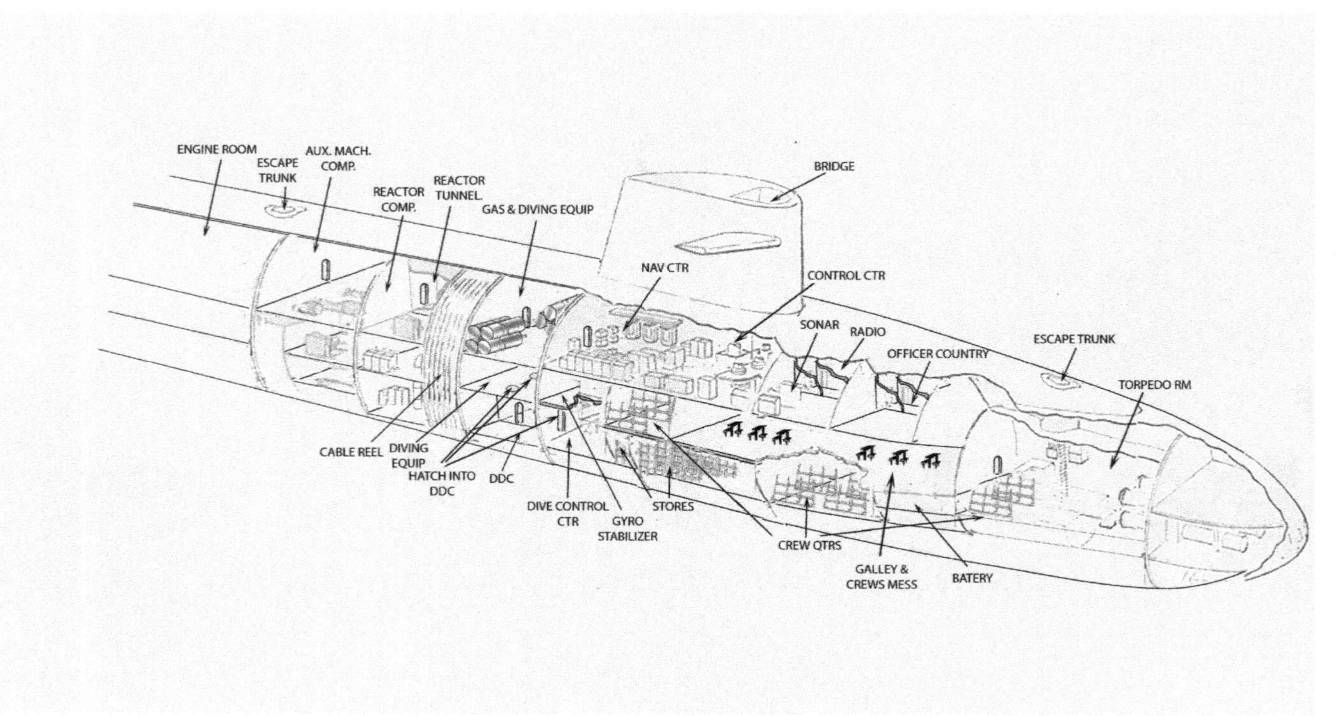

OPERATION ICE BREAKER

A Mac McDowell Mission

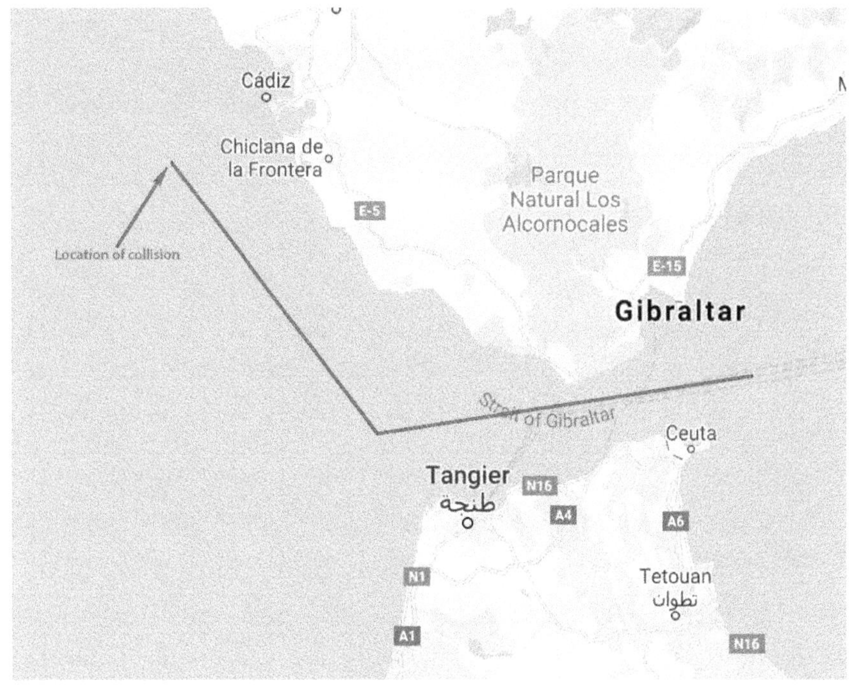

Off Cádiz, Spain

PROLOG

U.S. MISSILE SUB SUBMERGED—OFF CÁDIZ, SPAIN, EARLY 1970s

"Lieutenant McDowell, Sir…My planes are jammed at full dive!"

"Diving Officer, get a handle on that!" I ordered while checking my depth. Three hundred feet and dropping. I was doing twenty knots—depth was increasing fast. The stern planes frozen at full dive caused the 425-foot-long fleet ballistic missile sub to pitch down by the bow twenty-five degrees.

"Stern planes are still jammed!" My Diving Officer, Lieutenant junior grade (Lt.j.g.) Dick Franconi said. "Manual bypass doesn't solve the problem."

"Chief of the Watch…" I said.

3

"Working on it," Master Chief George Sedrick said. "Sonofa-bitch isn't responding!"

I checked the depth. "All stop!" I ordered as the sub passed 500 feet. "Back full!" Maybe I could shake it loose—whatever it was.

As the sub began to shudder from the reverse turns, the Captain charged out of his stateroom in his skivvies. "What the fuck's going on, Mac?"

I briefed him quickly as we passed 600 feet. "All stop!" I ordered. "Chief…?"

"Still jammed, Sir."

"Pump all forward tanks to sea!" I ordered. Perhaps I could bring the bow up that way. "Full rise on the fairwater planes! Try to get us level." We still had some forward motion, so that might help. I punched the Sonar intercom. "Give me your contacts, Sonar."

"Clear three-sixty, Conn. We had a tug off the starboard bow a half hour ago, but he's gone now."

Seven hundred feet.

"Get the Captain's jumpsuit from his stateroom," I told the messenger. Turning to the fairwater Planesman who controlled the fairwater planes, the rudder, and the engine order telegraph, I ordered, "Ahead one third!"

The Captain and I watched the bubble. We were still down about fifteen degrees. As the screw took a bite, the bow dropped another four degrees. "Ahead slow—make bare steerageway! Chief…pump water from all tanks!"

As the Captain donned his jumpsuit, a loud screech penetrated the hull from somewhere aft. A second later, the Control Center sound-powered phone warbled. With a nod, the Captain indicated I should answer it.

"EOOW here…something's scraping along the port hull back here. Making a hell-of-a-noise."

"Yeah, Jer…We hear it up here. Any ideas?"

"Nada, Mac, no fucking idea."

"Passing one thousand feet, Sir!" The Chief of the Watch announced.

"Can you free up the stern planes?" I asked the EOOW.

"They're jammed tight. Never seen anything like it," Lt. Jerry Dunston said. He was the Reactor Control Assistant—number two in the Engineering Department and the current Engineering-Officer-of-the-Watch. "Nothing we can do here right now, Mac, nothing."

"Passing eleven-hundred-fifty feet!" Master Chief Sedrick announced. "Tanks are dry…we're still headed down."

About a minute passed.

"Passing test depth, thirteen hundred feet."

Around us, the sub creaked loudly as the hull compressed from the extreme outside pressure. I looked at the skipper. "You have the watch, Mac," he said, "and you're running out of options. You know what to do."

I picked up the 1MC mike and looked at the skipper again. He smiled grimly and nodded. I was glad he was at my side ready to counter anything stupid I might do, but it was pretty clear the skipper wanted me to do it.

"Sound the collision alarm! Emergency blow all main ballast!"

A three-second rising sweep-tone filled the sub. Immediately after that, high-pressure air forcing its way into the ballast tanks surrounding the bow and stern drowned out every other sound.

"Passing fourteen hundred feet!" Master Chief Sedrick announced. "Slowing…"

The skipper and I stood quietly on the raised platform of the Conn, watching the depth gauge as the bow lifted to nearly level.

"Passing twelve hundred feet!" Master Chief Sedrick announced.

"Secure the blow!" I ordered as the sub continued its rise.

As the sound of rushing air subsided, the three-second rising sweep-tone of the collision alarm once again filled the sub.

"Passing nine hundred feet," Master Chief Sedrick announced, "rising fast!"

"Sonar, you got anything?" I asked over the intercom.

"Negative, Conn. Too much sound. I'm deaf."

"Secure the collision alarm," the skipper told me. Then he reached for the 1MC mike. "This is the Captain. We are on an uncontrolled ascent to the surface. We don't know what's above us, so grab hold of something and hang on!"

SURFACED—OFF CÁDIZ, SPAIN

It seemed to take forever, but in actuality, it took only about a minute. One moment we were rising like a skyscraper elevator, and the next, we slammed into something and stopped dead, surrounded by the awful sound of shrieking, tearing metal.

I tried raising the attack periscope, but it didn't move. The skipper tried the navigation scope, got it to rise about a foot, and that was it.

"Mac, go to the Bridge and see what's going on," the skipper told me. "Captain's got the Conn," he announced to the Control Room personnel as I donned a headset with boom-mike and started up the ladder leading to the Bridge.

I opened the lower trunk hatch. It swung up into the trunk. "Trunk's dry," I announced to the Control Room. I climbed the rest of the way and cracked the upper hatch. "Just a few drops of water," I announced as I let the spring open it all the way. I squinted into the bright noon sun. "Conn, Bridge," I said over the circuit, "it looks like we surfaced directly beneath something—a barge maybe. I can't tell for sure. Whatever we struck must have sunk." I scanned around the surfaced sub, gently rocking in the nearly calm sea off Cádiz, clearly visible to the northeast. "There's a tug two hundred yards off the port bow. A guy on the stern is chopping frantically at a steel tow hawser. It's stretched taut pulling down the tug's stern." I watched for several seconds. "The hawser just parted…disappeared below the surface immediately. The tug's on an even keel. Now the guy is screaming bloody murder, shaking his fists at us."

"I'm sending lookouts to the Bridge," the skipper said in my ears, "and the photographer."

"There's more," I said. "Two missile hatches are sprung, and the Bridge is pretty much a twisted mess."

"The screw and rudder work," the skipper said. "You got the Conn. Keep us away from anything else, but stay as close to where you are as possible. I'm on my way to the Bridge."

ATLANTIC SUBMARINE FORCE HEADQUARTERS— NORFOLK, VIRGINIA—TWO MONTHS LATER

It was a formal hearing—just the skipper and me. It seems the tug was towing an old WWII Victory Ship to a Mediterranean destination to be scrapped. The tug went DIW (that's dead in the water for you non-navy types), and the Victory ship drifted up on the tug. Sonar didn't hear anything because the tug had shut down its engines, and the Victory ship didn't have any. The steel hawser catenary dropped down 300 feet and wedged between our port stern planes and the sub's hull. That caused the hydraulics system to force the planes to full dive and keep them there. When we emergency-surfaced, we did so directly under the Victory ship, piercing its hull with the ice-hardened submarine sail, and sinking her. It was an unfortunate accident with no assignment of fault. That was the official finding of the Navy inquiry.

The skipper received a special commendation for saving the billion-dollar ballistic missile submarine with no loss of life, and I was given an official pat on the back and the opportunity to choose my next duty assignment. I chose the Man-in-the-Sea Program, not having any idea what it was really all about. I ended up as the Officer-in-Charge of a team of saturation divers. We shipped out on the *USS Halibut* for a highly classified mission that changed the course of the Cold War (as related in my account, *Operation Ivy Bells*).

MARE ISLAND NAVAL SHIPYARD—VALLEJO, CALIFORNIA—FIVE YEARS LATER

And that brings us to the present. Following the secret award ceremony in the Mare Island Rodman Theater described in *Operation Ivy Bells*, Defense Secretary John Lehman's aide motioned for me to approach his boss.

"We have a special assignment for you, Lieutenant Commander McDowell."

"Sir?" I said.

"That's right," Lehman said. You are herewith promoted to Lieutenant Commander. In sixty days, you, and in thirty days, your team will report for temporary duty to the Commanding Officer, *USS Teuthis* (SSNR-2), at General Dynamics Electric Boat Division in Groton, Connecticut." He looked left and right, and continued quietly, "This assignment is Top Secret/SCI.[1] Everything, including the vessel name, is classified. You and your team will be briefed on arrival." He shook my hand firmly. "Good luck, Commander!"

---

1 Sensitive Compartmented Information.

PART ONE

Carey Øer

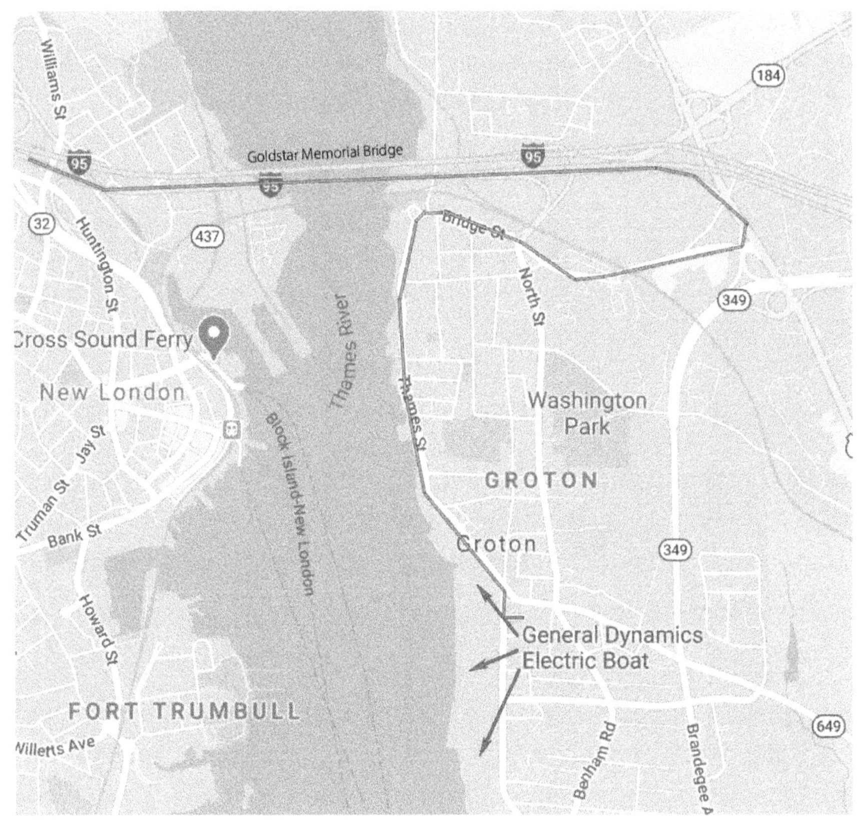

Goldstar Memorial Bridge to Electric Boat

CHAPTER ONE—*USS TEUTHIS*

GENERAL DYNAMICS ELECTRIC BOAT—GROTON, CONNECTICUT

I had pushed my red Vette from Vallejo across America's heartland for over 3,000 miles. Nice trip. Beautiful scenery. Even met a fun gal in Cheyenne. But I was glad finally to be crossing the Gold Star Memorial Bridge from New London to Groton. Down along the west bank of the Thames, New London's Winthrop Point pushed its way into the river, and ahead of me a bit to the south, General Dynamics Electric Boat dominated the river's eastern shore. An unusual fog bank blocked my view of the Groton Submarine Base to the north, but I knew where it was because I had spent a lot of time there learning how to be an enlisted submariner and later on the commissioned side of the business. It was almost like coming home.

A high overcast covered the October sky, and Interstate 95 was slick with fresh rain. The rain had stopped, however, and I had the top down and the collar of my fleece-lined flight jacket up around my chin. As I crested the Gold Star Memorial Bridge, I scanned southward. The morning river fog was dissipating, and in the southern sky, the late morning sun broke through. A shaft of light seemed to illuminate the Electric Boat assembly building about a mile to the south. For a moment, I thought I saw my new home, the *Teuthis*, floating in a slip, tied between two wharves projecting into the Thames River from that large structure.

I've got to tell you a bit about how *Teuthis* came to be. That boomer I served on, the one I emergency-surfaced right under the Victory ship, came here to EB for repairs and overhaul. Submarine Development Group One (SUBDEVGRPONE)—the Navy's top secret unit for underwater operations including espionage missions—got wind of the planned overhaul and conversion upgrading its loadout from the old Polaris to the new Poseidon missiles, which increased the number of warheads from three to ten per missile. Captain Dan Richardson (yeah, he got his bird) who had command of SUBDEVGRPONE, twisted the right arms. Instead of the damaged boomer undergoing repairs and upgrades for the new SLBMs, Richardson came up with funding to carry out a genuinely radical overhaul. Instead of relying on a makeshift old submarine near the end of its life cycle for his special operations, Richardson got himself a relatively modern nuke specifically modified and outfitted for deep-sea operations employing saturation diving.

✳

I took the first exit from Interstate 95 and whipped around to Thames Street along the river. I headed south for about a mile and pulled left into the EB parking lot. I had driven past this motley collection of buildings, shops, wharves, and piers, but had never been inside the compound. I put my top up, grabbed my orders, and crossed Thames Street to the main gate. My khaki uniform and ID card got me entry and directions to the *Teuthis* berth toward the north end of the complex.

I stepped onto the wharf, not knowing quite what to expect. Subs of the *Lafayette* class all look alike. Basically, they were *Skipjack*-class fast-attack subs with a 130-foot missile compartment stuck between the Operations and Reactor Compartments. *Teuthis* started out as a regular *Lafayette* class. Now, EB had removed the Missile Compartment with its damaged hatches and replaced it with a ten-foot Diving Operations Compartment (DOC) and a seven-foot Cable Reel Compartment (CRC)—together, giving the boat a true Special Operations capability.

From where I stood, *Teuthis* was indistinguishable from a *Skipjack* fast-attack boat—a bit longer, but that wasn't obvious. She was floating bow-out in a slip between two wide wharves with lines to each. The slip could easily have held three other subs. It was closed across the river end with a large, steel pontoon. A single topside watchstander guarded the spidery brow that stretched from the wharf to the sub's port side. He had a small guard shack to protect him from inclement weather.

I walked along the wharf toward the brow. The river fog had cleared, and the sun was high in the sky directly across the river, blocked by a bank of white clouds. Three seagulls swooped over the water just outside the slip endcap, skreeing and looking for flotsam coming down the river. As I reached the brow, the sun broke through the cloud bank so that the entire wharf, slip, and the sub it contained were bathed in bright pre-noon sunlight.

I walked up the brow, turned right to salute the flag on the stern, and then turned to salute the Topside Watch.

"Lieutenant Commander J.R. McDowell, reporting for duty. Request permission to come aboard."

"Seaman Joe Spanker, Sir. The COB is on his way topside." He was thin and tall, almost too tall for sub-service.

The Chief of the Boat (COB) emerged from the forward deck hatch, slipped on his fore-'n-aft cap, and strode toward me, hand outstretched.

"Brock Davis, Sir. Welcome aboard!" He stepped back and saluted. He was grizzled, medium height, fit, and sported a well-groomed handlebar mustache. "We heard rumors about you and your guys. We look forward to serving with you."

I followed him down the forward hatch into the Torpedo Room and then aft through the Crew's Mess, and up a narrow stairwell to the forward end of the Operations Center. We reversed direction, passed Sonar on the right, and the Radio Shack on the left into Officer's Country. First stop, Yeoman Brad Roman's cubby on the left, where I dropped my transfer orders and records. I stuck my head into Lieutenant Commander (Lt. Cmdr.) Lonie Franken-Ester's stateroom/office. I knew the sub's executive officer from the *Halibut*, where he had run Spec Ops.

The COB knocked on the skipper's cabin.

"Enter." Commander Fred Roken said.

The COB opened the door, came to attention, and said, "Cap'n, Lieutenant Commander Mac McDowell, Sir."

The Captain rose to his feet, his six-foot frame nearly filling the deck-to-overhead space, and held out his hand.

"Mac, nice to see you. Welcome aboard!"

He swept a hand through his sparse sandy hair and indicated his red Naugahyde couch. "Take a load off." He smiled briefly. "I understand you were aboard *Teuthis* during the collision?"

"More than that, Skipper, I was driving her."

"You'll have to give me the details. So, you qualified on this boat before the overhaul?"

"Yes, Sir. My first officer quals."

"You're familiar with what was changed?"

"Pretty much. The missile compartment has been replaced by the dive ops section and the Cable Reel Compartment," I said. "The reactor has been refueled, some of the older machinery have been replaced, and we got a new BQQ-2 sonar suite and some upgraded torpedoes."

"How long will you take to get up to speed on the new stuff?"

"By the time we get underway, I should think."

"Good!' He noted that the operations officer, Lt. Cmdr. Barry Jacobs, was the SWO.[2] I'll have him put you on the watchbill." The skipper unhooked his phone handset, dialed a number, and spoke

---

2   Senior Watch Officer

quietly into the handset, then hung up. "Petty Officer Rivera will get you settled in your stateroom."

Moments later, there was a knock on the door. Petty Officer Crisanto Rivera opened the door. He was a Filipino, a couple of inches shorter than me, with slightly longish, neatly trimmed black hair and displaying a professional smile. "Please accompany me, Commander McDowell," he said in flawless, unaccented English.

I shared my stateroom with two other officers, Jacobs, and his Communications and Sonar Officer, Lt.j.g. Seth Beaumont. As senior officer, Barry got the middle bunk, Seth got the bottom, and I got the top.

TEST OPERATIONS GROUP—*USS TEUTHIS*

If you read my previous mission account, *Operation Ivy Bells*, you know all about TOG—the Test Operations Group. We were initially formed to tap Soviet underwater communication cables in the Sea of Okhotsk. I think TOG got its odd name because of the overriding security associated with Ivy Bells. In any case, we were stuck with it.

Our unit at this time consisted of a well-trained group of saturation divers with me as Officer-in-Charge. Master Chief Hamilton Comstock, my Master Saturation Diver (whom we called Ham), was responsible for the divers and all the dives. Ham originally served with the Experimental Diving Unit at the Naval Support Activity—Panama City on the Florida Panhandle. He had been picked up for Ivy Bells and stayed on for Ice Breaker.

I lost Chief Petty Officer Jack Meredith, who was Ham's understudy on *Halibut*. He had moved on to a Master Saturation Diver position in SUBDEVGRPONE. The remaining six men were still with me. Bill Fisher made Chief, and Harry Blackwell and Jimmy Tanner made First-class rank. Melvin Ford (Whitey), Wlodek Cslauski (Ski), and Jeremy Romain (Jer) were still senior Second-class Petty Officers. I also had a new guy, Electronics Technician 2nd Class Jacob Palmer. Jake was an electronics genius and one of the sharpest guys on my team. This would be his first operational "sat dive" assignment.

*

As on the *Halibut,* we were assigned to *Teuthis* as TDY—temporary duty. For my team members, this meant their only duties were to become totally familiar with and maintain the sub's dive system. Since all saturation dive systems are basically similar, this was not a huge task. The most essential thing once they had wrapped their heads around this new system was to test it thoroughly during sea trials.

For all practical purposes, *Teuthis* was a new submarine. Virtually all the non-engineering enlisted personnel were new, which meant each of them had been busy on quals since they first stepped aboard. Over half the engineering guys were carry-overs, which aided immensely in the engineering spaces overhaul of the sub. The Engineer, Lt. Cmdr. Doug Watson, was a carryover from before as were the Damage Control Assistant (DCA) Chief Warrant Officer Bert Cobb and Lt. Cmdr. Jacobs as Navigator and Operations Officer.

And then there was me. I was the former Assistant Weapons Officer on the boomer version. This meant I knew everything about the torpedo and Polaris missile systems. And since I was a qualified Officer of the Deck, I had a solid knowledge of all the other ship's systems as well. On *Teuthis,* the missiles were gone, but the torpedo systems were virtually unchanged, except for the newer torpedoes. Functionally, I was fully qualified on *Teuthis,* which the skipper had alluded to when we talked briefly upon my arrival.

So, Eng, DCA, Nav, and I were the initially qualified watch officers. Weps, Lt. Waverly Denver, was fully qualified on two previous fast-attacks, so he would join the qualified list in a hurry. Special Operations Officer Lt. Cmdr. Franklin James had three previous fast-attack tours under his belt, but he had been away for a year getting his Master's in Marine Physics at MIT, so he had some catch-up quals before he could join the list. That left Lt.j.g. Zeb Trainer, the Reactor Officer, who was fresh out of Nuclear Power School, and Lt.j.g. Seth Beaumont, the Coms/Sonar officer, fresh out of Communications Officer School. They both had a solid year's work ahead before they would qualify as Officer of the Deck (OOD), and on top of that, Zeb had to qualify as Engineering Watch Officer first. No movies or card games for these two for quite a while.

USS TEUTHIS—GENERAL DYNAMICS EB DIVISION

Our team was part of a larger crew living aboard and operating a nuclear-powered submarine. It is a world that takes getting used to. Basically, a nuke sub is a long pressure cylinder with rounded, tapered ends. The narrower bow and stern are wrapped with a thin outer skin that covers ballast tanks between the skin and the pressure hull; these tanks are open to the sea at the bottom. Each has a series of large valves at the top. When the ballast tanks are filled with air, the sub floats; when they are filled with water, the sub sinks.

The forward part of the sub contains living quarters for the officers and crew, messing spaces, torpedoes and the mechanisms for loading and firing them, banks of emergency batteries, and the Control Center for operating and fighting the sub. The after part of the sub contains the reactor, machinery spaces, and the engine room. The pressure hull is made of 3½-inch-thick HY-80 steel, reinforced every two feet with circular frames. The individual spaces are separated by HY-80 steel bulkheads, creating watertight compartments. They are the Bow, Control, Reactor, Machinery, and Engine Room Compartments. Missile subs have the additional Missile Compartment between the Control and Reactor Compartments.

After the *Teuthis* in its previous life as a missile boat had crashed into the Victory ship off Spain, EB engineers had drastically changed its interior configuration, removing the missile compartment, and adding the two replacement compartments. A special feature of the ten-foot-long Diving Operations Compartment filled the bottom third of its space. Here, a Deck Decompression Chamber (DDC) featured three pressure airlocks that gave divers access to the ocean through their inward opening hatches. Each lock also had a separate upper hatch providing access to the interior of the submarine. Normally, only the port "Egress Lock" was used for divers operating outside the hull. This airlock contained umbilicals that passed breathing gas and hot water for maintaining body heat. In addition to hot-water suits, this small chamber also contained Unisuits, Mark 11 breathing rigs, Kirby-Morgan helmets, and miscellaneous diving equipment. The overhead hatches were used to transfer equipment into and out of the DDC locks when they were not pressurized. Hatches between each of the locks also allowed internal passage between the three. Figure 1—Kirby-Morgan Superlite 17 Diving Helmet

Normal entry to the DDC was through a hatch into the starboard lock, called the Entry Lock. This hatch connected the Diving Control Center, (Dive Control), to the Entry Lock. Dive Control was located in the bottom starboard side of the sub's Operations Compartment. The DDC middle lock, called the Main Lock, contained four bunks, a table, chairs, monitor, and other dive-related gear needed for long saturation dives.

Oxygen, helium, and argon gas flasks, compressors, hot-water pumps, and other diving equipment occupied the two spaces above the DDC. In addition, another small lock, the Medical Lock, connected Dive Control to the Main Lock for passing food, medicines, and other small items to and from the DDC when the divers were isolated under saturation conditions.

Kirby-Morgan Superlite 17 Diving Helmet

Dive Control was also home to Special Operations (Spec. Ops.) under Lt. Cmdr. Franklin James and his Chief scientist Dr. Amos Brand. Senior Chief Ocean Technician Morris Jones ran the department. The Basketball Console launched and controlled a basketball-size tethered vehicle with high-intensity floodlights and a TV camera. The Fish Control Console operated a tethered sidescan vehicle called the Fish. It was capable of presenting a detailed picture of the bottom and anything lying on the seafloor.

The second added section was the short, seven-foot-long Cable Reel Compartment, located directly aft of the Diving Compartment. It had a tunnel over the top to the Reactor Compartment tunnel and a cable feed pipe out the bottom for laying cable. During cable-laying operations, the CRC was open to the ocean. The reel and the cable pulling rollers at the bottom were operated by hydraulic motors.

One more feature confirmed the new *Teuthis* mission: Shipwrights had installed large, permanent skids on the bottom of the *Halibut* so she could sit on the bottom. Since she was speed limited anyway because of the dive chamber mounted on her stern, the skids made no difference. On *Teuthis*, we installed four skids that normally were flush with the hull, but that swung down hydraulically when activated. The skid supports were 9 feet, 11 inches tall at full extension. Their lengths could be varied to allow for a sloping bottom. In their extended position, they kept the sub far enough off the bottom for a six-foot, fully equipped diver to stand beneath the hull upon exiting the DDC main lock exit hatch.

USS TEUTHIS—GENERAL DYNAMICS EB DIVISION

I was eager to see the newly installed diving systems, so I called the Chief of the Watch in Control and asked him to send Master Chief Hamilton Comstock to the Wardroom.

"Ham, how the hell are you?" I asked as he entered the Wardroom. I shook his hand firmly. His dark, short-cut thinning hair and blue eyes were unchanged, and his grip was firm. We stood for a moment, eye-to-eye, comrades in combat, and then I gestured for him to take a seat.

"Wait till you see our toys," he said before I could say anything. "Beats anything I ever seen."

We spent a few minutes talking about the team—who got promoted and the new guy, and how much time we had before getting underway.

"We definitely need some training time on the new system," Ham said. "It's more flexible, but there's also more chance of screwing up."

"Walk me through the system," I said, getting to my feet.

✳

We walked aft to the Control Room, around the periscope stand, and through a watertight door (WTD) into the upper level of the Dive Compartment. It held gas bottles, a compressor, and other dive-related stuff. We dropped down an open ladder to the deck below. This level contained more dive-related equipment and three deck-hatches for access into the three locks of the Deck Decompression Chamber—the DDC. We dropped through the starboard hatch into the Entry Lock and then forward through a hatch into Dive Control, directly beneath the gyrostabilizer room.

Ham and most of his divers had been aboard for nearly two weeks already. He was thoroughly familiar with the Dive Control Console and was eager to show me his new toy. And a wonderful toy it was. Compared to what we had on *Halibut*, it was a Cadillac versus a V-dub. Because the system had three locks, we were able to run more than one decompression table at a time. We could be decompressing two divers in the Egress Lock while simultaneously locking out another two from the Entrance Lock. We could even press a guy down to a calculated ocean depth, lock him out to accomplish a quick task, and bring him back in with only a minimal decompression table, all without disturbing our ongoing regular dive.

We spent more than an hour going through the various systems, Ham answering my questions as they arose. I was impressed by how well he had already mastered this system. It looked like I had some catching up to do.

When we finished, Ham said, "Let me show you the CRC."

We ascended a couple of ladders—staircases, really—and then passed aft through a watertight door to the Dive Compartment. We crossed the compartment and through another watertight door.

"The cable reel is just below us," Ham said. "This hatch," he pointed to a watertight hatch in the deck, "gives access to the reel. Normally underway, the entire CRC air pressure is at one atmosphere. But during cable-laying operations, the reel below us is filled with seawater at ambient pressure. If something goes wrong, there's enough room for a diver to get inside and fix it. But," he added, "he would have to enter from outside down below since there is no lock here."

I could picture one of my guys getting stuck inside the CRC and being crushed by the reel and cable. "I'm going to want to get inside there myself to check it out before we do anything like that," I told Ham.

"I couldn't agree more," he said with a grin.

USS TEUTHIS—GENERAL DYNAMICS EB DIVISION

I needed to familiarize myself with the new and upgraded equipment in the engineering spaces. Bert Cobb was willing to take some time to give me a rundown. He stuck his grizzled gray head into Dive Control, where I was integrating the complex dive system into my psyche.

"Ready to do this, Mac?" he asked with a twinkle in his eyes.

Bert was easily the most experienced officer aboard *Teuthis*. He worked himself up to Master Chief Engineman on three fast-attacks and a boomer before being promoted to Warrant Officer. Everyone on board, including the skipper, deferred to him—kinda like *The Old Man of the Sea*. Bert remembered me from the submarine's last cruise as a boomer, and knew that I had come up through the ranks like himself, although on a different route. This gave us a common bond. I got to my feet and followed him.

We crossed through the CRC and Reactor Tunnels into the Auxiliary Machinery Compartment.

"That's the old diesel generator," I said, "right?"

"Yeah, but it's been overhauled," Bert said. "All the atmosphere equipment is new—oxygen generator, CO-H2 burner, CO2 scrubber. We still generate freshwater in the Engine Room."

✳

The simple reality of maintaining breathable air in a nuclear submarine makes a very complicated process: We use heat from the reactor to distill seawater to freshwater. We then break the freshwater apart by electrolysis into oxygen and hydrogen, storing the oxygen while dumping the hydrogen overboard.

Cooking, smoking, and certain other activities generate carbon monoxide, hydrogen, and methane. We routinely run the ship's atmosphere through the CO-H2 burner, that converts those potentially fatal gases either to water or carbon dioxide. Then we pass it through the CO_2 scrubber—basically, a lithium-hydroxide sponge that absorbs carbon dioxide. The Atmosphere Tech assigned to this station routinely monitors the sub's air and adjusts the components as necessary to keep the atmosphere safe and healthy.

✻

Although it had been a while since I had been involved in this routine but vital function, as Bert talked, it all came back. The oxygen generator was smaller, but otherwise, everything looked similar.

"You never qualified to stand watch back here, did you?" Bert asked.

"I was working on it when we had the collision," I said. "We're going to have a lot of time on this operation. Maybe I can complete it this time."

"Work through me. I'll make sure you get through it timely. We can always use another watchstander," Bert said with a grin.

We stepped through the WTD into the Engine Room.

✻

I'm not a shipboard engineer, but engineering spaces have always fascinated me. As a young Sonar Tech on my first boomer, I was assigned the task of identifying sound shorts throughout the engineering spaces. I did this by measuring the sound level on the machine side of a mount and compared it to the measurement on the hull side. If sound was leaking across a mount, it would be replaced. In general, that is one of the reasons our subs are so quiet. Virtually everything is sound mounted.

Much of an engine room consists of large, heavily insulated steam pipes leading from the reactor-fueled boilers to the two turbines. The insulation is padded, but you still have to watch out for head-bumps.

"The insulation is all new," Bert said, pointing to the bright white oversized pipes. The turbines underwent full overhauls, as did the reduction gears, but their exteriors are the same ones you knew."

We went into Maneuvering, from where everything was controlled—the reactor, the turbines, the generators. I could tell by the gauge indications that the reactor was shut down while we were hooked up to shore power.

"Bring back fond memories?" Bert wanted to know with a grin.

"Most of mine came from forward, you know," I answered. Then I told him about my sound short measurement job back in my early Sonar Tech days.

"Really," he said. "You know, we hated you guys, always disrupting our peace and quiet. Every time one of *you* showed up, we had work to do." He grinned at me again. "But they don't get any quieter than us, do they?"

We wandered among the equipment, touching this or that machine, lost in our own thoughts.

"Our new Chief Sonar Tech, King, has already briefed Eng and me," Bert said. "He's concerned about sound traveling under the ice. Said he wants *Teuthis* to be the quietest boat in the fleet."

"What do you know about our coming ops?" I asked.

"Not much. I guess we'll be briefed when the time comes."

"Yeah…sorry I can't tell you anything yet, but you'll know soon enough."

THE OASIS—NEW LONDON, CONNECTICUT

During my time at Mare Island with the *Halibut*, our favorite watering hole was the Winnie & Moo.[3] The Horse and Cow, its actual name, was a unique watering hole known to every sub-sailor on the west coast and most on the East Coast as well. There is nothing like it anywhere. But for guys stationed at the Coast Guard Academy or Groton Submarine Base, the Oasis Bar was the next best thing—even though it lacked that unique submarine atmosphere of the Vallejo fixture we all loved.

I parked my Vette on Bank Street outside the Oasis and pushed my way through the glass door. The light was dim, but I could see the bar across the smallish room with tables and chairs scattered around. The air was smokey, and someone had lit a pipe—smelled like Flying Dutchman.

"Over here, Mac!" I heard Ham's voice through the low din. The guys had pushed two tables together and looked to be on their second round of draft.

---

3 See chapter 5 of the 1st book in the Mac McDowell Mission series, *Operation Ivy Bells,* for the details.

I took a seat next to Ham, and someone slid a cold, foam-topped mug in my direction. I lifted it high. "To a job well done," I said. "You guys absolutely got the system down." I looked at Ham. "I mean that. You did a great job getting the guys up to speed on the system."

A pretty blonde was draped around Melvin Ford from the back, nuzzling his neck. As I sat, Whitey (that's what we called him) looked over at me, his pale blue eyes sparkling.

"Hey, Boss," Whitey said, "meet Maggie. We been pretty tight since we got here last month."

I lifted my mug. "Maggie," I said with a grin.

Harry Blackwell, who had recently made First-class, had a foxy girl with long dark curls on his lap. "This is Tina, Boss." He grinned at me.

I took in both the girls. "You know these guys are divers, right? They're the ones your mothers warned you about." All the guys hooted.

Then I felt a warm pair of arms drop down across my chest from behind.

"Haven't seen you before, Handsome," a throaty feminine voice whispered in my ear. I felt the flick of her tongue on my earlobe.

"Hey, Doris, he's the guy we've been telling you about, the Boss, Mac McDowell." That was Wlodek Cslauski or Ski, as everyone called him.

Ham interrupted with a scowl directed at Ski. "Lieutenant Commander Mac McDowell."

"I know that," Doris said with a svelte smile. "Bigtime hero, right?" She slipped her tongue in my ear. "No harm in dipping a bit of gold now and again."

"The Boss got something goin' with Doris?" Jake, the new guy, asked, looking at Ski and his buddy, Jeremy Romain.

Jer turned his dark eyes on Jake. "Boss don't trespass," he said. "He got class."

I pretended I didn't hear that and purchased another round for the table while gently moving Doris toward Ski and Jer, who had a reputation for sharing virtually everything.

I leaned over to Ham. "The guys going to be okay for fast cruise tomorrow?" I asked.

"Yeah, I'll get them back in one piece. You leaving?"

I nodded, stood up, and toasted the guys, "Hooyah!"

Hooyahs followed me out the door.

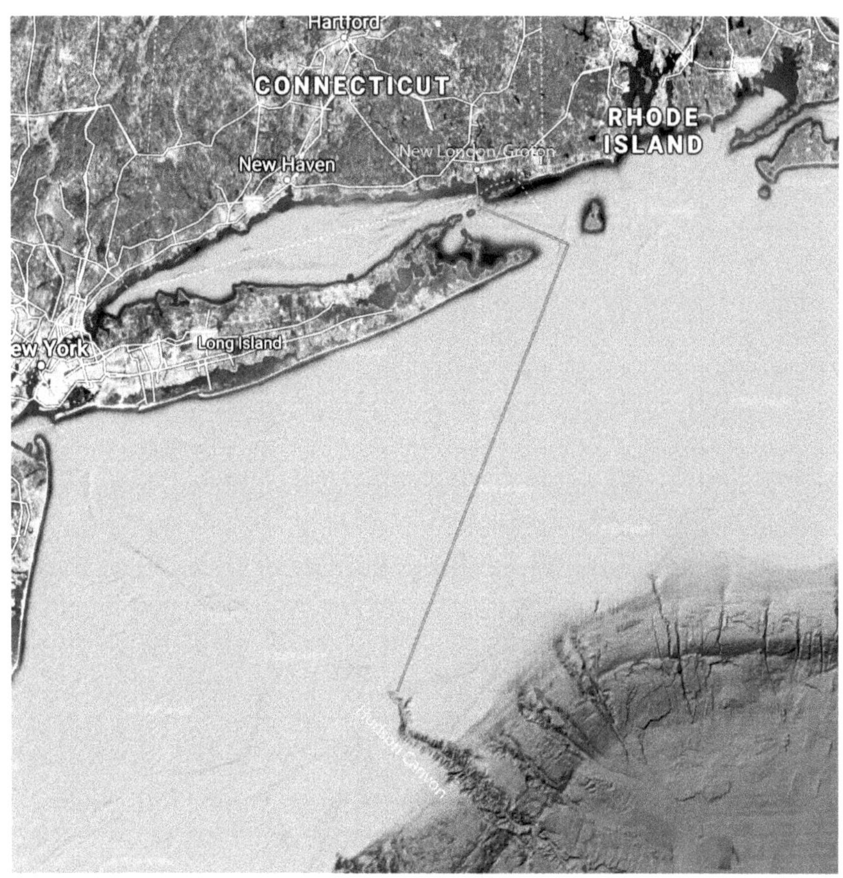

Electric Boat to Hudson Canyon

CHAPTER TWO—Angles & Dangles

FAST CRUISE—*USS TEUTHIS*—GENERAL DYNAMICS EB DIVISION

Ham held morning muster in Dive Control. Several eyes were a bit bleary, and Jake had a silly grin on his face. It seems that Doris had decided to give him his what for in the best way she knew how.

Ham reported that the team was ready and that his guys would use the twenty-four hours of fast cruise to test the entire system one more time, and then run through every wicked drill he could think of.

"I'm on the OOD watchbill," I told Ham. "I also have to catch up on some engineering quals, but I'll spend every possible moment with you here." I grinned at him. "Call me if you need me."

✳

The *Teuthis* was about to depart on sea trials. She had never been to sea in her current configuration, let alone tested her depth capability since the conversion. We all remembered the fast-attack *USS Thresher* (SSN-593)[4] and her ill-fated dive on April 10, 1963. There was not the slightest chance something like that would happen to *Teuthis*; nevertheless, before we took her to sea and took her to depth, we wanted to wring her out as thoroughly as possible while still tied up to the pier. Hence fast cruise—a full testing out of all systems while tied to the pier

At daybreak, the skipper set condition fast cruise. Eng brought the plant to full power, the electricians removed shore power, watch-standers closed all external hatches, and a shore party pulled the brow back to the pier. The Topside Watch, Joe Spanker, settled in for a long morning.

Between them, Engineer Doug Watson and DCA Bert Cobb had concocted a series of drills that would test the knowledge and skills of the entire Engineering Department for the next forty-eight hours. Forward personnel would not escape the tests either, particularly the radiation spill drills. Navigator Barry Jacobs and Waverly Denver (Weps) developed a similar list for the non-engineering personnel—torpedo loading and unloading exercises, navigation drills, sonar detection and evasion, radio reception, interference, and transmission problems, galley fire drills, collision and flooding drills. You name it, and they had it on their list.

Those of us serving as Officers-of-the-Deck supervised most of the forward exercises. We had help from our JOOD (Junior OOD) colleagues, three well-qualified senior chiefs, and on-the-job training help from Seth Beaumont (Coms/Sonar) and Zeb Trainer (Reactor) when he wasn't up to his eyeballs in one of Bert's wicked drills.

---

4 See Glossary entry.

Even the Mess Cooks found themselves in round-the-clock training of one kind or another—galley fire, radiation spill, toxic air, collision alarm, rig for ultra-quiet, among others.

✳

A day earlier, I had met with the skipper. His unease was understandable.

"I am concerned that your team members are unqualified as submariners," he told me.

"Actually Sir, only Ham and my medic, Jimmy Tanner, don't have a sub background. Even my new guy, Jake Palmer, earned his dolphins before becoming a diver." I took a breath and amplified. "Ham probably has more underwater time than most submariners, with his years in the Man-in-the-Sea Program."

"But their quals go back a way…"

I couldn't disagree, and I could see where he was going.

"We are undertaking a long and arduous operation that has never before been attempted. I need to know that every man on board can handle an emergency that strikes where he happens to be."

"No argument there, Skipper. Would you be satisfied with an abbreviated qualification regimen that covers all the areas my guys are likely to be?"

"Yes, with the proviso that Master Chief Comstock and Petty Officer Tanner complete the full set."

"Are you okay with me supervising their quals instead of the COB?" I was taking a bit of a risk, but it seemed worth it.

"Fine, but make it a priority!"

✳

Since I didn't have the Deck Watch as the fast cruise kicked off, I summoned Ham and Jimmy to the Wardroom.

"It's like this," I told them. "The skipper wants you guys to earn your dolphins."

"I saw this one coming," Ham said. "I got a lot done on the *Halibut*. Different boat, sure, but a lot's the same."

Jimmy's studious demeanor didn't change. "No big deal," he said. "I got nothin' to do anyway."

"I'll be supervising you both. Try to make regular progress. Let's show the skipper what sat divers can do!" I handed them their qual sheets. "The other guys need to do a shortened qual," I told Ham after Jimmy left. "I'll brief them in Dive Control."

✳

When I told them in Dive Control a few minutes later, I got a lot of groaning and grumbling.

"Been there, done that," Harry said to the nods of the others.

Looking directly at him, I asked, "Where's the Engine Room seawater isolation valve?"

"Ahh…I could find it pretty quick," Harry said.

"Really…and what happens before you do?" I asked.

"Okay…you made your point, Boss. I guess it does matter."

The others nodded in agreement, and I handed out their abbreviated qual sheets. "I'll be your quals supervisor," I told them.

"You, Sir?" It was Harry again.

I grinned. "Remember, I earned my silver dolphins on a boomer way back when, and I got my gold dolphins on this tub while she was still a boomer. So, I think I know what matters, and I'll get you guys through as painless as possible."

✳

During fast cruise, we had planned a simulated saturation diving excursion where we would coordinate with Control. When the time came, I was the OOD. I simulated being on station at a thousand feet, sitting on the bottom. Prior to this, Bill, Harry, Jimmy, and Whitey sealed themselves into the DDC and simulated pressing down to 1,000 feet. In reality, Ham pressed them down just to 40 feet, the distance of our keel above the bottom in our slip.

"Dive, this is *Teuthis*," I announced over the call box to Ham in Dive Control. "We are on the bottom at one thousand feet. Commence the dive."

"On the bottom, at one thousand feet. Commence the dive, aye," Ham responded.

"Launch the Basketball," I ordered.

Ocean Tech First-class Wally Dubbs had the Basketball watch. He opened the Basketball nest outer door outboard of Dive Control and activated the tethered vehicle thrusters. I slaved my monitor at the Conn to Wally's, but there wasn't much to see as the Thames River was very muddy. Wally drove the Basketball out about twenty yards to free up some tether. Then he dove it down to the keel and moved over to the port DDC hatch.

Several minutes later, a bright, diffused beam appeared under the hatch, and two divers exited, one after the other.

"Dive, this is Bill…in the water."

"Dive, aye."

"Dive, Harry…I'm wet."

"Use standard terminology, Harry."

"Dive, this is Harry…in the water."

"Dive, aye."

On a real thousand-foot dive, Ham would allow a great deal more latitude, but we were in training mode. He wanted things to go by the book, as we both had agreed beforehand.

"Bill, Harry, this is *Teuthis*. I have you on visual. It's fuzzy because of the muddy water." We had decided to identify the OOD as *Teuthis* when he talked with the divers to distinguish him from Dive Control and avoid any diver confusion.

"Bill, aye. Not much we can do about that."

"Harry, this is *Teuthis*…did you get my last?"

"Harry, aye."

They both swam around for about ten minutes, letting Jimmy and Whitey in the Egress Lock feed and retrieve their umbilicals. I checked my list, anticipating what would happen next. Faintly on the monitor, I saw Harry float to the bottom, not moving. I started my stopwatch.

"Harry, this is Dive…respond!"

Nothing.

"Harry, this is Dive…respond!"

Still nothing. On the monitor, Bill approached Harry and checked him over.

"Dive, this is Bill…Harry is unresponsive. I don't know what's wrong with him. I need assistance to get him back into the lock."

"Dive, aye. Whitey, this is Dive. Finish suiting up and follow the umbilical down to Harry. You and Bill get him into the lock."

"Whitey, aye."

I split my Conn monitor four ways, so I could follow the in-water activity, the Egress Lock, the Main Lock, and Dive Control. On the monitor, I heard Ham order Ski and Jer to lock into the Main Lock.

"Ski," Ham said, "you take over from Jimmy so he can check out Harry's condition."

Shortly thereafter, I had a clear view of Harry on his back on the Main Lock deck, his Kirby-Morgan helmet off, grinning from ear to ear. I clicked my stopwatch.

I called Ham on the ship's telephone system. "Five minutes was not bad," I said. "Do you think we can get it down to four or less?"

"Probably. Let's go through it again."

※

Over the next day and a half, we repeated that exercise with several variations, and a dozen more. The ship's crew conducted reactor scrams, spill drills, flooding, electrical and hydraulic failures, engine failures, and a whole list of other possible malfunctions and casualties. We spent several hours snorkeling, fought several simulated fires, and almost had a real one when Senior Chief Cedric Hurst, the cook, left his bread in the oven too long.

It was with a sense of relief that the skipper ordered me to secure fast cruise and station the Maneuvering Watch for sea trials.

For twenty-four hours, we had been practicing. Now it was on to the real thing. The crew would physically take *Teuthis* through her paces, take her out into the Atlantic, actually take her to test depth, and run her at high speed through steep angles. We would wring her out before she undertook her dangerous assignment.

My guys would press down to a thousand feet and exit *Teuthis* on the seafloor. We would push the physical limits for actual saturation diving—not a chamber dive aboard some test vehicle, but an actual dive to a thousand feet on the seafloor in the open ocean.

USS TEUTHIS—SEA TRIALS—HUDSON CANYON

When the Captain of the *Halibut* let me take her out from Mare Island about two years ago, it was a simple matter of making several straight legs down San Francisco Bay and then a hard-right turn under the Golden Gate and on into the Pacific. Not so here.

To start, we were moored bow-out to the left bank of the Thames River. In order not to get wedged between the two piers, we needed to keep our bow square to the current. We had two steerable outboard motors that lowered from the keel near the bow and stern; these would help. So would the tugs that would keep us in the ever-changing river channel. Then, there was the River Pilot that the Navy required us to use until we reached the sea buoy—the outer channel buoy. After that, we had about thirty nautical miles of rocks, shoals, and islands to traverse before we reached open ocean.

"Station the Maneuvering Watch for underway operations," the Chief of the Watch announced on the 1MC.

My Maneuvering Watch assignment was OOD, so I joined the skipper on the Bridge along with two lookouts out on the fairwater planes, secured with safety lines. A light rain was falling from a low overcast. We were all bundled up wearing ponchos with hoods. The sun showed no visible disk through the low overcast, but it was somewhere off to starboard in the southwest, getting ready to drop below the invisible horizon.

The skipper chose to take the boat out himself on this, our first time through the gauntlet, so he had the Conn while I retained the Deck. Barry was in the Nav Center, keeping track of our position. Senior Chief Quartermaster Alastair Forbes was backing him up, with Quartermasters Gary Fonzarelli and Ben Gross shooting lines of position through the main periscope and calling them out for Barry and Al to lay on the chart. Quartermaster Jubal Henshaw was adding radar lines of position from the radar screen right next to the chart table. Even with the River Pilot, who had joined us just before we got underway, things were a bit tense because it was everybody's first time with the boat actually underway, and there were lots of rocks, shoals, and islands around us.

The skipper had two tugs stay with us until we reached the channel entrance buoys to catch us if we got caught in an unexpected current. The pilot departed as we passed the buoys, and Barry recommended course 150 degrees to pass Race Rock Light down our port side in about eighteen minutes.

"Come left to new course one-five-zero. Make turns for ten knots," the skipper ordered over the squawk box.

"When Race Rock Light is broad abeam to port, recommend new course one-three-five, speed twenty knots," Barry called up from the Nav Center, "and watch out for some pretty heavy-duty riptides beyond the light."

The skipper acknowledged and then said to me, "Are you ready to take it, Mac?"

"Yes, Sir," I said, feeling excited to be taking control of the sub for the first time since the collision.

"Remember, Mac, there's not a lot of water under us, and the riptides will affect a sub much more than a regular ship."

"Aye, Skipper. That's been on my mind because I've run these waters before."

"Lieutenant Commander McDowell has the Deck and the Conn," the skipper announced to the Bridge personnel and over the squawk box to Control down below.

"I have the Deck and Conn," I repeated.

There wasn't much wind, and the water was pond smooth. The southwestern glow from the hidden sun was almost gone. After giving me the watch, as darkness enveloped the sub, the skipper perched himself on the sail, peering through his binoculars, his feet dangling into the bridge pit. Above his head on the raised radar mast, a white masthead light along with red and green lights on the fairwater planes, and another white light that shined aft on the rudder, told other vessels of our presence and our general direction of travel. Above the masthead light, a bright amber light flashed for three seconds, went dark for three seconds, flashed for three seconds, went dark, and so on. This told everyone out there that we were a submarine on the surface.

Shortly thereafter, the Chief of the Watch announced on the 1MC, "Secure the Maneuvering Watch. Set the underway watch, section three."

About five minutes later, section three JOOD Waverly Denver showed up. Shortly thereafter, with Race Rock Light about a quarter mile off the port beam, Petty Officer Ben Gauss, who had section three Nav Watch, announced, "Recommend new course one-three-five, speed twenty knots."

I put the recommendation into effect and pointed the sub at a spot about halfway between Montauk Point and Block Island, although all I could see from the Bridge were flashing lights. A quick calculation told me we would be there in about fifty minutes. I informed the skipper. He nodded.

I called Barry. "It's Mac. I'm happy to take your Bridge Watch. I've got Waverly with me, so there's no real work for me. This way, you can ride herd on your guys as we get ready for tomorrow morning's ops."

He accepted. I'm sure he wasn't looking forward to the weather topside.

"Time for me to go below," the skipper said. "It's getting a bit crowded up here." He climbed off the sail top and dropped through the hatch to Control.

"Captain's left the Bridge," Waverly announced, as I checked the darkening waters around me, making sure the lookouts had missed nothing.

✳

An uneventful hour later, Ben pointed me to course 190 degrees, aimed at our destination. Hudson Canyon—a deep, forty-mile-long underwater slash in the continental margin—lying ninety-four nautical miles ahead. The sun had fully set, and the sky was now pitch black. Long rollers from slightly north of east lifted our stern as they passed every fifty seconds. The ride was comfortable, but the Bridge had turned chilly with nightfall. The skipper had us remain surfaced until we reached Hudson Canyon because water depth on the entire route never exceeded 300 feet.

I guess we could have headed due south for sixty-four nautical miles where the bottom dropped off to over 3,000 feet to do our angles and dangles, but the skipper wanted to tie everything together—the sub seaworthiness tests and the diving system tests. That's why he chose Hudson Canyon. Its depth ranges from 400 to about 3,000 feet deep, twice as deep as we can go. The canyon is a bit under two nautical miles wide at the shallow end and three miles at its deepest. This would give us all the room we needed along the canyon length for angles and dangles, and all the depth we needed to wring out the dive system and test the divers.

I explained all this to Waverly. I was beginning to get a handle on his level of knowledge, which was right up there. I made sure he knew that I was there to mentor him into requalifying as OOD as soon as he could handle it. We spent some of our time discussing forward ops and emergency procedures. I even drilled him on nighttime ship recognition. To his credit, he had all the light configurations down pat—all of them I could think of anyway. The section three lookouts, Steve Becker and Billy-Bob Yokum, were experienced watchstanders and participated in helping Waverly come up to speed, much to his amusement.

Doug Watson (Eng) was next on the watchbill. He and his JOOD, Franklin James, showed up about 2340, dressed for the weather, wearing red goggles for night vision adaptation when below in white light. Waverly briefed them on our situation, pointing out a couple of contacts in the distance off our starboard bow—one ship moving into and one out of New York harbor. While he was briefing Doug and Franklin, the new lookouts, Julius Hoppenstein and Randolph Zimmerman, arrived to relieve my guys.

After the old lookouts left, I told Doug, "You got about four hours till we reach Hudson Canyon. The skipper wants to make a surface run along the canyon, and then toward morning, he wants to commence angles and dangles. Sometime in the early afternoon, we'll conduct our first dive near the head of the canyon. Between now and then, we'll be pressing the divers down to a thousand feet."

"I hear you say it, and it's hard to believe," Doug said. "A thousand feet…" He shook his head in amazement.

"I guess that'll be well past your watch," I said. "I headed below. I'll send up two cups of coffee before I hit the sack." I grinned. "I'm gonna turn in early. I got a long day tomorrow." I shouted to the lookouts, "I'll send some coffee up for you guys, too."

Doug gave me a thumbs-up as I dropped through the hatch into Control.

The Control Room was rigged for red and filled with the quiet hum of activity and the nearly inaudible high-pitched background whine from all the 400-Hertz electronic equipment in Control. I sent the messenger to get four cups of coffee to the Bridge, grabbed a chart of Hudson Canyon from the chart bin, and dropped down two ladders to Dive Control, where Ham and Bill were going over written plans while the rest of the divers were prepping for the press-down.

"Hey guys," I said. "I've got a chart of our op area. Let's see what we've got going." I rolled out the chart on the dive console desk while everyone gathered around. "We're going to do angles and dangles from here to here," I said, moving my finger from the shallow to the deep end of the canyon. "Then, we'll take her to test depth about here." I indicated the canyon end where water depth was 3,000 feet. "Sometime in the afternoon, we'll test the dive system at a thousand feet, which should be about here," I said, pointing to a spot near the shallow end of the canyon.

"What's this?" Bill asked, pointing to a notation of unexploded depth charges at about 200 fathoms just south of our dive site.

"The date says 1960 and 61," Ham said. "That's more than fifteen years ago. If it hasn't exploded by now, I don't think it's a problem."

"We'll be more than three thousand feet away from it anyway," I said, "in shallower water." I pointed.

"Probably couldn't see it anyway," Bill said. "It's gotta be silted over by now."

"Maybe Spook will see it with the Fish," Ham said. "They're going to test it, right?"

"They will," I answered. "I'll tell him about it."

✳

With that, the divers donned their Nomex jumpsuits, made their way through the Entrance Lock into the Main Lock, and settled in for the ten-hour trip down to 1,000 feet. Ham and Bill sat at the console, with Bill actually running the dive under Ham's close supervision.

The legal responsibility remained mine, but I trusted Ham, and I needed several hours of sleep before the next day's operations.

USS TEUTHIS—ANGLES & DANGLES—HUDSON CANYON

On the 1MC, the Chief of the Watch announced, "Attention all hands, rig the ship for dive. The senior petty officer for each watch station report to Chief of the Watch when your station is fully rigged."

Shortly thereafter, the skipper came up on the 1MC. "This is the Captain. We have scoped out the length and depth of Hudson Canyon. We are now near the deep end with about three thousand feet of water beneath us. Each of you keep in mind that we will be making the first dive since literally cutting the sub in half, taking out the missile compartment, and inserting the Dive and Cable Reel Compartments. Electric Boat has extensively tested every weld, every seam, and every seal. Nevertheless, only the real world will give us the final okay on what has been done.

"As we rig the ship for dive, be absolutely thorough. If you are not totally sure of something, check with someone who is. We're going to take a couple of hours to do this right. When I am satisfied that we can dive safely, we'll take her down to periscope depth. Some of you have been given specific monitoring assignments to make sure we don't have any water coming into the ship. If you see anything at all, notify the Chief of the Watch immediately!

"Okay…turn-to! Rig the ship for dive!"

✳

In principle, the process was simple. Secure every access to sea and otherwise make the ship ready for underwater operations. In practice, this involved securing all sea valves and their backups and tagging them appropriately, setting the ship's atmospheric system for submerged operation, setting the diesel for submerged operation but making it available for snorkeling, removing and stowing all topside safety lines, ensuring that the hawser stowage lockers wouldn't rattle underway, securing topside winches, and sealing all external hatches except the Bridge hatch. Every internal system had to be set for submerged operations, taking into consideration that the sub would be operating in three dimensions.

Even with the old hands applying their well-earned knowledge, the rigging process took the full two hours and then some. Finally, the skipper came on the 1MC again.

"This is the Captain. You all did a thorough job so that we are now ready to dive the *Teuthis*. Chief of the Watch, set the first watch section and dive the boat."

That was me. In anticipation, I had awakened forty-five minutes earlier, grabbed some chow and a cup of coffee, and was hanging out in Control, bundled for topside. After the skipper's announcement, I got my watch section organized with just myself and the two lookouts on the Bridge. I had Waverly remain in Control to handle things should something go wrong.

"Chief of the Watch," I ordered over the squawk box, "prepare to dive the ship."

The Navigator, Barry Jacobs, was in Control. Following normal procedure, he temporarily assumed the Watch from me so I could rig the Bridge for dive. Over the squawk box, he said, "I relieve you, Sir. Rig the Bridge for dive and lay below."

"Clear the Bridge!" I ordered the lookouts.

Jack dropped to Control while Fritz grabbed the squawk box and dropped down below the hatch; I kept the mike in my hand. I made one more quick visual scan around the boat, flipped up the Bridge fairing. I climbed through the outer hatch and pulled it down against the spring while Fritz held it tight with the lanyard so I could spin the handle. Then he tossed the squawk box to waiting hands and dropped to the deck while I followed through the lower hatch. He grabbed the lanyard for the lower hatch and pulled it down. As I spun the handle, I reported to Barry, "Last man down, hatch secured."

He acknowledged, and the Chief of the Watch announced, "Green board!" indicating that all the openings to sea were sealed, showing green on his monitor.

I assumed the Watch from Barry and told the Chief of the Watch to dive the ship.

"Dive! Dive!" he said on the 1MC and sounded two long *Aoogahs!* on the klaxon.

"Helmsman," I ordered, addressing Spanky, "ahead full, steer one-three-eight. Diving Officer," I said to Chief Torpedoman Jasper

Cedrik (whom everybody called *Tubes*), take her down; make your depth six-five feet."

✻

We all were rusty, and practicing a first dive on fast cruise is just not like the real thing. The skipper was on the periscope stand with me. Not that he didn't trust me as OOD, but it was his boat, and he wanted to be there in case something went wrong despite everyone's best efforts. Waverly stood off to one side of the periscope stand, keeping out of the way but paying close attention to everything happening, ready to jump in should he be needed. I liked his style.

Dokey, the Chief of the Watch, flooded the main ballast tanks. The skipper glued his eye to the main scope, swinging around checking for contacts. I took the attack scope, looking first aft, and then forward to ensure the ballast tank vents had opened. When the vents stopped spraying, I told Dokey to close the vents. In about a minute, I felt the sub level off, and moments later, Tubes announced, "At six-five feet, zero bubble, neutral trim."

"Make turns for five knots," I ordered. No need to put any excessive pressure on the more delicate attack scope. I glanced at the skipper's Night Order book, where he had listed the series of exercises he wanted to do.

"Chief of the Watch," I said, "prepare to snorkel." As he acknowledged, Waverly called Maneuvering on the sound-powered handset. Jay Swimmer had the watch back there. "Prepare to snorkel," he ordered.

"Snorkel is raised," Tubes reported. I acknowledged.

About a minute later, Maneuvering reported they were ready to snorkel.

"Commence snorkeling," I announced over the 1MC. On the sound-powered handset to Maneuvering, I said, "Load the diesel when ready." I could see that Waverly took a mental note of that order.

I made a sweep on the scope. I placed the scope on the bearing of the incoming five-foot rollers. "Breakers bearing…Mark!" I said.

"Zero-nine-three," Waverly said from the other side of the scope. "That's forty-five degrees off the port bow."

The next item on the skipper's list was checking the closing action of the snorkel.

"Diving Officer, make your depth six-seven feet," I ordered.

Five seconds later, the sub was at sixty-seven feet, and a moment after that, the first roller passed over the snorkel as I watched through the scope. The valve slammed shut, and the powerful diesel engine pulled several inches of vacuum in the sub before the roller passed, and the snorkel valve opened again. It did an excellent job of clearing everybody's sinuses.

I glanced at the skipper, and he nodded, holding up three fingers. I kept the depth steady at sixty-seven feet while we endured the next three rollers. Then I ordered, "Diving Officer, take us back to six-five feet."

The next item on the skipper's list was a crash dive to 600 feet at a steep angle. He got on the 1MC. "This is the Captain. We are about to undergo steep angles and rapid depth changes. Before we start, take a few moments to ensure that your area has nothing loose that can become airborne. The Chief of the Watch will make another announcement just before we commence."

"Recommend course one-six-eight," Al told me from the chart table.

"Depth," I requested.

"Twelve hundred feet," Al said. "Depth will reach eighteen hundred feet on this leg. You have five-point-eight-one nautical miles on this leg."

"Helmsman, come right to one-six-eight," I ordered.

I glanced at the skipper again. He nodded. I nodded to the Chief of the Watch.

"The ship will commence a crash dive in two minutes," Dokey announced on the 1MC.

The skipper made a final sweep with his scope, flipped the handles up, and dropped it into the well. I checked the time and did my final sweep. The horizon was empty all around under a gray overcast. I flipped up my scope handles and dropped the scope.

"Ahead flank! Thirty degree down bubble! Make your depth six-zero-zero feet!"

Teuthis jumped forward like a pent-up racehorse as the nose dropped rapidly to thirty degrees down and then continued to thirty-five degrees.

"Mind your angle!" I snapped at Tubes as a ceramic cup crashed to the deck somewhere behind me in the Electronics Nav Center.

I could hear some breaking noises down in the galley and something through the open Sonar Shack door.

"Sorry, Sir, we got a bit ahead of ourselves."

"That's why we're practicing this shit, Tubes," I said back.

"Depth two hundred feet," Dokey said. Moments later, he said, "Three hundred…" and then "Four hundred…"

"Don't slide through six hundred," I cautioned as we passed 500 feet. "Ahead standard," I ordered the helmsman.

"Zero bubble," Tubes ordered his planesmen.

As we hit 601 feet and then drifted back to 600, Tubes announced, "At six hundred feet, Sir, zero bubble."

"Very well. Make turns for five knots," I said and grinned at the skipper.

"Recommend course one-three-zero," Al said from Nav. "Depth eighteen hundred twenty-five feet—that's one thousand two hundred twenty-five feet below the keel," he added.

"Helmsman," I ordered, "come left to one-three-zero."

The skipper picked up the 1MC mike. "This is the Captain. Take fifteen minutes to clean up your messes, and then we'll do several in a row, including some tight turns."

✳

And so it went for the rest of the morning. No matter what the skipper said, each steep angle—down or up—caused at least one more object to crash. Finally, around 1100, the skipper took to the 1MC again.

"This is the Captain. Somehow, you gents are NOT taking this seriously. Two months from now, when we are beneath solid ice and need to dive quickly to avoid detection, one broken cup can get us all killed! We are going to continue these drills until nothing breaks anywhere in the sub, and we are doing it at Battle Stations. We'll remain at Battle Stations until we get it right!" He looked at the Chief of the Watch with a nod.

"Man Battle Stations! Man Battle Stations!" Dokey announced on the 1MC, and then sounded the General Alarm.

I was just about to come off watch, and my Battle Station was in Dive Control, where I was going anyway. I swung by the galley and grabbed a bag of tuna sandwiches—the skipper must have given the cook, Cedric, a heads up. When I got to Dive Control, Ham and Bill looked up from the console, and Bill passed the sandwich bag through the Medical Lock.

Ham reported on the Battle Station sound-powered phone, "Dive Control all present and accounted for. A reminder, Control, six divers are pressing down in the Main Lock."

It turned out that on the crash dive, someone had not properly secured an umbilical. It hit the deck in the Egress Lock with a lot of noise. And...Ham's favorite cup had slid along the console desk to crash off the end.

During the two hours that Barry—he was the Battle Station OOD—put *Teuthis* through its paces, Ham and I checked and re-checked everything under our control, so that nothing moved, even a fraction of an inch. You could have put *Teuthis* through a loop-the-loop, and everything would have stayed in place.

"That's how I want it from now on," Ham said to the guys in the Main Lock. "We're on a dive op, you free up whatever you need. But, the moment we're done, you put it back exactly like it is now. *We* are not going to be responsible for getting a fish up our ass!"

I couldn't have agreed more.

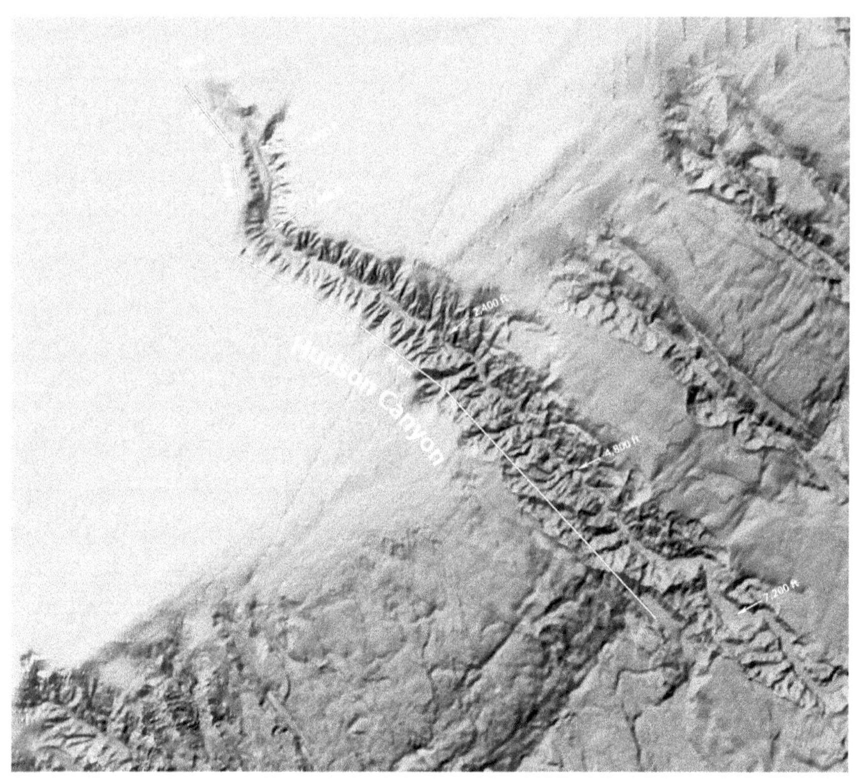

Hudson Canyon

CHAPTER THREE—Sat System Test

USS TEUTHIS—ENCOUNTER WITH CAMEROCERAS— HUDSON CANYON

Finally, the skipper was satisfied with how the crew performed during angles and dangles. I didn't blame him one bit for insisting as he did. I remembered only too well *Halibut*'s confrontation with the Soviet *Whiskey* in the Sea of Okhotsk. Our ability to be silent even when doing extremely complicated dive maneuvers, and Captain Jackson's tactical *chutzpa*, are the only reasons I am here to tell you about this follow-on operation.

"Secure from Battle Stations. Set the underway watch, section two," the Chief of the Watch finally announced.

The Dive Center telephone rang. I picked it up. "McDowell," I said.

"This is Bert. We're diving to test depth, and then we head for the dive ops area. We're going to hover at one hundred feet over the bottom and run a fish survey until we're satisfied we know what's down there. Once we're hovering, the Captain will join you in Dive."

✳

Taking a submarine to test depth for the first time after an extensive overhaul like ours is always a tense event. No matter how much faith you have in the people who did the overhaul, 668 pounds pushing against every square inch of submarine hull is something you cannot ignore. So far as I was concerned, the guys who did the welding on our hull should have been making this dive with us. Unfortunately, this wasn't navy policy.

Bert Cobb had the watch. I wished I were doing it, but the lot fell to him. If it had to be someone other than the skipper or me, I was glad it was Bert.

"This is the Captain," the 1MC droned. "We are about to descend to test depth of one thousand five hundred feet. We will not go to Battle Stations, but I want one person in each watertight compartment on sound-powered phones with Control. Report to the Chief of the Watch as soon as you are set up. We will descend to one thousand feet, check for leaks or other abnormalities, and then descend fifty feet at a time, stopping at each depth to check for leaks or anything else out of the ordinary."

"I'll be in Control," I told Ham. "Call the Nav phone if you need me."

I went up a level, forward to the galley, where I grabbed a sandwich and wolfed it down with a glass of bug juice (Kool-Aid) and then slipped quietly into Control and parked myself on the far side of the chart table. Fonzie had the Nav Watch, but Senior Chief Forbes was there as well, keeping back as I was. When Barry (Nav) joined us, it got a bit crowded. We pushed back against the firecontrol computer to leave sufficient room around the lighted chart table. I could feel the 400-Hertz vibration from the synchros that transmitted fire-control information from this monstrosity to its little brother in the Torpedo Room.

"Diving Officer, make your depth one-zero-zero-zero feet," Bert ordered, "ten-degree down bubble."

The sub nosed down and began to creak as we drove deeper.

"Passing five hundred feet," Senior Chief Ogden Winder, the Chief of the Watch, said. "Six hundred…seven hundred…eight hundred…"

"Ease your bubble," Bert ordered.

"Nine hundred feet…nine hundred fifty feet…nine hundred eighty feet…one thousand feet."

The skipper picked up the 1MC mike. "This is the Captain. We are at one thousand feet. Check each compartment fore to aft, top to bottom, and don't forget the bilges. Report your results to Control."

I went aft down the starboard side, down two ladders into Dive Control.

"What's your status?" I asked Bill.

"At five hundred ten feet, pressing to one thousand," he responded.

"Any problems?" I asked.

"We had to stop once at fifty for Jake. He cleared up with no problems since. Harry's done a lot of blowing, but he's been fine since two hundred. Jimmy's been blowing from the get-go, but I haven't had to stop for him. The others are just yawning from time to time. Harry claims he's hungry. Wants more sandwiches…with hot sauce. Says the first batch tasted like cardboard."

I called Cedric and asked him to send a plate of sandwiches to Dive Control along with two bottles of hot sauce.

From the Main Lock, Harry squeaked, "Toss in a six-pack with that order," his voice distorted by both helium and the increased pressure.

"You'll have to wait on that one," Ham said. "We're on back-order."

"Better hook up the descrambler," I said to Bill, "or the skipper will never understand them."

I headed back to Control. As I arrived, we hit a thousand fifty and were checking for leaks. I reassumed my spot against the firecontrol computer and kept my mouth shut.

"Eleven hundred feet," Oggy droned.

Ten minutes later, we started down again. It took about an hour to reach test depth—1,500 feet. It had been a long time since this old girl had experienced such pressure. But other than some surprisingly loud creaking, everything went fine. Technically, we had another 300 feet below us as a safety margin and maybe another 200 before the hull imploded—not something I wanted to contemplate.

The skipper said something to Bert that I couldn't hear. Bert picked up the 1MC mike.

"We are at test depth. We will remain here for thirty minutes while we test the hover system. Continue checking for leaks at your stations, and be sure to report anything unusual to Control." He turned to the Chief of the Watch. "What's your trim?"

"Neutral buoyancy, near as I can tell," Oggy answered.

"Let's see how close you are," Bert said to him. "Helmsman, all stop!"

As the sub ceased its forward motion, little-by-little, it began to rise. Oggy flooded several hundred pounds of seawater into both port and starboard trim tanks. The sub commenced sinking by the stern. He pumped a couple hundred pounds out of the aft trim tank. The sub leveled and stopped sinking at 1,510 feet. Oggy pumped a small amount from the port and starboard trim tanks, and as soon as the sub started to creep up, he flooded it back in. The sub halted at 1,501 feet. Oggy looked at Bert.

"Close enough," Bert said. "Well done." He looked at the skipper, who nodded and indicated a go-ahead.

"Activate the hover system and pump out a hundred pounds," Bert ordered the COW.

The sub commenced rising, but immediately the hover system sucked water in and then blew it out, sucked in less, blew it out, sucked in even less, and the sub stabilized at exactly 1,500 feet. For the next fifteen minutes, *Teuthis* remained there until Bert secured the test and ordered the sub to 300 feet at ten knots on a course to the dive location.

✳

The skipper arrived in Dive Control moments after Franklin James and his team.

"We'll be at the dive site in a few minutes," the skipper said. "I want to launch the Fish for a full left-right survey across the canyon from thirty feet over the bottom. How wide are your cuts?"

"From thirty feet over the bottom, about thirty-five feet," Lt. Cmdr. James answered. "We can drive the Fish at ten knots."

The skipper thought for a few seconds. "So, we can survey a half-a-nautical-mile square in about four hours and twenty minutes." He paused. How much tether do you have?"

"About two miles."

"We'll take station at three hundred feet above the dive spot and hover while you do your survey. Then we'll pick an exact spot, bottom the sub, and conduct dive operations." He looked around. "Any questions?"

He looked at me. "Where are your divers?"

I glanced at the middle of three large gauges on the console. "Eight hundred thirty-six feet, Skipper. We'll be ready to enter the water by the time you set dive ops."

"Good." He rose and left Dive Control.

✳

By mid-afternoon, we had set the 300-foot hover and by chow-time had completed the survey. Chief Ocean Tech Francis Oberst and Petty Officer Wally Dubbs laid out the printouts on the survey table and taped them together. What emerged was an image of a nearly flat, sloping bottom ending abruptly in steep slopes at both canyon sides.

I picked a spot 990 feet deep that was close to a nearly featureless rise from the ocean floor.

✳

We had done this many times before, but this time it was distinctly different. We had this fabulous oversized DDC. We were riding a vehicle specifically designed to support our operation. We were about to lock out of the sub in the open ocean at a depth never before attempted. We had been to a thousand feet before off the *USS Elk River* (IX-501) near San Diego, but this was entirely different. Before, we dove out of a Personnel Transfer Capsule (PTC) that had been lowered by a crane to our dive depth. Here, we were diving out of a submarine bottomed in a deep canyon at the edge of the continental shelf. As far as I was concerned, this completely redefined the meaning of cool.

Teuthis settled to the sandy bottom with a slight bump, her four skids finding good traction. Her heading was 138 degrees with a one-degree up-bubble. Barry Jacobs had the Deck, and Chief Ocean Tech Francis Oberst had left Dive Central to assume the watch as Diving Officer. Wally Dubbs remained in Dive Central to run the Basketball.

"Wally," Ham said, "you launch the Basketball and position it so we can record the divers exiting the DDC." He turned to Senior Chief Morris Jones, who ran the Spec Ops Department under Franklin James. "Make sure this gets recorded, Morris. We're makin' history here."

"Attention on Deck!" someone called out as the skipper entered Dive Control.

"As you were," the skipper said. "From now on, skip the formality during dive ops." He turned to me. "What's your status, Mac?"

"The Basketball is setting up to record the diver's first exit to the bottom. Harry Blackwell and Jimmy Tanner will be the first divers out. Whitey Ford and Ski Cslauski will tend them from the Egress Lock. Jer Romain and Jake Palmer—the new guy—will remain in the Main Lock with the hatch closed but not sealed." I picked up Ham's cheat sheet. "The divers will inspect the Engine Room seawater intake, check the screw, and then return to the Egress Lock. We'll rotate the teams to give everyone time outside. Then we wrap it up and give the boat back to you, Sir."

"Carry on," the skipper said and took a seat away from the immediate action.

✳

"Divers, enter the water," Bill Fisher ordered, running this dive under Ham's close supervision. "I'm using your names for this op: Harry, Jimmy, Whitey, and Ski."

"Harry, aye."

"Jimmy, aye."

"Whitey, aye."

"Ski, aye."

Their voices, affected by the higher speed of sound in helium and the effect of high pressure on their vocal cords, passed through the electronic descrambler to loudspeakers over the console. They still sounded strange, but they were intelligible.

"Tenders, verify your divers."

"Whitey tending Harry."

"Ski tending Jimmy."

About thirty seconds later, the speakers squawked:

"Harry on the bottom."

"Jimmy on the bottom."

"You got all this, Morris?" Ham asked, "video and sound?"

"Don't get your panties in a snit, Ham," Morris said. "I got your six!"

I was a bit tense since this was the first time this system had locked divers out at a thousand feet. We proceeded methodically. Ham checked Bill, and I checked Ham. There would be no mistakes on this watch.

It was pitch black outside, but the water was remarkably clear. The Basketball's beam was barely visible in the water column so that the circle of light it created almost seemed to appear and move by magic. Wally kept the Basketball about ten yards outboard of the divers as they glided down the starboard side. They swam parallel to the sub's keel, about seven feet above the bottom. Their strong fin down-strokes created tiny swirls on the bottom that picked up a bit of detritus, marking their path. There was no sound other than their easy breathing.

"There it is," Ski said, pointing to the seawater intake, a scoop protruding six inches from the sub's side.

Wally moved the Basketball in for a closer look.

"Dive, this is Harry. Look at this thing. If we was surrounded by slush, this could freeze up."

"Or if a piece of ice got sucked against it, slush could sorta weld it in place," Jimmy added.

The skipper got up and approached the monitor. "Try to get images from every direction and several close-ups as well," he said to Wally.

Ham looked at Bill and tapped the dive timer.

"Harry, Jimmy, this is Dive. Time to return to the DDC."

"Wally, pull the Basketball out so we can just see the divers," I said. "Let's get some big picture footage."

As I watched the monitor intently, in the right-hand corner, ahead and outboard of the divers, I saw something move—something big.

"Divers, stop!" I ordered. "Back up against the hull." And to Wally, I said, "Wally, focus in on whatever that movement is." I pointed to the corner of the screen. I turned to Ham and said quietly, "Better get Jer and Jake ready. We may need to put Whitey and Ski into the water."

Ham got on the sound-powered set into the Main Lock and brought Jer and Jake up to speed. In the meantime, Wally suddenly yowled, "What the fuck is that?"

Centered on the monitor was something right out of a monster horror movie. It looked something like the giant Humboldt squid that had attacked us while diving at a thousand feet off the San Diego Coast some three years ago.[5] Those guys were maybe eight feet long. Imagine one of those suckers, but instead of a soft squid body after the head, it consisted of a conical shell. From the pointy end of the shell to the tentacle tips was about twenty feet. No, that's not a mistake. As best as I could tell from the monitor, this creature was twenty feet long, and nearly half of that was its head and tentacles. As I watched, what looked like a thick proboscis extended from the center of its tentacles. The critter must have pumped water through the proboscis because it lifted from the bottom, raising a lot of silt, scattering the light from the Basketball.

As we watched on the monitor, it turned toward the Basketball, spread out its tentacles, pointed its nozzle to the rear, and jetted rapidly toward the Basketball. Wally pulled the Basketball back and up, avoiding the gaping beak, but one of the tentacles wrapped itself around the tether.

Before I could issue any orders, Harry faded out of the image and then appeared again from above, dive knife extended. Perhaps more than the other divers, Harry kept his knife razor-sharp. He whipped his blade through the capturing tentacle and then dropped back to the bottom with Jimmy beneath the curve of the sub's hull. Wally pulled the Basketball up and back toward the hull, keeping as much as possible in the field of view.

---

5 As described in Chapter 1 of *Operation Ivy Bells*, the first book in the Mac McDowell Mission series.

The creature whipped its tentacles wildly while it backed off a body length using its jet appendage.

"Ham, put Whitey and Ski in the water ASAP!" I ordered. "Have them carry gas-powered dart guns."

Bill quickly briefed the two while Jer and Jake scrambled into the Egress Lock. Less than a minute later, Whitey hit the water, Ski handed him four gas-powered dart guns and jumped through the hatch himself. Jer and Jake worked furiously to handle the umbilicals for the four divers.

It seemed to take forever for Whitey and Ski to appear on the monitor, but actually, only thirty seconds had passed since I decided to put them in the water. As they appeared, the creature launched another attack. Whitey had a gas-powered gun tucked under each arm. He fired both darts. One penetrated the creature's right eye, a grapefruit-sized orb, and the other disappeared in its gaping maw. He quickly severed the cords and reloaded new darts in both guns. Ski handed the other two dart guns, handle first, to Harry and Jimmy, and then dropped behind them under the hull, knife in hand.

The creature thrashed wildly, whipping its shell back and forth, frantically throwing its tentacles about, desperately seeking its tormentors. The shell swept toward Whitey, knocking him off his feet as he released another dart. It just bounced off. Two tentacles reached out, one grabbing the gun, the other Whitey's left arm.

"Get this fucker off me!" Whitey yelled, his voice squeaking through the speakers. He fired a dart from the gun in his right hand, striking a glancing blow to the creature's head. Then he dropped his gun and drew his knife from his chest sheath and started hacking at the tentacle around his arm.

Harry and Jimmy fired into the tentacle mess, and then Harry threw himself at the tentacles gripping Whitey. He pushed Whitey's knife away and sliced through the five-inch thick tentacle with his blade. The other tentacle dropped the dart gun and reached for Harry. Harry repeatedly sliced at its tip, removing a piece of tentacle with each swipe.

Jimmy and Ski retrieved the dart guns, reloaded them, and fired darts at the creature's head without much effect. As I watched, I realized the reason.

"Divers, listen up!" I said on the circuit. "Its brain is distributed throughout its body. Firing at its head doesn't do much."

"Tell me about it," Whitey squeaked, reaching out to stab its right eye as a tentacle grabbed his wrist.

Harry helped out again, severing that tentacle. The four divers cautiously backed toward the hatch from the thrashing monster as Jer and Jake frantically recoiled their umbilicals inside the Egress Lock. Whitey's head appeared first through the hatch opening. Jer literally pulled him up through the hatch and pushed him off to the side as Harry's helmet appeared. Jake grabbed him but needed a bit of help from Jer to leverage him inside the lock. Ski was next, all 5 feet 7 inches of him, almost making it up through the hatch without any help.

Jimmy handed the dart guns up through the hatch and started to pull himself up when he suddenly darted back down and disappeared.

"Sumbitch has my legs," he squeaked.

Harry pulled his blade and jumped through the hatch. All we could see on the monitor was brightly illuminated silt churning around the hatch.

"I see him," Harry said. "That fucker's dragging him off."

Wally pulled the Basketball off to the side, and the picture cleared a bit. Harry was pulling himself along Jimmy's body. "More umbilical for Jimmy," Harry squeaked, and Jake dumped several coils through the hatch.

This loosened up Jimmy's stretched out condition so that he could reach down to his feet and slash the grasping tentacles. Harry lunged forward and grabbed a fat tentacle near the creature's maw. As he sliced at the tentacle, he suddenly yelped.

"The fucker bit through my suit into my arm," he said through clenched teeth. "Jimmy's free. Pull him back." We heard wheezing and grunting. Then Harry said, "Increase my hot water flow and get me the hell back! I can't hold this sucker off much longer."

The guys pulled Jimmy into the lock with pieces of squirming tentacle still stuck to his legs. Then Jer and Jake pulled Harry's umbilical hand-over-hand as quickly as possible into the lock. Harry was literally airborne for a moment as they pulled him through the hatch.

The moment the hatch was clear, probably remembering what had happened with the Humboldt squid incident off San Diego, Ski lay down on the cover closing it against the spring. A wild thrashing in the opening stopped him. A five-foot tentacle whipped through the opening, wrapping itself around Jake's leg.

"What the fuck!" he yelled, reaching for his knife.

Harry beat him to it, slicing through the tentacle at the waterline, and Ski closed the hatch and cinched it tight.

"Whoa, whoa," Wally said as he zigzagged the Basketball with his joysticks. "You don't get a piece of me, you fucker!"

Wally played tag with the creature until he finally stowed the Basketball A loud clanging sound penetrated the hull. It repeated four times and then stopped.

"I think we really pissed him off," Lt. Cmdr. James said.

⁕

During all this activity, the skipper came to his feet, but stayed back, away from the action. That's what made him such an excellent commanding officer. He knew when not to interfere with his people, especially when they had their hands full. And if there ever was a time we had our hands full, that was it.

The skipper picked up a handset and called Control. "Lift us off the bottom, clear the skids and stow them, and bring us to one hundred fifty feet at five knots on course three-one-eight." He turned to me. "Get Harry's status and brief me," he said and left for Control.

⁕

Harry had a puncture wound in his right bicep. Jimmy treated it in the Main Lock under Dr. Janus Everest's supervision, closed the wound with three sutures, and put him to bed.

The divers had eight days of decompression ahead of them. Shortly, we would be on our way back to EB. When we arrived, they would still have a week to go.

USS TEUTHIS—GENERAL DYNAMICS EB DIVISION

"Surface! Surface! Surface!" That was Senior Chief Radioman Garth Walkman, *Sparks* for short.

Moments before at periscope depth, Doug Watson had done a quick look around for any close contacts and then given the order to surface. Too bad we couldn't remain submerged because the weather had gotten worse during our underwater stint. The rollers were from due east, about ten feet high. Doug set a course of 033 degrees, so they were crossing us 33 degrees ahead of our starboard beam. This caused *Teuthis* to roll fifteen to twenty degrees as each wave passed us, even though we were doing nearly twenty knots. I was glad he was on the Bridge and not me.

Within a half hour, virtually all the newbies were seasick as were nearly half the old hands. It boils down to this: There are two kinds of people, those who get seasick and those who lie about it. Since I had the 0600-watch, I was hunkered down in my bunk—fortunately, otherwise, I might have been seasick, too.

I slept soundly. So far as I know, nothing of any consequence happened. I was up and about by 0530, enjoying a hearty breakfast accompanied by one of Cedric's homemade English muffins, washed down with a couple cups of pretty good coffee, as shipboard coffee goes. Nothing like my favorite Kona coffee, but better than you can get at most restaurants.

By 0540, I was on the Bridge with my JOOD, Zeb Trainer, and lookouts Fred Jackson and Fritz Abelé. We had passed Block Island and were on course for Race Rock Light, about sixteen nautical miles ahead. We were doing ten knots, so we had about ninety minutes before we slowed and station the Maneuvering Watch for entering port.

I looked around as Franklin James, Doug's JOOD, briefed Zeb, my JOOD. Several trawlers were out on early morning fishing runs. The Block Island Ferry was just passing Race Rock Light, making a late-season, bad-weather run out to Block Island. Otherwise, the coast was clear. I accepted the watch and handed the Conn to Zeb.

The wind was really crisp, but it was at our backs, driving a light drizzle against our poncho hoods. I checked to make sure both lookouts were securely fastened to the Bridge safety rings. The last thing I needed in this crap was a real man-overboard exercise.

What I didn't know was what the skipper had in mind for us just a bit later.

※

As we passed Race Rock Light, I slowed to five knots and set a course of 330 degrees, while the skipper stationed the Maneuvering Watch. That was still me, but Zeb went below, and the lookouts changed. Down on the deck, the COB had the deck gang setting up a safety line, pulling hawsers from their bins, raising the fore and aft capstans, and generally making ready for port.

Suddenly, without warning, the COB threw an orange lifevest overboard to starboard and shouted, "Man overboard, starboard! Man overboard, starboard!"

On the deck, the men stopped their tasks and pointed toward the vest. So did the lookouts on the fairwater planes.

I ordered, "Right full rudder! Ahead full!" deciding on the spot to do a Williamson turn, a careful navigating maneuver designed to reverse the sub's course while tracing a curved track that would bring it back to the point where the mishap occurred. I glanced at the gyro repeater. When my bow was at 010 degrees, I ordered, "Shift your rudder to left full!" As the bow began to swing left, I then ordered, "Ahead two thirds!" As I approached 170 degrees, I ordered, "Ease your rudder, make your course one-five-zero. Ahead one third!" I followed my lookouts' pointing fingers with my eyes. I could just make out the bright lifevest about 300 yards directly ahead of us. "Come left to one-four-five." I watched the vest drift right. "All stop! Steer one-five-zero." We were approaching a bit fast. "Back one third!" I watched closely. "All stop!" We were still closing faster than I wanted, and the vest was too far to starboard. "Left full rudder, back two thirds!" As we came to a stop, the bow moved a bit to the right. "All stop, right full rudder!"

We came to a stop with the lifevest resting against the starboard bow as the sub drifted very slowly to the right.

The COB reached over the side with a boat hook and hooked the lifevest. Then he turned and gave me a thumbs-up. From him, that was a high compliment.

"Well done, Mac," the skipper said. "I see you haven't forgotten your basics."

I grinned and brought the sub back on course 150 degrees at five knots, relieved that I hadn't screwed it up.

Two tugs met us at the channel buoy, and the River Pilot jumped onboard as his tug pressed its padded bow against our side. He took over from there, but I remained on the Bridge because it was still my responsibility. When we reached our slip, I lowered both outboards, and with the tugs' help, lined up with the opening. A couple of guys on the pier caught our heaving line and pulled the hawser to the cleat. We used the rear capstan to winch ourselves into the slip. Fifteen minutes later, the Chief of the Watch announced, "Secure the Maneuvering Watch. Set the inport watch, section one."

✳

The *Teuthis* needed several repairs and a couple of minor modifications, including shunting a steam line to the seawater intake to clear potential ice accumulation. Ham and I had to top off our helium and oxygen tanks, and the supply officer and Cedric had to top off our food stores. We timed things so the divers would have one night in town after they surfaced and before we got underway.

Franklin took his tapes of the squid-like giant we encountered on the Hudson Canyon floor to Professor Maximilian Hedgepeth, who headed the zoology department at Massachusetts Institute of Technology. Franklin told me, "When Prof. Hedgepeth saw the images of the complete critter, he went apeshit!"

Franklin said the professor identified the critter as a Cameroceras, a giant orthocone that supposedly went extinct over 400 million years ago. "If there's one, there must be more," Hedgepeth told Franklin.

Franklin let the professor copy the tapes, and said he is preparing an expedition to find more of the creatures. "I think he sees a Nobel Prize in his future," Franklin told me with a grin. "I wish him luck!"

THE OASIS—NEW LONDON, CONNECTICUT

Like the last visit, I parked my Vette on Bank Street outside and pushed my way through the Oasis glass door. I've been in one or two bars in my time, some good, some bad. The Winnie & Moo ranks near the top, but I got to say, the Oasis did a pretty fair job. Submariner and Coastie wannabees hung out whenever they could. Through the smoke, I could see a couple dozen, each hanging out with their own kind. No uniforms, but I could tell the difference.

"Over here, Mac!" Ham called through the low din and the smoke.

The guys had pushed the same two tables together. They had obviously been there a while. That was fine with me. They deserved it, and ahead lay a long dry spell.

Harry handed me a cold, foam-topped mug with his left hand. He was still favoring his right. I sat next to Ham and lifted my mug. "You guys hear about the Cameroceras?" I asked.

"Camero-what?" Harry asked.

Obviously, they had not yet heard about Franklin's visit with the professor in Cambridge.

"Lt. Cmdr. James took the videos to MIT, to Professor Hedgepeth, their senior zoologist," I told them. "He said it was a Cameroceras, supposedly extinct for four hundred million years."

"The thing that grabbed my legs ain't no extinct critter," Jimmy said, clinking mugs with Harry.

"You got that right, Bro!" Harry said, grinning from ear to ear, as Tina kissed him soundly to the cheers of the other divers.

A back door opened, and Maggie entered with four of her friends, including Doris. The first thing Doris did was saunter over to me and greet my ear with her tongue. Then she settled in Jake's lap and proceeded to ignore everyone else. Jake did not seem to be complaining.

After a couple of rounds, it seemed like everyone had a companion, and I figured it was time for me to leave them to their fun for the rest of the night.

As I was making to leave, Doris jumped off Jake's lap and threw her arms around my neck, whispering in my ear, "You sure you can't trespass just once, Mac?" She kissed me.

"   I picked her up and twirled her around. "You're Jake's girl, right?" I asked. She nodded, and Jake grinned. "Then give him something to remember for the next few months," I said, patting her bottom and handing her to Jake.

As Doris settled into Jake's lap, I turned to Ham. "Make sure they make it back—all of them," I said.

"No problem, Mac. See you tomorrow morning at muster."

I grinned and toasted the guys with my empty mug. "Hooyah!" I said and turned toward the door.

Seven very masculine and six feminine *Hooyahs* followed me out the door.

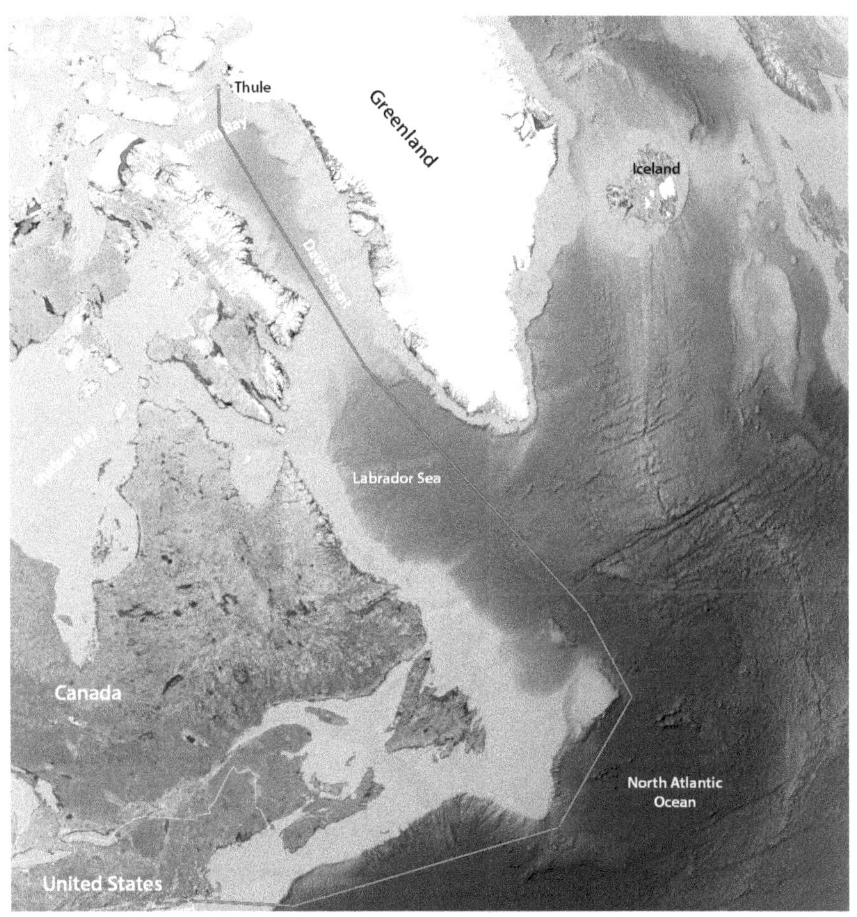

Transit from Long Island to Cary Øer

CHAPTER FOUR—Transit to Carey Øer

USS TEUTHIS—BLOCK ISLAND SOUND & NORTH-WARD

It was time. By any measure, it was time. Except for my guys, every sailor onboard had had about as much shore leave as he could handle. My divers had "surfaced"—returned to normal atmospheric pressure after the slow, methodical ascent—about noon yesterday. They had put in as much overtime ashore between then and this morning as Ham would allow. Fortunately, they were not needed for Maneuvering Watch. Out of respect for the rest of the crew, I required that they be present in Dive Control, but if they wanted to get some badly needed shut-eye in one of the bunks in the Main Lock, I had no objection.

"Station the Maneuvering Watch for underway operations," the Chief of the Watch announced on the 1MC. That was my cue.

"Ivy Bells was where we earned our chops," I said to Ham, "but Ice Breaker will go down in history with so many firsts that it boggles the mind." I grinned at him and left for the Bridge.

We transited the river channel without incident, dropped off the pilot, skirted Race Rock Light, and finally split the twelve nautical miles between Block Island and Montauk Point.

By this time, I had the OOD watch along with Lt.j.g. Zeb Trainer, the Reactor Officer, serving as my JOOD, along with Seamen Fred Jackson and Fritz Abelé as my lookouts on the fairwater planes. Down below in Control, Seaman Joe Spanky was on the helm, with Senior Chief Engineer Sam Dokey as Chief of the Watch, and Senior Chief Quartermaster Alastair Forbes as acting Navigator. The other immediate watch members were Chief Torpedoman Jasper Cedrik as Diving Officer, but since we were on the surface, he was manning the radar as a navigation backup and looking for surface traffic. Chief Sonar Technician Royal Bennett, who—with nothing to do right then—was manning the higher attack scope, also looking for surface traffic.

The thing to remember about all navy ships is that the commanding officer is the personification of the ship. *USS Teuthis* was Commander Fred Roken's ship—in our case, his boat. The crew, all of us, were accessories to his will, assisting him in carrying out his mission. He couldn't do it without us, but we were not independent agents. Rather, we were there to enable the Captain to complete his mission. In reality, of course, we all worked together as a team, but any good skipper ensures that his team knows who is boss.

Before we got underway, the skipper and the Navigator, Lt. Cmdr. Barry Jacobs, laid out the skipper's intended 2,710-nautical-mile track to the Labrador Sea, that separated Greenland from Canada. The skipper intended to run south from the mouth of the

Thames River to the edge of the Continental Shelf, then submerge and turn north to follow the shelf edge to where the Labrador Sea empties into the North Atlantic.

The Maneuvering Watch ended when we dropped off the pilot at the sea buoy. By the time we passed Block Island, half the watch was over. Unlike our experience during sea trials, the sky was powder blue with a crisp breeze from the north as I set a course of 183 degrees at twenty knots. With the wind at our stern, despite the eight to ten-foot waves, we had a comfortable ride as we headed south for the next 113 nautical miles. For me and my topside watch section, this meant three hours of sunshine and a last visual take on a blue ocean covered with foam-topped waves, with frolicking bottlenose dolphins playing in our bow wave.

The skipper looked at his watch. "Got to prepare a couple of dispatches before we dive," he said, climbing off the sail top and dropping down into Control.

"Captain left the Bridge," Zeb announced over the squawk box. In addition to the paperwork, the skipper made a habit of walking through the sub, chatting with sailors on their watch stations. He showed up back on the Bridge for the last two hours of my watch. I had turned the watch over to Zeb, except for my underlying legal responsibility, and was seated on the top of the sail with my feet dangling into the bridge open space, simply enjoying the view. After chatting with Zeb for a couple of minutes, getting an update of the overall status, the skipper plunked himself beside me, silently watching the dolphins play.

After a while, he asked, "How is Harry?"

"Still favors his good arm," I said, "but he didn't seem any the worse for wear at the Oasis last night."

"Do you ever miss it," he asked, "being one of the guys, being enlisted?"

I didn't answer right away. An honest answer deserved a little thought. Finally, I said, "Sometimes, like last night when one of the girls put the moves on me. But, I was out with the guys and had to turn her down. I left early with a couple of small regrets." I stopped talking and watched the dolphins for a minute. "This," I continued, sweeping my arm out over the ocean before us, "is what it's all about, this, and what we will be doing for the next several months." We both watched the dolphins for a bit longer. Then I added, "No, Sir! I wouldn't want to do anything else. If I'm lucky enough to get my own command someday…" I let my voice trail off, thinking about what it would be like to wear the skipper's shoes, carrying the full weight of the mission.

✳

About three hours later, I was in the Wardroom sipping a cup of coffee and reading some papers when Senior Chief Firecontrolman Ogden Winder, the current Chief of the Watch, announced over the 1MC, "Rig for dive! Rig for Dive!"

In reality, the crew had been rigging for dive ever since the end of Maneuvering Watch. For all practical purposes, all everyone had to do was make one final check (you never fail to do this, *never*!), and then report to Control.

I went aft and dropped to Dive Control, where I made a final check of its openings to sea—the three egress hatches in the DDC, the Basketball hatch, and the Fish bay. I had total confidence in Ham, but since the legal responsibility was ultimately mine, it was the prudent thing to do, and Ham expected me to do it. Had I not, he would have chastised me.

"This is the Captain," the 1MC blared throughout the sub. "We are about to submerge for our underway operation that will take us to the frozen waters off northern Greenland, then through the ice-clogged channels of the Canadian archipelago to Point Barrow, Alaska, and finally through the Bering Strait to our home port, Mare Island. We anticipate being submerged for the entire time until we arrive off San Francisco. We don't know precisely how long this will take—two to three months, at least.

"Anyone wishing to visit the Bridge before we dive, we will take you in groups of four for the next thirty minutes. I wish us all success in our endeavor and God's speed for a safe return."

✳

Twenty-five minutes later, the last bridge visitor had dropped into Control, where I was hanging out for the dive. The skipper dropped down the ladder and began sweeping the horizon with the nav scope. Chief Warrant Officer Bert Cobb had the watch. Lt.j.g. Seth Beaumont was his JOOD, and this was his big moment.

"Clear the Bridge!" Seth ordered over the squawk box.

Bert dropped into Control, stating, "This is Warrant Officer Cobb. I have the Deck." On the squawk box, he said, "Rig the Bridge for dive and lay below." He stepped onto the periscope stand and began sweeping around with the attack scope.

Seaman Jeremiah Walker, face black as coal, hit the deck moments later, looking up, followed by Seaman Greg Patterson's legs as he waited halfway down to handle the squawk box and hatch lanyard for Seth. I imagined Seth making one final visual sweep, securing the bridge fairing, and dropping through the hatch.

Greg pulled the lanyard while Seth spun the handle. Then Greg dropped into Control, and Seth's legs appeared as he pulled the hatch shut above him, and Greg pulled the lanyard. Chief Ocean Tech Bart Davidson took his place directly behind the planesmen, and Jerry scrambled to his stern plane seat while Greg stepped back out of the way.

As the lower hatch closed, Seth reported to Bert, "Last man down, hatch secured."

The Chief of the Watch announced, "Green board!"

"Chief of the Watch, dive the ship," Seth ordered.

On the 1MC, Oggy announced, "Dive! Dive!" followed by two long *Aoogahs!* on the klaxon.

"Make your depth six-five feet," Seth ordered as the main ballast tank valves opened.

A minute later, Bart announced, "At six-five feet, zero bubble."

Both the skipper and Seth scanned the horizon one final time and then dropped their scopes. Seth ordered, "Helmsman, come left to new course zero-eight-five, ahead full. Diving Officer, make your depth three-zero-zero feet."

✳

With a sigh, I left Control for the Wardroom, where I intended to spend several hours reviewing details of *Teuthis'* compartmentation, piping, hydraulics, and electrical runs and panels. It had been some time since I had qualified, and like everyone else, I needed to brush up.

For the next two days and 970 nautical miles, we charged northward at 300 feet and thirty knots. That speed through the water made us practically "blind" on sonar, but this didn't keep King and his sonar techs from continuously scanning our surroundings. Roughly every couple of hours, but randomly, we "cleared our baffles," slowing down for about fifteen minutes while radically changing course, while Sonar made a careful sweep, looking for anything out there.

Due to the improvements made during our overhaul, even at thirty knots, we were virtually undetectable by the best sonar systems available to the Soviets. The skipper was not willing to rely on this, however, so we cleared our baffles.

Near the end of day two, on Barry Jacobs' watch, we pivoted 35 degrees northward for fifteen hours, and then on my watch, we came around to 360 degrees for our 1,100-nautical-mile-run into the Labrador Sea.

✳

As anyone who has ever worn the dolphins insignia knows, submarining consists of endless hours of boredom interrupted by moments of sheer panic. This leg of our transit was the boring part. Under normal circumstances, there is virtually no ship traffic to and from the Labrador Sea. Thule Air Base in the far north of Greenland has a couple of supply runs, and Hudson Bay gets some limited traffic, but we were well into autumn. The northern waters were beginning to ice up. Furthermore, despite the general lack of surface traffic, we had to be alert for south-moving icebergs. These silent hazards to navigation could extend down well past our transit depth. We kept the under-ice sonar active. This was a high-frequency, short-range device that transmitted from the top of the sail. It would give us warning of the presence of an iceberg ahead, even at thirty knots, but the OOD had to be nimble to turn away quickly.

During our baffle-clearing intervals, King and his sonar techs picked up the occasional distant sounds of a cargo vessel or tanker transiting into or out of Hudson Strait on their way to or from ports surrounding Hudson Bay.

During Bert's watch late on the second day of the Labrador Sea transit, during one of our baffle clearings, Sonar Tech 1st Class Jim Orange called me, asking if I could come to Sonar. I interrupted my requalification studies in the Wardroom and walked aft down the passageway. I opened the door and stepped into the darkened room. Royal Bennett showed up just after me.

"What's up, Jim?" I asked.

"You used to be a Sonar Tech, right?" Jim asked.

"Yeah, but it was a long time ago."

"And you studied oceanography in college," Jim added.

I nodded. King just listened, probably wondering what was up.

"Listen to this," Jim said, turning on a reel-to-reel tape recorder.

Both King and I slipped on padded headsets. The first thing I heard was the unmistakable sound of Orcas on an orchestrated attack. I had watched a pod of Orcas in Puget Sound herd harbor seals into a compact group and then attack and consume them all. Their back and forth communication squeals and clicks were identical to what I heard on Jim's tape.

I held up a finger, and Jim stopped the tape. "That," I said, "was a pod of Orcas coordinating an attack against something. These guys do that. They work together, herding their prey into a clump, and then they attack and kill the entire batch—whatever it is." I grinned at them. "Okay, next."

Jim started the tape machine. What I heard next took some mental filtering. The Orcas were still present, doing their herding thing. The main sounds, however, were familiar but different—something I had heard back when we had transited under the Barents Sea ice several years ago.

"Play that second part again," I said. This time I got it. "Do you know what a narwhal is?" I asked.

King nodded, but Jim shook his head.

"How about a beluga whale?" I asked.

Same response.

"Okay," I said, "narwhals and beluga whales are very similar, two thousand pounds and maybe fifteen or more feet long. The main difference is that the narwhal has a five to six-foot-long ivory tusk protruding from its mouth. So far as I know, they live only in the Arctic and sub-Arctic. They communicate with clicks, whistles, and knocks." I removed my headset and took a breath. "What you just recorded, Jim, is a pod of maybe ten Orcas, herding together and attacking somewhere between six to ten narwhals."

"You're sure of this?" King asked.

"As sure as one can be with what we have."

"I'm keeping this tape," Jim said. "Shit! This is amazing!"

"You gotta play it for the Captain," King said.

"And the Officer of the Deck," I added. "Also, what this means is that we are near the ice edge. Narwhals never stray very far from there."

USS TEUTHIS—BAFFIN BAY

All the Control Room teams and sonar watch sections filled the seats in the Crew's Mess, chatting quietly among themselves. Lt. Cmdr. Lonie Franken-Ester, the executive officer (XO), assumed the watch in Control so Bert could join us. All the nav personnel were present, and Chief of the Watch Oggie assumed the Diving Officer position temporarily so Chief Bart Davidson could be there. Jim remained in Sonar so his watch section could participate. He stood in the door looking down the stairwell into the Crew's Mess so he could hear the briefing.

When sure everyone was present, I mounted the stairwell and turned left past Sonar. I knocked on the door to the Captain's Cabin, then opened it.

"We're ready for you, Skipper," I said and stepped aside so he could precede me.

The skipper stopped briefly at Sonar to say, "Great work, Petty Officer Orange. Can you make a copy that we can play in the Crew's Mess?"

Jim grinned and handed him a tape reel. The skipper took it and handed it back to me. "Play this after my briefing," he said, "and then leave it with the Mess Cooks so the rest of the crew can hear it."

✳

"Attention on deck!" the COB said as the skipper entered the Crew's Mess.

"As you were," the skipper said as the assembled sailors began to stand.

"We are at the edge of the Arctic ice pack," Roken commenced. "Petty Officer Orange recorded an interesting event that happened a short while ago near our location. Following this briefing, Commander McDowell will play the recording for you and narrate his best take on what you will be hearing, based upon his own significant oceanographic experience.

"Within the hour, we will no longer have clear water over us. Instead, the surface will be filled with increasingly heavy ice floes until—within five to ten miles—the surface will be solid ice six to eighteen inches thick. As we continue north, the ice will thicken to two feet or more. When we reach the permanent ice region, it may be as much as ten to fifteen feet thick." He paused to let those numbers sink in.

"I don't have to tell you that we do not want to surface through ice that thick. This will be our operating mode for the next two months, at least. You men are the best we have, the best submariners in the navy. You serve on the best submarine in the navy. I am asking you to be even more vigilant than your usual best.

"We will be bottoming west of Carey Øer, a group of small islands sixty nautical miles northwest of Thule, Greenland. There, Commander McDowell and his divers will lay a special hydrophone array that will integrate into our worldwide SOSUS network. Its location and purpose carry the highest possible security classification. You will not speak of this to anyone who is not here in this room, not to any other crew members, and especially not to anyone outside the crew.

"After that, we will transit through the Canadian archipelago to a location off Hope Point, Alaska, where Commander McDowell and his divers will lay another array. Then we will transit the Bering Strait on our way home to Mare Island.

"During our transit, we will have to surface occasionally to get a good navigation fix. If possible during those times, I'll allow some topside activity." The skipper stopped talking and looked around the

Crew's Mess. "Remember, no talk or discussion of the hydrophone arrays! Stick around to hear Petty Officer Orange's recording."

As the skipper turned to mount the stairwell, the COB said, "Attention on Deck!"

I mounted the tape on the reel-to-reel at the front of the crowded mess. The guys were fascinated and continued to ask questions until I had to cut them off.

"Drop by Sonar in the next couple of hours. You'll hear more stuff like this," I told them as I left.

*

I knew we would come to periscope depth soon for a nav fix, so I hung around Control after the meeting. Locating one's position on the globe is no trivial task. Ships at sea and aircraft normally use Loran-C, a radio navigation system that receives signals from ground-based transmitters. It is accurate to a few hundred feet, or even better if you take several fixes. Unfortunately, Loran-C signals do not normally reach the Arctic, and even if they do sometimes at night, the accuracy goes to shit. The Omega system is global, but even at best, it gives a two-mile accuracy, and in the Arctic, it's much worse. Fortunately, the Navy developed the SatNav system for its boomer fleet and the fast-attacks that chased Soviet missile subs. This system, called Transit, consisted of a bunch of satellites in polar orbits that broadcast info that could be used to calculate a fix within just a few feet. This was the accuracy the boomers needed to launch their missiles, and it was the kind of accuracy *we* needed to find our way through the iced-in Canadian archipelago.

To use the SatNav system, Barry needed to know our approximate position, a list of times a Transit satellite would be above the horizon where we were, a receiver for the signals, and a computer to process the signals and give a position. In principle, Barry and his guys could use the raw signal data to calculate a position, but this was tedious and prone to error. His SatNav receiver handled the entire task in minutes.

About a half hour later, Seth slowed to five knots, cleared the baffles, and ordered his Control crew to bring *Teuthis* to periscope depth. The sub had two scopes. Bert took one and the skipper the other. Barry Jacobs hurried through Control on his way to the Nav Center to make sure his guys got a good location fix.

The JOOD, Seth Beaumont, asked the skipper for his scope when he was done. After Seth had completed a couple full circles, I tapped him on the shoulder. "Let me take a couple of swings, and I'll give it right back," I said.

I saw calm, smooth water all around us and a white line several hundred yards off our port side to the north—the jagged edge of the sea ice. As I swung toward the bow, an Orca cleared the water, its entire 25-foot length suspended in the air for a moment.

"Look at this," I said, handing the scope to the skipper.

He watched for several seconds and then handed the scope back to Seth.

"The big ones are male," I said, "ten thousand pounds or so. Looks like they're still feeding."

"I just saw a narwhal clear the water," Seth said, "and an Orca right after it."

"Doesn't stand a chance," I said.

Barry approached the periscope stand and addressed the skipper. "I have a good sat fix, Captain. Recommend course three-four-zero."

✳

Bert glanced at the skipper for confirmation, and then he and Seth dropped their scopes.

"Helmsman, ahead full, come left to three-four-zero," Bert ordered. "Diving Officer, make your depth…" he glanced at the skipper again. The skipper raised four fingers. "…four-zero-zero feet, ten-degree down bubble."

The *Teuthis* heeled to port as the bow dropped. The skipper picked up his Night Order book and sat in his chair on the periscope stand, slowly writing his Night Orders in his classic, cursive handwriting.

As I left Control, the oncoming watchstanders were just finishing their evening meal—steak grilled to order, French fries, and fresh garden salad. I suspected this would be the last of the salad. There might be enough left to garnish "midrats"—midnight rations—sandwiches for a couple of nights, but that would be it. We'd still have fresh veggies and potatoes for some time yet, but fresh lettuce would soon be a distant memory. Cedric baked up a batch of fresh hot-cross buns that rounded out the meal to a T.

✳

By the time my 0600-watch rolled around, we had penetrated over 300 nautical miles further into the ice. We had just transited Davis Strait, between the southeastern-most point of Baffin Island and Greenland, 162 nautical miles at its narrowest. As I assumed the watch, we were entering Baffin Bay, still on course 340 degrees, doing thirty knots at 400 feet. The first thing I did was slow down and clear baffles.

As soon as we slowed down, King announced from Sonar, "Conn, Sonar. I have in intermittent contact twenty degrees off the port bow, bearing three-two-zero—designate Sierra-seven." This was the sub's seventh sonar contact logged thus far during the operation.

I picked up the handset. "What do you have, King?"

"Hard to tell, Sir. It's intermittent. Could have suppressed cavitation."

He was telling me it could be a submarine. Ships' propellers produce small gas bubbles as they spin. These bubbles collapse with a thrashy sound, like a top-loading clothes washer. Because any submarine is deeper, the collapsing bubble sound has a characteristic squeaky note.

"Can you get anything on it?"

"It's too intermittent, Sir. Maybe when it's closer."

I called the skipper's stateroom, but he didn't answer. I presumed he was having breakfast in the Wardroom and called there. Crisanto Rivera answered and handed the phone to the skipper.

"Skipper," I said, "can you come to Control? We may have picked up a submerged sub off our port bow."

"Be right there, Mac."

The skipper walked down the passageway past Sonar to Control. "Whadya have, Mac?" We stepped over to the chart table.

"We're here," I said, pointing to our position along our intended track. I laid out a line of position to the contact. "It looks like he might have come out of Parry Channel. SubLant knows what we're doing, right?" The skipper nodded. "I don't think it likely that they would put another sub in our operating area. That makes this guy Ivan."

"You've got a point," the skipper said. "SubLant specifically told me they would stay clear of our routes and operating areas."

I picked up a nearby mike. "Sonar, Conn, update your contact."

"Nothin', Conn. We lost him. He was intermittent... we'll probably pick him up again in a bit."

"Roger, stay on top of it."

"Let's slow our transit to ten knots," the skipper said, "and clear baffles once an hour randomly."

✳

We had 430 nautical miles left on our current course to put ourselves opposite Parry Channel—where we thought Ivan was. The fact that we heard him indicated that he was underway, probably in our direction.

In my experience, the Soviets had pretty much mapped out the general locations of our SOSUS arrays. They also had located blind spots where we could not see them. Their fast-attacks would rush pell-mell from one blind spot to the next, not really caring how much noise they made during their transits. The matter was that they knew we did not have any SOSUS arrays under the Arctic ice—that's what this operation was all about. So, the question was, would they move stealthily under the ice, or would they go hell-bent-for-leather? I certainly didn't know, and I didn't think the skipper knew either, although I'm certain he knew a lot more about it than I did. We might actually find out as we watched Ivan come in our direction.

If I assumed Ivan was doing ten knots so he could hear, and we were doing ten knots, then we could expect to be near each other in twenty-one hours.

About two hours into the watch, King called me from Sonar. "We picked him up again a bit to the left of his original bearing. This guy's definitely a Soviet sub. We're working on identifying him."

He was too close to our bow to get a good BQQ range. I called the skipper and suggested that we bring him broad on the port beam for a half hour to get a good range on him. The skipper concurred and told me to slow to five knots for the run.

"Ahead slow, make turns for five knots," I ordered. "Come right to new course one-three-zero."

"Nav," I said to Senior Chief Forbes, "keep me on this course for a half hour, and then lay a new course for our Baffin Bay endpoint."

I stuck my head into Sonar. "We're bringing Ivan on the beam. You got a half hour to get the best info you can."

✳

Thirty minutes later, I told Zeb to come to the new course Al had recommended and speed up slightly to ten knots. I left him with the Conn while I met the skipper in Sonar. King had pulled the "waterfall" chart off the BQQ machine and laid it out on a table. A couple of open books anchored the chart at the top. The chart displayed two sets of somewhat indistinct vertical lines consisting of clumped dots. Each line represented a distinct frequency. Together, they formed a unique pattern of one, and only one vessel, although only a trained Sonar Tech could distinguish one chart from another. The two sets of lines on the chart before us were identical to each other but offset by a small but measurable frequency difference. This represented the difference in the phase of the arriving signals and could be used to calculate the vessel's distance.

King pulled out his HP-45 calculator and ran the numbers. "Sierra-seven is at four hundred nautical miles, plus fifty, minus forty," he said. "We're talking a two-and-a-half-mile base at some four hundred miles. That's pretty shaky. I'd want to check this every couple of hours until we are sure of our results."

"You're calling the shots, King," the skipper said. Turning to me, he said, "Keep on top of it, Mac. Until we nail it down, run a half-hour baseline every hour, reversing directions each time. I'll put it in the Night Orders, but make sure your relief knows what we're doing."

It took the entire rest of my watch before King was satisfied with his numbers.

"Conn, Sonar, we got Sierra-seven nailed. He bears three-zero-eight, range two hundred sixty nautical miles, course one-six-zero at ten knots. He's an *Alfa class* Soviet sub, and…" King paused, and I could hear him grinning, "I think it's the *K-316*. We don't know much about these boats, but they're small, fast, and deep diving—perhaps up to three thousand feet." King paused. "Maybe we can add to the intel database while we're out here."

It didn't seem like a bad idea to me, but I had no idea how prophetic his comment would turn out to be.

USS TEUTHIS—CAREY ØER

Bert and Barry were on duty after my watch, keeping a careful eye on the *Alfa*. Instead of continuing on course for open water in the Labrador Sea, the small Soviet attack sub had stopped his forward motion. King suggested that he had heard us intermittently and was trying to find us. The skipper slowed us down during Doug's watch, so that by the time I came on watch again 24 hours later, we were about five hours away from the Carey Islands at our slower speed.

The skipper joined me after we had completed our turn-over and were into the routine of our watch.

"I have been thinking about our skirmishes with the *Whiskey* in the Sea of Okhotsk," the skipper said, recalling the cat-and-mouse games we played there two years ago. "That Soviet CO had an uncanny ability to arrive in our new operating area despite his inability to track us very well." He smiled at me. "I realize that you have not had the tactical training that a prospective CO receives. But you were with me in the Sea of Okhotsk, you have prior boomer experience, and you had a lot of experience as a Sonar Tech, and—I understand—you participated in a research project a couple hundred miles north of here. What are your thoughts?"

I thought about what to say before I answered, surprised that the skipper knew about my Arctic research while I was at University of Washington. "King says this guy is very quiet. Everything I know says we are even more quiet. I am guessing he picked us up two or three times—enough to give him an approximate track." The skipper and I walked over to the chart table. The *Alfa*'s last best position was marked on the chart. "If he was able to get an indication of our track, he may be heading toward where he thinks we are headed." I laid a track from his last known position to the Carey Islands.

Roken stood at the chart table for a couple of minutes, in thought, chin in his left hand. He pulled out a chart that detailed the vicinity of Carey Øer. Then he pulled out a chart that showed the northeastern Arctic and laid a line from the Carey Islands to the center of Parry Channel, west to Prince Regent Inlet, and south into the inlet. He pulled a chart of Prince Regent Inlet and laid a line south to the Gulf of Boothia and then east into the Fury and Hecla Straits. He pulled a chart of the Spicer Islands and laid a line generally eastward through Fury and Hecla Strait and down through the Labrador Narrows into Foxe Basin. He searched through the charts stashed next to the chart table and pulled out two that showed Foxe Basin to Foxe Channel on which he laid a line generally southeast, and Foxe Channel itself, where he continued the line. He pulled out one more chart, of Hudson Strait, on which he laid a line to the Labrador Sea, about 1,180 nautical miles south of the Carey Islands.

In effect, the skipper had drawn a rough circumnavigation of Baffin Island. "Nav follows you on watch, right?" the skipper asked.

"No, Sir, Bert does, but I'll get them to Barry."

"Okay, show these to Barry and tell him I want detailed tracks by the end of Bert's watch." The skipper turned and walked forward to his cabin.

✳

While I was up in this region during my university days, we were investigating a polynya— an area of open water surrounded by sea ice—that regularly appeared north of the Carey Islands between Greenland and Ellesmere Island. Sometimes it even extended south of Carey Islands. The *Teuthis* was now in the vicinity where we might expect clear or partially clear water above us.

We were moving at about ten knots to remain hidden from the *Alfa*, coming up on the southeast of the Careys, but the ocean currents in this area were strong and relatively unknown. We needed a good sat fix so we wouldn't bump into the underwater part of one of the islands.

I came up to 100 feet and activated the under-ice sonar. Because of the high-frequency, unless the *Alfa* were right next to us, he would not be able to pick it up. The display showed an ice cover at about eighty-five percent, less than a foot thick, with a smooth undersurface.

It looked like the polynya had spread to include the Carey Islands this year, and we were right at its southern edge.

I checked with Al—we had a Transit bird overhead—so I informed the skipper and requested permission to come to periscope depth to get a good sat fix. He gave me the okay.

I knew where we thought we were, but just to be sure, I wanted to head away from the Careys and Greenland. "Helmsman, come left to new course two-two-five; make turns for five knots."

When he acknowledged, I said, "Diving Officer, come to periscope depth, easy." I turned to the chart table. "Nav, prepare to get whatever fixes you can. I intend to remain at periscope depth for fifteen minutes."

Senior Chief Forbes could have done the fixes by himself, but he called Commander Jacobs to the Nav Center. I raised the attack scope as the skipper stepped onto the periscope stand and raised the navigation scope.

My Diving Officer, Chief Torpedoman Jasper "Tubes" Cedrik, called out the depth as we rose, "One hundred fifty feet…one hundred…seventy-five…seventy… at periscope depth, Sir, six-five feet."

I had been swinging the attack scope around from the time we reached seventy feet. The scope must have hit a small piece of ice because I felt it jiggle and then steady as it broke water.

"No contacts," I said, "broken ice in all directions."

"No contacts," the skipper echoed, "seventy percent broken ice in all directions."

I was looking aft as the navigation mast pierced the surface.

"Conn, Sonar, I've got a pod of beluga broad on the beam to the north."

I swung the scope to the left. There they were. "A hundred yards off the starboard beam, Skipper."

"What happens if the polynya freezes over?"

"I'm not an expert, Sir, but the polynya normally stays open year-round. If it really does start to freeze, the beluga can keep an area open so long as they find enough to eat." I grinned. "Another option around here is to follow an icebreaker track to open water."

The skipper looked at me with surprise. "Really?"

"They've been observed doing it." I thought of another option. "Bowhead whales can punch through two feet of ice and frequently do. Belugas and even narwhal are smart enough to seek out bowheads when they get trapped."

"Conn, Nav, I got my sat fix. Recommend course two-nine-zero."

That would take us just south of the Careys moving with prevailing currents that seemed stronger near the surface than at depth, according to Barry.

"Pass along the west of the Careys at ten knots tracking the thousand-foot depth curve," the skipper said. "Be sure to note it clearly on the chart. Then pick up Nav's plot for the Parry Channel, which he should have done by then. Once we're on that track, make fifteen knots at three hundred feet."

I looked at the skipper with a question on my face.

"I want the *Alfa* to hear us. We're going to lead him on a wild goose chase and lose him in the Canadian archipelago. We simply can't afford to have him around while we're on the bottom at the Careys."

✳

The rest of my watch consisted of steadying up on our track to pass around the Careys to the east. We were moving with the current, and so had to be careful we stayed on track. This required frequent small adjustments to our course, which kept Al and me busy.

I was glad when Bert relieved me about a half hour later. I gave him the skinny and then headed to the Wardroom for a well-deserved lunch of ham and swiss sandwiches with tomato-basil soup. As I've said before, in the Wardroom, we tend to eat what the crew eats—it's just that we pay for the privilege. For lunch, however, as a group, we decided to eat lighter fare. Since none of us were on a kosher diet, ham and swiss appeared frequently—who doesn't love that?

After lunch, I returned to my qualifications. I had worked my way through the Engine Room, Auxiliary Machinery Space, and the Reactor Compartment. I already knew the Cable Reel and Dive Compartments, so that left Ops and Torpedo, easily two more weeks of intensive study. It was interesting to me how much came back as I got into the details. Occasionally, I would discover a switch, actuator, or valve that had moved from my memory of its location. To be honest, I wasn't entirely sure whether this was a memory fault or an actual altered location. No matter though, I simply memorized the new location.

✳

The skipper was obviously relying quite a bit on my knowledge of this area. We had a pretty good library of publications that dealt in one way or another with under-ice operations and, more specifically, with the areas we would transit. I had no doubt that the skipper was absorbing as much as possible from these pubs. That meant that I had better be up on them as well. I took extensive notes to help me integrate what I had experienced in earlier under-ice excursions and my research time up here with information contained in the pubs—sometimes information I had not heard of before.

As it turned out, my studies and extensive notes would play a crucial role later on.

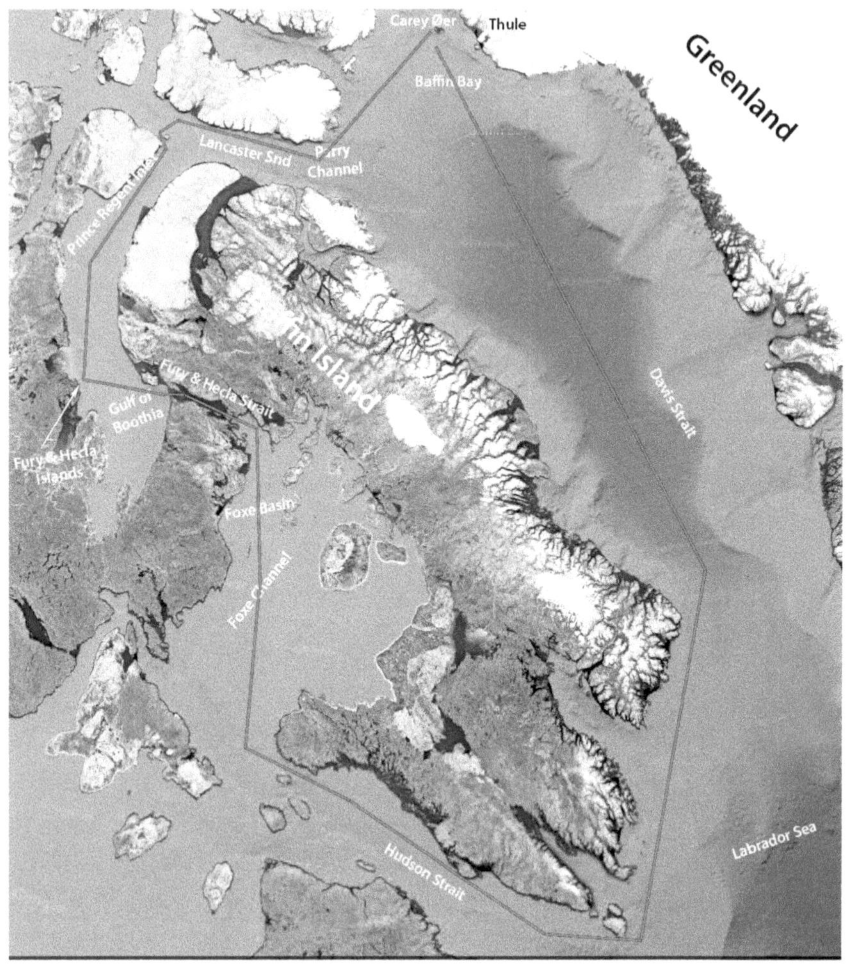

The diversionary chase around Baffin Island

CHAPTER FIVE—The Chase

USS TEUTHIS—LANCASTER SOUND

Bert's watch was taken up with passing the Careys and then coming around to the west to pass north of the islands. If we didn't detect the *Alfa*, the skipper decided to make three passes over the sloping plain west of the islands—north-south, south-north, north-south— using the secure depth-sounder to give us a sense of the bottom.

Secure depth-sounder? That was something left over from *Teuthis'* days as a boomer. Like the under-ice sonar, it used high-frequency sonar to look at the bottom, but with a difference. The secure depth-sounder also used spread-spectrum technology to disguise the sonar signals, where the signal is spread across the sound spectrum instead of being transmitted on a single frequency. Whenever there was any question about how much water we had below the keel, we used it.

Either the *Alfa* didn't know where we were, or he didn't let on that he knew. Bert completed the three transits, identifying the 1,000-foot curve about five miles west of Nordvestø and Fierø, on a moderately sloping bottom. Barry dropped a transponder at the thousand-feet curve between the islands. The transponder would remain quiet unless it received a coded signal from *Teuthis* when we returned to lay the SOSUS array.

❋

Barry assumed the watch from Bert, dove to 300 feet, and set a course of 218 degrees at fifteen knots. Roughly every hour at randomized intervals, he slowed to five knots and conducted several radical course and depth changes that finally brought us back on track and depth while Sonar thoroughly checked our baffles.

Ahead of us lay fifteen hours of the same. During Barry's six hours, Sonar detected the *Alfa* behind us three times, apparently following as far back as possible without losing us. On one of his baffle clears, he took the *Alfa's* range with the BQQ-2 sonar. The Soviet boat was fifty nautical miles behind us, which gave us a good idea of his passive sonar range.

Doug picked the *Alfa* up two times for sure, and maybe a third, but he didn't get a range. Sonar thought the *Alfa* might have dropped back a bit. We were in the cold, south-flowing Labrador Current by this time, which may have affected sonar range.

After a great breakfast of eggs over-easy, hashbrowns, and bacon—we still had fresh eggs—but they probably wouldn't last much longer either—Cedric's fresh buns, and two cups of very passable coffee, I came on watch at 0545. I brought a third cup of coffee with me and stepped to the chart table. We had three more hours of the same ahead of us. Despite the routine, there was always the possibility of finding the *Alfa* behind us when we cleared our baffles—a step from boring toward *very* exciting.

Finally, the three hours came and went without incident. It was now time to head into Lancaster Sound. First things first, however; we needed a good fix. Al informed me that we actually had two available Transit birds. I called the skipper on the sound-powered phone.

"We're getting ready to take a sat fix through the ice," I told him. Shortly thereafter, he came to Control and took his chair on the periscope stand.

"Helmsman," I ordered, "come right to new course two-seven-zero, make turns for five knots." Then I checked the under-ice sonar. We had eighteen inches of solid ice above us with a smooth underside. "All stop," I ordered, and then I addressed Tubes. "Diving Officer, rig the fairwater planes for ice penetration."

With our momentum from our earlier fifteen-knot speed, we still had some forward motion. "Back one third," I ordered, watching my indicators. "All stop."

We were DIW—dead in the water—at 300 feet.

"Chief of the Watch," I said to Senior Chief Sam Dokey, "bring us up slowly. I want to come to rest with the top of the sail resting against the ice cover."

Dokey got us there in about ten minutes.

"Okay, guys," I said, "this is a bit tricky. I want to drop down five feet and then give us enough upward momentum to crack the ice without pushing the sail through." I turned to Dokey. "Prepare to hover, Sam."

The skipper picked up the 1MC mike. "This is the Captain. We are about to break through the ice cover. You will hear a lot of noise, and things may shake a bit, but *Teuthis* is built to do this. Even though we will sound the collision alarm, we will not be in any danger." He nodded at me.

"Chief of the Watch, sound the collision alarm and crack the ice."

The collision alarm sounds like a police siren but at a higher pitch and a faster rate. Because it is also used for flooding, it sends shivers down the spine of every submariner, me included—even though I knew exactly what was happening.

We hit the ice rather gently—five feet is not enough to generate much momentum—accompanied by a little bounce and the sounds of cracking and scraping.

"Take her down a couple of feet, Senior Chief," I said, and eased the attack scope up. I broke through clear water and swung around quickly. "Nothing but ice all around. The sail pushed several chunks of ice onto the ice sheet. We have a few feet of clear water above us. You can raise your scope, Captain." Without removing my eye from the scope, I said, "Chief of the Watch, commence hovering at sixty-four feet."

I turned to Senior Chief Quartermaster Forbes. "Okay, Al, you can get your fix."

He went aft to the Nav Center. Both the skipper and I pointed our scopes toward the stern. The nav mast cleared the surface, remained there for about a minute, and disappeared.

"I got the fix," Al reported.

"That was quick," I said.

"Yeah…with two birds…"

I acknowledged and said, "Sam, maintain the hover, but drop down to one hundred feet." And then, "Sonar, report the *Alfa*."

"We got him on our track, Conn."

"I'm giving you a quiet hover at a hundred feet, Sonar. Get me your best range."

A few minutes later, Sonar reported, "We got the *Alfa* at twenty-five miles. No way he can hear us right now, so he's just chugging down our track."

I glanced at the skipper, and he nodded. "Let's give Ivan some breadcrumbs he can follow," the skipper said as he left for his cabin.

*

I had about two hours left on my watch. I dropped to 300 feet and headed due west at fifteen knots. I cleared baffles every hour or so as we had been doing, and each time, Sonar detected the *Alfa* in what I was beginning to call *hot pursuit*.

Bert's and Barry's watches went the same way. We were leaving a bright trail, and the *Alfa* was gobbling every crumb.

Just before Doug's watch, the skipper assembled the watch officers and nav watchstanders in the Wardroom. He laid out a chart on the table of the entire Canadian archipelago. He pointed his finger. "We're here." He moved his finger around Baffin Island along the path he had earlier outlined. "This is the path we intend to take." Then he moved his finger from our present position westward through Viscount Melville Sound and southward to the Bering Strait. "This is where we want the *Alfa* to think we are going, and here is how we will do that."

✻

Immediately upon assuming the watch, Doug went to 200 feet at flank speed—that's about thirty-one knots. We sprinted forward, totally blind, of course, but it would take the *Alfa* more than an hour to figure out that we were sprinting ahead. His logical assumption would be that we were sprinting toward the Bering Strait—precisely what we wanted him to conclude.

Doug kept it up for seventy-five minutes without clearing baffles. Then he changed course ten degrees to the right for another fifteen minutes. This placed *Teuthis* twelve nautical miles directly north of Prince Leopold Island. Prince Leopold is 3.5 miles across. Its southern end is just five miles north of Cape Clarence on the northeastern tip of Somerset Island.

I woke up from a dream about the red-headed Cheyenne gal I had met on my way to Groton as the Chief of the Watch announced, "Rig ship for ultra-quiet."

I checked the time: 0400.

Almost immediately, the soft whisper of circulating air vanished, the turbine hum disappeared, and the general submarine background noise—people, dishes, equipment, music—all stopped. You could have heard a pencil drop a hundred feet away. My curiosity got the better of me. I climbed out of my upper bunk, slipped on my blue jumpsuit and steel-toed, crepe-soled shoes, and left my shared stateroom, silently shutting the door behind me.

The sub was rigged for red. It was silent as a tomb. I quietly walked aft past the Radio Room on my right and the Sonar Shack on my left. Although red-lit Control displayed no white light, I could see everything clearly with my dark-adapted eyes. The only sounds were a quiet murmur from the 400-Hertz synchros in the Attack

Center and soft hissing from hydraulic valves controlling bow and stern planes and rudder.

Key people wore sound-powered headsets. When they spoke into the large, rubber-cupped mikes, it was in a quiet whisper.

"Come left to new course one-eight-five," Doug whispered. "Make your depth one-five-zero feet. Make steerageway turns—adjust turns to maintain bare steerageway."

I made my way back to the Engine Room. The engineers had shut down the turbine and its relatively noisy reduction gear and were driving the shaft at minimum turns directly with the much quieter electric motor. They had cut back reactor power to a minimum, so the primary and secondary coolant pumps were running at the lowest possible speed. Even though everything in the engineering spaces was fully sound mounted, the noise intensity now was dramatically lower.

I stopped in Maneuvering, where I found Chief Machinist Robert Daley. Whispering, I asked, "How long can we run like this?"

"Long as we want. If we seriously deplete the battery, we can bring the reactor up a bit to top it off or even run a zero-float" (meaning replacing battery power as it was being consumed). I hung around for a few minutes and then returned to Control.

Since I had the next watch, I grabbed some chow and returned to Control to relieve Doug early. I was up, so it made no sense for me not to assume the watch.

✳

I headed slightly east of south for four hours. When the bottom reached 500 feet below the keel several miles west of and a mile or so south of Prince Leopold Island, I walked over to the chart table. I pointed to the hundred-meter curve.

"Al, I want to follow this curve around Cape Clarence to here." I pointed to a spot about two miles off Cape Clarence, where the depth dropped to 900 feet.

"Left full rudder," I ordered. "Come to new course one-four-three. Make your depth one-two-five feet. Continue to adjust turns for bare steerageway."

Two and a half hours later, the bottom dropped off to 980 feet. I called the skipper. "We're ready to turn south, Sir."

The skipper joined me in Control. "Take her down to five hundred feet and ten knots," he told me. "When you run out of nine hundred feet, come up to four hundred feet, and follow the track."

I dropped the sub to 500 feet, set a course of 220 degrees, and turned the watch over to Bert and his crew—still at ultra-quiet. Then I dropped down to see Ham. We had some divers to press down to 500 feet and some preps to make.

HECLA & FURY ISLANDS—ON THE OCEAN BOTTOM

Twenty-four hours later, we had traveled 232 nautical miles south, passing through Prince Regent Inlet into the Gulf of Boothia. For the entire track, we were under ice from two to four feet thick, and we remained at ultra-quiet. The *Alfa's* chances of detecting us were somewhere between zero and nothing. We had lured him into believing we had continued west through Parry Channel into Barrow Strait on our way to the Bering Strait. At some point, we knew he would figure out that we had hornswoggled him. His first thought would probably be that we had turned south into McClintock Channel or Peel Sound, depending on how far west he got before figuring things out, since both those routes led to the Bering Strait.

The *Alfa* was faster than we were, although we didn't learn this until later. Also, he didn't care if we detected him since his job seemed to be to disrupt whatever we were up to. I suspect he dashed south into both passages looking for us. Then, depending on the *Alfa* skipper's mindset, he would either race to the Chukchi Sea off Point Barrow to intersect us there or return to investigate Prince Regent Inlet. If he chose the Chukchi Sea, he would eventually have to conclude he was wrong about our destination. That left Prince Regent Inlet, so one way or the other, eventually, the *Alfa* would investigate Prince Regent and Boothia. What we couldn't know was how he would do this. He had the option of following our route from the north or passing south of Somerset Island through Bellot Strait from Peel Sound.

By then, we hoped to be long gone, doing our job up at the Careys. If he passed through Bellot Strait, as I thought he might, the *long gone* would be a lot shorter. Nevertheless, when he didn't find us, he would figure that we had either headed around Baffin Island to the south or north, and head back to where he had first found us. We wanted to avoid that at all costs, so we needed to delay him in the Bay of Boothia as long as possible.

That's where my dive team entered the picture.

※

In 1821, William Edward Parry took the *HMS Fury* and her sister ship, the *HMS Hecla*, northwest through Foxe Basin north of Hudson Bay, looking for a northwest passage. He was stopped by an eight-nautical-mile-long narrow ice-filled stretch of ocean that came to be named the Labrador Narrows. On his next expedition in 1825, he penetrated the ice following the same path we took down through Prince Regent Inlet to the Bay of Boothia and the entrance to the sixty-three-nautical-mile-long straits that led to the other side of the Labrador Narrows. He named them the Fury and Hecla Straits. Unable to transverse the straits because of heavy ice, on his way back, Parry passed a small group of islands about ninety-five nautical miles almost due west of the straits that rise nearly straight up from a 550-foot-deep basin. He named them the Hecla and Fury Islands. Unfortunately, the *HMS Fury* never made it home. She became icebound about ninety-five nautical miles north just off the coast of Somerset Island, where Parry was forced to abandon her and take the crew aboard his ship for the return to England.

The Pentagon people behind our operation had put a lot of thought into the details. One of the requirements was a power source for the two arrays we would be placing. Radioisotope Thermoelectric Generators (RTGs) had been used for a long time, had been tested in space and underwater applications, were entirely safe, and were small and light—about the size of a large thermos flask. And perhaps the most important, they lasted for decades. We carried several onboard.

At the skipper's direction, Lt. Cmdr. Franklin James had his people construct a small sonar ping transponder powered by one of the RTGs. The transponder produced a ping at the same frequency as our active sonar. At random intervals, it would go active for several pings. Both the interval and the number of pings were randomized.

Furthermore, when it received a ping from an outside source, it would choose one of a dozen different response options, and returned pings that gave the ping source tracking information for a nonexistent target. Its responses could only show a target closing or opening on a specific bearing, but the differing tracks would serve to confuse the ping source—in our case, the *Alfa*.

We intended to place the transponder on the bottom at the north face of the largest of the Hecla and Fury Islands. The skipper figured, and I agreed with him, that this would confuse the *Alfa* for several days as it tried to determine precisely with what it was dealing.

The bottom line was that the transponder gave us a day or more beyond what we gained by our subterfuge, enough to let us depart the Carey Islands after laying the array and get underway for Point Barrow.

At least, that was the plan.

✳

The XO took my watch while I worked with Ham and Bill to get the divers ready for their excursion on the bottom at the base of one of the main Hecla and Fury Islands. We really had no idea what things would be like down there. Sounding data were virtually non-existent, except for two vessel paths that could very well have come from something under sail back in the nineteenth century. That would have been with lead lines. Taking lead-line soundings at 500 feet or more is tedious and not exactly accurate, especially in partial ice cover.

Bert assumed the watch as we approached our destination. He made several passes by the east side of the largest island, each a bit closer than the last. When Nav estimated that we were no more than a quarter mile from the island, Bert found the bottom starting to angle up. It was a 33-degree slope near the bottom that changed to 70 or 80 degrees, where the landmass rose from the water.

Bert brought *Teuthis* as close as possible to the upslope and set her on the bottom with something close to an even keel. That's some submarining!

✳

I arrived in Dive Control to find Lt. Cmdr. Frank James already there with Dr. Brand and Senior Chief Jones huddled with Ham and Bill. They were poring over a bottom contour chart of the largest of the

Hecla and Fury Islands. Penciled in on the chart were the soundings Bert had taken earlier. I joined them, crowding the table a bit. Dr. Brand was explaining his reasoning to the others.

"We have four distinct islands on the chart." Brand pointed at a spot to the southwest between the large island and the small one at the southern end. "This appears to be a shelf of some kind. Too shallow for our purpose." He slid his finger through the middle island to a spot at the northern end. "The whole thing is about four nautical miles long." He traced along the eastern side. "We want the transponder to be heard, but not obvious-in-your-face heard. The steepest slope seems to be here." He pointed to the easternmost extension of the largest island. "We should do a careful fish scan between us and the steep rise to find the best location for the transponder."

"Exactly my thought," a voice behind me said.

I turned to see Commander Roken grinning at us.

"Sorry, Skipper, I didn't hear you come in."

"You gents were pretty focused." He turned to Frank. "Get a really good bottom survey between us and the slope. I want to be as close to the slope as possible, so Mac's divers can remain closer to *Teuthis*. I'm not anticipating anything, but I really don't want a repeat of Hudson Canyon."

✳

Frank had his Fish team assemble in Dive Control. Chief Ocean Tech Francis Oberst set up a schedule with Wally Dubbs taking the first set and Derrick Jensen the second. Oberst supervised in the background with Senior Chief Jones, whom we called *Spook*, relieving him as necessary. This was Frank's operation, so I paid close attention but stayed out of it.

If there is anything more boring than a submarine transit, it's taking a series of sidescan sonar passes over mostly featureless seafloor. About six hours later, during which the engineering half of the crew took a well-deserved rest, Frank called me to Dive Control.

He had replaced the charts on the table with taped together sidescan printouts. It took a moment for my eyes to integrate the squiggles on the printouts, and then it came into focus. Then it was like I was looking through a window that changed everything to grayscale.

"What's our flight altitude?" I asked.

"Twenty-five feet."

The bottom was nearly featureless except for several yard-long oval lumps scattered here and there. Near the wall, a sandy slope rose about thirty to forty feet. Then rock took over, jagged and steep, heading straight up for about 450 feet to the surface.

"Let's get a visual sense of this," I said. "Are you ready to launch the Basketball?"

Frank had anticipated my request. A minute later, the device was jetting toward the rock wall under Wally's steady hand. The water was crystal clear, but it was pitch black. Light would not normally penetrate to 500 feet, and with a solid ice cover, there was no light at all. Wally rolled the Basketball around to give us a good visual image of the water column. Visibility extended at least out to 200 feet with crystal clarity.

Wally trained his light on the bottom and passed over one of the lumps. It moved with a ripple motion along the long axis, then lifted off the bottom and rolled ninety degrees.

"Be damned," Dr. Brand muttered, "That's a Greenland *Halibut*. Pretty good eating, but watch out for its teeth."

I looked at Ham. "Got it!" he said.

I picked up the handset and called the skipper. "It's Mac. Can you come down to Dive Control?"

When the skipper arrived, I showed him the sidescan printouts, and then Wally gave him a Basketball tour of the base of the slope.

The skipper turned to me. "Mac, get the Engineer down here, please."

I called around and found him in the Engine Room. "Doug, the skipper wants to see you in Dive Control."

"Be right up."

The Engineering Officer arrived several minutes later.

"Yes, Sir," he said to the skipper.

"Take a look at these," Roken said, showing Doug the Fish printouts. "Wally," he said, "take Eng on the same tour that you gave me."

When Wally finished, the skipper said, "Doug, I want to bottom as close as possible to the beginning of the slope. Either we can point up or down the slope, or we can bottom parallel to the slope. The slope is thirty degrees. If we bottom parallel to the slope, the divers will be much closer to the wall, requiring less vertical excursion. If we do this, I want to be pointed north, so the question is, can you port sufficient ballast to port to avoid any possibility of our rolling over?"

Now, that was a thought, doing a barrel-roll on the bottom in a nuclear sub. Of course, the sail would stop the roll, but that's not exactly something one would want to consider.

"Give me a half hour, Cap'n," Doug said. "I want to run some calculations with Bert and Sam."

✳

The skipper remained in Dive Control, chatting with Dr. Brand and me about effective placement of the transponder. He took a few minutes to exchange pleasantries with my saturated divers, Harry, Jimmy, Whitey, and Ski.

"While we did a Basketball survey," he told them, "we found a relatively large number of Greenland *Halibut*. So, while you're out there, try to bag three of them for a fresh fish meal for the crew. Dr. Brand says to watch out for their teeth."

While he was talking with the divers, Doug returned with his calculations.

"We can do it, Cap'n," he said. "The sand is rather soft so that our port skids will sink down a foot or so once we shift the water. We can monitor our progress with the Basketball."

Barry assumed the watch as we got ready to shift the sub up to where the slope met the wall.

The skipper joined Barry in Control. He opted to use the fore and aft position-keeping thrusters instead of the main screw. When the sub was bottomed on the skids, only a foot separated the extended outboards from the bottom. Any settling by the sub, and the outboards could be damaged. Barry's Chief of the Watch, Pots, gently lifted *Teuthis* off the bottom and extended both outboards. Wally checked the clearance of both units with the Basketball.

Most subs have no external vision—no windows, no TV cams, no nothing. We had the Basketball. The water was crystal clear, but black as sin. Fortunately, Wally's floodlight penetrated 150 feet through the clear water. The beam was virtually invisible. On the monitor, all we saw was the circle of light on the bottom created by the flood.

Seeing about two feet of clearance, Barry lifted *Teuthis* another ten feet. Wally placed the Basketball upslope, giving Barry a clear view of *Teuthis* above the slope as he approached the wall. We followed the progress down in Dive Control. Pots eased the sub up as Barry edged sideways, the two of them working as a close-knit team. When the monitor showed the sub's port flank to be fifteen feet from the wall, Barry went to a hover. Pots had so precisely controlled the sub's buoyancy that the hovering system had very little to do.

I went to Control to observe things directly, leaving Ham in charge of things in Dive Control. The skipper talked quietly with Barry and then announced, "I have the Conn."

It was pretty clear to me that should something go wrong, the skipper wanted the responsibility to be his alone. I admired that, but I also knew that Barry was disappointed, not that the skipper didn't trust him, but that the skipper would be doing it instead of him.

"Chief of the Watch," the skipper said, "we're going to bring the sub down slowly until it rests on the port skids. Once Wally reports that both skids are settled into the bottom, *and* we see this on the monitor, simultaneously bring water in and move water to port. Keep an eye on the monitor. We have a one-and-a-half-foot gap between the starboard skids and the slope. If we're lucky, we'll settle the port side into the sand until we two-block it. Then we'll lower the port skid supports until the starboard side gets a purchase on the bottom. If the port skids bottom out before they are two-blocked, we'll see if we have sufficient flexibility to keep the sub level. If not, we'll deal with that then." He paused. "Any questions?"

"What if we start to get a port list?"

"Move a bit of water starboard to compensate." The skipper smiled at Pots. "You're an old pro at the BCP, Pots," referring to the Ballast Control Panel. "If anybody can pull this off, *you* can."

The skipper addressed every Control watchstander. "Okay, everybody, this is a delicate, slow-motion operation. If we start sliding to starboard, we'll counter with the thrusters. Remember that everything we do will have a delay built into it. We're moving a lot of mass here, with a lot of momentum." He looked around the Control Room. "Any more questions? Now's the time to ask, *not* while we're doing it."

The watchstanders looked around, and at each other, and then at the skipper. No one asked a question.

"Okay, Pots, commence!"

I thought Pots looked a bit nervous at the skipper's order, but then he took a deep breath and focused on his task. Mostly, I kept my eyes glued to the monitor. Wally kept the floodlight on the forward port skid. As it began to take weight, whorls of sand squirted out the upslope side of the skid, and rivulets of sand flowed from the downslope side. Then the port side of the sub dropped about six inches, a jolt felt throughout the sub, and began a slow slide to starboard.

"Port full, both thrusters," the skipper said calmly. "Stop flooding."

On the monitor, the skid continued sliding to starboard several inches, but slower. Then it stopped.

"Port one half, both thrusters." After a few seconds, "Continue flooding."

On the monitor, the skid began to dig in. A trench formed, and the downslope edge of the skid disappeared. *Teuthis* began to assume a slight port list, but before the skipper could say anything, Pots moved water to starboard, compensating.

About fifteen minutes later, Pots said, "We've reached port trim tank capacity, Captain."

The monitor showed that port skid still had about two feet of exposed support, but it was not sinking further.

"We need a second Basketball," Barry muttered.

"Wally," the skipper said, "move to the starboard skid and place the Basketball so you can swing from starboard to port."

The monitor view shifted until we saw the starboard skid about eighteen inches off the bottom.

"Good, Wally. Now, swing to the port skid." The skipper turned to Pots. "Port one third, both thrusters. Retract the port skids eighteen inches, slowly." The skipper watched the monitor carefully. As the remaining skid support approached six inches, he said, "Swing to starboard, Wally."

As the monitor image steadied, we watched the starboard skid bite into the sand. *Teuthis* took on about a half-degree starboard list.

"Stop thrusters," the skipper said while closely watching the monitor. "Pots, slowly move a thousand pounds of water starboard."

As Pots did so, the sub took on another half-degree starboard list. You could have heard a pin drop in Control. I found myself holding my breath. The skipper waited a whole minute…then another…and then a third.

"Okay, Pots, move five hundred pounds from starboard to port."

The starboard list lessened to a half degree. Again, the skipper waited a minute…and then another.

"Pots, move five hundred pounds starboard to port and back to starboard. Do this three times total."

For five minutes, Control remained quiet except for the soft hum from the pumps. The list stayed at a half-degree starboard. Wally shifted the view back and forth between the skids, but they were steady.

"Commander Jacobs has the Conn," the skipper said. To Barry, he said, "Watch it closely for a half hour while Mac prepares for dive ops."

✳

Frank's people had set up the transponder with a state-of-the-art five-track, solid-state device filled with new-fangled integrated circuits that I really did not yet understand. It alternatively broadcast opening and closing *Teuthis* screw sounds, random ship's noise, active sonar pings in various combinations, and a reflected echo to any incoming ping that projected both closing and opening info. The transponder had no moving parts. It was powered by an RTG that was good for several decades. Before sealing the transponder, they filled it with dry nitrogen.

Frank told me that it would likely still be working fifty years from now.

While the skipper positioned *Teuthis*, Ham passed the transponder to the divers and got them ready to go. Ham and I had agreed to put Harry and Ski in the water with Jimmy and Whitey tending. We were right on the borderline for needing descramblers to communicate with the divers. Since the skipper was taking a more-than-normal personal interest in this dive, I decided to use the descramblers to make comms with the divers easier for him.

By the time the half-hour wait had passed, Harry, Ski, Jimmy, and Whitey were in the Egress Lock waiting to get wet. Barry called me from Control.

"You ready to go, Mac?"

"Yep."

The announcement followed over the 1MC: "Commence dive ops!"

Jimmy popped the hatch, and in moments, Harry and Ski were in the water. Wally illuminated them and their path forward.

"This is Dr. Brand. If you can find a tight slot about five feet above the sand."

"Roger that," Harry answered in his high-pitched helium and pressure altered voice made understandable by the descrambler. He was carrying the transponder, while Ski had a gas-powered dart gun in each hand.

Wally swept the wall in front of them. Within a few short minutes, they had located an ideal slot and wedged in the transponder.

"Can I tap this fucker with my knife handle?" Ski asked in a squeaky voice, handing both guns to Harry.

"No more force than you would use to drive a nail," Frank answered.

A metallic thunking sound passed through the descrambler virtually unaltered, synchronized with the image on the monitor of Ski pounding the transponder in place.

"Okay," Ski squeaked, "let's go fishing."

The Basketball wandered off to locate a Greenland *Halibut*. Shortly after, Wally said, "There you go, boys. Two of them side by side."

Each diver put a dart through a head with rotated eyes. Harry hoisted his above the bottom. "Shit, this fucker's heavy!" he said as he put it back and proceeded to drag it to the Egress Lock with Ski right behind him.

"I found another one," Wally said, sweeping his flood from the divers to the spot. "And a fourth," he added.

The divers handed the large fish through the hatch to Jimmy with darts still attached and inserted new darts into their guns. They moved about thirty feet off the starboard bow to where Wally's floodlight indicated. As before, they speared their catches and headed back up the slope, gliding a couple of feet above the bottom.

"Shit! What the fuck!" Harry yelped. "Something just grabbed my fins."

Wally swung the Basketball around as Ski squeaked, "Jesus, Mary, Joseph…what the fuck is that?"

The monitor was filled with the biggest shark I had ever seen, gaping mouth a full four feet top to bottom. It had a double row of smooth, razor-sharp teeth in its upper jaw. They looked like two-inch daggers, the front row pointed slightly outward, the back row slightly inward. The lower jaw seemed a bit disjointed and also held two rows of teeth. Unlike the top row, these teeth each had two cross members, looking so much like little saws.

Wally panned first to Harry's fins. Both were severed, just beyond his toes. Wally pulled up and back to give a view of the entire creature while Harry and Ski scrambled toward the hatch, halibut catch forgotten.

"That's a Greenland Shark, eighteen to twenty feet long," Dr. Brand said. He spoke into the circuit, "Harry, Ski, listen! You can easily outswim that guy. He cruises at less than a mile per hour. His fastest speed is only one and a half miles per hour. Stay away from his mouth, and you'll be okay,"

"So says the expert safe inside the sub," Ski muttered almost inaudibly, but clearly discernable through the descrambler.

"He masses at least three thousand pounds. He's after your halibut, *not* you. Don't argue with him," Dr. Brand added.

"I got no fins," Harry squeaked. "Fucker got 'em. Two of them halibut's more than enough for the crew. Let's get the hell out of Dodge!"

USS TEUTHIS—LABRADOR NARROWS

Thus far on this mission, the *Teuthis* and its crew had spent many long hours of routine stretching into boredom, but not now. For the next several days, boredom was the last thing on our minds. Capt. Parry on the Hecla had been stopped by jammed, thick ice floes stretching from Boothia Inlet in the northwest to Foxe Basin in the southeast. That was our route, and Labrador Narrows leading into Foxe Basin was only a couple of miles wide and dropped down to a half-mile at one point.

We had a good locus to commence our blind submerged transit—assuming the location of the largest of the Hecla and Fury Islands was accurate on the chart. Barry reset the Submarine Internal Navigation System (SINS), checked the Dead Reckoning Trace (DRT) a couple of times, and announced he was ready. Bill had hung Harry's clipped fins on the Dive Control bulkhead as a permanent memento of the Greenland Shark. My divers had about four days of decompression ahead of them, under Bill's able hand with Ham's oversight. Then, when we got to the Careys, they would press down again.

In the meantime, the skipper ordered us off ultra-quiet. He wanted to sprint across the Gulf of Boothia at 200 feet and into Fury and Hecla Strait before the *Alfa* began to work his way down Prince Regent Inlet—something the skipper was convinced he would do sooner or later. I could not have agreed more.

This was a bit tricky because eighty nautical miles ahead on a bearing of 115 degrees, a seamount rose to within 100 feet of the surface. Obviously, we needed to keep well south of the seamount, but we had no clue about the currents at the mouth of the Fury and Hela Strait. At twenty knots, the seamount was four hours distant.

Doug got us underway as he assumed the midwatch. The skipper's Night Orders had him running at 200 feet and twenty knots for three and three-quarter hours. Although I was sleeping, I knew that had to have been a bit of tedious boredom. There was little chance that another vessel of any kind was in our area, but Doug cleared his baffles every hour just to be sure.

I woke up early for my morning watch, just after 0400. I cleared my head and wandered to Control. Although he hadn't had a lot of sleep, Barry was there with the skipper poring over an ocean chart with the Nav Watch, Juby. The skipper looked up as I stepped into Control, steaming coffee cup in my fist.

"Mac, glad to see you. I was just about to send the messenger to get you."

"Great minds…" I said with a grin. "Anybody need coffee?"

"We're fine," Barry said.

"Look at this," the skipper said, pointing to our track from the Hecla and Fury Islands. "This was our aim point," he said, pointing to a spot four nautical miles due south of the seamount. "Here's where we are, based on the DRT and soundings." He pointed to a spot 2.9 nautical miles short of our intended position. "Obviously, we're dealing with a current. Do you have anything in that vast mental library of yours that addresses this?"

Okay, so I know a lot about the Arctic, but I don't think anybody had addressed the Fury and Hecla Strait currents. I shut my eyes and gave it some thought. *No…wait! I think Parry wrote something…* I concentrated hard. *Tidal flow and barometric pressure…*

"I may know something," I said hesitatingly. "When Parry's Northwest Passage progress was blocked in Foxe Basin, he wrote that when the tidal flow was westward, the Labrador Narrows was totally jammed with heavy ice. The ice opened up a bit when the flow reversed. He also noted that when the barometric pressure was higher in Foxe Basin, the Labrador Narrows ice was jammed tighter." I dug a bit deeper into my memory of what I had read. "During his sojourn in the Gulf of Boothia, when the barometric pressure was lower, he was able to work his way east to a polynya about halfway through the strait." I pointed to the spot on the chart. "I would have to assume that lower pressure to the west corresponded with higher pressure in Foxe Basin, forcing water under the ice through Labrador Narrows, opening up the ice in Fury and Hecla Strait." I paused and took a deep breath. "That may be what did this." I pointed to our plotted location.

"What do we know of the depth in the Strait and especially the Narrows?" the skipper asked.

Barry pointed to several lines of soundings through the Strait and a few isolated soundings in the Narrows.

"The Strait soundings probably originated with Parry," I said, "augmented by other explorers early this century—between the wars, after 1918." I slid my finger to the Narrows. "Nobody has yet transited the Narrows, so far as I know. These soundings were probably taken by Igloolik Inuit hunters through holes in the ice. The soundings themselves are probably accurate, but their placement might be questionable."

"Fortunately," Barry said, "depths are at least five hundred feet along most of the passage, except for this ridge leading south to Liddon Island. It shallows up to one hundred eighty feet."

The skipper stood quietly, chin resting in his left palm, deep in thought. I could almost read his thoughts. Was I hasty in opting for this route? Should I cut bait and run north? I've got skids. I've got sidescan. I've even got the Basketball. If anyone can do it, I can! He dropped his hand and leaned over the chart.

"Here's the plan," he said.

⁂

"I'll grab some breakfast and be back to relieve you," I said to Doug.

This morning, Cedric had made fresh popovers. Talk about good eating! I arrived back in Control, well-fortified for what lay ahead.

The skipper wanted to cover the initial fifty-four nautical miles at 200 feet and ten knots. I set a course of 084 degrees. With baffle clearing, that took my entire watch. It was not exactly boring, but it didn't really rise to a level of excitement either. Because of the paucity of depth information, I kept the secure bottom-sounder running. I did *not* want to discover an uncharted seamount the hard way.

When Bert assumed the watch, *Teuthis* was about four nautical miles due north of Purfut Cove, the northernmost point of Amhurst Peninsula, which is part of the Canadian mainland. He proceeded on a course of 113 degrees at five knots over the bottom at 200 feet. He compensated for the head current by making turns for eight knots, but he kept a close watch on the depth below his keel because he was coming up on Liddon Island Ridge. It took the better part of six hours to cover the twenty-four nautical miles.

We were in the general area where the polynya had been reported by Parry and several explorers following him. Following a burger and fries for dinner washed down with bug juice, I placed myself in Control so I could add whatever expertise I had to the mix. The skipper was there as Bert brought the sub to 100 feet and slowed to a hover. He had to maintain turns for about a knot to stay in one place, as indicated by the secure bottom-sounder. Barry showed up to assume the watch.

"Do you have a Transit bird overhead?" the skipper asked.

"Yes, Sir, for another twenty minutes," Barry answered.

The skipper told him to let Bert get a fix before relieving him. Barry went back to the Nav Center to get ready for the sat fix.

"This is the Captain…we are preparing to break through the ice to get a good navigation fix. Unlike the previous time, the ice above us is very thin. We will simply push the sail through the ice and then drop back to periscope depth and get our fix. We will briefly sound the collision alarm before breaking through the ice."

The ice cover was just a few inches thick, a non-issue for Bert. As the sub settled at sixty-five feet and he swung his scope around, he said, "There's clear water to the south as far as I can see. Diving Officer, make your depth six-zero feet." As the sub came up, he said, "I can just see land broad off the starboard bow."

"That's a small island off Liddon Island," Quartermaster 1st Class Gary Fonzarelli said. "That's three-point-four nautical miles—your maximum visible range at ten feet exposed. Give me an exact bearing, please."

"Bearing…Mark!" Bert said.

I stepped onto the periscope stand and read the bearing, "One-five-six."

A couple of minutes later, Barry announced that he had his sat fix. It coincided with Bert's line of position and maximum range circle—within about thirty feet, anyway. The main point was that the skipper—we—knew where *Teuthis* was.

Barry assumed the watch, eased the sub over Liddon Island Ridge, and dropped down to 200 feet. For two hours, he crept along at five knots while passing Liddon Island. Then he came slightly right to course 116 degrees for forty-five minutes. At the mouth of the Labrador Narrows, he came to a stop and hovered while checking the current. It was virtually zero, so there would be nothing pushing us off our path through the Narrows.

Neither the skipper nor I had left Control since Barry assumed the watch—the skipper because it was his ship, and me because I was absolutely fascinated by the process. Since I didn't have the watch, I wanted to be as much a part of it as possible.

"I'm going to grab a sandwich and a cup of coffee while you launch the Fish and Basketball," the skipper said.

I decided to do the same. Sitting at the Wardroom table with a tuna sandwich, the skipper with ham and cheese, I said, "You are making the first Labrador Narrows transit in history, but nobody will know about it, and only classified charts will display your soundings. That sucks!"

"Not really, Mac," the skipper answered. "I know. The crew knows. When we return, the Dev Group will know. With time, the word will get out." He smiled at me. "Let's go do this!"

✳

"I have the Conn," the skipper announced, as he did when we first broke through the ice cover. "Lower the skids to full extension."

Barry kept a close eye on the Fish and Basketball. He placed the Fish 100 feet in front of *Teuthis* and used the Basketball to investigate anything that seemed out of the norm. We had a bit over seven nautical miles through the Narrows. At five knots that would take 1.5 hours, but the way we were creeping along, stopping and starting as the Fish and Basketball gave us pause, we took a full three hours to transit the Narrows.

Not surprisingly, the floor was swept clean of nearly everything—a smooth, sandy bottom. We never really saw the sides. The skipper kept to the center, even in the wider parts to the west. Once we opened into Foxe Basin, the skipper secured the Fish and Basketball.

"Diving Officer, make your depth six-zero feet. Bring her up easy. Do not, I repeat, *do not* raise any scopes. Do not drop below sixty-five feet." The skipper was calm but firm. "Lieutenant Commander Jacobs has the Conn."

✳

The surface above was solid ice between three and four feet thick. The bottom was not very far down, less than 150 feet for the next 350 nautical miles. We kept our speed at ten knots while remaining only sixty feet over the bottom. Several times, we had to slow down and ease our way nearly to the bottom as we passed below a downward thrusting pressure ridge. Due to these slow-downs, we averaged only eight knots over the entire transit.

After forty-four hours of anything but tedious boredom, as I assumed the watch, we turned southeast into the Hudson Strait. Even this late in the year, Hudson Strait carried traffic—tankers and cargo ships accompanied by a Canadian icebreaker.

Within an hour of assuming the watch, Sonar called me. "Conn, Sonar, I have a contact just off the port bow, designate Sierra-eight." Shortly thereafter, "Conn, Sonar, Sierra-eight is two contacts. Sierra-eight is an icebreaker. The second contact is a cargo vessel, designate Sierra-nine. They're headed the same way we are."

"Sonar, Conn, range estimate?"

"Several miles, Conn. Best I can do right now."

I called the skipper. "We've picked up an icebreaker breaking ice for a freighter. They're headed out Hudson Strait. I think their destination is Thule."

The skipper came to Control. "Show me what you have, Mac."

We stepped into Sonar, where King walked him through it. "How fast is he moving?" the skipper asked King.

"Ten, fifteen knots. Depends on ice thickness. He's making good time."

"Skipper," I said, "can we get under the freighter and accompany them all the way to Thule? They are loud enough to mask us completely."

✳

The water was deep, and their speed was acceptable. It took me a couple of hours to catch up with them, then a half hour to nestle beneath the freighter. From that point, we did nothing more than station-keep under the freighter—for 1,500 nautical miles. I was right. The freighter's destination was Thule.

Five days later, as Doug was finishing his midwatch, we had reached a point between Thule and the Careys. As I came into Control to assume the morning watch, the skipper was in his chair on the periscope stand. The icebreaker and freighter turned east toward Thule.

"I have the Conn," the skipper said. "Make your depth one-zero-zero feet. Chief of the Watch, commence hovering."

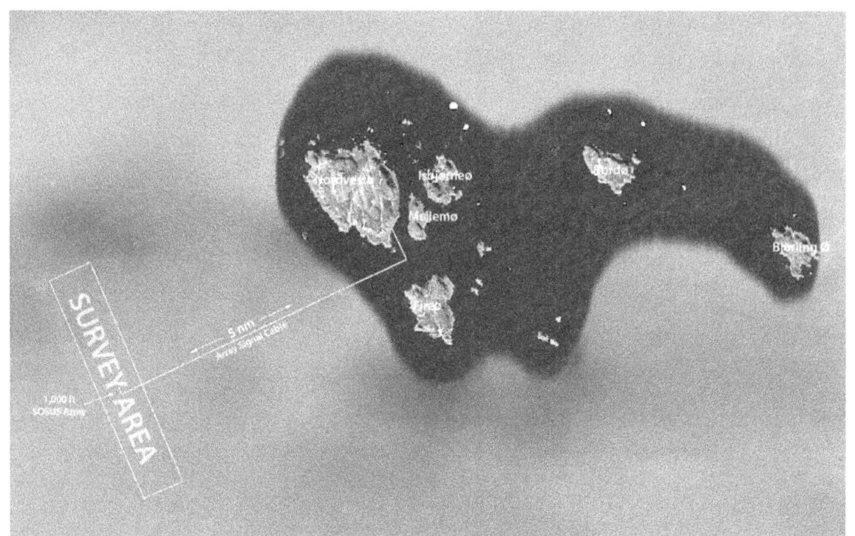

Carey Øer SOSUS Array placement

CHAPTER SIX—Carey Øer

USS TEUTHIS—CAREY ØER

The DRT placed us eighteen nautical miles due west from the harbor entrance for Thule and twenty nautical miles southeast of Björling Øer, the last known location of the ill-fated 1892 Björling and Kallstenius expedition's attempt to be the first to reach the North Pole.[6]

I knew a fairly strong current was pushing us northward, but in the short term, I didn't have to worry about it.

"Take us to periscope depth in the freighter's wake, get a good fix, and then drop back down to one hundred feet and take us to our survey zone five miles off Fireø," the skipper said to me. "Then descend to eight hundred feet, prepare for Fish ops, and call me," he added as he left Control.

Al confirmed we had a Transit bird available. I checked the under-ice sonar. It displayed clear water with chunks of floating ice. The wake had remained above us because it and we were moving

---

6 See Glossary entry.

with the current. Besides, the south end of the polynya still had to be somewhere above us. I wasted no time.

"Nav, prepare to get a fix. Diving Officer, make your depth six-five feet."

I had the scope up before we hit sixty-five feet and began sweeping around the moment it broke water. The wake trailed off to the east, with the freighter still clearly visible. As I swept astern, I saw the navigation mast at full extension. A minute later, Nav announced he had his fix.

I dropped the scope. "Diving Officer, make your depth one-ze-ro-zero feet." And to Nav, "Give me a course."

"Two-nine-zero, Sir."

"Helmsman, come left to new course two-nine-zero, ahead standard, make turns for fifteen knots."

We had about two hours on this heading. I planned to clear baffles about halfway through. Once we were settled on depth and course, I called Sonar.

"Sonar, Conn, in about two hours, we'll commence our survey west of Nordvestø. Keep a sharp ear…I don't want the *Alfa* to spring a surprise on us."

I called Ham in Dive Control. "It's time, Ham. As we discussed, within the hour, start pressing Harry, Whitey, Ski, and Jimmy down to a thousand feet."

"Got it," Ham said.

When we cleared baffles fifty-five minutes later, Sonar was unable to pick up the freighter or its icebreaker companion. By then, they were almost certainly tied up at the Thule pier, the crews headed for a beer at the local club.

✳

Barry and his quartermasters had prepared a detailed chart of our survey area centered on the transponder position, from 4.5 to 5.5 nautical miles off Nordvestø and Fireø, and five miles along the island fronts. Barry activated the transponder, and I eased down to 800 feet and steered toward it while readying for Fish ops. As I neared depth with the transponder directly below, I called the skipper. He came out to Control and settled into his chair on the periscope stand, but let me continue to run the operation.

I intended to run at bare steerageway across the slope that formed the rise from the seafloor to the Carey Islands while keeping 200 feet over the bottom. Once we crossed the thousand-foot curve, I wanted to follow it to enable the Fish to get a detailed bottom image because the array needed to be placed at one thousand feet for best performance. Dr. Brand and Chief Ocean Tech Bart Davidson would then pore over the sidescan images to locate the best lie for the 1,000-foot array.

When Dive Control informed me that they were ready, the skipper nodded to me, and I told them to launch the Fish. Wally maneuvered it along the starboard side, past the bow, and commenced its scan about a hundred feet in front of *Teuthis*. Ten minutes later, Nav announced that we were crossing the thousand-foot curve from shallow to deep at a ten-degree angle.

"Mark your head, Helmsman," I ordered.

"Three-one-zero, Sir."

"Come right to three-two-zero."

"You're drifting right, Conn," Nav told me.

"Come left to three-one-nine," I ordered.

And so it went for the better part of two hours—slight adjustments right or left as we remained atop the thousand-foot curve as closely as possible. When we reached the end of the run, I hovered at 200 feet above the bottom while Dr. Brand and Chief Davidson analyzed the results.

I called Ham in Dive Control. "What's your status?" I asked.

"A couple hours still."

"That'll work out about right," I said.

✳

About a half hour later, Dr. Brand called Commander Roken to Dive Control, where he had the scan images taped together and laid out on the table. A few minutes later, the skipper returned to Control with a sidescan strip in hand, followed closely by Dr. Brand. They went to the chart table, and the skipper gestured me over.

"Here's where Dr. Brand wants to lay the array," he said, placing the strip on the table and pointing to a spot on the detailed chart that Barry had made.

ON THE SEAFLOOR—WEST OF NORDVEST AND FIRE ØER

*T*uthis settled on the seafloor at 990 feet. We rested on a flat ledge about halfway up a slope that started on the abyssal plain a thousand feet below us and continued above through nearly two feet of solid ice to form the steep sides of Nordvestø and Fireø. Keeping in mind that the *Alfa* was still a worry, we were pointed generally southwest, about 30 degrees to the right of the face of the slope. This would allow for a quick exit with minimal maneuvering should that become necessary.

I joined Ham in Dive Control right after Bert and his team relieved me and my watchstanders. Chief Davidson had flooded the CRC. Bill had equalized DDC pressure with the outside, and the divers were dressed and ready to do some real work for a change. We had designated Harry and Whitey for the first dive, backed up by Ski. I held Jimmy back for his medical skills should anything go wrong. Jer and Jake would press down right before we were ready to anchor the upcable just offshore of Nordvestø and Fireø.

Under the Basketball's close scrutiny, controlled this time by Ocean Tech 1st Class Derrick Jensen, Harry and Whitey hit the bottom, wearing boots instead of fins. Harry carried a yard-long, U-shaped polymer anchor—like a U-bolt, but with non-threaded pointy ends. Whitey carried a hammer. They moved aft to the cable pipe directly below the CRC.

When we outfitted for this operation back at EB, the cable reel received two separate cables, one for Carey Øer and one for Point Hope, north of Bering Strait. Each cable set consisted of 1,000 feet of cable containing forty hydrophones at 25-foot intervals. This was permanently attached to sufficient armored cable to bring the acoustic signals to the monitoring stations. We carried seven nautical miles of armored cable to bring the signals to the monitoring station at Carey Øer.

The quarter-inch thick armored cable consisted of forty single nine-micron glass fibers, each with a 125-micron coating, jacketed with a waterproof, florescent orange plastic infused, aramid fiber sleeve. The cable was specially developed for this project under a Top Secret contract with Bell Labs.

The twenty-foot diameter cable reel in the CRC could carry 887 nautical miles of this special cable. We needed about seven and a half nautical miles for Carey Øer and about fifty-four nautical miles for Point Hope.

Using rollers built into the cable pipe, Bart Davidson had already lowered about thirty feet of cable to the seafloor beneath *Teuthis*. Harry grabbed the bitter end.

"I'll stretch this back," he squeaked. "You keep an eye out for anything hungry."

Since the cable design made it a bit heavier than seawater, Harry had no difficulty stretching it back thirty feet and laying it into the bottom silt. The hydrophone at the end was just a slight bump in the slender cable, and the other visible hydrophone looked like a small critter consumed by an orange snake. Back at the cable end, Harry placed his anchor over the cable just forward of the hydrophone, and Whitey hammered it into the bottom until it firmly anchored the cable end without pinching it.

Both divers returned to the egress hatch without incident and closed the hatch. I called Control.

"We need to move a hundred feet along the vector Nav laid out," I told Bert. "Derrick will guide you with the Basketball. You'll have the cable pipe on your monitor."

Bert lowered both outboards, lifted *Teuthis* off the bottom about five feet, and moved forward slowly. Initially, the cable took a slight strain on the anchor, but Bert slowed his forward motion to compensate. Then he called me.

"Okay, Mac, we got it. I'm on the bottom. You can send your divers out to set the next anchor."

Once again, Harry and Whitey set the anchor, wearing fins this time. Harry held the anchor, and Whitey pounded. While Whitey pounded, Harry looked around.

"There you are!" Harry squeaked. As soon as the anchor was secure, he darted fifteen feet upslope and grabbed a medium-size Greenland *Halibut*.

"You're supposed to be looking for things that can eat us," Whitey said.

"Yeah…but I got something *we* can eat." Harry pushed the squirming fish that was nearly as large as the hatch into the Egress Lock. "Gimme a couple of guns, Ski," he said.

Within a couple of minutes, Harry and Whitey had bagged two even larger halibut.

I grabbed the mike. "Stay alert, guys. This is Greenland Shark territory."

That stopped them in their tracks. They shoved their new catch through the hatch, and then scuttled through themselves and closed it. While Ham and the divers locked the fish into Dive Control, I called Cedric to send his messcooks to come get them. Then I informed Bert that we were ready for the next segment. It was taking us about thirty minutes to lay each cable segment, lock out the divers with fins since they were not trekking on the bottom, anchor the section, and then retrieve the divers. Without fishing, it went a bit faster. We were moving about a third the length of the sub for each segment. I estimated that we had about four hours remaining to finish.

Toward the end of the fourth hour, we were all getting pretty tired, especially the divers. Ski asked to participate in the last two dives. Neither Ham nor I could see any reason why not, so Whitey and Ski changed places. Wally had assumed driving the Basketball. Ski was on the bottom, and Harry was halfway out when Wally half-shouted, "Back in the lock, guys! We've got a visitor."

"What is it?" I asked. "A Greenland Shark?"

"Nope. Look at this." Wally pointed to the monitor.

There, in all its glory, was a male narwhal, about 17 feet long with a 7-foot tusk. I called the skipper.

"Sir, we've got a large male narwhal poking around near the egress hatch. They can breath-hold for twenty-five minutes, so he's probably got ten or more minutes left. If you wish to see him, you'll need to get to a monitor ASAP.

"Sir, Narwhals have never harmed humans, and their tusks are not dangerous. With your permission, I'm going to let the divers exit and place the anchor. It might be interesting how the narwhal reacts to them."

"Okay, Mac, but be careful. I don't want to lose a diver because of a miscalculation."

I turned around and said to Bill, "Put the divers into the water. The narwhal does not use its tusk as a stabbing weapon, but they are innately curious. It will definitely follow them and check out what they're doing."

Bill put Harry and Ski in the water, telling them to do their job quickly and return. "Mac says they do not use their tusks to spear prey, but I gotta guess it would hurt like hell if one hit you with its tusk."

Ski held the anchor, and Harry pounded it. Upon the first blow, the narwhal slid down under the sub and placed its left eye inches from their work. It examined the anchor, and then backed off and touched it with its tusk. While it did so, Ski and Harry returned to the Egress Lock. Immediately after Harry left the water, the narwhal swam right up to the open hatch and examined as much as it could through the relatively small, rigid opening, as seen from its perspective.

"Close the hatch, guys," I told them. "We gotta move along."

After we closed the hatch, the narwhal disappeared. To the guys' questions, I answered, "He's only got about twenty-five minutes of air, and open water is off to the southeast somewhere. He knows where it is, I'm sure. He'll be back before we're done. He's one genuinely curious critter."

A half hour later, as we settled into our final position, the narwhal suddenly appeared, swimming directly toward the Basketball. It seemed to recognize that it was not something to eat, and it was fascinated by the beam of light. Wally maneuvered the Basketball, so the light shined on the bottom beneath the hatch. The narwhal immediately went to the hatch, and when it popped up, the narwhal's left eye scanned inside the lock.

Harry reached down and gently pushed the narwhal away from the opening, and then he lowered himself into the water. The narwhal moved back slightly and rubbed his tusk along the entire length of Harry's body.

"He's sizing you up, Harry," Ski squeaked. "Maybe he wants to fuck you!"

"…and the narwhal you rode in on," Harry squeaked in response.

Ski joined Harry, and they pounded the last anchor into the seafloor, watched closely by the narwhal. Wally pulled the Basketball back.

"I'll be damned," Chief Davidson said. "There's another one… without a tusk."

"That's a female," I said. "Looks like he brought his girlfriend, guys," I said, chuckling.

"I guess he doesn't want you, after all, Harry," Bill said. "Too bad. I would have loved to see that!"

✳

I looked at Ham with a smile. "That was historic."

He grinned back. "Maybe we can tell our great-grandkids about it."

I got a call from Control. "Meeting in the Wardroom in ten—Lieutenant Commander James, Doctor Brand, Senior Chief Jones, Chief Davidson, Master Chief Comstock, and yourself."

I informed the people in Dive Control and left for the Wardroom. In addition to the people I already listed, Barry, Senior Chief Forbes, and the XO were present. Barry had laid out a hand-drawn chart on the Wardroom table. The skipper stepped through the door.

"Attention on deck!" the XO said.

"As you were," the skipper responded. "Frank…"

"What you will hear in the next few minutes is Top Secret—Special Access," Lt. Cmdr. James stated. "You may not discuss it with any of your subordinates or any of the other officers and crew." He pulled an extendable pointer from his breast pocket and pointed to a line running a bit north of northwest about five nautical miles from the shorelines of Nordvestø and Fireø. "This is the array we just laid." He drew a light penciled line from the southern end of the array to the gap between Nordvestø and Fireø, continued it into a small protected channel between Nordvestø and Mellemø, and terminated it slightly inland on the southeastern shore of Nordvestø. Then he placed his pencil tip on the line about a half-mile from shore. "We will lay the cable along this line until we reach the one-hundred-foot-deep-point. *Teuthis* will penetrate the ice here, creating an open area about a hundred feet wide. I will contact Thule, and they will dispatch a chopper with a Special Ops crew of SOSUS installation specialists. He circled the point lightly. "*Teuthis* will settle to the bottom here. Divers will anchor the cable firmly here and attach an RTG transponder. Then the sub will release the remainder of the Carey Øer cable."

"The chopper should be here about a half hour after they hear from me. The divers will attach a messenger line with a radio transponder buoy to the cable and release it. The chopper will retrieve the messenger line, haul up the cable until most of the slack is taken up, and then will lay it along this line and bring it ashore here." He pointed to where the light line crossed the Nordvestø shore.

"The Special Ops people already emplaced a small facility here to relay SOSUS signals to Thule," he pointed to the shore again, "along with the necessary equipment and a microwave tower for line-of-sight coms with Thule. When they are satisfied that they have the cable, that it has no excess slack, and that they have a signal from the array, the chopper will drop an M-80 at our approximate location. This will release us from the Carey Øer ops." Frank stopped talking and looked around the table. "Any questions?"

Ham spoke up. "Why not have the divers pop the buoy, and then the chopper lowers the hook into the water at the buoy above the anchor spot, and have the divers meet the hook at seventy feet and attach the cable?"

"We don't know how clear the area above the sub will be," Frank answered. "If it were clear enough, that would be an option, but we won't know until the chopper gets there. At that point, coms are difficult."

"At a hundred feet on the bottom, the divers would know how clear the surface is," I said. "If it's sufficiently open, the divers do as Ham said. If not, Ham's approach is still better than the chopper trying to locate and attach the buoy in heavy ice."

"That could work," Ham said. "We just need to make sure the chopper maintains a steady altitude and position."

"I don't think that's a problem unless we're in the middle of a big storm," Frank said. "We should be okay for a couple of days."

"So, what have we decided?" I asked.

"We'll do it Ham's way," Frank said.

The skipper cleared his throat. Everyone turned to look at him. "I want to put a wrapper around this whole thing," he said. "The Soviets know that we can track them virtually anywhere. They don't really know how. They know about our SOSUS arrays—at least in principle, but they don't know how we do it. By trial and error, they have mapped out blind spots in our network. They hide out in the blind spots, and whenever possible, they rush pell-mell from one blind spot to another. It has become increasingly difficult to place arrays to cover all of them.

"That's what we are doing. We just placed an array that will cover anything coming over the top into the western Atlantic. We're about to head to Point Hope north of Bering Strait, where we will do the same thing.

"Maintaining the secrecy of this project has the highest priority. Increasingly, the Soviets are coming over the top to maintain their first-strike capability. What we are doing will help keep our families safe for at least a decade…*if* they don't learn about it."

The skipper stood to leave the Wardroom. "Carry on," he said as he shut the door behind him.

※

By this time, Barry had assumed the watch, but he turned virtually everything over to his JOOD, the Weapons Officer, Lt. Waverly Denver. Waverly carefully brought the sub to 100 feet above the slope, keeping the outboards extended to lay the cable in as straight a line as possible,

Down in Dive Control, Bart paid out cable under Derrick's watchful eye through the Basketball. We had about five and a half nautical miles of cable to lay before we reached the anchor point. Chief Electrician William Panner—everybody called him *Pots*—was Chief of the Watch. He kept tight control of the sub's buoyancy. As we rose through the water column, the *Teuthis'* hull expanded, increasing its buoyancy. Pots slowly bled water into the rear trim tank, not only to compensate for the increased buoyancy, but also to give the sub a slight up-bubble, so we remained level to the slope. Barry kept bare steerageway, moving us forward at about one and a half knots.

About three and a half hours later, Barry turned the sub 90 degrees to starboard, so we were facing generally south across the slope, and gently set the sub on the bottom. Unlike the slope at Hecla and Fury Islands, this slope was gentle.

Ham put Jer and Jake into Unisuits and rebreathers, and pressed them down to a hundred feet in the Entry Lock. That took about five minutes. They locked out under Derrick's watchful eye. There was a fair amount of ambient light compared to the darkness at 1,000 feet. Nevertheless, Derrick illuminated their work area with the Basketball.

A shadow approached from the southwest. "Hey, Guys, you got a visitor," Derrick said.

As he spoke, a narwhal tusk and then head filled the monitor. Insofar as they could tell, it was the same one we had seen. Apparently, the bright orange of the Unisuits convinced the narwhal that Jer and Jake were not the same creatures it had dealt with earlier. While they coiled the cable and pounded seven anchors into the firm bottom, the narwhal nosed about, nudging first Jer and then Jake, forcing its 4,000-pound body between them to see what they were doing and stroking the anchors and cable with its tusk. Then it darted to the surface above them, grabbed some air, and returned, this time with the female.

Bart started to push the remainder of the cable through the cable tube, bur Jer stopped him.

"This isn't going to work," Jer said. "We're going to have a crazy rat's nest here. Can you move the sub several yards downslope and then pay out the cable?"

"There's a bit of a drop-off about twenty yards downslope," Jake added.

"We can hang onto the cable at the cable pipe while you move the sub," Jer added.

I looked at Ham and shook my head.

"Can't do that," Ham told them. "Return to the Entry Lock."

They did, under the watchful eyes of the narwhals. Waverly lifted the sub about five feet and moved it slowly downslope using the outboards.

"Stop!" Derrick said at the edge of the drop-off.

Ham sent the divers back out.

"This'll work," Jer said.

As Derrick fed the cable through the tube, Jer and Jake pushed it over the drop-off. The Basketball showed that the cable dropped only a few feet into a spread-out pile. Both the narwhals investigated the pile carefully, the male poking it with his tusk, moving the coils around.

"Is that a problem?" Derrick asked.

"No," Dr. Brand said. "He's just checking it out, and the cable is strong."

Jake picked a point on the cable about 200 feet from the anchor and attached the messenger line using a clove hitch. Then he released the buoy to the surface.

Waverly called Dive Control and relayed his reports directly to the divers. "The chopper acquired the buoy…He's hovering above the buoy…He's lowering the hook…"

The hook appeared in the Basketball monitor along with the female narwhal's nose.

"Got it," Jer said. He figure-eighted the messenger line around the hook, floating about twenty feet above the slope surface. He pulled back from the marriage and said, "Okay, take her away."

On the monitor, we saw the messenger line rise to the surface, followed closely by the curious narwhals. Then the cable lifted off the bottom and broke the surface a short time later.

I could imagine but did not see the Special Ops guy in the chopper attach a tension sleeve to the cable. The tension sleeve allowed the cable to slip through the sleeve while maintaining tension on the seaward side of the cable so the chopper could maintain control of how it would be placed in the water.

I recalled the divers. As they entered the Entrance Lock, the male narwhal paid his respects, his left eye scanning around the interior of the lock he had not yet seen. Jake closed the hatch. While Bill continued to monitor the decompression of Harry, Whitey, Ski, and Jimmy, Ham slowly surfaced Jer and Jake, following a decompression schedule we had worked out before we put them into the water. Twenty minutes later, they rejoined us in Dive Control.

Now we waited…and waited. It took the Special Ops guys twice as long as I had anticipated, but finally, three hours later, a sharp *CRACK!* in the water above us told us we were free to depart.

It was nearly zero-dark-thirty. Doug had assumed the watch. He had Juby reset the SINS, stowed the outboards, lifted *Teuthis* off the bottom, retracted the skids, set a course of 220 degrees, and dropped to 300 feet at ten knots.

USS TEUTHIS—UNDERWAY OFF CAREY ØER

The entrance to Parry Channel lay 175 nautical miles ahead of us. With baffle clearing, that would take about twenty hours. That meant that Doug, myself, and Bert would have the joy of re-experiencing the tedious boredom part of submarining.

By the end of my watch, I was almost hoping Sonar would detect the *Alfa*. At least that would give us something to do. Despite the boredom, however, the watchword was vigilance. For one, the *Alfa* could still appear, although I suspected he probably was hanging out near Bering Strait. Secondly, something could go wrong. We were a big, complex ship running submerged at nine atmospheres of external pressure. A lot could go wrong, so we drilled just like I did back in my boomer days. Each Control Room watchstander had the opportunity to come up with a mechanical failure. He would give us the symptoms, and as a team, we would work our way through to a solution.

What we didn't know was that one of these drills would come in handy before we got home.

PART TWO

Arctic Transit

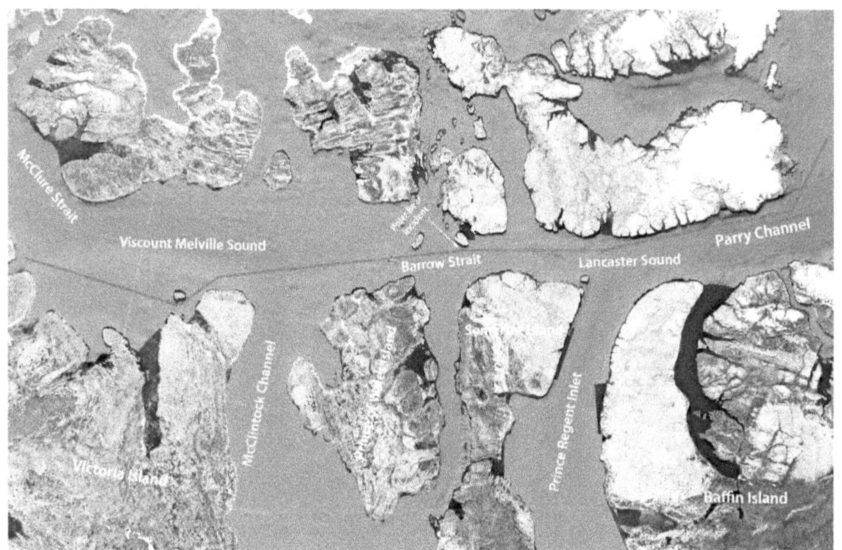

Parry Channel Transit

CHAPTER SEVEN—Parry Channel

USS TEUTHIS—LANCASTER SOUND

I was in Sonar chatting with King, comparing notes about narwhals, belugas, and bowheads. Benny Simms had the watch.

Sound filled the room—a background hiss, sharp transient cracking, even an occasional whistle. While King and I talked, part of me slipped back in time to my days as a Sonar Tech on the boomer. I was much younger in those days. Everything was new—a big adventure. Every unfamiliar sound widened my horizons as I sought to master my strange new world. Much of that wonder had remained with me, so that even now every time I awakened, it was to a sense of excitement about what the day would bring.

As I stood in the darkened Sonar Shack, out of the incoherent background noise, a repeating pattern began to emerge. I found myself counting the beats of a large propeller—four-bladed, it sounded like.

"Conn, Sonar," Benny said, "I have a contact ten degrees off the starboard bow, designate Sierra-ten."

"Sonar, Conn, what is Sierra-ten?" Waverly asked from Control.

"Wait one, Control."

In Sonar, Benny concentrated on the sound. What I could hear over the speaker was a set of beats that seemed to split and then synchronize, and I heard a bit of suppressed cavitation.

"Conn, Sonar," Benny said a minute later, "Sierra-ten is actually two contacts. The first, Sierra-ten, is a tanker low in the water, slightly cavitating four-bladed screw. Sierra-eleven is an icebreaker, apparently breaking ice in front of Sierra-ten."

"Sonar, Conn, I will locate their track through the ice and come up for a fix. I'll turn broadside so you can get a range."

"Sonar, aye."

✳

We were used to the process by now. Since the icebreaker and her charge were to our starboard, and since we had not crossed their track earlier, Waverly figured that they had entered Parry Channel from the south and were headed to a settlement on one of the northern islands. Rather than changing course, he remained on his present track, believing he would cross theirs shortly.

That's exactly what happened. When the under-ice sonar indicated clear water with broken ice overhead, Waverly and Barry set about obtaining a good fix without having to penetrate the ice cover.

Either Barry called the skipper, or he came on his own, but Commander Roken was present for the coming shallow and fix taking. When they were finished, and Barry had reset the SINS, the skipper told them to settle beneath the tanker and match speeds.

"Might as well use all the cover we can find," he said as he departed for his cabin.

Quartermaster 2nd Class Ben Gross, Barry's Nav Watch, was Barry's junior quartermaster, which was why Barry assigned Ben to his watch.

"What are the possible destinations for that tanker?" Barry asked Ben.

"Only two make sense, Sir, Dundas Harbor, about forty-three nautical miles ahead to starboard, and Resolute, about two-hundred-thirty-eight miles."

"Sonar, Conn, do you have a range on the contact?"

"Sonar, aye, he's at fifty miles, Sir."

"I guess they're headed for Resolute," Ben said.

"It could be Resolute and then one or more other communities," Barry mused.

I stepped into Control. "I have some info on that subject." I walked over to the chart table and rolled out a chart that covered the entire Canadian Arctic archipelago. I pointed to Cambridge Bay at the south end of Queen Victoria Island, and then across Coronation Gulf to Umingmaktok at the head of Bathurst Inlet and Qingaut at its foot, both on the Canadian mainland but accessible only by sea or air, and to the Hudson Bay Company trading posts Tuktoyaktuk and Paulatuk near the Alaska border on the Bering Sea.

I picked up a pair of dividers and stepped off the distance between Resolute and Cambridge Bay—480 nautical miles distant. Then I measured the distance to Umingmaktok—115 nautical miles, and from there to Qingaut—sixty.

"Tuktoyaktuk and Paulatuk are almost certainly serviced by road," I added. "These guys around Coronation Gulf—that's a long way to go through heavy ice. I gotta believe they are normally provisioned during the high summer."

"That means," Barry said, "that our tanker's destination is Resolute."

"He'll probably stay there for the rest of the winter," I added.

"We got about a day before we pass Resolute," Ben said.

"I'm going to guess that we'll be on our own from there until we round Point Barrow," I said. "That's where we'll likely reacquire the *Alfa*."

USS TEUTHIS—BARROW STRAIT

On the charts, Barrow Strait really is just a continuation of Lancaster Sound, and they're both parts of Parry Passage. Technically, Resolute Bay, along which the tiny hamlet of Resolute nestles, is a deep-water harbor on the south side of very large Cornwallis Island, about eight nautical miles across from much smaller Griffith Island. Resolute Passage rests between them. Griffith is one of two larger islands and five smaller ones along with a host of rocky islets that hamper passage through Barrow Strait.

Barrow Strait is ice covered year-round. Pressure ridges form, pushing both above the surface and below, sometimes as much as a hundred feet. For a ship trying to press through with the help of an icebreaker, the rocky islets are virtually impossible to see. For a submarine beneath the ice, things are different.

Teuthis was equipped with the under-ice sonar that could detect ice ridges pushing down from the surface, but realistically we would have to move at bare steerageway for it to be useful. It was way better for us to remain below the extent of these ridges—that would be 200 feet with a margin of safety. *Teuthis* was also equipped with the secure bottom-sounder, and unlike the under-ice sonar, it served to help us avoid the obscured rocky islets. We couldn't charge through Barrow Strait at twenty knots, but if we could remain at 200 feet and had a good SINS reset before we started, we could safely transit the Strait at ten knots, keeping a close eye on the bottom-sounder for any unexpected rises.

Barry set a path that would take us south of the bulk of the islands in Barrow Strait.

✳

We arrived off Resolute Bay in the final quarter of Bert's watch. As expected, the icebreaker and tanker turned into the bay, and we moved on until Griffin Island lay between us and Resolute. Barry needed an accurate fix to reset the SINS if we were going to thread our way through Barrow Strait.

The skipper and Barry arrived in Control at about the same time.

"How thick is the ice?" the skipper asked Bert.

"Four feet or more, Sir."

"It's fairly smooth on this side of the islands to the west," Barry said, "but I suspect it will be more jumbled and rough on the other side."

"Why's that?" the skipper asked.

"The surface current flows generally west to east in Parry Channel. That should level things out where we are east of the islands."

The skipper checked the time. "We've got about two hours of daylight and three hours of twilight. Let's surface and give the crew some time on the ice."

✳

"This is the Captain. We will be breaking through the ice in a few minutes and surfacing. The COB and the deck gang will clear the ice from the Bridge and the main deck aft of the sail, clearing the hatch. As assigned by your division leading petty officers, crew members may leave the sub in groups of five for a maximum of fifteen minutes. Dress warmly. It's about minus ten outside. Each group will carry an air-horn. By the time we are ready to do this, you will have about an hour of daylight and two hours of twilight left.

"We will be surrounded by four feet of ice, so there should not be any open water around us. Nevertheless, be very careful. Should you fall between the sub and the ice, you will likely not survive. The COB will ensure that leaving and returning is safe. Stay within one hundred feet of the sub. Listen for a recall blast from the ship's whistle. If you hear it, return immediately.

"One more thing. This part of the Arctic is dominated by Polar Bears. They are curious, they will be hungry, and they are very fast. Should you see one, sound your air-horn and return to the sub immediately. We will sound a recall for everyone else. Just in case, a sharpshooter will be on the Bridge.

"We will sound the collision alarm before surfacing. The ship will remain rigged for dive."

The skipper turned to the OOD. "You've done it before, Bert. This time will be a bit different. Set the fairwater planes for penetration. Come up to the ice slowly with a twenty-degree up-bubble. Commence pushing air into forward main ballast until the ice starts breaking. Then do the after main ballast. Once the decks are above water and the sub is stable, get to the Bridge with lookouts and a sharpshooter, and turn the COB loose on deck."

I decided to hang out in Control while we surfaced. The COB showed up with Seamen Spanker, Jackson, and Raker to work topside, and Seaman Billy-Bob Yokum as sharpshooter. Yokum brought an M-21 sniper rifle with him. Bert's Chief of the Watch, Senior Chief Firecontrol Technician Ogden Winder—everyone called him *Oggy*— lowered the fairwater planes to vertical and brought *Teuthis'* bow snug against the ice cover. Then he sounded the collision alarm and dumped high-pressure air into the forward main ballast tank.

At first, nothing seemed to happen. Then a snapping, cracking, banging sound filled the entire submarine, and moments later, the bow burst through the four-foot-thick ice while simultaneously, the sail cut through the ice with a shrieking, rending sound followed by two loud bangs as thick chunks of ice slid down the sail and bounced off the deck. Bert and his lookouts, dressed for the -10 degrees cold, climbed to the Bridge, followed by Billy-Bob with his rifle.

The COB and his guys followed, attached safety lines, and clambered down the rungs on the side of the sail to the deck below.

In Control, Seth Beaumont manned the attack scope, and the skipper manned the nav scope. They scanned around the horizon while Barry got a multiple satellite fix for the best possible SINS reset.

It took the COB and his seamen fifteen minutes to clear the after hatch and set up knotted hawsers from the centerline safety-track to the ice below. The ice alongside *Teuthis* was hard against the sub but did display some cracking radiating out away from the sides. Several large slabs angled from the deck to the ice, creating an easy path down. A few minutes later, fifteen men climbed out of the hatch onto the deck and clambered over the sides using the hawsers. I watched them through the attack scope as they found their footing and slid around on the ice, acting like a bunch of boys on recess. While they were out, the COB sent another fifteen to the other side.

Fifteen minutes were up for the first group and then the second all too soon. The COB called them back and sent out another thirty. They had been on the ice for about five minutes when Jerry Walker's voice sang out from the Bridge over the electric megaphone.

"Bear! Bear! Polar Bear broad to starboard!" After several seconds, he called again, "There's a whole bunch of them, and they're makin' tracks to the sub!"

Bert sounded one long blast on the ship's whistle. Thirty sailors on the ice beat feet for the sub, clambered up the slabs, turned around to help shipmates, and then dropped below.

"Clear the deck!" the COB shouted. "Drop the hawsers over the side…get below!"

I trained my scope on the approaching bears. I counted six, two full-grown females and four large cubs, most likely two for each female. The females were large, over 500 pounds each. The cubs were half their size, probably in their second year of cubhood.

By the time the bears arrived at the sub, only the Bridge was occupied. In less than two minutes, all four of the cubs had climbed on deck, checking things out. One of the females walked entirely around the sub, examining everything closely. The other female went to the stern where some free water was visible between the rudder and the deck. She slipped into the water, dropped below the surface, and then propelled herself up out of the water and grabbed the aft end of the rudder in her teeth. Struggling to gain a foothold, she pulled herself nearly to deck level while leaving hind claw marks in the paint, and then she dropped back into the water. Undaunted, she tried again, and this time, using teeth and claws on all four feet, she made it to the deck.

Two of the cubs ran up to her. She swatted them soundly, sending them tumbling to the ice. Then she turned toward the sail and looked up at Bert and his lookouts, Jerry and Jake, and Billy-Bob the sniper. Billy-Bob put the M-21 to his shoulder, but Bert put out his hand and pushed the rifle down.

"No need for that. We're safe up here."

The female approached the sail and walked around it, sniffing it, checking its surface carefully. When she came to the rungs that led to the Bridge, she stood on her hind legs, reached up as far as she could with her front paws, and bellowed a fierce roar. She wrapped her front paws around a rung nearly halfway up the sail, about ten feet, and tested its holding capacity. It held. She tried to climb but couldn't keep her hind paws firmly on the bottom rungs. Several times she tried, roaring her frustration between attempts. Finally, she gave up the attempt to reach us.

Down on the ice, the other female called her cubs. They joined her and commenced rolling on the ice, mock-fighting each other while she watched attentively. The second pair of cubs joined them, squealing, grunting, and growling loud enough to be heard on the Bridge. The female who had tried to reach us slid down one of the slabs and joined them. She sat near the other female, licking first one forepaw and then the other.

The skipper arrived on the Bridge, spending a few minutes watching the six bears. Then he ordered everyone below, sealed the sub, and told Barry to relieve Bert and submerge the sub.

I hung around long enough to watch Barry submerge through the thick ice chunks surrounding us.

"Chief of the Watch," he said to Pots, "submerge the ship."

Once the ballast tanks were full, he ordered, "Make your depth one-five-zero feet using buoyancy." When we reached 100 feet, he ordered, "fairwater planes to normal." That took about fifteen minutes. Then he ordered, "Ahead standard, make turns for ten knots. Come left to course two-four-two."

And with that, we ended our adventure with the Polar Bears and set our sights on Point Hope.

USS TEUTHIS—VISCOUNT MELVILLE SOUND

I was near the end of my requalifications. I left Control to study, knowing that Barry had to thread a needle between Hamilton Island, one of the small islands obstructing Barrow Strait, and Russell Island, a larger island separated from the north coast of Prince of Wales Island by Baring Channel. At closest approach near the end of his watch, he would have only four and a half nautical miles between *Teuthis* and land on both sides. To make matters more interesting, a horseshoe-shaped ridge connected the islands, extending to the southwest just 260 feet below the surface. This caused Barry to set his depth at 150 feet instead of 200.

Several study hours later, I slipped into Control to watch Barry thread the needle before heading out into Viscount Melville Sound. As I left to get some midrats before hitting my rack, Barry ordered, "Come right to new course two-six-zero. Ahead full; make turns for eighteen knots. Make your depth two-zero-zero feet."

This would take us about ten nautical miles north of Stefansson Island on a direct path toward the entrance to Prince of Wales Strait between Banks Island to the northwest and Prince Albert Peninsula on Victoria Island to the southeast, some 270 nautical miles distant.

The Prince of Wales Strait is a 144-nautical-mile *so-called short-cut* to Bering Strait. The entrance is eight nautical miles wide, and it gradually widens to twenty-two nautical miles at the southern end where it opens into Amundsen Gulf. I called it a *so-called shortcut* because the trip through the strait was, in fact, about a hundred miles longer. It had the advantage, however, of keeping Banks Island between *Teuthis* and the Beaufort Sea—open water all the way to Russia. We were less likely to be detected by the *Alfa*, especially as we moved along the north coasts of Canada and Alaska, where we hoped to blend into the coastal noise of ice, occasional shipping, and marine life.

One more thing: About halfway through the strait, the Princess Royal Islands pushed their way through the surface right in the middle of the strait. The passage to the northwest was fairly shallow, so the skipper opted to pass the islands on the southeast side. What we did not anticipate was what we would find when we got there in about twenty-six hours.

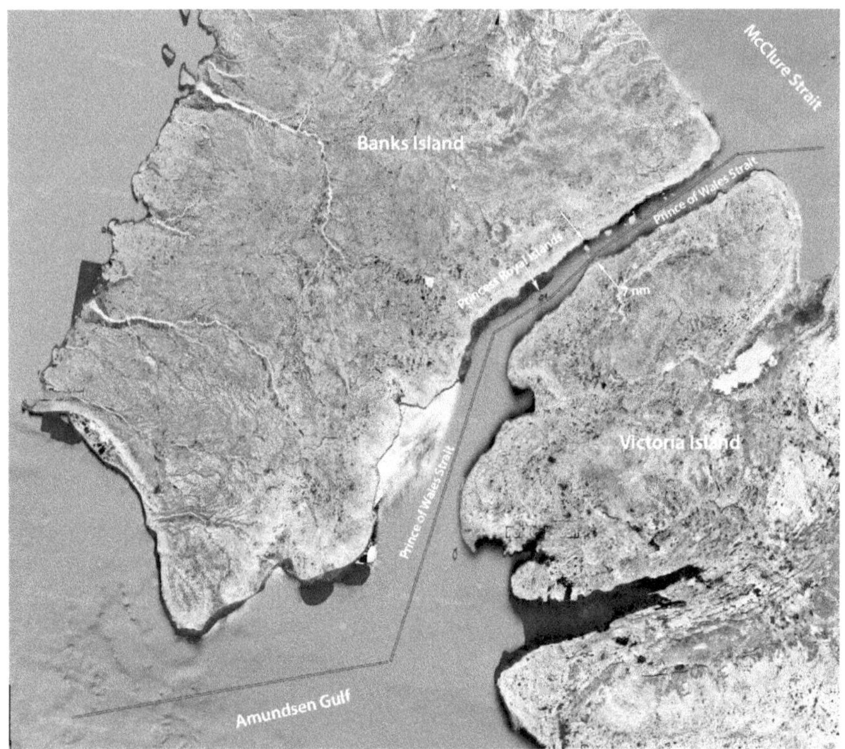

Prince of Wales Strait transit

CHAPTER EIGHT—Prince of Wales Strait

USS TEUTHIS—MCCLURE STRAIT

The skipper's cabin on *Teuthis* was smaller than CO's quarters on virtually any other navy vessel. Still, it did have room for a maroon Naugahyde-covered couch and overstuffed chair, a fold-down desk, a bookcase, and a small bathroom with a shower and fold-up sink.

Chief Sonar Tech Royal Bennett and I seated ourselves on the couch. The skipper made himself comfortable in the overstuffed chair, set at an angle to the couch.

"Gentlemen," the skipper commenced the conversation, "I want your opinions on something that has been on my mind. King," he said to the chief, "you are the best Sonar Tech I know, and you, Mac, well, you're Mac." He smiled slightly.

King grinned, and I felt a bit uncomfortable.

The skipper rolled a chart on the deck between us that displayed the entirety of the Canadian archipelago. "We're here, headed for here," the skipper said, pointing to our present position fourteen miles north of Stefansson Island and then to the entrance of Prince of Wales Strait. "The *Alfa* is out here somewhere." He swept his hand from Point Barrow, Alaska, across the Beaufort Sea to the McClure Strait, where Parry Passage emptied into the Beaufort Sea. "He seems bound and determined to track our activities. Should he acquire us as we approach Point Hope" —he pointed to a cape about midway between Point Barrow and Bering Strait—"we would have to pass right on through the strait and try to lose him in the Bering Sea or even the North Pacific. We already did that once around Baffin Island. I don't want to do it again." Roken paused and leaned back in his chair. "We fooled the *Alfa* once before. Maybe we can do it again. If he's hanging out in the Beaufort Sea, and if we do some energetic activity here," he pointed to the middle of McClure Strait, "as if we were heading through the strait to the Beaufort Sea, how far out do you think he could detect us?" He glanced from King to me and back to King.

"I'm told his sonar is as good as ours," King said. "He doesn't have anything like the BQQ-2, though."

"The sound will channel under the ice," I added. "If we make the noise at three to four hundred feet, I think he can pick it up as far as five hundred miles."

"He would know that," the skipper said. "If he thinks we're no longer worried about him, he might place himself out here," he pointed to where the Beaufort Sea becomes the Arctic Ocean. "If we can convince him we're coming toward him and then gradually reduce our noise profile until he loses us, he may very well think we are still headed in his direction, but moved out of the deep sound channel." He placed his finger back at the middle of the McClure Strait. "Can we get from here to the entrance of the Prince of Wales Strait undetected?"

I got down on my knees to check the soundings along the path he had indicated. "The depth along the track is deeper than thirteen hundred feet for most of it," I said. I took a quick measurement.

"That's about sixty nautical miles. If we remain within seventy-five to a hundred feet of the bottom at five knots, I don't think he could find us." I checked the soundings at the entrance to Prince of Wales Strait. "It starts shallowing up about fifteen miles out, but we would be moving sufficiently slow to keep up with it and still remain close to the bottom." I looked at the skipper. "I think you can do it, Skipper, don't you, King?"

"I agree, Capt'n. We do it how the commander said, he'll never hear us."

"Once we exit the channel," I added, "we can hug the coastline to our south. We'll be shallower, but ice noise and marine life should mask us."

"Thank you, gentlemen," the skipper said as he rose to his feet. "We'll do it. I'll issue the appropriate orders." He looked at me. "You have the next watch, right?"

"Yes, Sir."

"Grab a bite, and I'll meet you in Control."

✳

Popovers again. I had no doubt why the skipper made sure Cedric came to *Teuthis* with him. When I arrived in Control, Barry was there with the skipper.

"How comfortable are you with our SINS position?" the skipper asked Barry.

"Depends on what your plans are," Barry answered.

The skipper told him.

"Let's get a good three-satellite fix," Barry said.

I checked the under-ice sonar. It was a godawful mess up there. With the current and the wind coming through McClure Strait, the ice was jumbled all along the northern coast of Stefansson Island.

"Skipper," I said, "I think we need to move away from the coast about ten miles before we get our fix."

"Make it so," the skipper said, "and then follow Barry's track. As we discussed, take her down to four hundred feet and kick her. Run at flank on two-eight-zero, clearing baffles hourly, to here." He pointed to a spot broad off the southern coast of Melville Island. "Then run for fifteen miles on three-one-eight. As we discussed, near the end of the run, slow gradually to five knots and drop slowly to near the bottom. Wake me if I am not up and about when you start these maneuvers."

❋

I ran out at twenty knots and 400 feet, keeping my eye on the under-ice sonar. Sure enough, starting about eight miles from our starting point, the surface ice smoothed out. Unfortunately, it was six or more feet thick. I brought the sub to seventy feet and cruised in an expanding circle, looking for a thinner spot.

The skipper was up, so I called him and explained what I was doing. "Good thinking," he said. "Carry on."

About an hour later, the ice above us thinned to three feet. I didn't want to surface, just break the ice so Barry could extend his mast and get a good fix. I brought us to a stop.

Senior Chief Engineman Sam Dokey, my Chief of the Watch, swung the fairwater planes to their ice penetration mode and stood by for my orders.

"Okay, Sam," I said, "ten-degree up-bubble. Take her up gently until she rests against the underside of the ice."

"Captain's in Control," someone said as we moved up slowly.

A gentle bump, and we were there.

"Chief of the Watch, blow forward main ballast gently…just until the ice cracks."

"Forward ballast is dry, Sir. This ice is a lot harder than before."

"Old ice, Sam. It's been around a while."

Finally, after three minutes, a sharp report told us we had breached the ice.

"Ease her down to a level six-five feet, Sam," I said.

Two minutes later, Sam reported, "At six-five feet, zero bubble, Sir."

I grabbed the attack scope while the skipper raised the nav scope.

"Clear," I said.

"Clear," the skipper said.

"Nav, raise your mast, and get your fix." I wanted this over as soon as possible. Our scopes and mast were the only metallic objects within many hundreds of miles of our position. Small though they were, they would pop on any radar screen.

"It's gonna take ten minutes," Nav informed me. "We want a three-satellite fix…that's the minimum window."

So, we waited. That was a long ten minutes, but finally, Nav said, "We got the fix, Conn. Mast down."

The skipper and I dropped our scopes, and I turned to Sam Dokey. "Chief of the Watch, fairwater planes to normal. Diving Officer, make your depth four-zero-zero feet. Helmsman, ahead flank, come right to course two-eight-zero."

The skipper hung around until we reached depth and speed. "Keep a sharp eye on the water beneath the keel. Clear baffles every hour."

✳

With the ocean floor 900 feet below me and the ice 400 feet above me, flying along at over thirty knots was the cat's mEOOW. Roughly every hour, I slowed to five knots, made a figure-eight while King did a thorough search in all directions. Nothing at the end of the first hour. Nothing at the end of the second. Nothing after the third and nothing after the fourth. Then we changed course and ran for another twenty minutes.

I called the skipper to Control before gradually slowing while assuming a twenty-five-degree angle for the bottom.

I did a quick calculation. It would take us about ninety seconds to reach our depth. I kept one eye on my stopwatch and another on the depth. At one minute and twenty seconds, I ordered, "Zero bubble, ahead slow, make turns for five knots, come left to course one-eight-six."

As we settled into our new course, Sonar notified me, "Conn, Sonar, while we were descending, passing six hundred feet, I picked up suppressed cavitation on a bearing of two-eight-zero. I heard it for only five seconds. I'm running analysis right now."

Two minutes later, "Conn, Sonar, it's the *Alfa*. He's way out there, but it's him for sure."

✳

Bert relieved me right after that, and we spent the next ten hours hugging the seafloor at five knots, while Sonar kept getting intermittent hits on the *Alfa*. It seemed to be closing.

Two hours after Barry took over, the water began to shallow. Once he reached 400 feet, Sonar was able to get a really good bearing on the *Alfa*. It was definitely moving into McClure Strait. As Barry rounded the corner into Prince of Wales Strait, the under-ice sonar indicated very thin ice to starboard.

The skipper joined Barry in Control, and together, using the outboards, they moved *Teuthis* starboard into the lee of Passage Point, the northeasternmost tip of Banks Island, where the water was a bit less than 100 feet deep. Overhead was a thin skim of ice just a few inches thick. Pots, Barry's Chief of the Watch, inched the sub up until the top of the sail just popped the thin ice film.

Pots kept *Teuthis* exactly at depth and in position while Barry and Fonzie got a good satellite fix. While Barry got his fix, Waverly and the skipper scanned the surface and shore for anything.

"We got the fix," Fonzie announced.

"That should hold us through the one hundred forty-four miles of the strait," Barry said.

Barry slipped south into the channel while dropping to 125 feet on a course of 226 degrees at ten knots.

USS TEUTHIS—PRINCESS ROYAL ISLANDS

Barry pushed farther into the Prince of Wales Strait for his entire watch, remaining at 125 feet while keeping a watch on the water beneath the keel. He cleared baffles four times, but Sonar heard nothing except the noise of ice along both shores. Because *Teuthis* was only about five miles from land on both sides, sonar noise was substantial. Despite the tiring effect of this constant noise on a Sonar Tech's hearing, Barry instructed Benny to keep a close watch astern for the *Alfa*.

Realistically, it could have taken the *Alfa* fourteen or so hours to get to the entrance of Prince of Wales Strait—or a lot less, depending on how far out he was when we first picked him up. Prudence dictated that we placed him at the entrance. If he detected us, he would be on us like white on snow unless we could somehow shake him.

Doug Watson, the Engineer, took over from Barry just seventeen miles from the Princess Royal Islands. He came left to 224 degrees, and shallowed up to 100 feet. He really didn't know what to expect. The best info I could supply from my research was that currents ran from south to north and from north to south in Prince of Wales Strait, for all the good that information did. We really didn't know if it was an under-over or side-by-side flow, or if it was tidal, first one way and then the other, or even some crazy combination.

Because I had the next watch, I tried to get some sleep. I found out later that after five miles, Doug slowed to eight knots, and after another seven, to five knots. I finally got up, grabbed some early breakfast with three cups of coffee. I went to Control with my third cup since I had nowhere else to be, and just maybe my research would be of some help. The skipper was in Control poring over the charts trying to make something appear that simply wasn't there. He nodded to me as I approached the chart table.

The skipper put his finger on the narrow passage between the islands and Victoria Island, where the chart said the depth was a bit less than 200 feet.

"It just doesn't feel right," he said. He glanced at the under-ice sonar. The undersurface was jumbled rough, sometimes extending down forty or fifty feet. Why all the ridges?" he asked. "What's going on up there?"

"I have a thought, Skipper," I said, tentatively. "I have records showing currents flowing both directions here. What if they're accurate? What if the surface is a swirling jumbled mass of ice and water trying to go both directions at once? With the kind of cold that's up there, I would think the result would be massive ridges pushing both up and down—perhaps even a hundred, hundred fifty feet."

Franklin James was Doug's JOOD. He walked over to the chart table. "Let me get this straight," he said. "*Teuthis* is fifty-five feet from the keel to the top of the sail. The water is one hundred ninety-five feet deep. The ridges extend to one hundred fifty feet. My math says we got ten feet more sub that we got room."

"That's about it," the skipper responded. "And we don't know what's on the other side…"

"Except the bottom is a bit deeper," I added.

✳

My first thought as I was getting ready to assume the watch was that we really needed eyes on the situation. We were doing too much speculating. The skipper was still in Control, so I walked up to him and said, "Skipper, I recommend we launch the Basketball to investigate what we actually have ahead of us, and that we get divers ready to deal with whatever it finds."

"Let's do it," the skipper said. "You go to Dive Control and set things up. Leave Zeb in charge up here. I'll stay in Control until you get back. But I want you here for the op."

I spoke briefly with Zeb and then announced, "The Captain has the Deck, Lieutenant Trainer has the Conn."

I met Ham in Dive Control along with Senior Chief Ocean Tech Morris Jones. "Spook," I said, "the skipper wants to use the Basketball as eyes while moving up to and through the ice ahead. We figure we got a big mess. Put your brightest, widest flood on the Basketball."

I explained the details of what we thought lay ahead to Ham. "Check with Sam Dokey—he's the Chief of the Watch right now. See if he has a pneumatic drill that will work underwater at two hundred feet and can drill a two-inch hole in ice. Ready two divers for one-hundred-eighty-foot diving—rebreathers should be fine. And round up several sticks of explosive."

I then outlined what I wanted the divers to do. "They will want to review the situation on the monitor before they get wet," I added.

"You think?" Ham said with a grin.

✳

"I have the Deck and Conn," I announced after arriving back in Control. I looked at the skipper. "I want to inch forward slowly until we encounter ice pushing down," I said. "Then, I'll lower the skids and settle to the bottom." I glanced at the secure bottom-sounder. The seafloor was fifty feet below us.

"Carry on," the skipper said. "I'll jump in if I see a problem."

I called Dive Control. "Are you ready to go, Spook?"

"Yes, Sir, I got Wally on the Basketball."

"All stop…Back one third…All stop. Helmsman, are we D-I-W?"

"Yes, Sir."

"Chief of the Watch, lower the skids to full extension."

"Full extension, Sir."

"Roger. Settle us to the bottom using buoyancy."

I grabbed the mike. "Spook, launch the Basketball."

The monitor displayed twisting, tumbling shapes as the Basketball stabilized, replaced shortly by a clear view of the sub's starboard side as Wally moved forward.

When the Basketball reached the bow, I said to Wally, "Bring it up slowly until we can see the ice underside."

Wally tilted the Basketball so the flood illuminated upward at about 45 degrees. About forty feet above the sail, several large chunks of ice filled the monitor.

"Now, move forward," I told him.

Almost immediately, the ice jumble began angling down. At fifty feet ahead of the bow, the ice was twenty feet above the sail.

"Chief of the Watch, extend both outboards and adjust the buoyancy to neutral."

Three minutes later, "Done, Sir."

"Walk us forward at a slow pace. Be prepared to stop instantly and drop into the silt."

We moved ahead slowly, about the speed of a toddler's walk as the skipper and I stared intensely at the monitor.

"Move the Basketball about ten feet above and twenty feet ahead of the top of the sail," I said.

We continued to inch forward. A large, jagged piece of ice appeared on the monitor.

"Stop!" I ordered.

I could sense no difference, but Sam announced, "On the bottom…not moving."

"Wally," I said, "you ever do any spelunking?"

"Yes, Sir! Bunches."

"Okay. Make like you are in a crawl with a very low ceiling. Use the Basketball to survey it left to right and front to back to see if you have room to wiggle through. You ever done that before?"

"Lots, but we had no Basketball, just lights and our mark-one mod-zero eyeballs."

"Okay, Wally, show me what you can do."

The Basketball moved to the right following the ice contour. It remained pretty much the same for a hundred feet to the right. Then it followed the ice to the left. The ice went up for about forty feet and then dropped to within twenty feet of the bottom. The Basketball returned to the point where the ice went up and began to move forward through the tunnel. As it moved forward, the ceiling dropped to within forty feet of the bottom. Once again, the Basketball moved right and then left. For about sixty feet of width, the ice ranged from an average of sixty feet from the bottom to a low of forty feet.

Wally explored around the one-hundred-sixty-foot projection. It was about twenty feet thick and was the only projection that descended that far. All the others terminated about sixty-five feet above the bottom.

"Wally, I'm going to move *Teuthis* until it is just this side of that long projection. I want you to guide me by saying *Come right a foot… come left two feet, etc.* You got it?"

"Yes, Sir. Ready when you are."

To the Chief of the Watch, I said, "You got that, Sam? Bring us to neutral buoyancy and follow Wally's prompts."

"Aye, Sir."

After twenty minutes of careful maneuvering, the projection hung just ahead of and above the bow. I called Ham in Dive Control.

"Did you get the drill?"

"And the explosive sticks," he answered. "We've been following you down here. I think we know what to do."

"Just the same, Ham, I want to talk with you and the divers face-to-face first."

I looked at the skipper. He nodded.

"The Captain has the Deck, and Lieutenant Trainer has the Conn," I announced.

As I walked aft from Control, I heard the skipper say, "I have the Deck," and Zeb say, "I have the Conn."

✳

Spook had sketched a drawing of the downward projecting ice. His sketch made it clear that it was a slab of seven-foot-thick surface ice. It had twisted and rotated so that one corner had been pushed down to within forty feet of the bottom. Spook and I studied the sketch for a few minutes. I marked seven spots across the slab, twenty feet up from the corner.

"If we drill at these points and insert seven charges, it should break the entire corner off," I said.

"The broken piece should move up and out of the way," Spook answered.

I brought over Ham and the divers—Harry and Jake. Ham wanted to give Jake more experience and decided to send Harry with him just in case. I walked the divers through their task.

"Any questions?" I asked.

"Any narwhals around here?" Jake asked.

"Not likely," I answered. "Ice is too thick to break through, and there aren't any open spots nearby."

"Well, shit, I was hoping Harry could meet his boyfriend."

It took the divers two hours to drill the holes and set the C-4 explosive sticks. They wired the sticks in parallel so they would blow simultaneously and fed the wires back to the egress hatch.

I called the skipper in Control. "We're set to go."

"I've been watching on the monitor. Your divers are inside the DDC, right?"

"Yes, Sir."

"Very well…initiate!"

✳

King said the explosion nearly overwhelmed Sonar, but inside the sub, we only heard the slightest pop, barely distinguishable from the ice noise around us. I looked up at the monitor.

"Wally, check that out," I said.

Wally gave us a tour of the result. The corner had broken off cleanly, but it had jammed in such a way as to project into the plane *Teuthis* would have to penetrate. I called Control.

"We need to do it again, Skipper. I think three charges will do it."

"Before we take that step," the skipper answered, "have Wally do another round over the top of the broken-off piece."

"You heard the man," Spook said to Wally.

After ten minutes of Basketball examination, the skipper said, "I think that piece is just balanced. If we nudge it with our sail, I think it will break free and move up and out of our way. What's your opinion, Spook?"

"Does look that way, Capt'n."

"How about you, Mac?"

I swallowed my pride. "I was too hasty with my first recommendation, Sir. Upon re-examination, I agree with you. I think we can push through…with Wally's guidance."

"Good…I need you back in Control."

"Sam, as before, neutral buoyancy, inch ahead following Wally's prompts."

"Neutral buoyancy…ready to go, Sir."

"Wally, take us through this maze."

We commenced forward motion, very slow forward motion.

"Bring the sail against the ice chunk," I said.

On the monitor, the sail pushed up against the large chunk of ice.

"Okay, move forward slowly," I said.

Just as the skipper figured, as we pushed, the ice chunk rotated and slid up and out of sight. We continued inching along the bottom while keeping a close eye on the ice above us. By the end of my watch, the jumble above us was gone. I stowed the skids and outboards and brought *Teuthis* up until we had a hundred feet below us. Barry laid out our ninety-nautical-mile path to Amundsen Gulf, and I turned the watch over to Bert and Seth.

USS TEUTHIS—AMUNDSEN GULF

The Amundsen Gulf is defined by Banks Island to the north, Victoria Island to the northeast, and the mainland Northwest Territories to the south. To the east, south of Victoria Island, five linked waterways—Dolphin and Union Strait, Coronation Gulf, Dease Strait, and Queen Maud Gulf—form the southernmost stretch of the so-called Northwest Passage that Roald Amundsen finally traversed back in 1903.

Our intent was to head the other way, west toward Point Barrow, the same route that Amundsen took after working his way through the ice in the Dolphin and Union Strait. The big difference, we were beneath the ice. Our only problem was avoiding the *Alfa*.

We had no way of knowing what the *Alfa* was doing. The skipper thought, and I agreed with his reasoning, that the *Alfa* had followed us into Prince of Wales Strait. Unlike us, however, the *Alfa* skipper had no way of investigating the immediate environment ahead of him. My personal fantasy was that when he reached the Princess Royal Islands, he ran smack into the jumbled ice through which we had picked our way. He simply would have had no way of knowing that the ice extended so far down. Conservatively, he might have been doing between five and ten knots. I believed he hit the ice, did some damage, but not enough to disable him, and that he turned around, headed back out the strait, and headed west around Banks Island.

Transit from Amundsen Gulf to Demarcation Point

CHAPTER NINE—Beaufort Sea

USS TEUTHIS—LEAVING AMUNDSEN GULF

It was now over thirty days since we had left Groton, ten days since we began deploying the first SOSUS array, and eight days since we began threading our way across the Canadian Arctic. Once we passed south of Banks Island, the only things north of us were 1,930 nautical miles of ice-covered open ocean stretching between us and the Russian Arctic island of Severny—and probably the *Alfa*. Ahead of us was Point Barrow, Alaska, 580 nautical miles as the fish swims, but we wanted to blend into the coastal noise. This would add fifty nautical miles or so to our track.

Forty-three nautical miles west of our position and twelve due north of Cape Bathurst is the entrance to a five-mile-wide shipping channel recently defined by Canadian maritime people. It passes south of, for the most part, a spread-out grouping of pingo-like protrusions from the seafloor.

On land north of the permafrost zone, pingos are a type of frost heave where ice forms on top of the permafrost, pushing the ground above it into a mound that can rise as high as 180 feet. The Tuktoyaktuk Peninsula, between 90 and 175 nautical miles west, is home to a very large number of these formations.

Just offshore of Tuktoyaktuk Peninsula, extending for fifty miles right to the edge of the drop-off into the Beaufort and Arctic basin is a large number of gas-hydrate pingos that bubble methane from the tops of their structures. They are not very well understood but might indicate the presence of oil beneath the seafloor. The Canadian-surveyed shipping channel lies south of most of them, and those in the channel are well charted. The channel runs for 187 nautical miles along the coast to Mackenzie Bay with depth ranging from eighty-five to a hundred feet. The ice surface is mostly smooth and fairly thin—six to eighteen inches for the most part.

We could handle the transit at just below periscope depth at five knots. Because of the precision navigating, we would need to avoid the pingos in the channel; however, the skipper wanted to reset the SINS before commencing the run.

USS TEUTHIS—PINGOS TRANSIT

Barry and Waverly assumed the watch two hours away from the entrance to the shipping channel. They continued the twenty-knot run until the bottom began to shallow up as they approached the entrance. The skipper joined them in Control as they prepared to push through the ice to take a fix.

By this time, pushing through the ice cover, especially a thin cover, was nearly routine. Barry instructed Waverly to handle the process and gave him the Conn. The skipper didn't interfere, but he remained on the periscope stand in his chair, and when the scopes went up, he took the nav scope as he usually did. Quartermaster 2nd Class Ben Gross had the watch with Barry, and he successfully got a three-satellite fix that nailed our position. He reset the SINS, and Barry laid out a path that followed the deepest part of the channel and avoided the submerged pingos by the widest possible margin.

Creeping along at five knots with the secure bottom-sounder running continuously, we went through a complete watch cycle plus two, so that as *Teuthis* exited the channel fifteen nautical miles north of Mackenzie Bay, I was coming on watch with Zeb Trainer. Zeb had been carrying most of the load for several watch cycles. Legally, I had to retain the Deck, but he did most of the work.

Barry had laid a course track to a point about twenty nautical miles north of Herschel Island. Zeb was studying the chart.

"What depth do you think?" he asked.

"How deep is the water?"

He traced his finger along the track. "Looks like he keeps us twenty-thirty miles from the coast. Shallowest appears to be about two hundred thirty feet."

"So, what do the skipper's standing orders say?"

"No less than a hundred feet beneath the keel. More if possible."

"So…?"

"One hundred twenty-five feet, I guess."

"You guess?" I was giving him a bit of a hard time.

"Diving Officer," Zeb said, "make your depth one-two-five feet."

USS TEUTHIS—DEMARCATION POINT

King called from Sonar. "Commander McDowell, can you come to Sonar?"

I stepped off the periscope stand and into Sonar. "What's up, King?"

King handed me a set of headphones. "This is the starboard side," he said.

I heard sound, lots of it, much more than we heard up in Parry Channel. It formed sort of a background crackling hiss.

"This is the port side," he said.

The noise was two or three times as loud, subjectively anyway. It was pretty overwhelming. I suspected it would tire out a pair of ears pretty quickly.

"I don't think anybody can hear us against that noise," King said. "I'm thinking we tell the Captain we're go for more speed."

"I get that, but the water isn't very deep here. I'll check with the skipper to see if we can move out several miles so the depth will support higher speeds. Then we can see if the background noise still masks us."

Back in Control, I detailed the suggestion to Zeb. "If we could travel near the fifty-fathom curve while still being masked, that would work. Check the chart, get the details in mind, and then call the Captain and explain it to him."

Zeb was relatively new to the Navy. He had a lot of respect for the skipper, tinged with just a bit of fear. He called the skipper on the dial-up. I could see the concern in his eyes.

"Captain, it's Zeb Trainer…Yes, Sir, J-O-O-D.I…I have a thought, Sir, that will allow us to make faster time…No, Sir. It's a bit complicated. Can you come to Control so I can show you?" He replaced the handset on the hook and looked at me with a question in his eyes.

"You did fine, Zeb," I told him with a warm smile.

The skipper joined us at the chart table. As Zeb started to explain, the skipper got it immediately, but he let Zeb finish his presentation.

"You want to move out to the fifty-fathom curve, let Sonar check out the sound, and then we'll make a decision? Is that it?"

"Yes, Sir, exactly."

"Make it so," the skipper said to Zeb, glanced at me, and returned to his cabin.

✷

Zeb moved us out another eight nautical miles until the secure depth-sounder indicated 175 feet below the keel—fifty fathoms. I stepped into Sonar and told King. He handed me the headset again and reached for his reel-to-reel.

"This is live off the port side," he said and then switched to the tape deck. "And this is from before." He switched back and forth several times.

Frankly, I could barely tell the difference. King showed me the actual difference on the decibel meter—a bit less than a DB. That was below the threshold the human ear could hear. I went back to Control and informed Zeb.

With more confidence this time, he called the skipper. "Captain, there is virtually no difference in the noise level. I think we can stay out here and raise speed to twenty knots."

A moment later, the skipper joined us in Control. "I trust you," he said to Zeb, "but I want to see for myself."

He spent a few minutes looking at the chart and then stepped into Sonar. When he returned to Control, he said, "Okay, two hundred feet, twenty knots."

✳

About two and a quarter hours later, we passed Demarcation Point that defined the bay of the same name, the first identified harbor on the American side of the border—that is, if anything could be called a harbor on this ice-choked shoreline. Despite the ambient noise, the skipper wanted to clear the baffles every hour, if for no other reason to listen carefully outward for any signs of the *Alfa*.

By the end of our watch, we had passed Barter Island and had our sights set on Point Barrow, 200 nautical miles ahead.

✳

Doug Watson and Franklin James assumed the watch shortly before we arrived in the waters north of Point Barrow, the northernmost point of the United States. Their first task was to reset the SINS to enable *Teuthis* to move safely through the shallow waters around Point Hope to lay the second SOSUS array.

In addition to a satellite fix, Point Barrow had several rotating beacons on towers that would give the quartermasters a backup to their satellite fix.

Twenty nautical miles north of Point Barrow, the ice was a foot thick, mostly solid, and without ridges. When Doug broke through the ice, he raised the attack scope.

"Bearing…Mark! White and green. Bearing…Mark! Red-red."

Juby laid out the lines on his chart and awaited the SatNav results. "Got it! Pinpoint!"

The skipper had joined Doug and Frank and was draped over the nav scope when Sonar called.

"Conn, Sonar, I have a faint, intermittent contact at three-three-zero. I think it's the *Alfa*."

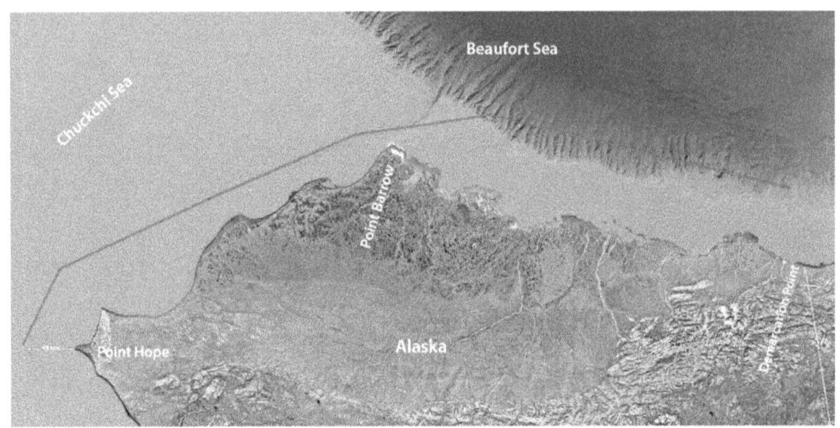

Transit from Demarcation Point to Point Hope

CHAPTER TEN—Point Hope

USS TEUTHIS—CHUKCHI SEA

Sonar had intermittent contact with what might be the *Alfa*, but it was too flaky to get a range. As I had done earlier, Doug turned over most of the watch responsibilities to Frank, who was well qualified in principle, but still needed some knowledge of fine points on *Teuthis.*

Frank reported the *Alfa* detection to the skipper, paused to listen, and then responded, "Aye, Captain. I'll pass it along to Doug." He turned to his Diving Officer, Chief Electronics Technician Rusty Jackson. "Diving Officer, make your depth two-zero-zero feet quietly. Helmsman, ahead standard gently, make turns for eight knots, come left to new course two-four-six."

The 1MC came alive. "This is the Captain. We have picked up our Russian friend again. We will not go to ultra-quiet right now, but I want you to be as quiet as possible while carrying on with your normal tasks. Be ready to go to ultra-quiet instantly when the time comes."

✳

Frank walked to the chart table and beckoned Doug. "The Captain said to maintain this course, speed, and depth until the fifty-fathom curve shallows out…" he pointed, "right about here. From then on, we're dealing with water a hundred twenty or so feet deep. That puts us near periscope depth. He wants five knots."

"How long before all this happens?" Doug asked.

"About ten hours with baffle clears."

"Okay, then. That makes the rest of our watch easy."

✳

When Zeb and I assumed the watch, we still had four hours to go on this leg. I continued to let Zeb handle the watch. He was doing great. I suspected that by the end of this cruise, the skipper would qualify him as an official watchstander.

During our second baffle clearing, Sonar called. "Conn, Sonar, I got the *Alfa*—still intermittent, but more steady. I suspect he is somewhere beyond Point Barrow. If you can give me a fifteen-minute broadside, I may be able to get his range."

Zeb called the skipper, and I joined them in Sonar.

"Tell me what you know," the skipper said to King.

"I think he's beyond the continental margin, probably deeper than three hundred feet, which is why he still is intermittent."

"I recommend we wait until he is solid," I said. "He'll be inside the fifty-fathom curve. We can get a more reliable range."

"I agree," the skipper said.

✳

Four hours later, Sonar informed us that the *Alfa* was no longer intermittent. We came to a stop and hovered at 200 feet for fifteen minutes, pointing toward the northwest while Sonar tried to get a range.

"We got a range, sort of," King told me. "The *Alfa* is between seventy and a hundred miles astern."

"Stay on depth, course, and speed until the fifty-fathom curve," the skipper told Zeb.

Two hours later, Alastair Forbes, who had the Nav Watch, announced, "Fifty-fathom curve, Sir. Recommend we come to one hundred feet and slow."

"While we're still at two hundred feet," I said to Zeb, "let's come to all stop, turn broadside to the *Alfa*, and see what we get."

A few minutes later, King called from Sonar. "We got a good range on him—seventy-five nautical miles. But there's something wrong. I'm hearing mechanical noises that don't belong with an *Alfa*. I don't know what they are yet, but the *Alfa* is moving rather slowly."

"What do you think would happen if the *Alfa* bumped into the ice wall we crawled under?" I asked.

"Depends on how fast, I guess. It'd mess up his sonar, that's for sure. Could fuck up his drive train, too. We don't know a lot about these guys, Sir."

I called the skipper to brief him about the *Alfa* and told Zeb to listen to my side of the conversation. When I was done, I nodded to Zeb.

"Diving Officer," Zeb said, "make your depth one-zero-zero feet. Helmsman, ahead slow, make turns for five knots."

And with that, we commenced our very stealthy approach to Point Hope.

USS TEUTHIS—POINT HOPE

Point Hope juts out about ten nautical miles into the Chukchi Sea from Lisburn Peninsula. It is about 160 nautical miles slightly east of north of the Bering Strait. The Chukchi Sea is quite shallow all the way to Russia. The waters off Point Hope are not particularly well suited for a SOSUS array. The area was so strategically important, however, that we were tasked with placing an array that would see traffic to the north, east, and south.

Because of the necessarily shallow location of the array, we would have to lay it with all possible stealth. Hence our creeping approach and worry about the *Alfa*.

We had to cover 205 nautical miles, but in stealth mode, we were moving at five knots, plus we had to clear baffles roughly every hour. This added up to fifty-one hours of slow-walking along the bottom in about 120 feet of water. It's not particularly difficult, but it required full focus and concentration the entire time. That can be exhausting.

We cycled through the Control watch cycle twice before Zeb and I brought *Teuthis* to a stop forty-five nautical miles west of Point Hope in 180 feet of water. Bert and Seth would have the fun of surveying out a thousand-foot-wide flat area for the array.

Barry laid out a survey field 2,000 feet on a side. Chief Ocean Tech Francis Oberst worked out the details of the survey. The Fish would run thirty feet above the bottom across the field, making thirty-five-foot swaths. *Teuthis* would cruise slowly a hundred feet above the field while the Fish would run fifty-seven swaths at ten knots. Total time about two hours.

Franklin set up the survey in Dive Control with Derrick at the Fish controls. Once we had selected the ideal location after the survey, my divers would go through substantially the same drill as they did off Carey Øer, anchoring the array every hundred feet.

Under Bert's watchful eye, Seth ran the survey and worked with Dr. Brand, Chief Ocean Tech Bart Davidson, and Lt. Cmdr. Franklin James to designate the best position for the array. Then he set the *Teuthis* on the bottom at the south end of the array, pointing along the bearing of the array, and notified me in Dive Control that we could commence dive operations when ready.

ON THE SEAFLOOR—WEST OF POINT HOPE

Because we were in late autumn, ice covered most of the Chukchi Sea, but a couple nearby polynyas remained ice-free, and many areas near land were covered by easy-to-break thin ice. This allowed air-breathing marine mammals to range from south of Bering Strait north into the waters above Point Barrow.

Ham and I decided to put Whitey and Ski into the water for the first half of the array, and Harry and Jimmy for the second half. We put the divers in hot-water suits breathing a standard tri-mix of nitrogen, helium, and oxygen. This gas mix protected them from nitrogen narcosis, allowed a short decompression time, and conserved helium.

Wally focused the Basketball on the egress hatch as we commenced. Whitey entered the water carrying an anchor, followed by Ski with the hammer. They both headed aft to the cable pipe. Bart had already lowered several feet of array cable. The divers stretched out a few feet of cable along the sub's axis, and then Whitey placed the croquet wicket-like anchor over the cable just aft of the first hydrophone.

As Ski lifted the hammer to seat the anchor, he shouted, "What the fuck!" his voice sounding nearly normal through the tri-mix. "Something jerked the hammer right out of my hand."

Wally panned the Basketball around. As he did so, something very white flashed briefly in the beam and then disappeared. He brought the light back on the divers and panned around the seafloor. About five feet away lay the hammer. Ski stretched over and retrieved it. He lifted it again.

"Dammit!" he shouted. "Fucker took it again."

Wally backed the Basketball away, increasing the coverage of its light beam. Floating in the light with what looked like a silly grin on its face was a fifteen-foot white whale with a big bump on its forehead.

"That's a beluga whale!" I said, my excitement pretty obvious to everyone in Dive Control. "He won't hurt you, Ski," I said. "He just wants to play." I turned to Jake, who was standing behind me. "Jake, see if you can find a short piece of two-by-four. Hurry."

Jake returned a couple of minutes later with a four-foot piece of wood.

"Run it through the Entrance Lock," I told him.

About three minutes later, the 2x4 appeared through the egress hatch.

"Push it toward the beluga," I said.

As the wood moved forward and up, the whale chased it, grabbed it in his mouth, and actually brought it down to Ski.

"I'll be golldamned!" Ski said as he shoved it away again, but harder.

While the beluga retrieved the wood, Ski pounded the anchor into the bottom.

"Okay, guys, we got work to do," Ham said. "Return to the lock."

Like the narwhal off Carey Øer, the beluga followed the divers to the hatch and then tried to get a look at what was beyond that bright circle of light.

Seth called King, who arranged for the Basketball view to appear on monitors throughout *Teuthis*, so the crew could enjoy the antics. of the beluga.

Seth moved *Teuthis* for the first five anchors while Whitey and Ski, accompanied by their beluga friend, set them into the seabed. Four times during the course of this activity, the beluga disappeared for several minutes, apparently to get a gulp of air. On his last return, four other belugas joined him, jousting with each other for the 2x4 after Ski pushed it toward them. When they came down near the divers, they were gentle as tame dolphins.

✳

When Barry and Waverly assumed the watch, Ham switched Harry and Jimmy for Whitey and Ski. Someone had located another 2x4. For the next two hours, the crew continued to be entertained by the divers and their aquatic friends.

Finally, Harry and Jimmy were crouched around the last hydrophone, preparing to set several anchors close together to prevent the array from being pulled up by the shore cable. Three belugas were watching intently when, suddenly, a large black and white creature swept into view, smashing viciously into the side of one of the belugas, tearing a huge chunk of flesh from its flank. The beluga whipped away wildly, trailing massive amounts of blood.

"Divers…Into the hatch immediately!" I barked. "Now!"

In five seconds, both Harry and Jimmy were safe inside the Egress Lock. Wally swam the Basketball down to the hatch, and Ski pulled it inside the lock.

"What the fuck…" Harry said.

"Yeah…what the fuck," Jimmy echoed.

"That was an Orca," I told them. "Up here, Orcas feed on narwhals and beluga, and even bowhead."

"And divers?" Jimmy ventured.

"Not normally, but this one was in a feeding frenzy. These guys never travel alone, so his buds were nearby. They would not deliberately attack you, but if you are in the midst of a pod of beluga with blood everywhere…what do you think?"

"We didn't set all of the last set of anchors," Harry said. "Will it be safe to go out to set the rest?"

"Actually, yes," I said. "We'll give them fifteen minutes. They all will need air, and the belugas will be long gone. The dead one will be floating at the surface under the ice, so that's where the Orcas will be."

✳

Twenty minutes later, Ski dropped the Basketball through the hatch. As soon as Wally got it stabilized with a good picture, Harry dropped into the water. As he did, an Orca with an oversize dolphin head slipped under *Teuthis* and nudged him.

"Shit!" Harry yelped. "He's gonna eat me!"

Harry backed up, stuck his head through the hatch, and the other three guys pulled him into the lock. As they looked down through the hatch, the Orca's bill appeared. It was on its side and stopped to peer into the hatch. Then it rolled over to peer with its other eye. Its curiosity was apparent. It wiggled around for a bit until it was on its back. Then it rolled forward and stuck as much of its head through the hatch as possible. Its eyes moved in their sockets as it took in the four divers. It opened its bill about three inches and uttered a loud, piercing squeal followed by a three-second-long chitter. Then it dropped back into the water and vanished.

I gave them five minutes to pull themselves together and then sent Harry and Jimmy back out to finish their job.

USS TEUTHIS—WEST OF POINT HOPE

The next part of the operation was routine but tedious. We would lay the armored cable along the bottom, anchoring it every quarter mile for forty-five nautical miles until the sub could no longer operate submerged. From there, our divers would bring a messenger line to the beach.

In Control, Barry and Waverly handled the first four hours running on the outboards, keeping the skids extended. Ham divided the divers across the time so that everyone had a chance to brave another Orca encounter, but none occurred.

Twelve hours later, during my watch, Zeb set *Teuthis* to a hover at periscope depth while the XO assumed the Deck so I could be in Dive Control for this final, crucial operation.

Seth, Sparks, and the skipper recorded and encoded a brief message that gave the location and approximate time the divers would surface. When they completed the message, Sparks compressed it into burst message format. Then he raised the antenna and sent the message. The transmitter was active for less than a second. A few minutes later, Sparks sent the burst message again, and then once more twenty minutes later.

ON THE SEAFLOOR—ONE MILE WEST OF POINT HOPE

Jer and Jake entered the water nine-tenths of a nautical mile from shore and a hundred feet below the thin ice crusting the surface. They wore bright orange Unisuits and rebreathers and Kirby-Morgan helmets with limited range underwater sound communication. Their first task was to fake out a mile of cable across the seafloor in hundred-foot loops.

The pair temporarily anchored the bitter end to the seafloor a hundred feet from the cable pipe.

"Okay, Bart," Jer said, "start feeding out the cable."

Under the watchful eye of the Basketball, Jer pulled a loop of cable forward a hundred feet to the right of the bitter end. Then, as Jake pushed cable toward him, Jer laid a neat, hundred-foot length of cable against the previous fake, moving toward the cable pipe until sixty-one loops lay nicely faked on the seafloor.

"Got it, Bart. Stop feeding cable," Jer said.

Jake returned to the hatch, where Ski handed him a reel of strong messenger line. He swam out to Jer, followed closely by the Basketball.

"How's your knot-tying?" Jake asked.

"This cable ain't heavy," Jer said, "but they'll be pulling a mile of it. We better do it right, or this whole exercise will be wasted."

I jumped into the conversation. "How about a double sheet bend?"

"A sheet what?" Jake asked.

"I know what it is," Jer said. "Watch me. If I do it wrong, you can 'splain it to me."

Wally moved the Basketball close.

"Okay, that's fine, but finish it with a couple of half hitches around the cable."

"Like this?"

"Yeah, that's it."

"Okay, Boss. We're ready to swim."

"You're swimming by compass. You got your variation set right?" I asked.

"Checked it with the gyrocompass."

"Okay, but you were inside the sub. Our heading is zero-eight-seven-point-zero-three. Line yourselves up with the sub about a hundred yards ahead of us and make sure your variation is correct."

"You got it, Boss."

"I don't want you swimming toward Bering Strait."

Jer took the lead using proper compass swimming procedure. It was obvious he had done this before and was comfortable doing it. Jake followed with the messenger line reel.

Wally ran out of Basketball tether 200 feet beyond the sub's bow. I watched Jer and Jake disappear into the underwater gloom, moving at a comfortable pace. I calculated that they would reach shore in about twenty minutes. Their instructions were to hand off the messenger line and wait until the shore guys they met had retrieved the cable. I figured another twenty minutes for that, then another twenty minutes for their return to *Teuthis*. An hour, give or take.

Fifty-four minutes later, the Basketball began to pick up a faint shadow ahead. Gradually, the divers' images emerged from the darkness.

"Dive party, this is Dive Control, comm check, over." I wasn't exactly impatient, but I wanted to get the status as soon as possible.

"Dive Control, this is Jer and Jake. Mission accomplished. We'll be home in a couple."

PART THREE

The Alfa

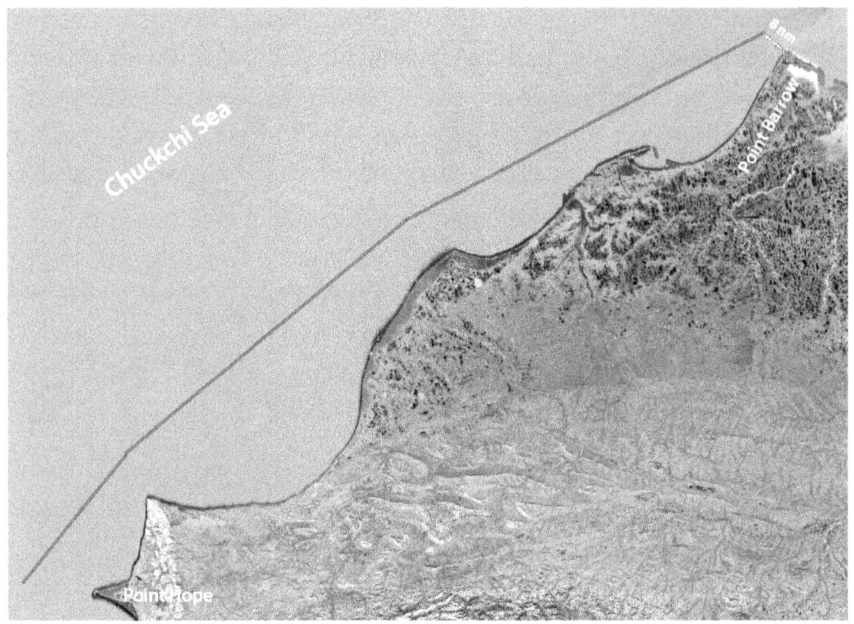

Transit from Point Hope to Point Barrow

CHAPTER ELEVEN—The Hole

USS TEUTHIS—TRANSIT TOWARD POINT BARROW

Our work was done—at least we thought it was. Because the *Alfa* was somewhere north of us, Commander Roken decided to head north toward Point Barrow. Once there, we would make sufficient noise so the *Alfa* would pick us up, and then we would let him follow us south through the Bering Strait, down through the Aleutians, and across the North Pacific to San Francisco.

Bert let Seth do most of the driving. Even though the water wasn't very deep, by sticking to the path we used coming south, we were able to do a stealthy eight knots northward with safety. Point Barrow lay some 270 nautical miles ahead of us. That would involve thirty-three hours of transit time plus eight hours of baffle clearing. From our point of view, the only thing of interest anywhere in our vicinity was the *Alfa*, and it lay ahead of us to the north. To be fair, we had no idea about what else might be lurking in the waters around us. To the south, the Kamchatka Peninsula harbored the Soviet's largest submarine base, Petropavlovsk-Kamchatskiy. To the northwest lay the entire northern coast of the Soviet Union. The ice cover and shallow water helped us remain undetected, but they also limited our ability to detect anything at long range.

Zeb and I had the watch as we slipped silently into the waters off Point Barrow. Submarine crews are always in a quiet mindset, but since leaving Point Barrow earlier, the crew had been in an enhanced quiet mode just short of ultra-quiet. This had put a damper on normal operations, but it had been necessary to prevent the *Alfa* from detecting us.

And at that moment, we had no idea where it was.

USS TEUTHIS—OFF POINT BARROW

As Zeb hovered a hundred feet over the bottom near the edge of a 500-foot-deep hole eight nautical miles northwest of Point Barrow, King called me by sound-powered phone.

"The *Alfa* is nearby," his voice whispered in my ear.

Without waiting to inform the skipper, I sent the word throughout the sub by sound-powered phone to set condition ultra-quiet. The engineers secured the turbine and generators and shifted to the battery. Others shut down the fans and blowers throughout the sub. Everyone who was not actively engaged in watchstanding or another critical activity went to bed.

In Control, a soft 400-Hertz tone from the Attack Center synchros permeated the air, accompanied by an occasional quiet hiss from the hydraulic system as the planesmen shifted planes or rudder. The only other sound was the nearly silent shifting of water into or out of ballast tanks to keep *Teuthis* at depth. Sam Dokey, my Chief of the Watch, had trimmed the sub with such skill that very little water shifting was necessary.

"Conn, Sonar, the *Alfa* is within several hundred yards. I hear mechanical noises and shouting, but the turbine is not running, and their screw is not turning. They definitely have a problem, Sir."

The skipper went into Sonar for several minutes and then joined us in Control. He examined the chart briefly and then said, "Zeb, ease the outboards out, slowly and quietly." He walked back to the chart table. "Move very slowly to here," he pointed to a spot on the seafloor near the southern edge of the 500-foot hole. "While transiting, drop slowly so that you settle on the bottom here." He tapped his finger on the same spot.

Zeb lowered the outboards and skids. Pumps kept the hydraulic pressure up, but the engineers had slowed them down to minimize their noise output. As *Teuthis* slowly sank to the bottom, the only perceptible sound was the quiet creaking of the sub itself as the hull compressed from the increasing external pressure. In the stillness of ultra-quiet, it sounded deafening.

USS TEUTHIS—BOTTOMED 8 NAUTICAL MILES NW OF POINT BARROW

Over the sound-powered phones, King asked, "Conn, Sonar, can we reset our axis, so we have a broadside view to the northeast?"

"Are we still at neutral buoyancy, Sam?" I asked.

"Yes, Sir."

"Zeb," I said, "Work with Sam to point us at three-one-five. Then set it down and have Sam make the sub heavy, so we won't shift on the bottom."

Zeb and Sam completed the operation in virtual silence. I could not imagine anyone hearing us through the ice noise along the Point Barrow coast and the general noise of a moving ocean covered with ice plates surrounding us in all directions.

I donned a sound-powered headset to make communications with Sonar easier. King whispered in my ears again, "Conn, Sonar, the *Alfa* is above us and off our starboard. I don't speak Russian, but I can hear words, and I hear angry shouts…"

"Hold one, Sonar," I said.

I turned to the skipper. "King says he can hear people speaking Russian, but he doesn't understand Russian. I do, Sir. Would you take the Deck so I can spend a few minutes in Sonar?"

"I have the Deck," the skipper announced quietly. "Go ahead, Mac."

✳

King handed me a headset as I entered Sonar. I donned it, and I heard in Russian, "…shaft misaligned…damned prototype…sound-mount shifted…keep the reactor hot…" Then I heard a shrill alarm that was cut off almost immediately, followed by, "reactor scram, reactor scram…oh shit, oh shit…keep it hot…reinsert the rods… omygod…omygod…keep it hot…Emergency Blow…Emergency Blow," followed by the sound of rushing air for a few seconds, followed by five minutes of silence.

King interrupted me. "She bounced off the undersurface of the ice, and now she's headed for the bottom, Sir." King paused for a minute, listening. Then he said, "She's on the bottom, about a hundred yards away."

I held up a finger as I heard more Russian: "Abandon ship… ready the pod…all hands…goddamned stupid engineers…" From that point, the talk was drowned out by noise from within the *Alfa*. A couple of minutes later, I heard loud mechanical cranking and a very loud hiss followed, after a few seconds, by a distinct thump and cracking sound. Then nothing except background noise from the ice.

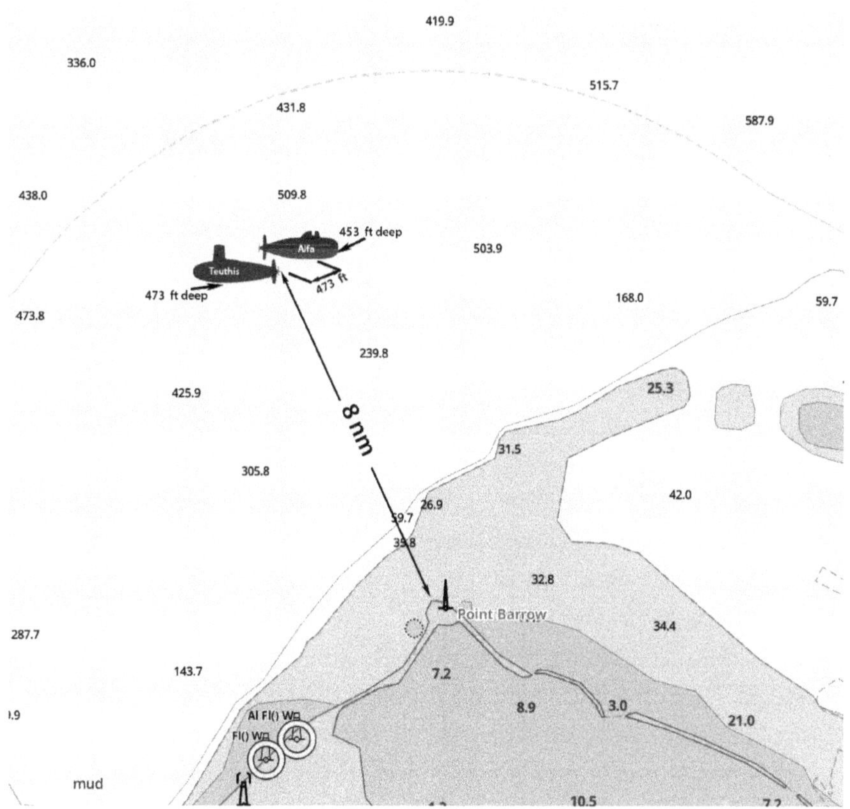

USS Teuthis *& the* Alfa *in 500 ft hole 8 nm off Pt. Barrow*

CHAPTER TWELVE—The Sting

USS TEUTHIS—BOTTOMED 8 NAUTICAL MILES NW OF POINT BARROW

"So, what do we have?" the skipper asked me when I returned to Control from Sonar.

"I can only give you my best guess, Sir."

"That's all I can ask for."

"King says this is the same *Alfa* that's been dogging us all along—the *K-316*. I think he followed us into the Prince of Wales Strait and bumped into the ice wall that we crawled under. This damaged his sonar and started a chain of events in his powertrain that resulted in a driveshaft misalignment and displacement of some kind of mount. Somehow, all this scrammed his reactor. I kept hearing the phrase, *"keep the reactor hot."* The unresolved scram seems to have been a reason to emergency surface. Apparently, that attempt was uncontrolled, and he didn't make it through the ice."

"I've heard," the skipper said, "that the Soviets have been playing around with different reactor cooling systems. Know anything about that?"

"No, Sir. Nothing." Then I added, "One more thing, Sir. I've read some intelligence that they have been testing escape pods that will carry an entire crew. An *Alfa* crew is small—twenty or so. I think they installed a pod on their *Alfa*s. I thought I heard them abandon ship… into a pod of some kind. I've read that they have installed escape pods on their new subs. That works for an *Alfa*, but I don't see it for one of their missile boats. I'm pretty sure a pod left the sub, but I don't think it penetrated the ice."

"It sounds like we have a small crew of enemy submariners stranded in a pod that is trapped beneath the ice. Unless we do something, they're going to die." He sighed. "Have Seth meet me in Radio."

I sent the messenger to locate Seth. He found him in the Wardroom studying his quals.

ON THE SEAFLOOR—8 NAUTICAL MILES NW OF POINT BARROW

"We have a unique opportunity here," the skipper told me. "Let's put your divers out and have them examine the outside of the *Alfa*. They can sever any comm link with the pod. Maybe we can find a way to get inside her, figure out what she's all about."

It was near the end of our watch. Bert showed up early so I could initiate the dive. Ham met me in Dive Control.

"I want two divers on long umbilicals to locate and investigate the *Alfa*," I told him. "We'll play it by ear from there."

"Probably should use our most experienced divers for this," Ham said, "Harry and Whitey. Let's hold Jimmy back for possible medical complications."

"He'll be disappointed."

"How long do you think we will be here?"

"Long enough. So much depends on what we find," I said. "Let's get them ready."

* * *

Two hours later, Harry and Whitey entered the water, got their bearings, and commenced swimming toward the *Alfa*. Derrick accompanied them with the Basketball, running out ahead of them looking for the bottomed sub. King had determined that it was close aboard, a hundred yards or so.

After a few minutes, the murky outline of the *Alfa*'s silhouette appeared on my monitor. The skipper showed up in Dive Control.

"How long are their umbilicals?" he asked.

"Five hundred feet, Sir," Ham answered.

"We got her!" Harry squeaked, helium and pressure distorting his voice even after descrambling.

The Basketball swooped down to the divers' location. Whitey checked his umbilical, pointed to a marker, and said, "She's about four hundred seventy-five feet away."

"Twenty feet shallower than *Teuthis*," Harry added.

The Basketball showed her starboard side pointed about fifteen degrees away from us.

"First thing," I told them, "check the entire perimeter. I want to make sure she's stable."

"If she rolled," Ham commented to me, "the water surge would probably push them away, but I agree, survey first."

The divers made a slow swim circuit forward on the starboard side and around the bow.

"Holy shit! Look at that!" Whitey squeaked.

Derrick swept across the bow.

"Looks like you called it, Mac," the skipper said.

Half the bow fairing was ripped open like a tin can. The sonar sphere was obviously damaged. It was impossible to tell by looking at it if it still worked or not.

"That must have been exciting," Ham remarked wryly.

"A collision at sea…" I said, letting the words hang in the air, finishing the thought in my head: *… can ruin your entire day.*

The divers continued their survey with Derrick looking over their shoulders and occasionally darting the Basketball in for a closer look or out for a wider view. When they reached the stern, Whitey said, "Look at them little propellers on the…what are they? Horizontal stabilizers…"

"Those are the stern planes, dumb shit," Harry said. "But yeah, a four-bladed screw about three feet across on the rear tip of each stern plane."

Derrick showed us what they were talking about.

"Divers, Control, you need to reverse your survey direction. You're about to run out of umbilical," I told them.

They returned to their starting point and then headed aft on the starboard side.

"Come forward along the deck," I told them.

They swam up to the deck and followed it to the streamlined sail.

"Whoa, look at this," Harry said. The Basketball showed him peering down inside the sail. "This thing is completely open," he said.

"That has to be the pod location," I said to the skipper. "The part that faired into the sail is missing. It must be attached to the pod."

"The way it's shaped," Dr. Brand commented, "It could function like a trimaran's outriggers if there were flotation at the bottom of each wing." He had quietly joined us in Dive Control.

That was when I realized that Dr. Brand's interest had really perked up once we actually made physical contact with the *Alfa*. He was traveling with us to supply potentially needed expertise for laying the two SOSUS arrays, but he really hadn't much to do for most of our trip. The *Alfa* seemed to have changed all that.

"We got a tether and a comms cable," Harry said.

"Recommend we cut the comms cable but keep the tether for the time being," I said to the skipper.

He nodded without speaking.

"Cut the comms cable, Harry," I said. "Whitey, locate the escape hatch. It should be right below you on the hull at the bottom of the sail. Look for a pressure connector."

"Found it, Boss. It's a standard metric high-pressure nipple."

Derrick zoomed in on the fixture. We were in luck. Doug's people would have a way to marry one of our own HP hoses to that nipple.

The skipper watched the divers for several minutes, and then perhaps a minute later said, "Bring your divers back, Mac. We need to go up to send a burst message."

USS TEUTHIS—BOTTOMED 8 NAUTICAL MILES NW OF POINT BARROW

The message read:

TOP SECRET—TOP SECRET

TO: COMSUBDEVGRUONE
FROM: USS TEUTHIS SSNR 2

SUBJ: ABANDONED SOVIET ALPHA CLASS
      SUBMARINE

1. CURRENT TEUTHIS LOCATION: LAT 71.488085 LON -156.909747, ON BOTTOM, 473 FT.

2. CURRENT ALFA LOCATION 475 FEET NORTH OF MY POSITION. THE ALFA EARLIER EXPERIENCED AN UNKNOWN CATASTROPHIC FAILURE RELATED TO PROBABLE COLLISION WITH AN ICE WALL. SHE HAS SEVERE DAMAGE TO HER SONAR DOME. INTERCEPTED CONVERSATIONS FROM WITHIN THE SUB INDICATE PROBABLE DRIVE TRAIN DAMAGE AND A NON-RECOVERABLE REACTOR SCRAM. THERE IS NO INDICATION OF RADIATION LEAKAGE OUTSIDE THE SUB (BASED UPON ACTUAL MEASUREMENTS) OR INSIDE (BASED UPON OVERHEARD CONVERSATIONS).

3. THE ENTIRE ALFA CREW ABANDONED THE SUB IN AN ESCAPE POD. THE POD RESTS DIRECTLY ABOVE THE ALFA UNDER TWO FEET OF SURFACE ICE. POD IS CURRENTLY TETHERED TO ALFA.

4. THE ALFA IS UNAWARE OF TEUTHIS' PRESENCE, BUT ALFA (BELIEVED TO BE K-316) HAS DOGGED TEUTHIS SINCE CAREY ØER. IT IS LIKELY ALFA NOTIFIED SOVIET NAV HQ OF GENERAL LOCATION AND INTENT.

5. REQUEST SOONEST POSSIBLE RESCUE OF ALFA CREW BY BREAKING UP ICE AROUND THE ESCAPE POD WITH EXPLOSIVES OR OTHER MEANS AND REMOVING CREW FROM ESCAPE POD.

6. SIGNAL TEUTHIS WITH TWO SMALL EXPLOSIVE CHARGES IN SHORT SUCCESSION WHEN ALFA CREW SAFELY AWAY FROM ESCAPE POD.

7. UPON RECEIVING SIGNAL, TEUTHIS DIVERS WILL WINCH ESCAPE POD TO BOTTOM AND SECURE.

8. UPON SECURING POD TO BOTTOM, TOG OIC LT. CMDR. J.R. MCDOWELL WILL ATTEMPT TO PRESSURIZE ALFA MAIN COMPARTMENT TO 15 ATM, AND THEN TO ENTER THE ALFA. IF SUCCESSFUL, HE WILL PHOTOGRAPH AND RECORD AS POSSIBLE AND WILL COLLECT ALL AVAILABLE DOCUMENTS FOR RETURN TO TEUTHIS.

9. UNLESS OTHERWISE DIRECTED, TEUTHIS WILL MARK ALFA LOCATION WITH A TRANSPONDER FOR FUTURE INVESTIGATION.

10. TEUTHIS WILL REMAIN AT PRESENT LOCATION UNTIL RECEIPT OF RESPONSE TO THIS MESSAGE. TEUTHIS WILL EXTEND AN ANTENNA EVERY THREE HOURS ON THE 12, 3, 6, 9, PST.

TOP SECRET—TOP SECRET

✳

Five hours later, we received a message from CINCPAC-FLT—the Commander-in-Chief, U.S. Pacific Fleet. That's as high as you can get in the operational Pacific Navy. I suspect that most of the high command had no idea that we were in the

Arctic and no clue about what we were doing. The DevGroup must have carefully picked how to forward our message so that need-to-know protocol was strictly followed, while it got to the right hands as soon as possible. Believe me, that was a tricky accomplishment.

Their message read:

TOP SECRET—TOP SECRET

TO: USS TEUTHIS SSNR 2
FROM: CINCPACFLT
VIA: COMSUBDEVGRUONE

SUBJ: ABANDONED SOVIET ALPHA CLASS
    SUBMARINE
REF: YOUR MSG SAME SUBJECT RECEIVED
    5 HRS AGO

1. DO NOT, REPEAT, DO NOT PRESSURIZE ANY ALFA COMPARTMENTS.

2. THE AIR FORCE HAS SENT AN EXTRACTION TEAM FROM FAIRBANKS TO POINT BARROW. THAT WILL ARRIVE APPROXIMATELY TWO HOURS FROM THE TIME OF THIS MSG. THE TEAM WILL FOLLOW YOUR RECOMMENDATIONS REGARDING THE EXTRACTION.

3. ONCE YOU HAVE SECURED THE POD ON THE BOTTOM, NOTIFY COMSUBDEVGRUONE BY BURST MSG, AND PROCEED POST-HASTE TO WOMAN'S BAY, KODIAK, ALASKA.

4. YOU WILL BE MET BY A SUBDEVGRUONE REP WITH EYES ONLY ORDERS.

5. YOU WILL RECEIVE A TEAM OF DIA SPECIALISTS AND WILL ALSO ONLOAD SPECIAL EQUIPMENT.

6. WHEN READY, AS DIRECTED BY THE SPECIAL ORDERS, TEUTHIS WILL PROCEED WITH UTMOST STEALTH TO ALFA LOCATION.

7. WHEN ON LOCATION, CO TEUTHIS, OIC TOG, AND DIA TEAM WILL PROCEED AS DIRECTED BY THE SPECIAL ORDERS.

7. UPON COMPLETION OF ONSITE OPERATION, CONTACT COMSUBDEVGRUONE BY BURST MSG FOR FURTHER INSTRUCTIONS.

TOP SECRET—TOP SECRET

The message was simple enough, but I wondered how much of a shakeup our message had caused. The new Soviet *Alfa* sub was pretty much of a mystery to the West. Getting our hands on one where there was a distinct possibility that the Soviets would not be aware that we had it was a very big deal.

Barry assumed the watch as we awaited the explosions that would signal the extraction team had arrived on the ice. If the message we received contained an accurate timeline, we expected to hear the explosions at any time. I was pretty sure the Air Force had an extraction team based at Eielson Air Force Base. I figured that CincPacFlt probably issued deployment orders within two hours of receiving our message. The remaining three hours before we received their response were bureaucratic nonsense. This meant the extraction team had departed Eielson within three hours of our message, four at the outmost. Their C-130 would have arrived an hour and fifteen minutes later at Barrow Airport. Allow a half hour to unload, another half hour to drive the eleven miles to Point Barrow. I presumed they would have brought Zodiac boats and snowmobiles, but I had no idea of the shoreline conditions at the point. They either drove the Zodiacs through icy water for some distance and then dragged them across the ice with the snowmobiles, or they pulled the Zodiacs with snowmobiles right from the shore. In any case, I gave them an hour from the point to the rescue spot.

Add it up. The extraction team would arrive above us an hour and fifteen minutes to two hours and fifteen minutes from our receipt of CINCPACFLT's message. I checked the time. We were already in the window.

I put the divers in standby mode so we could deploy them the moment the *Alfa* crew was gone.

✳

While I was in Dive Control with Ham readying Jer and Jake to retrieve the pod, backed up by Whitey, Ski, and Harry, with Jimmy in the DDC but not getting wet, a string of explosions penetrated the hull. I can only imagine the desperation the *Alfa* crew members must have been feeling as they bobbed below the ice cover with no way to extricate themselves from their situation. The explosions must have been terrifying. They were loud in Dive Control, 570 feet away as the fish swims. They would have been deafening in the escape pod. Further, they had no idea whether they were being rescued or sent to the bottom.

Forty-five minutes later, I heard two distinct low-power explosions in short succession. That was the all-clear. The twenty-five or so *Alfa* crew members would have been transported ashore at Point Barrow and hustled inside a couple of trucks. One Zodiac would have remained on-site to drop the charges. By now, it would be well on its way to Point Barrow.

I called Control and spoke to Waverly. "We're commencing dive operations," I told him. "You can follow on your monitor. Let us know if there is something you wish to examine more closely."

ON THE SEAFLOOR—8 NM NAUTICAL MILES NW OF POINT BARROW

By the time Jer and Jake entered the water, the Basketball, under Wally's steady hand, was flooding the seafloor under the hatch with light. The large underwater marine mammal visitors we had come to expect were nowhere to be found. I suspect the explosions chased them away—for the time being, anyway.

Jer moved to a forward deck locker that contained a hawser and untied the stays. With control T-wrench in hand, Jake moved to the forward capstan and raised it to its operating position and flipped a nearby cleat upright. Jer wrapped the hawser four times around the capstan and attached the bitter end to the cleat. Together, both divers wrestled the hawser out of the locker and over the starboard side of the sub—the side toward the *Alfa*.

They picked up the other free end and, holding it between them, began swimming toward the *Alfa*. Once there, they swam the bitter end into the gap in the sail created by the absent pod. Aided by light from the Basketball, they tied off the hawser to a stanchion with a short piece of line and then located the tie-down point of the pod tether.

"Let Wally get a close-up of the tether," I said to the divers. It was slender, about half the thickness of a little finger. After several seconds I asked, "Does it look like a multi-function tether to you or just a steel strength member?"

"Strength member," they both said.

"Just a steel cable," Jake added.

"Any way to remotely decouple it from the sub?" I asked.

"Just a stainless swivel joint," Jer answered. "The cable is under slight tension that varies as waves pass overhead. It never goes to zero."

"They must be able to release the cable at the pod," Jake said.

"Ham, you figure we can follow the plan?" I asked off the circuit.

"The hull is titanium, right?" Ham asked.

"Titanium alloy, I think."

"What about the superstructure and sail?"

That stumped me. I had no idea.

"Jer, are you sure that swivel joint is stainless? Could it be titanium?" I asked.

Jer pulled his dive knife and scraped along the side of the joint. "Ain't stainless," he said. "The cable's stainless. Everything else seems to be titanium."

"Okay," I said, "we'll follow the plan Ham discussed with you before you got wet—we'll cut the eye in the wire rope."

Jake dropped to the *Alfa*'s deck and flipped two deck cleats. He pulled the hawser around a cleat and swam it to Jer, who carried it up the tether about thirty feet from the swivel and attached it with a tautline hitch. Jer signaled Whitey and Ski to take a strain on the hawser. I turned to Ham.

"Time to put Whitey, Ski, and Harry in the water." Ham nodded to Bill, who carried it out.

As we watched the monitor, the hawser began to tighten until it was taut.

"Hold it," Jer said.

Under the Basketball's watchful eye, Jake retrieved his mini-torch and proceeded to cut the cable eye. Because the cable was stainless, the process took a full five minutes. As he reached the end of the burn, Jake said, "Take more strain before it gets away from us."

On the monitor, the hawser vibrated a bit as a wave passed overhead, putting a strain between the tautline hitch and the swivel joint.

A sudden *POP!* interrupted everything.

"Shit! Motherfuck!" Jake yelped.

"Jer, report condition of Jake," I ordered.

"The cable eye popped loose and struck Jake's faceplate. It's cracked. His helmet is flooding."

Jake turned toward the Basketball and gave two thumbs-up. He pointed to his ears and then his mouth, and then drew a finger across his throat.

"Looks like his comms are out," Ham said, "but he's breathing. We better bring him back to replace his Kirby-Morgan."

"Jer, this is Dive, you and Jake return to hatch immediately," Bill said. "We'll replace Jake's helmet and put him back in the water."

Jer and Jake headed back toward *Teuthis*, with the hawser stretched out below them. They split at the sub with Jer heading for the after capstan and Jake for the hatch.

"Wally," I said, "stay with Jake until he enters the hatch. Then proceed to the capstan."

✳

Jimmy pulled Jake through the hatch while Harry brought him another Kirby-Morgan. Before Jake donned the replacement helmet, Jimmy looked him over and checked his vitals.

"You okay, Bro?" he asked. "Anything hurt, feel funny?"

"Gimme a fuckin' break, Doc. They need me out there."

"Easy, Jake. Just makin' sure," Jimmy said. "Okay, good to go," he said, slapping the top of Jake's head.

"Wally," I said, "join Jake and Harry and stay with them to the capstan." And to Jake and Harry, I said, "To the after capstan."

Jer had already raised the capstan. Jake and Harry flipped a cleat and set the hawser before dropping it to the seafloor. Then Jer and Jake swam it to the *Alfa*. Once there, Jake wrapped it around the second cleat while Jer swam to the opening in the sail.

"Haul in the forward capstan until Jer stops you," I said."

While we watched on the monitor still showing Jer in the *Alfa* sail, Whitey and Ski commenced hauling the hawser. In less than a minute, the tautline hitch came into view.

"Stop!" Jer said.

The tether stopped moving, and Jer swam thirty feet up the tether and hauled the hawser thrice around the tether and tucked it under itself twice in a traditional tautline hitch. Then he said to Harry, "Harry, take some tension on your capstan."

As Harry hauled on the capstan, the first hawser began to slack, and Jer undid the tautline hitch and tied off the hawser on a stanchion.

"Okay, Harry, haul away until I stop you."

A minute or so later, the pod was sixty feet below the ice. We still had to repeat the process fourteen more times. I checked the clock on the bulkhead. We were taking about fifteen minutes per cycle, so it would take us about three and a half hours to bring the pod back to the *Alfa*. I pointed this out to Ham.

"Good thing our guys are in excellent shape," Ham commented with a grin.

"By the time they get back, they're gonna be beat to shit," Bill added somewhat wistfully. I suspected he would rather have been outside with the guys.

I called Control. "Waverly, we've got four hours more to secure the pod. Then a half hour to stow the hawsers, cleats, and capstans. Once everything's shipshape outside, Ham will bring the divers back onboard. I'm going to grab a bit of sleep in the meantime."

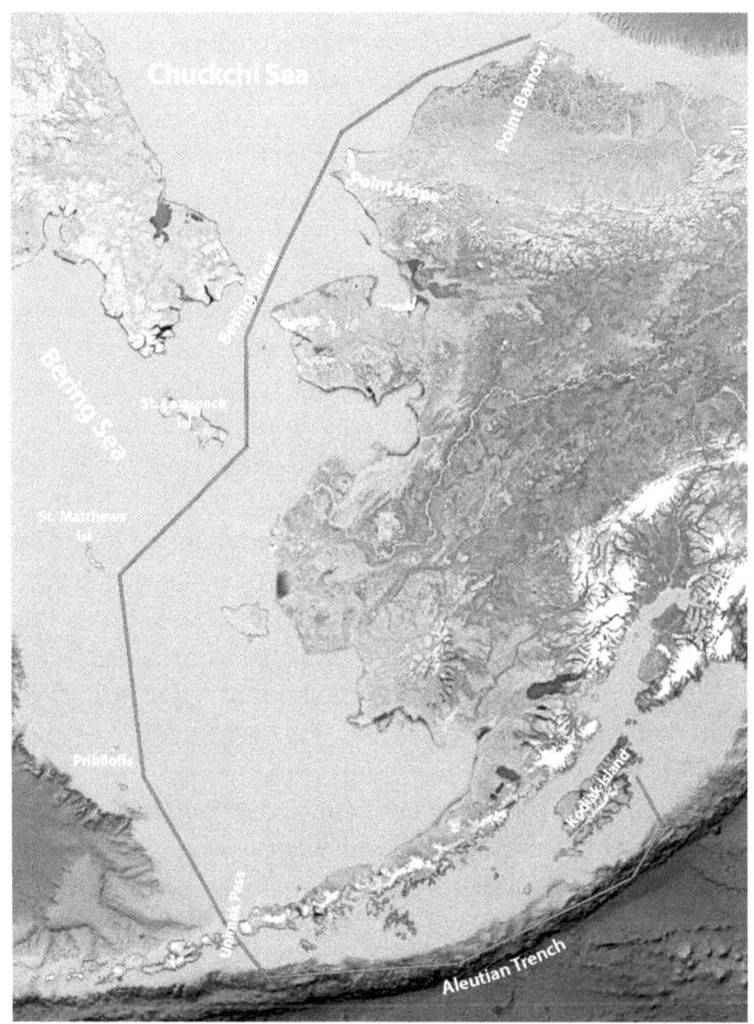

USS Teuthis & Mystic *transit from Pt. Barrow to Kodiak Island*

CHAPTER THIRTEEN—Transit to Kodiak

USS TEUTHIS—TRANSIT TO BERING STRAIT

We had been submerged for weeks except for our brief tangle with Polar Bears at Barrow Strait. All of us were nose blind to the smells that permeated the sub's air. Every time we blew sanitaries to

169

sea, we had to vent the pressurized tanks inboard. Sure, they vented through a set of activated charcoal filters, but that didn't do much. Everything inside the sub was permeated with that smell. We couldn't smell it, but it was there. Then there were cooking smells, also filtered, but also everywhere. Furthermore, most of the guys smoked, adding stale tobacco smoke on top of the other smells.

We couldn't smell it, but were you to step aboard the sub, you would quickly become overwhelmed by the oppressive odors. We badly needed to ventilate the sub, since it looked like we would be underway submerged for quite some time still.

Doug and Franklin had the watch as we wrapped up our diving ops. Topside was ready for ultra-quiet running, and the divers were stowing and securing their equipment. Jake and Jer were busy replacing the shattered Kirby-Morgan faceplate.

Franklin gingerly lifted *Teuthis* off the bottom and brought her to sixty-five feet, periscope depth. After a visual scan revealed nothing, he raised the snorkel mast and started venting the sub while Juby got a good fix. The incoming air was crackling cold, and the sub got downright chilly during the half hour we ventilated. Nobody complained. The fresh air was wonderful—we couldn't get enough.

Finally, every molecule of bad-smelling air had been sucked out of the sub. Some of the guys had laid their clothing on their bunks to air out. Most did not, but it probably made no difference anyway. You can go into any bar frequented by sailors and watch the B-girls walk behind the guys on the barstools, sniffing at each. When one of the girls picked up that peculiar submarine smell, she would latch onto the guy. As a submariner, he had more jingle in his jeans.

Franklin dropped us down to ninety feet, which put us fifty feet over the bottom on average all the way to Point Hope. We had taken this track twice before, and the SINS was on the mark, so following our track a third time was relatively easy. Ahead lay 445 nautical miles of Chukchi Sea that funneled everything headed south through the forty-three-nautical-mile-wide Bering Strait. It was a near certainty that the Soviets had at least one, and probably two or three subs patrolling the waters north of Bering Strait. Our southward route took advantage of the deepest waters between Point Barrow and Point

Hope. This trough was ten to fifteen nautical miles wide, which meant that any other sub at our latitude would be relatively close to us.

South of Point Hope the bottom dropped down another forty feet on average, which would give us more speed latitude, and spread out across most of the width of the strait, which would give us more room to remain hidden.

The skipper set our speed to Point Hope at eight knots. This meant we would be crawling along for nearly two days, taking our hourly baffle clearing into account.

✳

When we arrived off Point Hope again, Doug and Franklin were back on watch with their team. As recommended by Juby, Franklin set a course of 188 degrees, heading for a point forty nautical miles just slightly west-of-north from Cape Prince of Wales—our side of Bering Strait, and set turns for thirteen knots at ninety feet. That point was the beginning of a narrow shipping lane that headed due south between Cape Prince of Wales and Little Diomede Island—our half of the two islands that marked the middle of the strait. Since this channel lay along the deepest part of the strait, the skipper wanted to keep to the bottom of the lane until it opened out into the Bering Sea.

Shortly after we arrived at the head of the shipping lane, Barry and Waverly took over. They turned due south to follow the lane. I was in Sonar reviewing intel on the *Alfa*s when they conducted our first baffle clear. Benny Simms had the Sonar Watch, but King was with me reviewing the intel. Benny picked up a faint contact directly astern of us.

"Conn, Sonar," he said, "I have a new contact bearing due north, directly astern, designate Sierra-twelve."

"Whatcha got, Benny?" King asked, reaching for a set of headphones.

"It's gotta be a sub, right?" Benny asked. "It's all ice back there."

"Chances are…" King said. "Let's figure out what it is."

King broke out a volume that illustrated the waterfall display patterns for Soviet subs. Benny compared them with what he picked up from Sierra-12.

"Shit, Man! That's a Sierra-I!" Benny's excitement was palpable.

We didn't know very much about Sierra-Is. Probably a titanium alloy hull. Deep diving. Not so automated as the *Alfa*—but this was speculation. Better sonar and more weaponry than the *Alfa*. Noisier, too. That was why we detected this one.

The skipper stepped into Sonar and listened to the Sierra. "He doesn't really concern me," he said. "I just want to know if he follows us into the Bering or if he remains in the Chukchi."

USS TEUTHIS—BERING SEA

The north end of the Bering Sea is like a great river delta. Relatively shallow water in the Bering Strait spreads out in a great 300-nautical-mile-arc across the Bering Sea and then continues down the eastern side for another 200 nautical miles. The relatively shallow water terminates in a steep drop-off into the Bering Sea Basin, where depths exceed 12,000 feet.

The Aleutian Islands stretch in a southwesterly curve from the Alaska mainland nearly to the Kamchatka Peninsula in Soviet Russia, cutting through the north end of the Bering Sea Basin. The Aleutian trench, on the south side of the island chain, drops down to 22,000 feet or more.

After passing through Bering Strait, we split the difference, passing east of St. Lawrence Island, and then veering west toward St. Mathews Island and the Pribilofs, St. Paul and St. George Islands. This way, the depth averaged about 240 feet, allowing us to transit at 140 feet and twenty knots in safety. We would more than compensate for the extra miles with our added speed. For the initial 175 nautical miles after transiting Bering Strait, we remained at thirteen knots and ninety feet. To our good fortune, it appeared that the Sierra-I had remained in the Chukchi Sea. Then we dropped down to 140 feet and kicked the speed up to twenty knots.

We took nearly two and a half days to travel from Bering Strait to Unimak Pass that cuts through the Aleutians. I had the watch with Zeb as we approached the pass. By this time, he was conducting the watch entirely without input from me. I was there because I had to be, legally. We were about ten miles out from Unimak Pass when Zed pointed to the under-ice sonar.

"It looks like we have broken ice above us," he said.

I checked. It did.

USS TEUTHIS—UNIMAK PASS

"Conn, Sonar, we have a contact dead ahead, designate Sierra-thirteen. This guy is a tanker, deep draft, moving at a good clip, fifteen to twenty knots at least."

"What the fuck?" Zed said to me. "What's that all about?"

"Come here," I said, walking to the chart table. I pulled out a chart that covered the entire North Pacific. "These guys regularly transit from here," I pointed to Puget Sound, "to here." I pointed to Japan. "Tankers and container cargo ships, twenty-four hours a day, every day. The great circle route passes through here," I pointed to Unimak Pass, "and here," I pointed further out along the island chain.

"I'll be damned," Zeb said. "I guess I never thought about it." He passed his finger along the route. "Doesn't ice ever hinder their passage?"

"Occasionally," I said, "but they have hardened bows. The ice has to be pretty heavy to stop them. If necessary, they'll hire an icebreaker to open things up."

We went back to the periscope stand. "This guy's got a hefty draft," I told Zeb. "Check with Sonar to see where we need to be in case he runs overhead."

Zeb talked with King and then came back to me. "He could have a sixty-foot draft. Call us sixty-five feet with a safety margin… that's a hundred twenty-five feet. If we're at one hundred forty feet, that's a fifteen-foot margin." He looked at me with a slight frown. "That's not enough, is it?"

"What's the depth?" I asked.

"Shit! It's twelve hundred feet."

"What's the shallowest depth in Unimak Pass?"

"Uh…one hundred fifty-six feet. That sucks."

"What do you want to do?"

Zeb was silent for a minute considering his options. "I'm going to drop to two hundred feet to let the tanker pass. Then I'll track the bottom, staying as deep as possible, but less than two hundred. If we're clear of transiting big guys, I'll push past the shallow hump and drop down on the other side. It gets pretty deep real fast."

"I agree," I said. "Let's do it." I turned to find the skipper smiling at us and nodding his head. I guess he concurred.

That's what we did, and three hours later, the bottom dropped from under us to 13,590 feet.

✳

"Come to periscope depth long enough to send a burst message to CINCPACFLT announcing our arrival," the skipper told Zeb, not ignoring me, but giving Zed the feel of actually running the sub as OOD.

No need to give the details. Zeb did it right, as he should have by that time. Fifteen minutes later, we were on our way back to depth.

USS TEUTHIS—TRANSIT TO KODIAK ISLAND

For the first time in a long time, we had the luxury of running deep and fast. Before we turned over the watch, the skipper told Zeb to take it to 700 feet and flank speed. Al set a track that kept us over the edge of the Aleutian Trench. It quickly drops down to 22,000 feet—that's over four miles down. Even that extreme depth is still a couple of miles shallower than the deepest oceanic trenches. At 700 feet, we were just skimming the surface.

We were traveling around the north edge of the Alaska Gulf, one of the stormiest pieces of ocean on Earth. As Zeb and I and our team turned over the watch to Bert and Seth and their watch section, the under-ice sonar gave us a picture of the surface above us. It was a chaotic, jumbled mess. Instead of running in one direction with the wind, the waves were running into each other creating unpredictable peaks and troughs. The peaks sometimes exceeded twenty feet. I was glad we weren't up there on the surface, having to deal with that shit.

For the next eighteen hours—during Bert's, Barry's, and Doug's watches—we were pedal-to-the-metal, slowing down roughly every hour, of course, to do a baffle clearing. Sonar picked up several tankers and container ships running for Japan and points west. By the time Zeb and I came back on watch, Sierra-20 was fading behind us.

The surface turbulence had subsided somewhat, but the waves were still ten feet or so. We turned left toward Woman's Bay, came up to 200 feet, and slowed to fifteen knots. At this depth, *Teuthis* was rocking around with the topside wave activity. It was tolerable but uncomfortable.

Four hours later, we arrived at the outer bounds of Chiniak Bay. The sea surface had quieted because of the protection offered by fingers of land embracing the bay. Although we were still several miles from the pilot pickup buoy, it was time to surface.

"Sonar, Conn, give me your contacts," Zeb ordered.

"Conn, Sonar, we just detected Sierra-twenty-one dead ahead several miles. It's a small vessel. I believe it's the pilot craft."

"Make your depth six-five feet," Zeb ordered. "Ahead slow, make turns for five knots."

As we reached sixty-five feet, Zeb swung the attack scope around while I followed suit with the nav scope. The skipper arrived in Control just then, so I turned the nav scope over to him.

As Zeb passed the bow, he said, "Mark."

I checked the bearing and called it out. "Three-zero-one. Designate Victor-three."

"Chief of the Watch," I said, "Raise the radar mast."

As soon as the radar mast was up, I asked, "Al, what's Victor-three's range?"

"Four miles, Sir., bearing three-zero-one."

"Very well," I said. "Sierra-twenty-one and Victor-three are the same contact—the pilot craft. Designate Mike-one."

The skipper picked up the 1MC mike. "This is the Captain. We are a few miles off Kodiak Island. We will be surfacing and setting the Maneuvering Watch. We will be here for the day, remain the night, and the next day and night, and get underway the following afternoon. Each of you should have a few hours ashore but stay close by. It's bitter cold and stormy. I don't want to send a search party out looking for you."

I turned to the skipper. "Request permission to surface, Sir."

He nodded.

I looked at Zeb. "Get the people who will be topside ready for the foul weather. When they're standing by, surface the sub."

❋

Seamen Jackson and Abelé joined the skipper and me on the Bridge, bundled for the sub-zero, early morning temperature. We were still on East Coast time—a five-hour difference. When we docked, we would set our clocks back four hours to Pacific Standard, ignoring the hour difference to Alaska Time. That way, when we finally arrived at our homeport, Mare Island in Vallejo, California, we would not have to adjust to a new time zone.

The Pilot Buoy with the pilot boat standing off several yards was clearly visible through the dawn light. We had not yet called for a pilot, so apparently, someone in our chain-of-command arranged for his presence, or he spent his daylight hours, as few as they were, at the buoy. I suspected the former. It was too cold and the weather too stormy for anyone to spend any unnecessary time out here.

Radio hailed the pilot. He had received word of our arrival two hours earlier through the local Coast Guard commander. Sometimes the system worked better than expected.

"Station the Maneuvering Watch," the skipper told me. "Make sure everyone topside has a lifejacket and is tethered—NO exceptions."

I understood the skipper's concern. The deck was slippery with half-frozen slush, and anyone who fell into the water had about three minutes before serious hypothermia set in. That was a problem we simply didn't need.

I brought *Teuthis* to a slow glide with the buoy and pilot boat just off our port bow. The COB, Brock Davis, dropped a couple of bumpers over the port side, and the boat skipper skillfully brought it alongside without actually touching them. Two deckhands on the boat slid a gangway with a single lifeline across to our deck. The pilot clipped a safety line to his harness and gingerly crossed to *Teuthis*. The COB grabbed him, and as soon as he unclipped himself from the pilot boat, fastened his harness to one of our tethers. The gangway slid back to the pilot boat, and it peeled away from us.

"Never done this for a sub before," the pilot told the COB. "Where do we go?"

The COB, walking him to the port side of the sail, gestured with his thumb. "Up the ladder, Sir," he said. "Once they clip you in up there, unfasten this tether and toss it to me."

As the pilot clambered over the sail into the bridge well, I took a good look at him. He was short, dressed in foul-weather gear, wearing a woolen watch cap. His weathered face made guessing his age difficult. I made him for sixty-plus. His close-cropped full blond beard was peppered with gray, and his crinkled eyes showed permanent smile lines. He held out a weathered hand to the skipper.

"Master Pilot Sven Jakobsen," he said in a vaguely northern European accent, raising his voice above the whistling breeze.

"Commander Fred Roken, Commanding Officer," the skipper replied. He turned to me. "Lieutenant Commander Mac McDowell, my Officer of the Deck."

The pilot shook my hand. "How deep is your draft?"

"Thirty feet," I responded, fudging by six inches.

"That's cutting it a bit close in the channel. It's dredged to twenty-eight feet, but mostly it's deeper. Can you raise her up a bit?"

I glanced at the skipper.

"Matter of fact, yes," the skipper said, and turning to me, "Have the Chief of the Watch pump out as much ballast as possible."

I passed the order on, and in five minutes, we were pulling a draft of twenty-seven feet. That gave us a foot; not much, but the pilot seemed satisfied.

"I never handled a sub before. Mind if I take her in a figure eight? To get the hang of how she handles?"

"No problem, Sir," I said. I spoke into the squawk box, "Master Pilot Jakobsen has the Conn." I turned back to him. "We have one screw astern center. We can lower two extendable maneuvering thrusters from the bow and stern. They take two feet. Ahead speeds are slow, one third, two thirds, full, and flank. Same in reverse, except it's back emergency, not back flank. You'll have a slight delay between order and execution—one second or so."

The pilot took *Teuthis* through her paces in a figure eight. "Ungainly beast, isn't she?" he said. "I'll bet she's way better underwater."

"That's her home," the skipper said. "Would you like to take an underwater ride?"

"Can I?" The pilot's excitement was palpable.

"I'll clear it with my superiors, and when you pilot us out, we'll take some time to give you a dive."

❋

The pilot didn't use a chart to bring us in. Al followed our track carefully from Control, using radar fixes, and two of his quartermasters taking continuous visual sights.

At one point right near the start of the twenty-eight-foot channel, the pilot said, "Sensitive to current, isn't she?"

From what I could tell, he had already compensated for what he expected from our nearly fully submerged hull. This guy definitely knew his stuff.

Two hours later, we moored port side to the main cargo dock. Woman's Bay is a nearly perfect natural rectangle a nautical mile long and a quarter wide, lying southwest to northeast in a protected cove on the northeast side of Kodiak Island. The cargo dock is halfway along the southeastern side of the bay, dredged to twenty-eight feet at lower low tide. The dock is on a quarter mile-wide peninsula that separates Woman's Bay from the incoming channel. Across the bay from the cargo dock, Old Woman's Mountain rises fourteen hundred feet of steep, slippery-sloped shale to a plateau that runs the full length of the bay beyond the rectangle. The northeastern end of the bay housed a Coast Guard facility and the Kodiak Airport.

The pilot left as soon as the deck gang pushed the brow across to the dock. Immediately thereafter, the Commanding Officer of the Coast Guard Station boarded, accompanied by Captain George Jackson, the former CO of the *Halibut*, and a navy lieutenant I didn't know but whose breast insignia I did—the Deep Submergence pin. They were followed by five men, four civilian DIA specialists, and another man out of the past I knew very well, Sergyi Andreev.

On the dock was something I had half-expected but wasn't sure that enough time had elapsed to make it happen—the small, cylindrical minisub formally known as the Deep Submergence Rescue Vessel-1 (DSRV-1) or *Mystic* as she was informally called. The lieutenant, clearly, was her pilot.

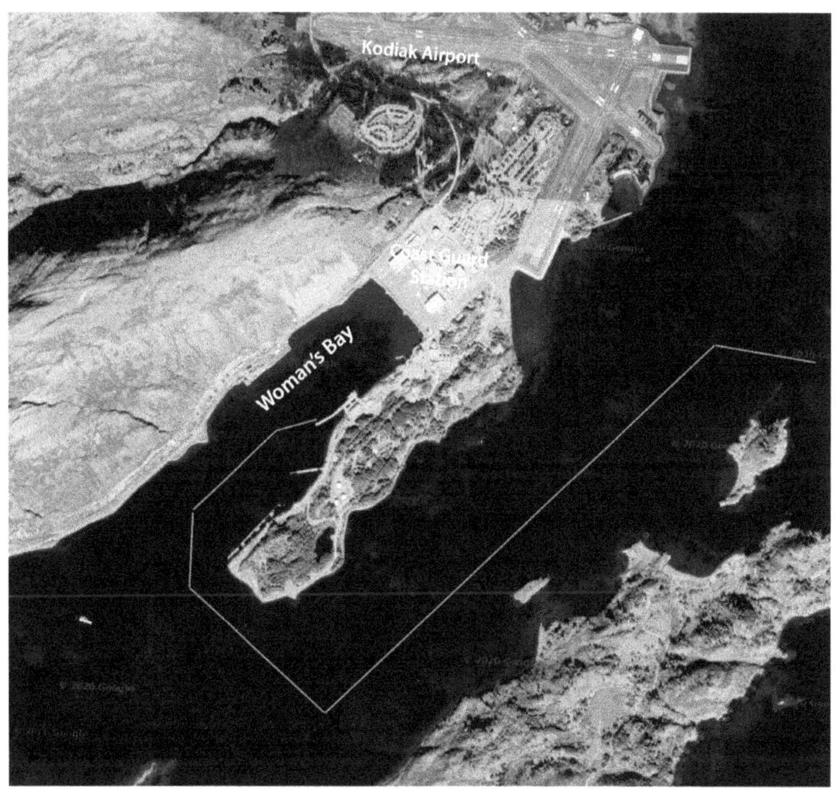

Transit into Woman's Bay, Kodiak, Alaska

CHAPTER FOURTEEN—Kodiak Island

KODIAK—WOMAN'S BAY—MYSTIC

During Operation Ivy Bells on one of our underwater operations from the *Halibut* in the Sea of Okhotsk about two years back, we captured Ukrainian saturation diver Sergyi Andreev. He ended up saving my life, and over time, we became fast friends.[7] At the end of the *Halibut* operation, Sergyi was snatched up by the NSA for a thorough debriefing. Apparently, when the NSA heard about the *Alfa*, he was detailed back to *Teuthis* and my team because of his extensive

---

7   See the first book in the Mac McDowell Mission series, *Operation Ivy Bells*.

knowledge of Soviet equipment and operations. So, there Sergyi was, standing on the foredeck of *Teuthis* in remote Kodiak, Alaska, waving at me. I looked at the skipper, and he nodded.

"Set the inport watch," I said to the Chief of the Watch over the squawk box.

Then I clambered over the sail edge and down the rungs on the port side. I walked up to Sergyi, grinning from ear to ear. He looked at me, snapped to attention, and saluted.

"I see you have been promoted," he said, his eyes twinkling. Then he reached out to me with both arms and gave me a bear hug.

✳

The skipper followed me down from the Bridge. Sergyi again came to attention with a salute. I caught his eye and shook my head slightly, so Commander Roken did not receive a bear hug. Nevertheless, he welcomed Sergyi warmly. Sergyi stepped back, and the skipper approached the Coast Guard Station commander, who stood with Captain Richardson and the *Mystic* pilot. They exchanged salutes and handshakes, and the skipper introduced me to the station commander. Lt. Robert Taggert, the *Mystic* pilot, introduced himself to the skipper and me.

While this was going on, Ham came topside and joined the rest of the *Mystic* crew dockside. They were Lt. James Deckhart, Senior Chief Sonar Technician Gaspard Abelé, Electronics Technician 1st Class Parker Flanger. From the way Ham and Lt. Deckhart greeted each other, it was clear they were old friends. He brought the three of them aboard and was ready to take them below when the skipper signaled him.

We turned to the other four civilians. A tall, gangly man in his late thirties with close-cropped brown hair stepped forward with outstretched hand. "I'm Wyatt Cook, nominally in charge of these lunkheads," he said with a wide grin. "I'm the *Alfa* specialist. This," he indicated a short, slightly chunky nerd with longish brown hair, "is our Soviet sonar specialist, Matthias Hart."

Hart, who looked to be in his early thirties, shook our hands but didn't make eye contact.

Cook continued, "This is Gilbert Edwards. He knows more about Soviet reactors than they do."

We shook hands with a short, tough naval engineering expert who looked like the "snipe" he was. He had a ready smile and receding brown hair cut short. I put him in his mid-thirties.

Finally, Cook presented Kendrick Long, tall, athletic, full head of auburn hair, late twenties. "Our Soviet submarine hull expert," Cook said.

After shaking everyone's hand, the skipper said, "Welcome aboard. You gents are in for an exciting sojourn on *Teuthis*. I'll leave you in the capable hands of Master Chief Comstock. We," he indicated the station commander, Capt. Richardson, Lt. Taggert, and me, "have to review some logistics down below." He turned and beckoned us to follow.

✳

We arranged ourselves in the skipper's cabin as best we could. Taggert remained standing. Capt. Richards handed the skipper a 9x12 brown envelope. He wore a regulation-length red beard, and his red hair was close-clipped. The skipper opened the envelope and extracted a second envelope labeled TOP SECRET—EYES ONLY. He laid it on his fold-up desk and turned to the station commander.

"Would you please work with Lieutenant Taggert and his people to get the *Mystic* loaded onboard *Teuthis* as soon as possible?" The skipper stood as did the station commander.

"Of course, Captain."

After the station commander and Taggert left, the skipper opened the second envelope, removed two sheets of paper, and slowly read their contents. Then he passed them to me. The orders were utterly remarkable. I had expected something like this, but seeing the words on paper was another level entirely.

"Do you have any questions?" Capt. Richardson asked.

"Well, Dan, you had your Ivy Bells moment, and it looks like I will have an *Alfa* moment. And you, Mac," his eyes twinkled at me, "will have been part of both."

✳

I joined Ham and the five civilians in Dive Control. Sergyi was in the midst of everyone. The divers crowded around with a lot of back pounding and happy chatter. Ham had introduced Sergyi to Jake. The guys were filling Sergyi in on their activities till then.

"Need-to-know, guys," I said, raising my voice to be heard above the chatter. "Sorry, Sergyi. You guys know what to leave out of your stories. The same goes for these guys." I indicated the four DIA specialists.

✳

The *Mystic* had arrived during the night at Kodiak Airport in an Air Force C-5A Galaxy complete with her special transport trailer. A Kodiak trucker had towed it to the cargo dock on Woman's Bay before *Teuthis* arrived. The station commander sent a large crane to lift *Mystic* with its cradle from the trailer bed onto *Teuthis'* stern, where she would be seated against the after hatch, and the cradle firmly lashed to the deck.

Both the COB and Ham were present. The COB supervised the deck gang, who held steadying lines to keep *Mystic* from swinging or rotating as the crane lowered her to the hatch seal. The crane operator was used to loading big things onto ships. The deck gang was used to loading torpedoes on the sub. Since *Mystic* was like an oversize torpedo, the guys had no trouble with what they were doing.

An hour and ten minutes after they started, *Mystic* and cradle were firmly lashed to *Teuthis'* after deck. Lt. Taggert's crew, Lt. Deckhart, Senior Chief Abelé, and Petty Officer 1st Class Flanger thoroughly checked each fitting and the seal. Then Lt. Taggert checked everything himself again, just to be sure.

I liked what I saw. It gave me confidence in how these guys would do their job on the *Alfa*.

KODIAK—WOMAN'S BAY—PARAFFIN

Around noon in the foreshortened Alaska day, a truck arrived at the dock with six fifty-five-gallon drums. Lt. Taggert approached me, explaining that the drums were filled with paraffin.

"And why six drums of paraffin?" I asked.

"We have no idea what kind of seal we can make with the *Alfa*," he replied. "The paraffin gives us options. We've played around with the concept but have not actually used it operationally yet."

"But six drums?"

"We talked with NSA. They want to cover all options. If we cannot establish a seal, we will not be able to remove any of the *Alfa*'s equipment. In this case, DIA will try to encapsulate equipment they want with paraffin and swim them to *Teuthis*."

"How much do those suckers weigh?"

"Four hundred fifty-three pounds each," Lt. Taggert said.

"Hey, Bob," I said, "do you know what you're asking? We can drop those fuckers into the Torpedo Room with a crane, no problem. From there, we have to haul them all the way to the Dive Compartment tunnel, and then we'll have to rig a block and tackle to get them below." I considered the logistics. I retrieved a small daily diary and reference volume that I routinely kept in my breast pocket. "The density of paraffin is fifty-six-point-one-nine pounds per cubic foot," I said. "The density of seawater is sixty-four-point-two-four..." I did some quick calculating, checked on the dimensions of a 55-gallon drum—23 inches diameter by 34.5 inches high—and said to Taggert, "Those paraffin-filled drums have just under twenty pounds of positive buoyancy in seawater." I grinned. "I got a better way to get them aboard and stowed where we need them."

✳

An hour later, Whitey and Ski in dive gear were on the bottom under *Teuthis* digging a three-feet-deep, three-feet-wide trench that passed directly below the three DDC hatches. They used a hose with a pressure nozzle fed from an HP water pump. The soft silt bottom blasted away with very little effort.

This was not a diving operation that needed tethered divers with hot-water suits and Basketball supervision. The Basketball would have been pretty useless anyway because Whitey and Ski were kicking up a ferocious cloud of silt.

Ten minutes into blasting, Whitey said on the acoustic comms system, "Dive, Whitey, we're getting close. Where are the drums?"

In the meantime on the dock, Ham supervised lifting one drum at a time and lowering it into the icy water under my watchful eye—along with Sergyi, who was with me. Each drum had a diver's weight belt cinched around its middle with twenty-one pounds of weight attached. Jer and Jake were in the water, taking control of the drums as they were lowered. Jake fumbled around for a minute, figuring out how to control the drum's descent while the crane kept it on the surface.

"Okay," Jake said, "I got it. Slack it off."

He unhooked crane hook from sling and dropped to the bottom with the drum, which with the dive weights attached, now weighed about two pounds.

"Can't see for shit," Jake said as he approached the trench. "You guys done kicking the bottom up?"

"Bring it to the outboard side of the trench," Ski said. "We'll take it from there."

Jake slid the drum into the trench, where Whitey removed the dive weights and pushed it to Ski under the Egress Lock. Ski turned it and let it bob up through the hatch. Harry and Jimmy had rigged a block and tackle directly over the hatch. They hooked onto the sling and hoisted the first drum into the Egress Lock, where they secured it to the outer bulkhead with line and tie-downs.

By the time they secured the first drum, the second was poking its head through the hatch. The next two drums went into the Entry Lock and the final two into the Main Lock, where they were secured horizontally to the deck between the bunks.

Immediately following the last drum, Ski felt something bump his back. He turned around. "I'll be golldamned! Look what we got here," he said as two narwhals poked down under *Teuthis* to investigate what all the fuss was about.

The narwhals' single tusks and large size made close investigation difficult for them with only a foot of clearance beneath the sub. Yet, they poked around and then found the trench. One turned on its side and passed through the trench, stopping to peer through each hatch. The second watched and then duplicated the trick. It accidentally caught its tusk in the Entrance Lock hatch and was having trouble pulling it back out. Jimmy grabbed the tusk and firmly pushed the narwhal back into the trench until the tusk was free of the hatch. The narwhal didn't swim away but pushed its left eye up against the hatch, possibly trying to identify what had helped with its tusk.

✳

Sergyi and I watched the drum-loading operation first from the dock and then in Dive Control.

"Your Dive Control much better than the Can," Sergyi said, referring to the fake DSRV that *Halibut* had carried on her stern.[8] His English was much improved, but he still retained his distinctive Russian accent. He would object to calling it *Russian*, insisting that it was *Ukrainian*.

"I couldn't agree more," I said. "All we are missing are several more divers."

"You got me now," Sergyi said.

"You're right. At least we won't have to babysit you like we will with the other four."

✳

One more thing. Upon our arrival, Dr. Brand had left *Teuthis* to return to the States. We no longer needed his special services, and he was happy to go home. I think he might have enjoyed what lay ahead of us, but he lived in his own little world. He never said so, but I suspect our antics with the *Alfa* had terrified him.

Of course, not even I really knew what was coming.

KODIAK—BREAKER'S BAR

The shortened day had long since turned to night by the time we had everyone briefed, all gear stowed, and were ready to hit the beach. The skipper set a port and starboard watch for that night and the next to give every crew member a chance to go ashore. I decided to accompany the divers, at least for a while, on their first night on the town in quite some time.

The divers asked around and quickly discovered the bar they wanted to visit—Breakers. Located in an otherwise empty parking

---

8 See the first book in the Mac McDowell Mission series, *Operation Ivy Bells.*

lot, Breakers was an ugly, low building with blocked windows and a sloping flat roof. We pressed through the inward-swinging double doors and were greeted by concrete floors and walls, tables and stools fixed to the floors, and a horseshoe-shaped bar made of polished concrete against the back wall. The beverage glasses were plastic. There was nothing breakable except for shelves of bottles on the wall behind the concrete bar.

As the guys disbursed around two of the immovable tables, the bartender beckoned to me, apparently having surmised that I was the leader.

"You guys don' wan' be here after seven-thirty," he said. "This be the local fishermen's bar. They don' take to no strangers, and they fight at the drop of a hat."

Ham saw us talking and joined me. "We're not looking for trouble," I told the barkeep. "We're deep-sea divers from the submarine that just docked in Woman's Bay." I handed him a hundred-dollar-bill. "The drinks are on me until this runs out."

"For everyone?"

"Yeah. As they come in, ask them to join us."

"This may not last very long," the barkeep said.

I slid him another fifty. "Let me know if it starts to run low," I told him as I glanced at my watch.

✳

Ham and I joined the divers, Ham at one table and me at the other. "Listen up, guys," I said. "This bar belongs to the local commercial fishing boat crowd. They're the tough guys in this neighborhood. I need you people alive and whole when we depart. I've set the stage tonight by setting up the house for drinks until my money runs out. Just remember who these guys are. They earn their living doing the most dangerous job in the world, every day the water is not frozen. Give them the respect they deserve, and once they learn about what you guys do, you'll get their respect."

Ham had told the guys to stick to beer to stretch the evening out. We were still on our first round when the initial group of locals arrived.

They barged through the double doors, saw us immediately, and one of them bellowed, "Who the fuck are you guys?"

"Yo, Jack!" the barkeep shouted. "Those deep-sea divers bought the bar. Your money's no good tonight!"

"Deep-sea what?" Jack countered.

"Divers. Jackass," the barkeep said. "Divers. They been diving under the ice north of the Bering for months." He laughed. "They be havin' their first drink since tyin' up in Woman's Bay." He laughed even louder. "You got nothin' on these blokes. They be tough as they come. Divin' out of a submarine…go figure. You do that, Jack?"

"No shit! Come on guys, let's meet these crazy fucks."

A couple more groups swaggered in, got a similar story from the barkeep, and joined us, now scattered around four tables. Two who spoke Russian were deep in conversation with Sergyi, who spoke fluent Russian even though he was Ukrainian.

Jack, who had tossed back several shots by then, jumped onto a table and, raising his glass high, shouted, "Cheers to our crazy new underwater chums!"

The fifteen or so commercial fishermen in the bar shouted their approval.

Jack had latched onto Ham, and they appeared to be swapping sea stories from their lifetimes at sea. I heard Ham say, "Come here, Jack, meet my boss." They wedged next to me at my table.

"Lieutenant Commander Mac McDowell, meet Master Mariner Jack Petrikoff."

I was prepared to shake hands and so did not anticipate Jack's bear hug.

"It's Mac, right?" he asked with a broad grin. "We alike. You come up from seaman to senior officer, me from Ordinary Seaman to Master."

I lifted my glass in acknowledgment just as a couple of gals walked into the bar. It took them a minute or so to discover why all the hubbub, and then they moved in on my guys. I saw a couple of locals start to get ruffled. I turned to Jack.

"Yo, Jack," I said, "you collar your guys, I'll tame mine."

"Don' work like that," Jack said. "These guys do what they want… always."

I turned to Ham. "Get the guys under control. We better be thinking about leaving."

A couple more gals joined the crowd. None of these women would take a prize in a Florida beach contest, but we were in the far north, and every sailor understands *any port in a storm*. Just then, one of the new gals, somewhat more attractive than the others, walked up to me and gave me a liplock. No introduction, no preliminaries, no nothing but a sloppy liplock.

Immediately, one of the locals shouted, "Hey, diver boy! That's me girl you're kissin'!"

While trying to untangle myself from her, I turned to look at the shouter. He was my height and age, twenty pounds heavier, and it wasn't fat. A Bowie Knife was balanced in his left hand, and he was coming for me. The divers rose in alarm, and Sergyi shouted a Ukrainian curse.

I stepped back, turned to my right, and raised my hands slightly. "I've got this," I said to Ham. "Keep the guys back."

I watched the fisherman's movements. He'd been drinking (on my dime), but he wasn't out of control. He moved toward me, knife in his extended left hand. Without warning, I lifted to the balls of my feet, tilted toward him, and spun on my left foot into a roundhouse kick with my right. From his perspective, my right foot seemed to come out of nowhere as it smacked into his left hand and sent his knife flying. I continued around again, lifting my right foot, so it connected soundly with the right side of his head. He dropped to the floor and remained there.

It was over almost before it had started.

Jack looked at me in astonishment. "Can all you guys do that?"

"Most of us," I answered. "We train for it." While thinking to myself, *I'm not sure any of my guys could do that.*

I looked at the barkeep. "I got any money left?" I asked. He nodded. "Drinks all around," I said loudly as my guys and the fishermen crowded around me, slapping my shoulders, and pounding me on the back. The gals kept clear, but I was okay with that.

"Yo, Diver Boy!" echoed around the concrete room as everybody drank up.

Two fishermen propped their downed companion against one of the anchored stools. One slapped his face lightly. "Come on, Tony, wake up. You still got some drinkin' to do."

Tony opened his eyes groggily and rubbed the side of his face. I walked over to him and squatted. Sergyi joined me. *Shit*, I thought, *I hope I didn't go too far. Let's see if he's alright.*

"Hey, Tony," I said, "you okay?"

He nodded, his eyes still not fully clear. Sergyi reached out and steadied his shoulder.

"You got a nice girl, Tony. She was just greetin' me. She tol' me she's yours. I got no interest, buddy."

I got to my feet, reached down with my right hand, grabbing his in a lifting grip, and pulled him to his feet. "Come on, Buddy, it's all good," I said. Sergyi and I walked him to the bar as his head cleared.

"Give Tony his favorite drink—a double," I said to the barkeep.

I lifted my beer mug. "To Tony! Ain't afraid of nothin'!"

Cheers of *Yo, Diver Boy!* and *Yo, Tony!* rang out across Breaker's concrete interior.

✳

Ham and I got the guys back to *Teuthis* somewhat the worse for wear. Every one of them high-fived me as they headed toward their bunks for a well-earned sleep. I heard one or two loud whispers of, "Yo, Diver Boy." I pretended not to hear them.

KODIAK—RENDEZVOUS

I got up early the next morning because I wanted to visit the town of Kodiak during daylight hours. I pulled on jeans, western boots, and a warm leather jacket. I dropped down to Dive Control to find Ham and Bill going over our dive inventory to see if there was anything we might need and could get from the Coasties.

"Have the guys assist with stores onloading this morning," I told Ham. "Breaker's is probably safe now that the locals know the guys, but try to get them back early. We'll be leaving on the morning high tide around ten hundred."

I stuck my head into the skipper's cabin. "Request permission to go ashore, Sir," I asked, following a centuries' old tradition for seagoing officers.

"Granted," he said with a smile. "Nice job onloading the paraffin yesterday."

"Thank you, Skipper."

✳

I dropped down to the messdeck and went forward to the Torpedo Room hatch. As I stuck my head through the hatch, I saw Master Mariner Jack—my new buddy from Breaker's— standing on the pier, talking with the topside watch, Seaman Joe Spanker.

"Hey, Jack!" I said. "What's up?"

"I were just talking with Spanky here. I say I take you to town. He say you be out shortly. So I wait."

I grabbed the handset on the squawk box and dialed the skipper.

"I met a fishing boat skipper last night, Master Mariner Jack Petrikoff. His Kodiak family goes all the way back to the 1790s. He's on the dock right now to take me into town. Would you be okay if I gave him a tour of *Teuthis*?"

"Sure. Just have the Chief of the Watch announce his presence, so watchstanders can cover sensitive gauges."

"Thank you, Sir."

I called the chief, and shortly over the 1MC, he announced, "Rig ship for visitors. Rig ship for visitors."

I approached the brow and beckoned Jack aboard. Spanky followed him up the brow and stepped back into his topside watch role.

"So, Jack Petrikoff, what brings you here this morning?"

"I think I show you my town, Diver Boy. I have friend you should meet."

I liked this guy. A bit rough around the edges, but who am I to speak? It was his town, and he wanted to show it to me.

"Jack," I said, "how would you like a tour of the *Teuthis*?" I pointed to the deck beneath my feet with both forefingers.

"For real? You do this for Jack?"

"Let's do it," I said, dropping down the forward hatch.

He imitated me by grabbing onto the rails and dropping all the way to the deck below. He grinned at me while slapping his hands together, and we started the tour. Jack had been to sea as a fisherman most of his life. He knew the local waters, the local catches, and what he could take sustainably. He had never seen a nuclear submarine before, let alone explored the interior of one.

I showed him the torpedoes and how they were launched. We checked out the galley and crew's quarters.

"These guys, they got to like each other," he said. "It's tighter than my fishing boat."

We spent some time in Control. I let Jack sit in the helmsman's chair, where he moved the fairwater planes stick/combination rudder back and forth and left and right. Then I let him raise the attack scope and peer around Woman's Bay. He was like a kid in a toy store. We visited Dive Control, and I let him enter the DDC. I took him into the Egress Lock and had Ham seal it so we could open the egress hatch. He couldn't get enough of it, and I had to drag him back into Dive Control, where he and Ham chatted for a few minutes.

We crossed over the Cable Reel Compartment, but I didn't even mention it, and over the Reactor Compartment.

"You know," I said, "that our radiation dosage here on *Teuthis* is less than yours out there in Kodiak or at sea on your boat."

"You kidding, right?" He had trouble believing this.

I showed him my radiation badge and explained that the doc checked them every week, so I knew for sure that my dosage was virtually nonexistent. He loved the Auxiliary Machinery Compartment—the cleanliness and the quiet.

"How you make so quiet," he asked.

I pointed to the Engine Room, showed him the turbines, reduction gears, and driveshaft. Jack was completely overwhelmed and impressed beyond measure. We headed back forward through Control to the Wardroom, where Crisanto Rivera served us coffee. The skipper stuck his head through the door and joined us.

"Captain Roken," I said, "please meet Master Mariner Jack Petrikoff."

"Captain Petrikoff, welcome aboard my sub."

"Totally my pleasure, Captain Roken. I always remember this courtesy, always." Jack pumped the skipper's hand.

The skipper excused himself, and we finished our coffee. Then I took Jack to the Bridge where he took in the view through a pair of binoculars normally stored there while in port. I could see him imagining himself as the skipper of the submarine on its way to sea. We climbed over the side of the sail and down the rungs to the deck, and then over the brow to the dock.

"Now I have something to show you," Jack told me.

✳

The sun was up, and the sky was clear of clouds, unusual for this time of year, but you take what you can get up here. Jack drove me in his pickup several miles into Kodiak. We chatted, getting better acquainted.

"Last year, end of fishing season," Jack told me, "I be out in my boat with me crew in big storm. Worst storm ever—forty-foot waves. I break my arm, bad break, serious problem. S-O-S to Coast Guard. They send Cutter, but too rough to help, so they send chopper. They lower stretcher; crew lashes me in. Cutter standing by few yards off. Chopper lifts stretcher. Big wave hits Cutter, washes XO overboard—Lieutenant Junior Grade Josh Perry. He sucked under me boat. We never find him." Jack's voice trembled. "Josh really nice kid. Gave his life to save me."

Jack pulled his pickup into a strip mall parking lot across West Marine Way from the small-boat harbor. We approached a small shop displaying a rustic driftwood sign that read, *Kate's This & That.* We stepped through the door to the sound of a jingle from a small bell above the entrance.

The shop walls were covered with a fishing motive—driftwood, nets, a harpoon, several glass floats. A slightly musty odor permeated the air, reminiscent of old fishing nets and dried deck planks. Behind a glass case filled with scrimshaw, a statuesque, startlingly pretty woman raised her face to greet us. Her golden hair was braided and wrapped tightly around her head. Her neck was long and supple. She wore a fitted light-blue sweater that matched her eyes and displayed her small, unsupported figure to advantage. She rested her hands on the counter, slender fingers splayed, with faintly colored, manicured nails.

As she recognized Jack, her face and eyes broke into warm, welcoming smiles.

"Jack, how nice to see you." She stepped around the case and leaned down to hug Jack and kiss both his cheeks.

"Kate," Jack said, his eyes twinkling, "I want you to meet my friend Commander Mac McDowell." He turned to me. "Mac, meet Kate Perry. Her husband lost life saving mine."

Kate straightened, meeting me eye-to-eye.

"Mac is on the submarine in Woman's Bay," Jack said. "We met last night, and I know right away, you two should meet."

Kate extended her hand. We shook. Her grip was firm, and her skin was cool. "It is a real pleasure, Mac."

Her voice was a mellow contralto. I detected a faint spicy scent but couldn't tell if it was perfume or just Kate. For a moment, I was speechless, somewhat awed by this unexpected creature. Then I found my tongue.

"Wow! I would never have expected to meet someone like you here."

Her blue eyes twinkled. "You say that to all the girls, don't you?"

I almost stuttered. "Seriously, Kate, you are not what I expected when we walked through your door."

"Really…what did you expect?" Her eyes were laughing at me.

"I don't really know," I said, "certainly not you."

"I got things I gotta do," Jack said, squeezing both our shoulders. "You kids get to know each other."

✻

Kate and I spent the rest of the morning talking, drinking coffee, getting to know each other. I've known a girl or two in my time, but nothing like Kate. When I gazed into her eyes, I found myself drawn into a bottomless whirlpool. She was barely twenty-five, but her sensuality and maturity belied her youth.

While we were sharing lunch at the next-door café, Kate's fingers crept across the table to touch my hand. It was like an electric shock—we both felt it. Her big, blue eyes took in my face, and she reached out and stroked my red beard with her fingers. At that moment, we both knew where this was going.

We didn't finish our lunch. Kate drove me across town in her Datsun roadster to a small cottage with a white picket fence. I have no clear memory of going inside, nor do I distinctly remember the events that followed. What I do recall is waking several times to the soft touch of lips on my body, to the urgent thrust of passionate hunger, to the sweet lingering of passion spent, and finally, the pungent smell of fresh coffee and the unforgettable image of Kate's bare silhouette outlined by sunlight streaming through the curtained window of her small cottage.

We dressed slowly, reluctantly. I followed Kate to her little sports car. She drove through town, past the harbor, and across the airport to the cargo dock on Woman's Bay. *Teuthis* was clearly readying for departure. I turned to look at Kate. Tears tumbled from her blue eyes and spilled down her cheeks. She kissed me wetly and deeply.

"Don't you forget me, Mac McDowell, don't you dare forget me," she said, her contralto voice trembling. "You and I both know what happened back there."

She kissed me again, even more passionately, and pressed a small cylinder into my hand. I clambered out of the passenger seat and blew her a kiss. She wiped her tears and smiled as the morning sun broke through the clouds.

I turned and crossed the brow. As I lowered myself through the forward hatch, Kate blew me a kiss. I waved. I went below to my stateroom to change into my uniform jumpsuit. Once I was alone, I opened my hand to reveal the small ivory cylinder carved with scrimshaw she had placed there. I twisted it open, and Kate's faint spicy scent filled my nostrils. Stuffed inside, I found the silk panties she had worn before we tumbled into bed.

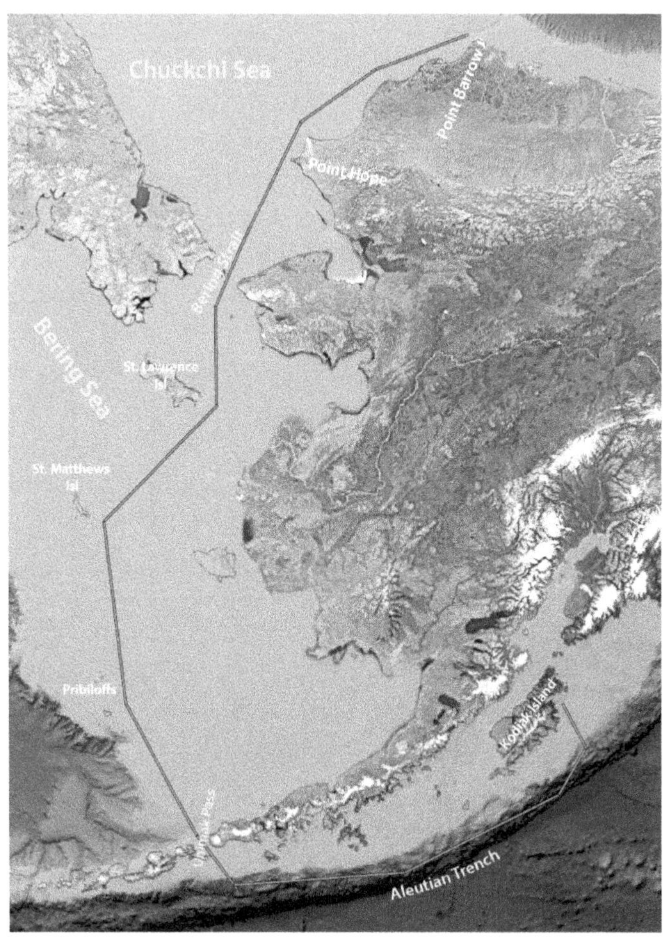

USS Teuthis & Mystic *transit fromKodiak Island to Pt. Barrow*

CHAPTER FIFTEEN—Transit to Point Barrow

USS TEUTHIS—WOMAN'S BAY

As I arrived on the Bridge, the Chief of the Watch announced, "Station the Maneuvering Watch! Station the Maneuvering Watch!"Throughout the submarine, sailors hurried to their designated slots. The COB and his topside deck crew raised the fore and after capstans, although they probably would not be necessary. Master Pilot Sven Jakobsen crossed the brow and clambered up the sail to the Bridge. Two men hauled in the brow and stowed it. Coasties placed themselves at both bollards on the dock, ready to handle lines from dockside.

Clouds swallowed the sun that had appeared briefly as I left Kate's Datsun. The wind picked up and swept across the frozen bay as the temperature dropped to just above zero.

The skipper joined me on the Bridge, looked out over Woman's Bay as its thin ice cover cracked from the force of the wind, and greeted the pilot. "Good day for a dive, Mr. Jakobsen."

"Yes, Sir." Jakobsen looked at his watch, a waterproof stainless chronometer. "High tide is at ten twenty-nine, Captain—seven and a half feet." He checked his watch again. "That's in twelve minutes. We'll want to ride it out through the channel. You've taken on a bit of extra weight, I heard."

"Three thousand pounds of cargo, fourteen hundred pounds of personnel, five thousand pounds of provisions, and thirty-seven tons of mini-submarine," the skipper said. "We still cleared the bottom by a foot last night at low tide. Seven and a half feet should give us plenty of room."

"Maneuvering Watch set," the squawk box announced.

I looked at the skipper, and he nodded.

"Single up all lines," I called to the COB.

The Coasties tossed off the extra turn of line around the bollards, and the deck crew hauled the slack line aboard and took turns around both cleats.

"Lower the outboards," I told the Chief of the Watch.

"Cast off the bow line," I called to the COB.

"Forward thruster, starboard full; after thruster starboard easy."

"Cast off all lines," I called to the COB.

The *Teuthis'* bow angled away from the dock. When the stern was about ten yards from the dock, I ordered, "Ahead slow, right full rudder."

I kept an eye on the stern as *Teuthis* angled out into Woman's Bay, pushing thin sheets of ice aside as she moved. I wanted to ensure the stern cleared the dock before I turned over the helm to the pilot. When we were twenty yards from the dock, I turned to the pilot.

"You ready to take it, Mr. Jakobsen?"

"Aye that," he answered.

"Master Pilot Jakobsen has the Conn," I announced through the squawk box.

I glanced up at the two periscopes. They were rotating and stopping, rotating and stopping, as Barry's people took bearings to prominent objects. The radar mast turned slowly, while they captured range and bearing to radar points as they traced our track out of Woman's Bay and into the channel. As we turned left into the channel, Jakobsen said, "Let's take her to ten knots."

"Ahead two thirds, make turns for ten knots," I ordered over the squawk box.

Our wake stood out against the thin ice cover. It was practically ice-free except for a few small ice-pads that floated back into the wake farther behind us. We were headed into the wind, so our extra speed dramatically lowered the chill factor on the Bridge. I called the lookouts from the fairwater planes into the bridge well and ordered hot coffee for everyone.

Fifteen minutes later, we turned right at the end of the channel and threaded our way between a couple of islands toward the Pilot Buoy about three nautical miles out. The ocean was throwing ten-foot waves at our bow, mostly from the southeast out of the Alaska Gulf. As we crossed the fifty-fathom curve, the wave intensity began to lessen a bit. The skipper directed Radio to notify the pilot boat to meet us at the buoy in two hours.

"Are you ready to see what it's like beneath this mess, Mr. Jakobsen?" the skipper asked.

"You betcha, Captain."

✳

I pointed *Teuthis* toward deeper water and rang up ahead full. We set the underway watch with about an hour remaining in section one—my watch.

"Rig the ship for dive!" rang throughout the sub while Zeb readied the Bridge, and everybody dropped to Control. Zeb manned the attack scope while the skipper allowed Jakobsen to man the nav scope. Zeb set course for 135 degrees and asked, "Chief of the Watch, status?"

"Green board, Sir."

"Helmsman, make turns for ten knots. Diving Officer, dive the ship! Make your depth two-zero-zero feet smartly."

Jakobsen pulled back from the scope to see what was happening around him, his eyes as wide as saucers. The skipper grinned at him.

The 1MC blared, "Dive! Dive!" followed by two long *Aoogahs!* on the klaxon. Zeb and the skipper lowered their scopes, and Tubes, the Diving Officer, quickly dropped *Teuthis* beneath the waves and then tilted to a fifteen-degree angle and drove to depth.

"At two hundred feet, zero bubble," Tubes announced.

"How deep is the bottom?" Zeb asked Al.

"Five thousand feet and dropping," Al said, checking his chart.

I glanced at the skipper. He nodded with a twinkle in his eyes. I walked over to the helmsman, Joe Spanker, and spoke quietly to him. "Spanky, give your seat to Mr. Jakobsen, but stay right by him to coach him."

"Mr. Jakobsen," I said, "would you like to take *Teuthis* through her paces?"

His eyes lit up. I took him to the helmsman console and introduced him to Tubes and Spanky.

"First, you should know that because we have the minisub mounted on our stern, we are limited to ten knots, very much less than our top speed. Consequently, what you will experience will not be so dramatic as it might otherwise be.

"Zeb will issue helm orders directly to you. He will issue dive orders to the Diving Officer, Tubes, who will tell you what to do. Spanky will be right beside you to coach you if things get confusing." I grinned at him. "Any questions?"

He shook his head and took Spanky's seat. Spanky adjusted the seat closer to the console to accommodate his shorter stature. I looked at the skipper. He raised ten fingers.

"Okay, Zeb," I said softly. "Remember that Mr. Jakobsen is both excited and probably rather nervous. Issue your orders slowly and clearly and follow Control protocol exactly. Got it?"

Zeb grinned at me, remembering—I'm sure—his first time on the planes.

"Okay, go for it!"

"Helmsman, come left to new course one-two-five. Diving Officer, make your depth one-zero-zero-zero feet, thirty-degree down bubble."

Spanky whispered to Jakobsen, and he said, "Come to new course one-two-five, aye," as he put the rudder left ten degrees.

Tubes echoed Zeb's depth order. "Make my depth one thousand feet, thirty-degree down bubble, aye." Then he said to Fred Jackson, the stern planesman, "Thirty-degree down bubble, Jack." To Jakobsen, he said, "Mr. Jakobsen. make your depth one-zero-zero-zero feet."

Coached by Spanky, Jakobsen said, "Make my depth one-zero-zero-zero feet, aye."

Spanky spoke quietly to Jakobsen. "Jack controls the sub's angle, the *bubble*. You control the depth. When you move your fairwater planes, it affects what Jack is doing. You guys have to work together to make it happen." As the sub's angle went beyond thirty degrees, Spanky said, "Woops, back off a bit…that's it…now give it a bit more…okay, that's it, you got it."

As *Teuthis* plunged past nine hundred feet, Spanky said, "Ease it off now. Jack will pull the bubble back, and you will glide right down to one thousand feet—no more, just one thousand."

And then Tubes announced, "One thousand feet, zero bubble."

It was really fun to watch Jakobsen's excitement as he realized what he had just participated in, and where the sub actually was right then.

Zeb glanced at the skipper. He nodded. Zeb stepped over to the chart table and checked the chart. He spoke quietly with Al and then issued his next set of orders.

"Helmsman, left full rudder."

Jakobsen answered, "Left full rudder, aye."

"Diving Officer, make your depth one-zero-zero feet, smartly, thirty-degree up-bubble."

"Make my depth one hundred feet smartly, thirty-degree up-bubble, aye." Then Tubes told Jakobsen, "Full rise on your fairwater planes."

"Full rise on my fairwater planes, aye," Jakobsen answered.

Teuthis heeled sharply to the left as her bow popped up thirty degrees. We were racing for the surface.

"Watch your depth, Tubes!" Zeb said. "Keep it under control." He waited a few seconds and then ordered, "Helmsman, ahead slow, rudder amidships."

"Ahead slow, rudder amidships, aye," Jakobsen repeated as he set the engine order telegraph and centered his rudder.

Tubes brought *Teuthis* to an ever-decreasing bubble, sliding her neatly to zero at one hundred feet.

"Helmsman, right full rudder, come to new course three-zero-seven."

Jakobsen repeated the order, bringing *Teuthis* smartly to the new heading.

"Where are we, Nav?" Zeb asked.

"Two miles southeast of the buoy, Sir."

"Sonar, contacts," Zeb said.

"One contact, dead ahead, Sir. I make it the pilot boat."

"Diving Officer, come to periscope depth, six-five feet."

Zeb manned the attack scope as it broke the surface while the skipper was on the nav scope.

"Mark," Zeb said, "pilot boat."

I noted the bearing, "Three-zero-five."

"Surface the ship," Zeb ordered.

"Surface! Surface! Surface!" the 1MC blared, followed by three long *Aoogahs!* on the klaxon.

Zeb remained in Control while the lookouts and I climbed up to the Bridge, followed by the skipper. The seas were still rough, although they had quieted somewhat over the past hour.

"All stop," I ordered. "Back one third…" I waited a few seconds for *Teuthis* to cease her forward motion. "All stop."

We were DIW right beside the pilot boat. I leaned over the starboard side to get a closer look. To my astonishment, Kate stepped out of the pilothouse onto the open bridge and waved at me, blowing me kisses.

"Yo, Kate," I yelled. "What's this?"

The COB and two deck guys appeared through the forward hatch, safety lines securely attached to the track, and dropped two bumpers between the ships. Two crew members on the pilot boat tossed a line to our guys, and then they push-pulled a brow across to

Teuthis. The guys on both sides steadied it while Jakobsen clambered out the forward hatch, safety line attached. He switched his safety line to the brow and then darted across before it could drop into the icy water as the two vessels surged back and forth against each other.

The pilot boat crew immediately retrieved the brow, and the boat shoved off from *Teuthis.* The COB and his guys dropped back inside the sub—topside was secure. As the pilot boat turned toward home, Kate ran to the fantail where she remained waving a scarf in the wind until they disappeared. I reached into my jumpsuit right pocket and fingered her ivory cylinder as I watched her waving scarf vanish.

"Okay, Mac," the skipper said, "she's gone. Dive the boat and get us on course for Unimak Pass."

USS TEUTHIS—UNIMAK PASS

The general idea was to return the way we came. There were possibly shorter routes, but we had not traveled them, and so we were reluctant to return on any path that we had not traversed before, even at ten knots. At ten knots, we were quieter than any Soviet sub at five knots. This gave us a huge advantage. We would always detect them before they could detect us. By clearing baffles randomly about every hour as we routinely did, should a Soviet sub come into range, we would absolutely know about it before it could detect us.

The mostly iced-over Bering Sea was noisy. It was sufficiently large so that storms could develop entirely within its boundaries. The resulting wave action typically resulted in a miles-deep ice edge and the regular cracking and breaking of the larger ice sheet. This, in turn, generated grinding noises as ice floes pushed against one another. This noisy background generally limited passive sonar reception. Unlike the Soviets, we had developed ways to filter out this background noise. It still limited our range, but not nearly so much as for the Soviets.

Our path to Unimak Pass kept us over the continental rise with several thousand feet under the keel. The skipper put us at 500 feet and ten knots for the 480 nautical miles that brought us a few miles southeast of Unimak Pass.

Barry and Waverly had the watch when we came to periscope depth to check our position and reset the SINS. Surface traffic was surprisingly heavy, consisting almost entirely of tankers and container ships heading to and from Japan—approximately an hour apart both ways. The occasional trawler gave Sonar something else to do.

The shallowest part of Unimak Pass is just over 150 feet deep. With supertankers sporting drafts of up to ninety feet, we would have no free space at all, were such a tanker to pass directly over us. Consequently, Barry and Waverly coordinated carefully with Sonar to avoid any close encounters. With the recent SINS reset, Barry was able to follow our earlier track closely so that even near the bottom, he maintained eight knots.

Halfway through the pass, Doug and Franklin took over with their watch section. Once through, they set a course for the Pribilofs and—because the bottom deepened to 240 feet—dropped to 130 feet at ten knots.

Besides getting us through Unimak Pass safely while dodging tankers and freighters, their major accomplishment was slipping under the ice edge into the relative calm of the ice-capped Bering Sea in winter.

USS TEUTHIS—TRANSIT TO BERING STRAIT

We were twenty-six hours to the Pribilofs, which actually gave Doug and Franklin something to do near the end of their watch. Not a lot, really; they came right fifteen degrees to aim for St. Matthew Island.

Ahead lay twenty-seven hours of nothing except the hourly baffle clears, during which Sonar detected not one contact. The end of this stretch gave Zeb and me the one real change since Unimak Pass. We made a major course change to the right, pointing toward St. Lawrence Island, and came up to 100 feet because of the shallowing bottom.

We cycled through two entire watch cycles during this leg, coming shallower all the way to seventy feet as the bottom rose. Zeb and I got to make the next big change as well. We swung left to course

340 degrees, pointing toward the shipping channel with a depth of at least 156 feet and eased down to eighty feet.

This final leg before the channel was thirty-eight hours. Doug and Franklin had the first half of the second day of the leg. Zeb and I had the second half, and during our third hour, Sonar announced, "Conn, Sonar, I have a submarine contact directly on the bow, drifting left to right, designate Sierra-one."

The skipper had told Sonar not to catalog the pilot boat nor all the vessels in Unimak Pass, so this contact was the first since we got underway from Woman's Bay.

"Sonar, I'll give you a starboard beam, so you can get more info."

About ten minutes later, King came out to Control with a book of Soviet submarines. "This guy is a newer Soviet sub, a Sierra-I class fast-attack. It's bigger than the *Alfa*, but it's slower, and it can't go as deep. I don't know for sure, but I think his sonar suite is better than the *Alfa*'s. He's a hundred nautical miles out on a course for the western side of Bering Strait—the Soviet side. He's doing twenty knots, so he's blind as a bat. These guys do Crazy Ivans every hour or so. We'll watch him carefully. When he changes aspect, we'll let you know right away. By the way, I think this guy is the *Carp*, what they call Project 945."

Just before Bert and Seth took over the watch, Sonar called. "Conn, Sonar, Crazy Ivan! Crazy Ivan!"

"All stop," I ordered. "Set emergency ultra-quiet!"

In five seconds, *Teuthis* went totally quiet. Sound ceased through-out the sub—everything stopped. The skipper walked silently to Control.

"What's happening?" he asked.

I told him about the *Carp*. "He's a hundred miles away. He should not be able to hear us, but I wanted to be sure. He's going to where we expect to be soon."

"Good!" he said. "Carry on."

King stepped out to Control. "We lost him, Sir, just as he com-menced his Crazy Ivan. He's too far away and too quiet now."

"Okay, we'll wait another ten minutes and then start up again."

We didn't pick the *Carp* up again, and I figured that was the last of him. Little did I know.

USS TEUTHIS—TRANSIT TO POINT BARROW

All roads lead to the Bering Strait, at least in this part of the world. Good thing the strait was solid ice. We didn't have to worry about surface traffic. As for the Carp, it was one of the newest Soviet fast-attacks. It could have been headed to Polyarny—the Soviet submarine base straight across the Arctic near the Norwegian border. More likely, it was on some kind of patrol out of Petropavlovsk-Kamchatskiy on the Kamchatka Peninsula. Just the other side of Kamchatka was the Sea of Okhotsk, where my team had locked out of the *Halibut* on the seafloor to tap into Soviet underwater communication cables—Operation Ivy Bells.[9]

Ivy Bells was an operation dealing with underwater communication cables permanently placed on the seafloor. It came about through several years of careful planning with multiple cover stories. One cover was the *Man-in-the-Sea* Program that produced trained saturation divers that would be needed for Ivy Bells. Another was the entire DSRV submarine rescue program—two DSRVs, two motherships, several fast-attacks modified to carry the DSRV, and a complete fly-away system to transport a rescue vehicle anywhere in the world. Anyone who gave some thought to the DSRV system would have realized that it was designed to rescue crewmen from submarines disabled in relatively shallow water, but in actuality, virtually all subs normally operated in waters many times deeper than their maximum operating depths. In other words, the DSRV submarine rescue system was useless for rescuing submarine crews in their normal operating environment.

On the other hand, it was an excellent cover that allowed subs like the *Halibut* to look like they were practicing sub-rescue ops when they were actually carrying saturation dive chambers outfitted to look like DSRVs. These systems, with their saturation divers, have been successfully used to gather intel that has meaningfully shortened the Cold War.

Unlike Ivy Bells, we found ourselves involved with Soviet property this time entirely by accident. We were the same guys, mostly, on an entirely different mission. We found ourselves deeply enmeshed

---

9 See the first book in the Mac McDowell Mission series, *Operation Ivy Bells.*

in a serendipitous situation that would call on every skill my divers and the *Teuthis* crew could muster.

✳

Ahead of us lay sixty-nine hours of ten-knot minimum-height-over-the-bottom cruising to Point Hope along a path we had covered once already, and twice from there to Point Barrow. Our concerns about the *Carp* were small: At ten knots, we were quieter than anything the Soviets had. And, at that speed, our forward-looking ears were excellent. If the Soviet sub's plant were live—a near certainty—we would detect him long before he detected us. That is, if he was ahead of us, of course, and *that* also was a near certainty.

So we cruised along, clearing baffles every hour or so, keeping as close to our old track as possible. Sonar detected no contacts. The ice overhead was solid, at least three feet thick, in some places four. We passed under an occasional pressure ridge, but nothing that extended downward more than ten feet. Other than the focused attention required by *Teuthis* being sandwiched between ice and bottom and our special passenger lashed to the stern, our transit to Point Barrow was one of the more relaxing legs of our total journey thus far.

The DIA guys and the divers got to know each other, something that is important for men depending on each other out on the seafloor. Matthias Hart, the sonar specialist, spent a lot of his time in Sonar. He knew virtually everything there was to know about Soviet sonar systems, but he had never observed a U.S. submarine sonar system in action. He confided to King that he was terrified about the forthcoming saturation dive. King told me, and I spoke with Ham. Obviously, we had some work to do before we put Hart out on the seafloor.

The *Mystic* officers and their two enlisted technicians, along with the DIA guys and me, developed as many scenarios as we could think of for the *Alfa* operation. They used perhaps half the time to tweak the DSRV systems they could access from inside. Otherwise, they roamed the sub, getting to know various crew members and watch stations.

Sergyi and I caught up on each other's happenings since the award ceremony back in Rodman Theater at Mare Island. We played a lot of chess. I won about half the games, but I still suspected that Sergyi let me win.

Two and three-quarter days later, as Barry and Waverly were completing the first half of their watch, Sonar activated the transponder we had left near the *Alfa*. Barry zeroed in on the bearing, and a half hour later, *Teuthis* settled to the bottom on her skids in 470 feet of water, her bow pointing to 315 degrees as we had before. A few minutes later, Sonar reported that we were only 200 feet away from the *Alfa*.

At the time, sitting so close to the *Alfa* seemed like a good deal, but that was then.

PART FOUR

The Carp

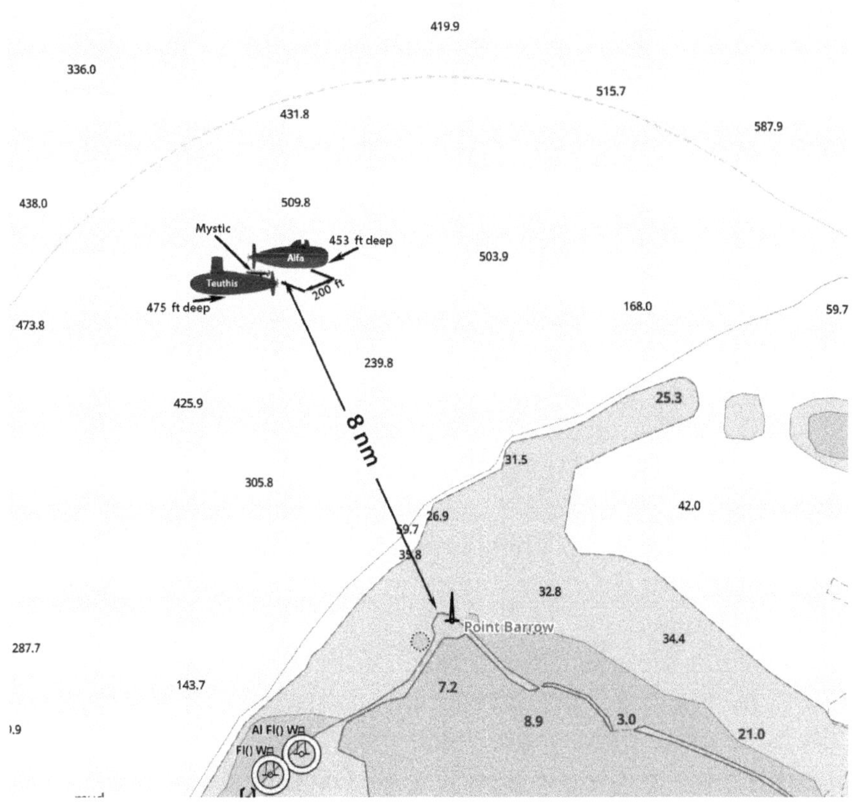

USS Teuthis *with* Mystic *on seafloor with the* Alfa

CHAPTER SIXTEEN—The *Alfa*

USS TEUTHIS—BOTTOMED AT THE *ALFA*

"**O**fficer's Call," on the 1MC followed by, "Spec Ops personnel, *Mystic* pilots, and Master Chief Comstock to the Wardroom." It was a bit tight, but everyone found a place. For the interim, the XO took over as OOD.

"You've had several days to get acquainted," the skipper said to the four DIA guys and the pilots, "and to discuss among yourselves how you intend to proceed. For the time being, I consider *Teuthis* a tool put at your disposal." He stopped and smiled around the group crowded into the Wardroom. "This is subject to several provisos. Diving and *Mystic* operations are under the absolute control of Lieutenant Commander McDowell. Nothing, and I mean *nothing*, happens outside this submarine without his personal approval." He stopped again, looking around the group. "Is this understood?" He waited. "Are there any questions about this?"

Hart looked like he wanted to say something, but Ham—who was sitting beside him—whispered to him, and Hart settled back in his seat. The skipper looked at Ham with a question in his eyes.

"Nothing, Sir," Ham said.

"Our job," the skipper continued, "is to learn what we can about the *Alfa* and to take what is possible out of her. But our number one priority is safety. Do not forget, not for a moment, that men will be outside *Teuthis* in four hundred seventy feet of nearly freezing water. Their *only* safe haven is back in the DDC. Any other option, I mean *any other*, is a painful death. That's not going to happen.

"What we are attempting has never been done before. Don't be brash. If you have an idea, pass it by Mac and Ham. We have some of the best, most experienced diving expertise on this planet and the world's best submersible pilot skills right here in this room. Make use of it. Let's learn what we can from this opportunity that has tumbled into our hands. Let's get into Ivan's shorts and teach him a lesson he'll long remember.

"One more thing. We know the *Alfa* crew was rescued, but we do not know about their repatriation. Once they are home, their skipper will ensure his high command knows the position of the *Alfa*—and that it's inside the twelve-mile limit. Once that happens, it is only a matter of time until a Soviet submarine starts nosing around this vicinity. The *Carp* apparently did not get the word. Otherwise, she would be here right now. What I can guarantee is that the *Carp* or another Soviet sub will be here before long. We want to be long gone by then.

"Mac is off the watchbill for the duration of our operations here. The XO will take his place." The skipper stood and left the Wardroom.

ON THE SEAFLOOR—AT THE *ALFA*

Dive ops this time were considerably more complicated. I called everyone together in Dive Control to lay out the plan.

"I know that Ken and Matt were planning to brave saturation to get a personal look at the *Alfa* hull and sonar dome. With the real possibility that the *Carp* might show up, putting all you DIA guys inside the *Alfa* has become more urgent than Ken and Matt getting a personal look at the sub's exterior," I began. "If I put you two in the water now, you would need about five days of decompression before you could enter the *Alfa*. We don't have five days." I stopped talking and looked around the group. Ken's face showed genuine disappointment. Matt looked relieved.

"You DIA guys deserve a lot of admiration for undertaking this operation," I told them. "My guys all went through a year's training before being designated as saturation divers. Beyond that, each diver has participated in numerous saturation diving operations. Due to their training and experience, their reactions in an emergency are instinctive. Yours would not be. When you are out there, in fact, what your instinct tells you to do would probably kill you.

"When you are on an umbilical with a hot-water suit, we control you unless you disconnect yourself from your umbilical—you can ask Ski about that.[10] When you're using a rebreather with a Unisuit, you're pretty much on your own. If you screw up or if something happens beyond your control, *you* have to solve it—you and your dive partner.

"During deep lockout training, we connect a trainee to his experienced partner with a buddy line. If we can put you in the water after the *Mystic* ops, we'll use buddy lines. Rely on your buddy! One more thing. Comms when you're on an umbilical go through our descrambler. It makes it much easier to understand one another. With the rebreather, you are communicating through the water—no descrambling. Talk slowly and clearly. You will get used to it, but it will take a while. Any questions?"

"Who has been inside the *Alfa*?" Cook asked.

---

10 See chapter 22 of the first book in the Mac McDowell Mission series, *Operation Ivy Bells,* for the details

"Nobody yet," I answered. "Before we picked up you guys, I was going to pressurize the interior and enter, but our high command nixed that idea in favor of you guys and the *Mystic*."

Gilbert Edwards, the DIA Soviet reactor specialist, raised his hand. I nodded at him.

"The guys have pretty much explained the saturation diving concept to us, but I'm still unsure about the ceiling. Can you talk to that for a couple of minutes?"

"Sure. If you are saturated to thirty-three feet, you can come right to the surface without suffering any consequences. But if you saturate at forty feet, you cannot come shallower than about seven feet without suffering the bends, when the dissolved nitrogen or helium (if you are breathing mixed gas) in your body comes out of solution to form bubbles. The bends are very painful and can be fatal. A body can tolerate a one-atmosphere difference between its saturation level and the ambient pressure. That's the background information. In practice, we have discovered that there is increasing leeway as your saturation depth is deeper.

"What this means for you outside *Teuthis* is that you will be saturated to four hundred sixty-five feet. The *Teuthis* is at four hundred seventy feet, but the egress hatch is five feet shallower. We have learned experimentally that you can actually ascend to three hundred sixty-nine feet without any consequences when saturated to our depth. There's a little bit of wiggle room in these numbers, but I don't want you to take any chances. *DO NOT* ascend above three hundred sixty-nine feet! That is your ceiling.

"Does this answer your question?" I asked.

I got a thumbs-up from all four DIA guys.

"Any more?"

Matthias Hart lifted a finger. "How does the rebreather differ from the umbilical?"

"At our depth, the oxygen percentage in your breathing gas is one-point-four. That's the same number of oxygen molecules that you breathe on the surface, but, obviously, the percentage is a lot smaller. On the umbilical, the gas console operator in Dive Control controls your oxygen percentage. On the rebreather, the electronics in your rig control your oxygen percentage. Should your oxygen cylinder begin to run low, your oxygen gauge will start to creep down. If your buddy can't fix it, you must return to *Teuthis* right away. If it begins to creep up, you're getting too much oxygen. Your dive partner should be able to fix that on the spot.

"But all this is hypothetical. For now, anyway, the DIA guys will stay dry. We're going to put Harry and Ski in the water to get as many external photos as possible. After that, we'll put you DIA guys inside the *Alfa*. I'll be joining you."

✳

Ham pressed down the entire dive team. He designated Harry and Ski to get the photos, Whitey and Jer to tend them, and Jimmy and Jake in reserve in the Main Lock.

The skipper joined us in Dive Control. "Listen up," he said as he took the mike so the divers in the DDC could hear as well. "I don't want any of you to think that I don't trust you with the photos you will be taking and with the documents that Commander McDowell will bring back from the *Alfa*. Each of you has my utmost respect and full confidence. Nevertheless, we can't make the photos nor any of the documents available for your personal perusal. We are dealing here with a strict need-to-know. All of you understand that. Our technological and military superiority depends on everyone in the chain-of-command right down to the deck gang fully complying with the spirit of what need-to-know means. Without the efforts of each of you, we could not be pulling off this remarkable intelligence coup. Thank you for that."

The skipper handed the mike back to Ham and leaned back against the bulkhead to watch the proceedings.

Harry dropped to the seafloor first, and then Ski followed. Between them, they carried four waterproof cameras. Wally illuminated the bottom ahead of them with the Basketball as they moved toward the *Alfa*.

When they arrived, Gil Edwards, the reactor specialist, said, "Check out the scoops. See if anything clogged them."

The divers first went to the scoop on the starboard side halfway between the sail and the screw, snapping photos along the way.

"The scoop looks normal," Harry said. He shined his light into the scoop, snapping more photos. "Looks clear."

They went around the bow to the port side, where Ski inspected that scoop. "It's clear," he announced. More photos.

"Hey, Ken," Harry said, "the hull is covered with some kind of acoustic tile. You should be able to see it on the monitor. Here and there, tiles are missing."

"Check the after hatch," Bob Taggert, the *Mystic* pilot, said.

The divers went to the after hatch where the *Mystic* would hook up. "There's a tile-free ring around the hatch," Harry commented. "Looks like it will accommodate the *Mystic*."

I turned to Taggert and said, "You guys need to get ready for your excursion. How long will it take to be ready to decouple from *Teuthis*?"

"A half hour."

"Okay, I'll send the DIA guys back shortly, and I'll join you right before you decouple."

The divers swam forward, lingering at the bow for several minutes while they inspected the damage carefully and poked around inside the sonar dome. Matt followed their progress on the monitor.

As luck would have it, a local narwhal pod that kept the ice cover broken somewhere nearby decided to investigate the divers' activities. The first I knew about it was when Hart yelled, pointing at the monitor, "Holy shit! What the fuck is that?"

"It's a curious narwhal, Matt," I told him. "It won't hurt the divers."

Another appeared in the circle of light. And another, without a tusk.

"You sure?" Hart asked. "They won't stab the guys?"

"Those aren't weapons, Matt, they're sensing probes."

"Really…?"

"Yeah… They'll stay with the divers till they need air. They must have a polynya nearby."

Hart directed the divers' attention to several items in the dome that particularly interested him. Harry and Ski used up the rest of their film on Hart's requests.

"Okay," I told them, "return to *Teuthis*. Stay wet in case we need you for the *Mystic* launch."

I turned to the DIA team. "Showtime," I said. "I'll meet you in the *Mystic* in ten minutes."

I looked at Ham. "You got it, Ham. If you really need me, you can reach me by communicating with Lieutenant Taggert." I sighed. "I want this over and done. With the *Carp* out there somewhere—I really have no idea how much time we still have."

ON THE SEAFLOOR—*MYSTIC* OPS

I decided to put all the DIA guys inside the *Alfa* at one time so they could interact, and so we could save time. I would accompany them because I knew submarines and I knew diving, and—frankly—because I could.

Mystic was clamped into a cradle that was lashed to the deck with multiple tie-downs. "The *Mystic* can unclamp itself from the cradle and clamp itself back into the cradle from within the minisub," Bob Taggert told me. "It has multiple ways of attaching itself to the *Alfa*, but the primary way is the external fifteen atmospheres of pressure holding it in place. Once we get the hatch open, we will figure out exactly how to clamp *Mystic* down as a backup safety measure."

I called the skipper. "We're ready to commence *Mystic* ops. I'll be transferring to the *Alfa* with the DIA team."

"Thank you, Mac. Keep the *Carp* in mind. We're just outside our territorial waters, but it isn't as if there were a major military installation nearby to back us up."

"Aye, Sir."

✳

I had ridden aboard *Mystic* years earlier—before Operation Ivy Bells—while serving aboard the DSRV mothership *USS Pigeon* (ASR-21). Even though the entire DSRV-based submarine rescue system was a cover for Ivy Bells and subsequent operations, it still had to function. On the *Pigeon*, we were working out some of the bugs in the system. Now, here we were actually using a DSRV in a manner never anticipated by the developers, most of whom had no clue about Ivy Bells or what we were undertaking.

I went aft to the Engine Room and clambered up through the escape hatch into *Mystic*. The interior of the vehicle comprised three metallic spheres linked by access hatches: the forward sphere for the

DSRV operators, and the rear two for passengers and equipment. The DIA team had brought with them cameras and film, and several tool kits, trying to anticipate whatever fittings, bolts, and screws they might find on the *Alfa*. The pilots, Bob and Jim, were in the forward sphere, the piloting module. They settled into their chairs in front of a complex instrument panel that incorporated monitors, gauges, dials, and read-outs. The DIA guys entered the after sphere and took seats on the spare benches, while Senior Chief Abelé and Petty Officer Flanger joined me in the mid-sphere.

"Everybody ready?" Bob asked.

He received a chorus of *Ayes, Let's do its,* and *Okays.* One of the *Teuthis* engineers sealed both trunk hatches, and Flanger sealed the *Mystic* hatch. Shortly thereafter, several quiet clanks indicated that *Mystic* was free of her constraints. I placed myself in the open hatch between the pilot-sphere and the mid-sphere. I followed our progress on the video displays from the fore and aft cameras. We lifted off the cradle, rotated to point toward the *Alfa*, and then applied a burst of speed. Since we had only 200 feet to cover, Bob commenced reverse thrusting the moment the shadow of the *Alfa* appeared on the forward monitor. Shortly thereafter, we could see part of it through the other monitors.

Bob eased over the hatch, examining carefully his display that showed an actual image of the hatch with a superimposed outline of the skirt. "It's tight," he said, "but it will fit."

He slowly lowered *Mystic* over the hatch until we heard a solid clunk. Petty Officer Flanger opened a valve that allowed the water captured in the skirt at fifteen atmospheres to flow into a drain tank on *Mystic*. Once the pressure equalized, he pumped the remaining water into the same tank.

"Looks like we got a good seal," Flanger said. "Skirt pressure equalized, skirt dry. Request permission to open hatch."

"Open the hatch," Bob answered.

I stepped back into the mid-sphere to watch the hatch opening. It opened inward, dripping with water. Below was the hatch of the Soviet *Alfa* submarine. Despite myself, I felt a thrill. We were about to conduct a game-changing first.

What we didn't know was whether the *Alfa* was at one atmosphere or not. She could have been flooded. Flanger attached a pressure gauge to a recessed nipple on the hatch apparently put there for just this purpose.

"One atmosphere inside the *Alfa*," Flanger reported.

The *Alfa* hatch had a recessed fitting that looked like it could be turned with a ratchet handle with the proper attachment.

"That's a standard Soviet fitting," Cook said. "I'm certain we have one in our tool kits."

"I got one," Long said, "and the matching ratchet handle." He handed them to Senior Chief Abelé.

Abelé started to place the wrench on the hatch fitting.

"Hold it," I said. "We don't know anything about the air inside the *Alfa*. I want everyone out of the mid-sphere except myself and the senior chief. We'll wear breathing masks. You guys seal the spheres."

It made a lot of sense, and nobody argued. It might have helped that I was the senior officer present, but submariners never were compliant sheep, and I'm sure the DIA guys could think for themselves.

The others quickly sealed the hatches between the spheres. "Here," Abelé said, handing me a full-face breathing mask attached to a manifold.

We both donned our masks.

"Let's do it," I said.

Abelé lay flat on his stomach. He was just able to reach the hatch fitting. He grunted a couple of times, and then the fitting began to turn clockwise. He worked the ratchet for what amounted to several turns of the fitting. He placed his left hand flat on the hatch and pushed downward while he twisted the ratchet a final bit. As he eased the pressure with his left hand, the hatch swung up on its springs, emitting a slight hiss.

Abelé dropped a probe attached to a wire into the open trunk. He checked the readout on an instrument attached to the sphere bulkhead.

"No radioactivity, oxygen normal, no unusual organics," Abelé said. "It looks like normal air." He reported the finding to the pilot. "Okay, now for the big one."

Abelé climbed down the rungs in the trunk and placed himself so he could spin the wheel to open the bottom hatch while remaining out of its way when it opened.

It opened easily on its springs. The compartment below was dark. Abelé lowered his probe into the darkness. "Again, no radioactivity, oxygen normal, no unusual organics," he said. "We're good to go, Lieutenant," he told the pilot.

ON THE SEAFLOOR—INSIDE THE *ALFA*

Abelé opened the hatch to the aft-sphere. The DIA team crowded into the mid-sphere, eager to get into the *Alfa*.

"Each of you has your headlamp and voice-activated recorder?" I asked.

Nods from everybody.

"Camera and spare rolls of film?"

Nods again.

"Guys, this may be our only chance to gather the intel down there." I pointed down the hatch. "Keep your wits about you. Talk into your recorder, and key your audio notes to the photos you take. If Bob gives us an emergency evac order, get the hell out of Dodge…right now… immediately. All our lives may depend on this." I turned my headlamp on and stepped onto the rungs in the trunk. "I'm headed inside. Wyatt has assigned tasks to each of you. Let's turn-to!"

I started talking into my miniature voice-activated cassette recorder as I dropped into what turned out to be the front of the *Alfa*'s Engine Room. As I hit the deck, the lights came on—apparently sensing my motion.

"I see a closed watertight door just ahead of me," I dictated. "I am opening it. I have stepped into a space…the lights came on…it is an auxiliary machinery space. I'm walking down the port side of a large generator. There is a passage on the starboard side as well. I'm at the forward bulkhead. A WT door has a radiation sign on it." I cracked the door and stuck a radiation probe through the opening. It indicated no radiation.

"I am entering the Reactor Compartment. The lights came on. There is no radiation. I am passing through a lock near the center on the port side. I am stepping into a space filled with electronic cabinets, and looking forward, I can see a series of consoles in a U-shape with the open end toward me. We'll designate this space the Control Compartment."

I continued to state my observations into my recorder. "I will call the U-shaped console area the Control Center. The 'U' consists of eleven instrument/control panels with built-in desks. Each panel has a seat attached to the deck that swivels and moves in-and-out and up-and-down." I examined each panel. "It appears that all ship operations are controlled from these panels. The forwardmost panel and the one to its left, manned by two operators, control the sub's speed, direction, depth, and attitude, including ballast control. Between them is the chart table connected to their version of the SINS. Going around to the left are electrical control, then power plant and reactor control, and then radio comms. On the right side are sonar and radar acquisition and tracking, torpedo loading and launching, navigation control, and consolidated ship's information console. In the middle of the 'U' is the periscope tower. Aft of the 'U' is an open equipment space filled with the navigation center, including their SINS, electronic cabinets, and document storage.

"Although there are eleven control panels, I think the sub can run normally with only four or five actually manned, except for Battle Stations. Add a couple of cooks and some techs to back up the sonar and comms panels, and that makes a crew of less than thirty."

I stepped a few paces past the Control Center.

"Forward of the 'U' is a watertight door that appears to access more equipment and torpedo stuff.

"I am descending a stairwell into a galley and messing space, and forward of that, berthing. So far as I can tell, access to every other part of the submarine is sealed or labeled as non-entry except for an emergency." I paused and looked around.

"As I stand in the galley, I am beginning to believe that I am inside a fully automated underwater fighting machine that bends to the will of her Captain and small crew. Obviously, something went terribly wrong, but it appears to have been caused by external circumstances, not the automated systems that run the sub."

I saw no documents of interest in berthing or messing spaces, so I returned to the Control Center, where I continued to record. "A safe in the equipment space is not something I can deal with. Several cabinets, however, contain documents organized by purpose."

I spread them out on the deck and separated them into docs relating to the *Alfa* and its engineering, Soviet intel about the U.S. and allied navies, and other stuff. I crammed as many of the *Alfa* and intel docs into my waterproof duffel bag as possible.

I snapped thirty-six photos, mostly in the Control Center. Then I opened the watertight door forward of the space.

"I have entered the forward compartment. It is filled with electronic cabinets that probably are part of the sonar and radar suite." I opened a door at the end of the compartment.

"I have stepped through a non-watertight door into a complex automated torpedo loading and launching system. I will leave its description to an expert."

That was it. There really was nothing more I could do except check with the DIA guys to see how they were progressing.

Carrying my document-filled duffel bag over a shoulder, I walked back to the after trunk. Flanger grabbed the duffel bag and pulled it up into *Mystic*.

Hart was in the forward compartment figuring out the sonar installation. Cook, Long, and I joined Edwards in the Reactor Compartment. Edwards was visibly excited.

"Here's what I think happened," he told us. "Whatever caused that mess to their bow—ice or whatever—misaligned their driveshaft—not a lot, just a bit. Over time, however, this fed back through their automated mechanical drive system until the reactor scrammed. This reactor," he pointed to the large cylinder occupying a significant part of the compartment, "is liquid metal cooled—lead-bismuth." Edwards gave us a broad smile.

We just stared at him.

"Don't you see?" he said. "If this reactor shuts down for more than a few minutes, the liquid coolant solidifies." A broad smile again.

I still didn't get it, and apparently neither did the others.

"Once it solidifies," Edwards said with a satisfied voice, "it's nothing more than an expensive dead weight. You can't start it up again. Even in a shipyard. You have to remove it and junk it."

That's when I got it. "So, these guys limped along all the way from the Princess Royal Islands, and when they reached here, their plant died. They had no choice. They had to abandon ship."

"Yeah," Edwards said.

"Shit, man," Cook said slowly. "Imagine having to do that up here, under the ice."

Edwards opened a deck locker near the hatch. "Here's the shore-power cable. Let's take it with us. It might come in handy."

"Do you guys have full film cassettes and full audio tapes?" I asked as Hart came wandering back, looking for us.

Nods all around.

"How long we been down here?" Long asked.

I looked at my watch. "Four and a half hours," I said. "Let's go home."

USS TEUTHIS—BOTTOMED AT THE *ALFA*

We had a huge number of photos from both the dive around the *Alfa* and the hours we spent inside her. The ship's photographer's mate was up all night, creating contact sheets that the DIA team and I could index to our tapes. He developed the color slide strips in canisters to keep the toxic fumes out of the sub's atmosphere. Then he made monotone contact sheets from the slide strips that he distributed to the DIA team members and me. I speeded up my playback to double, but it still took more than two hours to create the index.

We met in the Wardroom with the skipper and the Special Ops team to review our findings and decide our next course of action.

"We really would like to get the *Alfa* into a secure American controlled port where we can fully analyze all her equipment," Cook said. "Dragging her behind *Teuthis* doesn't really seem like an option."

"Not hardly," the skipper said. "How about removing selected pieces of equipment?"

"That's doable, I suppose," Cook said.

"There is another option," I said. "What if we charged her batteries to full, and then put a crew aboard her to drive her to Mare Island?"

The reaction was astonishment.

"You're serious, aren't you?" the skipper asked in a disbelieving tone.

"Doug's people can make a waterproof adapter to attach our shore cable to their shore fitting. I figure her battery charge will last for thirty-six hours at ten knots, give or take. Doug can give you a better number. We stick to littoral water all the way down the coast since we'll be limited to ten knots anyway. We stop and charge the *Alfa* every thirty-six hours or so. We might even be able to reset the escape pod before we leave." I shut up to let everyone think.

"It's the only solution that really makes any sense," the skipper said after several minutes of silence. He picked up the handset and called Seth Beaumont. When he arrived, the skipper said, "Get with Mac and draft a burst message to COMSUBDEVGRUONE. I want to send it as soon as possible."

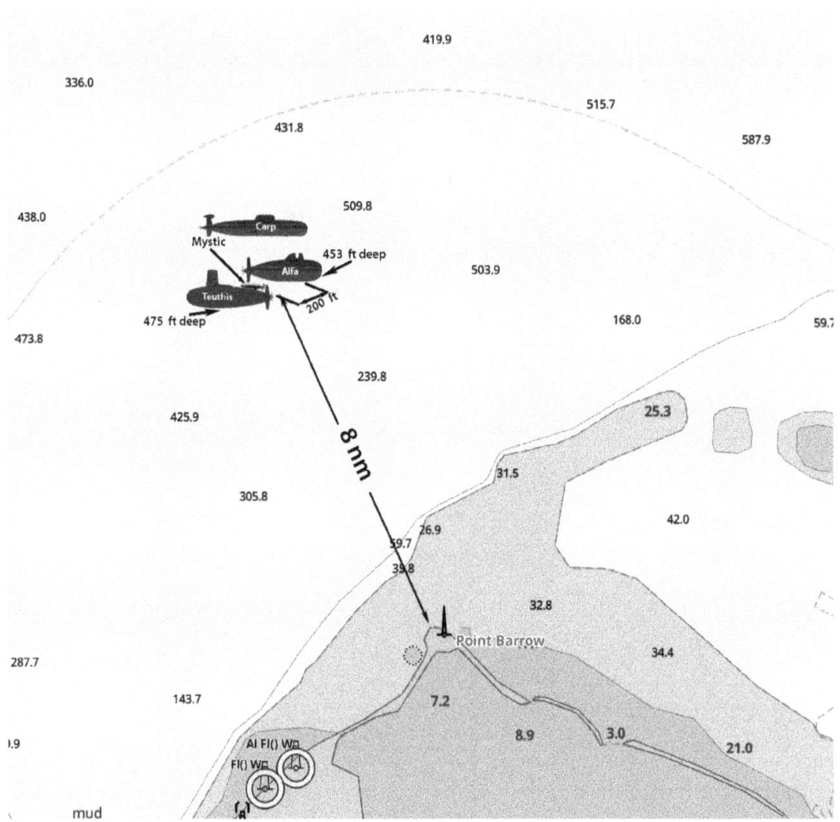

USS Teuthis *with* Mystic, *and the* Alfa *and* Carp *in the 500 ft hole*

CHAPTER SEVENTEEN—*Carp* Encounter

USS TEUTHIS—BOTTOMED AT THE *ALFA*

"Conn, Sonar, I've got a contact bearing three-four-five—it's the Carp, Sir."

"How far?" Seth asked. He and Bert had the watch.

"Difficult to tell, Sir. Less than a hundred miles," Jim Orange, the sonar watch section leader, answered.

I happened to be in Sonar at the time they picked up the *Carp* again. I went out to Nav and pulled a polar chart that showed the entire polar basin. I drew a line on a bearing of 345 degrees from Point Barrow. It pointed straight across the Arctic Sea to Polyarny near the Russian-Norwegian border. I called the skipper, and he arrived in Sonar shortly thereafter. I showed him the chart.

"I think the *Carp* was on its way from Petropavlovsk-Kamchatskiy to Polyarny when it received word to hightail it back to here," I said, pointing to our position off Point Barrow. "The *Carp* knows there is an *Alfa* down somewhere near here." Again, I pointed to our position. "I think they're coming to investigate."

Two hours earlier, just before Bert and Seth came on watch, we had popped up just below the ice cover and pressed through the ice so we could extend an antenna. We sent the burst message three times. In essence, it contained my recommendation that we man the *Alfa*, bring her systems online, and drive her to Mare Island, or any other port COMSUBDEVGRUONE wanted. In an hour, we were due to check for a response.

"Petty Officer Orange, how far away is the *Carp*?" the skipper asked.

"Less than a hundred miles, Captain. We're working on a better fix, but he's pretty faint."

✳

The skipper went to Control to talk with Bert. I tagged along.

"I want the antenna up five minutes before the next hour. In the meantime, go to ultra-quiet, come to two hundred feet, and hover."

"Rig ship for ultra-quiet, Oggy," Seth told his Chief of the Watch.

I parked myself in Sonar as we slowly rose through the water column. We passed through a temperature layer at 230 feet.

"Conn, Sonar, we got a good signal on the *Carp*."

Seth held *Teuthis* at 220 feet and notified the skipper. Jim conducted a quick but thorough analysis of the incoming data. Ten minutes later, he called Control by sound-powered phone.

"Conn, Sonar, the *Carp* is at forty-seven miles, closing on a bearing of three-four-five at thirty knots."

He was ninety minutes away. I checked my watch. It was ten minutes to the hour, and Seth was taking us up.

We cracked through the ice with our sail and immediately dropped back down to sixty-five feet. Then we extended our antenna through the pool of water we had left on the surface.

While Bert and Seth took us through the ice cover and set us up to receive a response, the skipper composed another burst message detailing the arrival of the *Carp*, and his intention to interfere with their investigation of the *Alfa*. The response, granting permission to bring the *Alfa* back to Mare Island, arrived as he was composing his message. He acknowledged receipt of their authorization and indicated that he would carry out the plan, subject to the outcome of whatever happened following the *Carp*'s arrival.

Radio sent the message, and Seth brought *Teuthis* back to the bottom, about 300 feet south of the *Alfa*.

The skipper spoke with the Control Center watchstanders. "Pass the word throughout the ship by sound-powered phone to set extreme ultra-quiet condition. I want there to be zero chance that the *Carp* detects us when he arrives," the skipper checked the time, "in less than a half hour."

✳

"Mac," the skipper told me in his cabin, "I want your divers pressed down and ready to enter the water if it turns out we need to address a situation brought on by the *Carp*."

"I already did that, including Sergyi," I told him. "We think the *Carp* has a limited lockout capability, and she may be able to fly a sidescan fish."

"If we can pull it off," the skipper said, "I don't want them to find the *Alfa* or to know about our presence."

The skipper's sound-powered phone chirped softly. He picked it up.

"Thank you." He turned to me. "The *Carp* has settled to the bottom beyond the *Alfa* about three hundred yards north of our position. We've launched the Basketball with lights extinguished. Get down to Dive Control and take charge of the situation. Talk to me before putting divers into the water."

As I walked through Control, Sonar reported that the *Carp* had launched a device. "It sounds like a tethered sidescan fish," Orange told Conn.

USS TEUTHIS—BOTTOMED AT THE *ALFA*

"Ham," I said, "locate the DIA guys and get them here." When they arrived a few minutes later, I briefed them on how my divers had disabled the Soviet *Whiskey* sub during the Ivy Bells operation.[11] I explained how Ski had entangled their topside safety line and antenna wire into their propellers, forcing them to blow to the surface. I kept the details of Ivy Bells out of my telling.

"We have a similar situation here," I told them. "The *Carp* is bottomed on the other side of the *Alfa* and a bit to the north. It's beyond umbilical distance, but we can easily reach it with rebreathers. The Basketball is somewhere near it, but we dare not turn the lights on for fear they already have divers in the water.

"We know the *Carp*—a *Sierra-I* class—is similar to the *Alfa* but larger. Is there any way to disable her?"

Edwards spoke up. "I don't think the Soviets would have put a liquid-metal-cooled reactor in another sub class. I'm guessing pressurized water. Look at this photo." He opened a classified book that displayed photos of Soviet subs. "Someone risked his life to get this one." He pointed to a scoop near the stern. "That's almost certainly a coolant scoop." He put the book down. "If we could get close to one of these with a heated drum of paraffin, their pumps would suck the liquefied paraffin into the cooling system where it would solidify and block the coolant flow. This would scram their reactor and force them to surface through the ice. They're sufficiently larger so that it's very unlikely they would hang up like the *Alfa*."

"How would they deal with that?" I asked.

"Who knows?" Cook said. "Soviet subs have been plagued by reactor problems for years."

---

11 See chapter 22 of the first book in the Mac McDowell Mission series, *Operation Ivy Bells,* for the details.

"With a scrammed reactor," Edwards said, "the paraffin would slowly soften until it flowed out. After a couple of hours, without having a clue about what happened, they could restart their reactor."

"I'm guessing," Cook added, "that they would then limp home—probably to Petropavlovsk-Kamchatskiy. No way they would risk a submerged transit under the ice to Polyarny. Besides, it's seventeen hundred nautical miles to Petropavlovsk versus twenty-three hundred to Polyarny. The crew would probably mutiny."

"So, why did they bottom right here?" Ham asked.

"The *Alfa* crew gave them a good fix, I would presume," I said. "The *Carp* knew exactly where the *Alfa* would be. Now they seem to be confirming that with a sidescan fish. My guess, in two hours, they will have a sidescan map of the *Alfa*. The *Alfa* is between them and us. Let's hope that when they find the *Alfa*, they stop searching."

✳

"Doug," I said to the Engineer a few minutes later, "I need two heaters that will melt paraffin in fifty-five-gallon drums with the surrounding water about twenty-eight or twenty-nine degrees—in other words," I grinned, "out there. I'll need a long extension cord—about three-hundred-fifty yards."

"That's a tall order, Mac."

"I need it to be really hot, so it stays liquid while it's being sucked up into the *Carp* cooling system."

"You're shittin' me!"

"Nope. And I need it A-S-A-P." I held my grin. "Oh, yeah…I'll also need two hand pumps that will attach to the drum bungs to pump that shit into their coolant intakes."

Doug stared at me for nearly thirty seconds. Then he clapped my shoulder.

"I'm on it, buddy…"

ON THE SEAFLOOR—NEAR THE *ALFA*

When we were ready, a surprisingly short time later, I called the skipper to Dive Control. When he arrived, I pointed him to the monitor from the Egress Lock. Standing beside the open hatch was a paraffin drum with an insulating jacket around it. The jacket was partly open, revealing tight coils of cable. Extending from the bung near the edge of the cover, a hand pump with a five-foot hose coiled on top of the cover looked strangely normal. Three garbage weights were strapped to the top of the drum. A neat pile of electrical cable was figure-eighted on the deck.

"Captain Roken, meet the *Carp* scrammer," I said.

Then I explained to him how it worked and what we intended to do. He remained in Dive Control to observe the operation.

✳

Ham assigned Jimmy and Sergyi on rebreathers as standby, Jer on rebreather, and Jake on umbilical as tenders. Ham put Harry, Whitey, and Ski in the water. Harry and Whitey were on umbilicals, and each carried a gas-powered dart gun across his back. Ski wore a rebreather and carried two gas-powered dart guns. All three divers carried an extra five darts each, and all wore headlamps.

Wally was flying the Basketball and was hovering above the *Carp* with lights extinguished, looking for anything moving.

The three divers moved across the distance between *Teuthis* and the *Alfa* with the drums, trailing two umbilicals and the power cord for the heaters. The liquefied paraffin in the drums caused them to move with a gyroscopic sway. Harry and Whitey quickly learned to compensate for this, but it slowed their progress.

Just as the divers reached the *Alfa*, Wally announced, "I've got two divers in the water from the *Carp*. They exited from beneath the bow. They got high-power spots. They're carrying three tanks on their backs and are not leaving a bubble trail. They're headed straight for the *Alfa*."

I examined the monitor image. It looked like they were armed with gas guns similar to what our guys had. They had no reason, however, to expect anyone else in the water unless, somehow, the *Carp* had gotten wind of us.

"Divers, Dive Control," I said, "you got two *Carp* divers headed toward the *Alfa*. They are armed."

I glanced at the skipper. "Deadly force authorized?" I asked.

He nodded. "They're armed close to our territorial waters."

"You need to take them out," I told the divers. "Deadly force is authorized, but if possible, disable and bring them to *Teuthis*."

I received a Roger from all three divers.

"Harry and Whitey, move under the *Alfa* bow and stay hidden from the divers. Pull sufficient umbilical, so you have freedom of movement. Ski, stay on this side of the *Alfa*, ready to cross over to confront them. Watch your ceiling, Ski. Attack together on my order. If you must, shoot to disable. Acknowledge."

"Harry, aye."

"Whitey, aye."

"Ski, roger."

"Wally, drop the Basketball down to the *Alfa* deck at the sail."

We waited.

I called Sonar on the sound-powered phones. "Do you have any comms transmissions from *Carp* or their divers?"

"Negative, but maybe they're just not talking."

"Divers, if you see any evidence of comms, rip it off ASAP."

Sonar called me. "We just picked up a modulated sound transmission." Sonar played it to me.

I looked at the skipper. "They just announced that they have arrived at the *Alfa*."

"They got comms, guys. Rip off their headgear."

The monitor showed the divers reaching the *Alfa* about deck level.

"Stand by," I said to the divers. "Attack!"

Harry and Whitey must have appeared out of nowhere, from the Soviet divers' perspective. One moment they were reporting their status to *Carp*, and the next they were sans headgear, faces exposed to near-freezing water.

"Lights, Wally!" I ordered.

As the area flooded with light, one *Carp* diver headed toward the surface, a stream of bubbles trailing from his mask. They had been breathing mixed gas for at least fifteen minutes by this time. He had no chance, and we made no attempt to stop him. Ski darted in from the flank, grabbed the second diver's arms, and whipped them behind him, tying them together with a cord from his leg pocket. Then he grabbed the diver's bubbling facemask, looked inside, and ripped out a small mike. The Russian diver's eyes were wide with fright as Ski pressed the facemask against his face, making sure the nose and mouth cup was properly seated.

"Harry and Whitey, bring that diver back with you now. Let him breathe, but remind him of his precarious situation," I said.

I turned and spoke briefly with the skipper. He listened carefully and then said, "Are you sure, Mac?"

I nodded. "I need divers in standby, Harry and Whitey have their hands full, and Ski is out there by himself. We have a job to do, and we need to do it quickly."

"I'm relying on your expertise and judgment, Mac. Don't let me down!"

USS TEUTHIS—BOTTOMED AT THE ALFA

Several things happened while I was out, as recorded by Sonar. The Carp reactor scrammed, as we expected it to do. About an hour later, the Carp emergency blew its main ballast tanks and shot to the surface, breaking through the ice easily, just outside U.S. territorial waters. What took place during that hour is anybody's guess, but it's fun to speculate.

Soviet subs have had a history of reactor problems, with more than one having to surface because of internal radiation. I have to believe that the typical Soviet sub crew was jumpy at best. An unexplained reactor scram accompanied by an inability to bring the reactor back online would probably freak out a crew. I'm not suggesting a mutiny, but the Captain would be under a lot of pressure to bring the sub to the surface and replace all the air in the interior. I'm not sure they would want to submerge again.

When they surfaced, two things would have happened. Fighters would have scrambled from Eielson Air Force Base to investigate the surfaced Soviet sub, and the *Carp* would have signaled Petropavlovsk. But what then? I became fully conscious with four more days of decompression ahead of us. I remembered Wyatt saying earlier that the *Carp* would "have to limp home—probably to Petropavlovsk-Kamchatskiy." I knew it was a 1,700 nautical mile trip. What would they do?

✳

I called Sonar. King had the watch. "How's your shoulder?" he asked.

"I'll live," I said. "Got any details for me?"

"We recorded all of it," King said. "Don't speak Russian, but it was pretty obvious what was happening."

He walked me through the events I had missed. After the *Carp*'s reactor scrammed, its crew spent about a half hour trying to communicate with their four missing divers. This was accompanied by a lot of mechanical sounds that probably were the engineers trying to get their plant up and running again. Then there was a lot of shouting—a lot of anger that came right through the *Carp* hull. Things quieted down for a while, and then suddenly they blew their main ballast tanks—no lifting off the bottom first, no alarm sounds, just the sudden rapid evacuation of their ballast tanks that resulted in the *Carp* heading rapidly to the surface.

Fifteen minutes later, King called me back. "They're starting up, Sir. Their reactor is working this time."

I heard King call Control on the sound-powered phone. "They're starting their plant. Sounds like they're getting ready to get underway."

"Can you keep an open mike for me, King?" I asked.

Zeb had the watch with the XO because I was officially still off the watchbill. He called the skipper, who joined them in Control to see what transpired.

The *Carp* emitted various sounds that were really difficult to interpret. Then I heard the distinctive sounds of the main ballast tank vents venting.

"She's diving," King said. "She's drawing left…picking up speed. She's doing turns for ten knots."

King did some calculations. "Conn, Sonar," he said on the sound-powered phone, "the *Carp* is on course of two-three-two, doing ten knots, range three miles and opening."

Fifteen minutes later, Sonar called again. "Conn, Sonar, the *Carp* has commenced active pinging, and he increased his speed to fifteen knots. He's in a hurry, Sir. He's ranging ahead of himself to detect possible obstacles."

I thanked King for bringing me along and disconnected.

ON THE SEAFLOOR—NEAR *CARP*

"Mac to Ski, Jimmy and Sergyi are joining you as soon as they can get there. I will be along in as much time as it takes them to get there plus five minutes to press down." I turned to Ham. "Drop me down fast. I'll dress on my way down. I want to be in the water on my way six minutes after you shut the hatch."

"You're sure, Boss?"

"You know it!"

I stepped through the hatch into the Entrance Lock. As he shut the hatch, Ham said, "Jimmy and Sergyi just reached Ski. It took them a bit over two minutes. Neither seemed winded."

I thanked Ham and started suiting up. It helps to have someone assist in donning a Unisuit, but I got it sealed with my keepers on my feet in ninety seconds. I slipped into my buoyancy compensator, checked the weight load, donned my rebreather, and pulled gloves over my wrists. That was the most difficult part, and I would want one of the guys inside to tighten them before I entered the water.

I don't have any problems clearing my ears, so Bill was able to press me down quickly. Our protocol required a minimum of ten minutes for 500 feet, but I had already told Ham to get me down in five.

Once I hit bottom, the guys in the Main Lock pushed the door into the Entrance Lock and welcomed me with high-fives. I checked my neck and wrist seals, and Jimmy pulled each three-fingered glove securely over the seals. Except for the Kirby-Morgan helmet, I was ready to go. Jer helped me with my headgear and did a quick check of my complete rig. The last thing I did before entering the water was to check my oxygen percentage. Jake strapped a bandola of darts around my right thigh and handed me two gas-powered guns as I entered the water.

I took a moment to orient myself and turn in the direction I wanted to go. As I did so, Harry and Whitey arrived with their prisoner. I assisted them in pushing the Russian diver through the hatch. They followed. On the through-water comm system, I checked with Jimmy and Sergyi at the *Alfa* and briefly noted the presence of a curious narwhal. Then, I struck out for the *Alfa*. Two minutes later, the four of us were exchanging high-fives, although, in the Unisuit with its three-fingered gloves, I guess it really was high-threes.

"Mac, Dive Control, state your condition."

"Fine. We're moving the drums to the *Carp*."

✳

The drums were virtually weightless. Ski and Jimmy lifted them off the bottom a foot or so where they floated. Then they pushed them toward the *Carp* while I pulled the electrical cable along behind them, all the while Sergyi was keeping watch for other divers. The Basketball remained above and ahead of us looking for unwanted guests.

We had about 700 feet to go. I estimated our progress at about 1.5 feet per second; thus, eight minutes or so lay between us and the *Carp*. You have no idea how long eight minutes can be. Following several hours of subjective inching along the bottom toward the *Carp*, we finally saw the looming shadow of the bulbous nose materializing ahead of us. I checked my watch. Surprisingly, it said eight minutes had passed.

As we moved down the *Carp's* starboard side, a thought popped into my mind. This sucker was a hundred feet longer than the *Alfa*. If the behemoth beside us were the *Alfa*, the scoop we were seeking would lie well beyond the *Alfa's* screw. Finally, we found it. Ski and Jimmy wrestled the two drums directly below the intake that was at head level while I pulled the remaining power cable to our feet.

Ski and Jimmy each grabbed a hose and held them to the scoop. I flooded my BC until I was firmly pressed onto the bottom. Then I grabbed a pump handle in each hand and commenced pumping with all the energy I could muster. Wally illuminated the scoop, and I could clearly see a large volume of liquid paraffin flow into the opening and get sucked up inside.

For five minutes, I pumped furiously. Suddenly and simultaneously, Sergyi shouted, "DUCK!" and I experienced a deep, excruciating pain in my left shoulder. I turned to my right as I ducked and saw a diver between the seafloor and the upward curve of the keel with a dart piercing the side of his head, pinning him to the bottom.

"Ski, behind you!" Sergyi shouted.

Ski twisted while drawing his knife with his right hand. A diver lunged at him, plunging his knife through Ski's Unisuit into his right shoulder.

Although my pain was pretty intense, I simply had to help Ski. He was injured, and his suit was filling with freezing water. So was mine, but I hadn't figured it out yet, and besides, my leak was a lot smaller. I pulled my knife and propelled myself into the attacking diver. I keep my knife razor-sharp with a needle point. I pierced the airbag on his chest and swept my blade upward through whatever fittings and electronics might have been there and sliced open the bottom part of his full-facemask. I watched his eyes through his faceplate fill with fright as he tried to disengage. Perhaps he thought he could make it to the hatch located on the underside of the bow. That wasn't going to happen!

With my left hand, I ripped his faceplate out of its damaged frame and pulled off his nose and mouth cup. Then, with every remaining ounce of strength I could muster, I punched him in the stomach. His eyes opened wide in total surprise and his mouth opened to release a stream of bubbles as he sank to the seafloor, lungs filled with ice-cold seawater.

While all this was happening, Jimmy kept pumping paraffin into the scoop until both drums were empty.

"We got to get the hell out of here," I squeaked, beginning to feel a bit faint from pain, the blood loss, and the icy water that was percolating throughout my suit. "Ski won't last if we don't get him inside."

I grabbed Ski's harness with my left hand, ignoring the pain, and started pulling both of us along the cable that had powered the drum heaters. Sergyi came up to my right, and Jimmy grabbed Ski's harness from the left. As Sergyi grabbed my harness, I began to fade.

"Stay with me, Mac!" Sergyi squeaked. "Keep kicking!"

"The paraffin," I mumbled. Then I gasped as a wave of pain swept through my body. "Hold on, Ski," I whispered as Jimmy and Sergyi wrestled us through the water, our path illuminated by the Basketball.

That's the last thing I remember until I opened my eyes in the DDC main lock. My Unisuit was gone, and Jimmy was wrapping my left shoulder with a white bandage. Lying at my side was another bandage, soaked red.

"Ski," I muttered.

"Just fine, Mac," Ski's voice floated across the aisle from his bunk to mine. "A prick is all. I'm just fine." I tried to give him a thumbs-up, but instead, I drifted off again.

ON THE SEAFLOOR—NEAR THE *ALFA*

We had just returned to the seafloor near the *Alfa* from a brief time at periscope depth to send a burst message.

I called the skipper on the regular handset. "I have a serious concern that's been on my mind as I sit here slowly returning to surface pressure." I paused, not entirely sure it was my place to bring it up. "The *Carp* has gone to the barn, but I'm pretty sure that's not the end of the matter. They had plenty of time on the surface to let their bosses know what happened."

"Do you believe they knew about our presence?"

"Probably not, but their first two divers definitely saw the *Alfa* and had plenty of time to report that they sighted it. Remember, the *Carp* was communicating with its divers over something like our *Gertrude*—unreliable and spotty. The divers likely would withhold a full report until they returned to the sub. They would have reported our divers the moment they spied them, but I think we got them before they could make the report. We simply can't know for sure. I think they sent out the second pair of divers to look for the first pair. We got a lot done before they found us. They probably went to the *Alfa* because the first pair would, at a minimum, have reported they found it. Did they see our lash-down of the escape module? If so, the divers knew about us. Even if not, they probably found our power cable and followed it back to the *Carp*. Did they report our presence then or when they reached the *Carp*? If then, they know about us. If not, at the *Carp*, it all happened so fast. Sergyi nailed the diver who got me almost immediately. Did he report before he shot? I would have shot first. Plenty of time after to tell you what happened. Same with the second diver. If he was in an attack-first-tell-later-mode, then I stopped his report, too.

"The bottom line is, Sir, we can surmise that they know about the *Alfa*, but not us…but do we stake our lives on this?"

"I agree with your logic, Mac, but where does that leave us? We told the DevGroup that we would try to bring the *Alfa* back with us. We got the DIA team. You are as qualified as anyone to drive the *Alfa*. You take Bert, Dokey, Pots, and Sergyi with you."

"Thanks for the vote of confidence, Skipper. I agree we could do it. But I keep thinking about Ivan. Worst case scenario, they know we fucked them, and they're hungry for revenge. One rung up, they suspect us. One more rung, they really don't know about us, but they know we know where the *Alfa* is, and they want it back really badly.

"Their *Alfa* is in our waters, and they want it back, no matter the scenario. They want it back. If you were the Ruskies, Sir, what would you do?"

"I definitely have my thoughts on that, but first, I want to hear the rest of your proposal," the skipper replied.

"Okay…Well, whether we *were* there or not, they *know* we will be. They know about the DSRV. I think they believe we will try to bring the *Alfa* to a secure American port—make that Anchorage, Puget Sound, or Mare Island. If I'm the Soviet high command, there's no way the Americans will get one of my *Alfa*s. I would spread my subs south of Bering Strait and a couple north of it. I then bring my icebreakers into the Bering Sea to open things up for every surface combatant I've got. I plug the Bering so tight not even a cod could get through. My orders are to sink the *Alfa*, and I'll push right to the brink of war to make this happen."

I paused to let my comments sink in. The skipper folded his arms and then put his chin in his left hand.

I added, "There's no way on earth we will make it through the Bering Strait. Based on whatever report the *Carp* probably sent, the Soviets already have subs moving in. If we're going to pull that one off, we go back the way we came."

"Well, Mac," the skipper said, "I reached the same conclusion several hours ago. That burst message we just sent laid out virtually everything you just told me. I informed Dev Group that we would be returning to Kodiak to reprovision, including the oxygen and helium you requested, and drop off our prisoner. I recommended that we should then return to the *Alfa* and transport her through the Arctic to a secure East Coast port of their choosing. I also recommended that they send another sub up here to fend off any Soviet sub until we return."

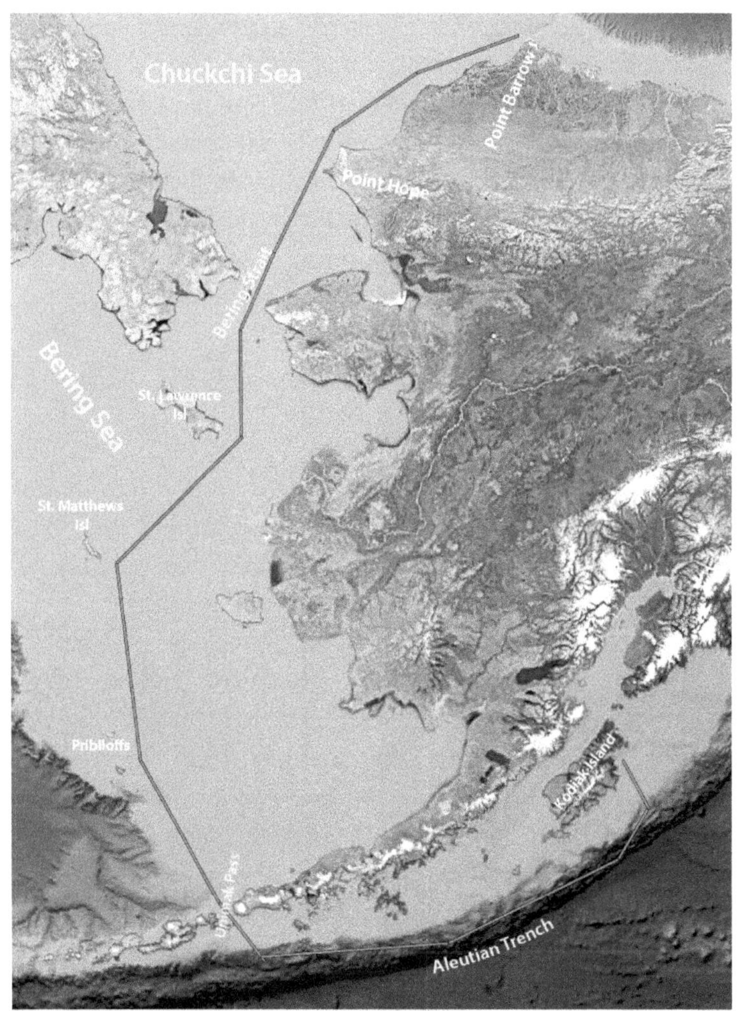

USS Teuthis & Mystic *transit from Pt. Barrow to Kodiak Island*

CHAPTER EIGHTEEN—Transit to Kodiak

USS TEUTHIS—BOTTOMED AT THE *ALFA*

Ham collected the DIA and Spec Ops guys in Dive Control for a briefing. Sergyi and I, with the rest of the divers, joined the meeting from the DDC, where we were slowly decompressing.

I spoke to the group. "The skipper has just sent a message to the Dev Group that lays out our current situation and his recommendations moving forward. What's important from our perspective is that we really don't know whether or not the Ruskies know the *Teuthis* was here." I repeated my conversation with the skipper. "Here's the thing. If they come back and find the divers' bodies or other evidence of our activities, they will be operating from an entirely different perspective. They will know we were here.

"So…we're going out there to police up the entire bottom—no bodies, no drums, no cables, no lines, no anything."

The guys murmured among themselves. Then Long raised his hand. "What about the escape pod?"

"That's the critical question, isn't it?" I responded. "Right now, it's lashed to the sail." I looked around the group but saw no sudden inspiration. "If they know about us, this entire discussion is moot. If they don't, however, we want to maintain the illusion."

The skipper had decided to flood the escape pod and leave it attached to the *Alfa* but lying on its side on the seafloor. That way, it would appear that the rescuers of the *Alfa* crew had flooded the pod before they left the ice. I explained this to the guys.

"Our job will be flooding the pod and unlashing it from the *Alfa*. This will be our last dive for a while. Do any of you DIA guys want to get in the water?"

Edwards and Long volunteered.

"Jer and Jake will join them," I said, giving my two most junior divers a chance for one more dive. "Ham, press down the DIA guys to our current depth in the Entrance Lock, and then take us all back down to the bottom."

✳

Ham put Edwards with Jer and Long with Jake. The divers followed the power cable to where the *Carp* had sat on the bottom. The *Carp*'s emergency blow had tipped over both drums. Watched over by Derrick with the Basketball, they located the bodies of the two Soviet divers Sergyi and I had dispatched. The ocean floor critters had already started to do their thing with the bodies. Several curious narwhals and beluga whales joined them. They seemed interested in the bodies but didn't bother the divers, other than the belugas nudging them and the narwhals stroking them with their tusks.

While they brought the bodies back, accompanied by their cetaceous friends, Ham got three body bags from the corpsman and locked them into the DDC.

When they arrived, I told them, "While still in the water, strip the dive gear off the bodies and shove the gear into the third body bag. Then put each body into a bag and drain the water from the three bags as they are lifted from the water. Try to keep any of the contamination from the bodies out of the lock."

They complied, and then the inside guys used a hose to wash down the entire Egress Lock.

The four divers followed the cable back to the drums, where they disconnected the power cord and then attempted to lift them.

"Divers, Dive Control," I told them, "the empty drums weigh forty pounds, and they each carry an extra twenty-one pounds of garbage weights. Try rolling them."

That worked well, although the pump handles kept getting in the way. That turned out to be more of an annoyance than anything else. They had the drums upside down under the egress hatch fifteen minutes later.

Whitey placed the tip of his knife in the middle of the first drum bottom and struck it with a hammer. Then he and Jimmy lifted it into the Egress Lock and placed it along the bulkhead in the space it had originally occupied. They did the same with the second.

While Whitey and Jimmy were hauling the drums into the Egress Lock, the four divers returned to the site. They checked the area carefully. Long found two gas-powered guns, and Edwards found several darts. Otherwise, the site appeared clean. Jer picked up the power cable bitter end, and they swam back to *Teuthis*.

✳

Harry, with an umbilical, joined the four divers as they approached the *Alfa*. He brought along a forty-foot long, two-inch hose. Long swam up under the pod and located the locking wheel for the hatch.

To ensure he knew what he was doing, I asked, "Ken, what will happen when you unseal that hatch?"

"External water pressure will push it open, and the pod will flood until internal pressure equals outside."

"And what happens to you if you are anywhere near the hatch?"

"Shit! Glad you asked. We'll be sure to do it right."

Harry swam back to the *Teuthis* and grabbed some heavy-duty line. He dragged it to the *Alfa*. The divers secured one end of the line through the pod hatch handle and tied it off to a large titanium stanchion in the sail. They used a deck cleat to gain as much leverage as possible as they tightened the line.

It appeared that the pod would fall to starboard once it flooded, so the divers placed themselves at the base of the sail on the port side. Long stretched himself out on the hinge side of the hatch and slowly turned the locking wheel. After several turns, it spun freely. He kept spinning until it reached its extent of travel. Harry, who kept his knife very sharp, handed it to Long. Remaining stretched out on the spring side, Long commenced sawing at the hawser. Derrick kept the Basketball away from the action, but sufficiently close to give us a good view on the monitors.

With a sudden loud POP, the hawser parted at Long's cut, and the hatch snapped upward. The Pod rapidly filled with water, leaving about 1.5 feet of air at the top, compressed to fifteen atmospheres.

Harry said to Ham, "Have Jake swim the float end of the hose to a couple of feet above the pod, please."

Ham passed the instruction on to Jake. Then Harry pushed the other end into the pod up into the air pocket. In a few seconds, bubbles started to flow from the float end until all the remaining air was siphoned out of the pod. The pod tilted to starboard.

Jer checked to ensure no one was near any line or cable nor under the pod. Then he sliced through the line cinching the pod to the sail. The pod slid down the starboard side of the *Alfa*, bounced about a foot off the bottom, did a half roll about its long axis, and settled.

"Okay, everybody," Ham said over both circuits, "make sure nothing remains of our activities. Pick up and return everything you left on the seafloor. Find the end of the anchoring cable that popped Jake's faceplate. Return it to the anchor point and try to make it look normal."

"Not gonna be easy," Harry quipped.

Ham sent Hart to see if the engineers had any plumber's putty. They did. He sent it to the divers, and it helped a lot. According to Harry, "It made the fitting look normal."

"We still need to locate the body of the diver who went to the surface," I told the divers.

They conducted an area search coordinated by Derrick with the Basketball. About an hour later, they found the body, swollen and partially eaten. Ham sent out another body bag.

Finally, all the divers returned. Harry made one final short tour around the egress hatch for anything that had been missed. Good thing he did. Whitey's dive knife had tumbled out when he pierced the drum bottoms. That would have been a dead giveaway.

From our point of view in the DDC, all that remained was a routine five-day decompression. Well, maybe not so routine. We had our six divers, the two DIA guys, the prisoner, and Sergyi and me—and the DDC had four bunks.

We worked it out.

USS TEUTHIS—TRANSIT TO KODIAK ISLAND

Our nine-day transit to Kodiak was as routine as could be expected—ten knots all the way as deep as we could go. Sonar detected nothing until we reached the freighter and tanker convoy route at the Aleutians.

We had a problem, though. We knew it, but it wasn't obvious at first. With eleven of us inside the DDC, keeping track of our prisoner was not particularly complicated. As was Sergyi back in Operation Ivy Bells,[12] our prisoner, Leonid Volkov, was grateful to be alive.

In the DDC, we watched several movies, played a lot of chess, even played several poker games. We surfaced just after we transited Unimak Pass. Ski was pretty much healed, thanks to Jimmy's attentive care. I still had a way to go.

The *Teuthis'* hospital corpsman was waiting for both Ski and me when we stepped out of the DDC. He took us straight to his boss,

---

12 See chapter 35 of the 1st book in the Mac McDowell Mission series, *Operation Ivy Bells*, for the details.

Dr. Janus Everest, the ship's doctor, who gave us both a clean bill of health. He put my left arm in a sling and told me to wear it for a week and put me on limited duty. He told Ski with a chuckle, "Take two aspirin and see me in the morning."

Sergyi worked out a deal with Volkov and Ham. Ham arranged for a cot in Dive Control for the Russian diver. Volkov gave his word not to cause any trouble, and one of the divers would be with him at all times. This satisfied me because I trusted Sergyi implicitly.

Next, I went to see the skipper. But on my way, I managed to get a hot shower and wolf down a couple of Cedric's popovers with maple syrup. Frankly, I was a bit nervous about talking with the skipper. My getting shot and Ski stabbed had not been part of the equation when I told the skipper that I needed to be on scene for the paraffin transfer. I knocked on his cabin door.

"Enter," he said.

To my utter surprise, because Commander Roken was one of the most straight-laced officers I had ever served under, the skipper offered me a chair and then pulled a bottle of single-malt Islay from his safe.

"Your preferred beverage, I believe," he said with a twinkle in his eyes. He poured two shots in water glasses. "These will have to do," he said.

"Jimmy and Sergyi both told me that you saved Ski's life and that you were instrumental in getting him back to *Teuthis*."

"That would be with their spin," I said. "Actually, I got shot first, and Sergyi nailed the shooter…pinned his face to the bottom with a dart. When that diver stabbed Ski, I became enraged. I don't exactly remember what happened, but when it was over, Ski was alive, and the Russian was dead. I knew that Ski was going hypothermic. All he had was three or four minutes before it was all over. I remember grabbing him and pulling us along the power cable toward *Teuthis*. That's about it. I guess Jimmy and Sergyi got us back. If it hadn't been for them, both of us would be dead."

The skipper lifted his glass. "I'm honored and proud to have you on my team, Mac."

*

Several hours later, I stepped into the Wardroom for a cup of coffee. The skipper was there, getting himself one. "Skipper," I said, "I know the doc put me on restricted duty, but I don't need my left arm to stand a deck watch, and I'm not taking pain killers, so I don't have any cognitive impairment—other than that resulting from all my time under pressure." I snapped a grin at him.

The skipper grinned back. "So that's what I've seen since you reported to the *Halibut*[13] what seems so long ago now." He chuckled. "You're sure? You've earned the right to a bit of rest."

"More than sure, Skipper. I'll have more than sufficient time to rest when I'm retired."

"Okay, I'll have a word with the SWO."

✳

Finally, we surfaced a mile from the Pilot Buoy off Woman's Bay. I got a watch under my belt, but Bert had the privilege of bringing *Teuthis* in this time. He's an old hand. He did just fine. As we were tying up, Kate's Datsun roadster pulled up to the dock. I stroked the ivory cylinder in my pocket and could not believe the level of excitement I felt.

I asked the skipper for leave to take off early. I assured him that Ham would get the helium and oxygen aboard, and I would be back the following morning, ready to jump into whatever was required before we got underway again.

"What about Volkov?" the skipper asked.

"Wyatt told me that someone from DIA will be here shortly to take charge of him. He's no Sergyi, but Wyatt thinks they can wring a lot of good intel from him. They'll probably offer him asylum once they finish with him."

"Take care of your shoulder," the skipper said as I left.

✳

Kate looked like she was getting out of her roadster. I waved to her. "Don't!" I said as I jumped into the passenger seat. "We need to get the hell out of here before something else comes up." I looked through the windscreen. "Like that," I said as a black car flying Sec-Nav's flag drove onto the dock.

---

13 See chapter 4 of the 1st book in the McDowell Mission series,
    Operation Ivy Bells, for the details.

Once past the Kodiak Airport on the road to town, Kate stopped, pulled off the road, and threw her arms around my neck. After we surfaced from her ministrations, she saw my left arm.

"Oh my god! What happened? Oh my god!" She started crying.

"A bit of trouble with some bad guys," I said. "I'll live." I brushed away her tears and kissed her softly.

She put the roadster in gear, and we drove on in silence, holding hands.

"How long can you stay?" she asked finally.

"Uncertain," I answered, stroking her cheek. "We'll know better after tomorrow."

We drove straight to her place without stopping anywhere. We made it to the bedroom, but I'm not sure how, with clothes strewn everywhere. I must have smelled like a sewer, but that didn't seem to matter to Kate. Sometime during mid-afternoon, I stumbled into the bathroom and managed to spend several minutes in the shower before Kate joined me for the best shower experience I can ever remember having.

I think we ate something, and we may even have gotten a bit of sleep, but I'm not entirely sure. Kodiak daylight is in short supply during the winter, so I was missing the diurnal signals I normally received when ashore. Besides, Kate so completely monopolized my time that I totally lost track of it.

My pager buzzed at 0600. It was a Kodiak number, but I didn't know it. I called on Kate's Princess Phone by her bed.

"Mac here," I said.

"It's Ham. The XO told me to call you. SecNav arrived yesterday. He's hosting an award ceremony at noon in the Coast Guard Armory auditorium. I had Rivera spruce up your dress blues. You should go straight to the auditorium. Kate will know its location. She can be there as your guest. Things are moving pretty fast. Believe it or not, the sub is fully provisioned. We got the oxygen and helium. We finished up about seventeen hundred. We may be getting underway sometime tomorrow."

"Okay, tell the XO I'll be there. Ham, is there any way one of the guys can bring me my dress blues?"

"I thought you might ask. Sergyi has volunteered. What's the address?"

I told him, and then I hung up the phone and rolled over, shaking my head.

"We're going to an award ceremony with SecNav at noon today."

"The Secretary of the Navy? Really…Wow!" She paused. "We or you?"

"We, Baby, we!" I told her. "You need to put on your Sunday-go-to-meeting outfit. One of the guys is bringing my dress blues … Sergyi, a Ukrainian—you'll like him."

She stuck out her tongue at me. "How much time do we have?"

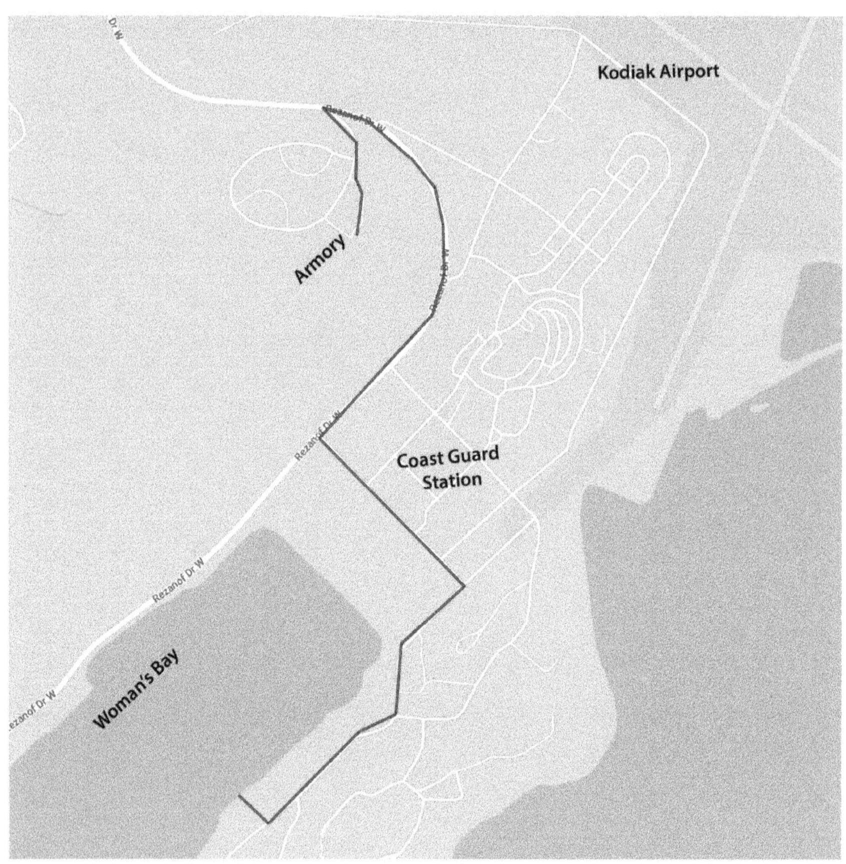

The 2-mile path to the Coast Guard Armory

EPILOG

COAST GUARD BASE KODIAK—ARMORY AUDITORIUM

The entire crew of the *USS Teuthis* was assembled in the first few rows of the Armory Auditorium at the Coast Guard Base Kodiak. Behind them were their immediate families—wives and girlfriends, children, fathers and mothers, brothers and sisters—flown in overnight by the Navy and sworn to secrecy as a condition of being present on this occasion.

Mac and Kate arrived several minutes before the ceremony was to commence. Mac seated Kate with the guests and found his way to the front with his divers.

Outside the auditorium, with the temperature hovering just above zero, wind-driven snow had slowed the arrival of a black limo festooned with the flag of the Secretary of the Navy. The people in the auditorium had been waiting for about ten minutes, when Master Chief Brock Davis, *Teuthis'* Chief of the Boat, called out, "Attention on deck!"

The assembled crew came to attention in rigid silence. The guests straggled to their feet, looking at one another and around the room with curious interest.

A moment later, the Secretary of the Navy stepped onto the stage without fanfare or flurry. In a quiet voice that carried to the small crowd at the front of the auditorium, he asked them to be seated, and welcomed the officers, crew, and visitors. Then he opened a leather folder that he had brought with him.

For the next half hour or so, the Secretary of the Navy presented the following citations and awards:

The Presidential Unit Citation to *USS Teuthis* (SSNR 2)

The Navy Cross to Mac (his second award)

The Bronze Star to each member of the TOG dive team (their second award except for Jake, his first).

The Navy Commendation Medal to Ham (his second award).

The National Security Medal to Mac and each member of the DIA team, including Sergyi.

Navy Unit Commendation to *Mystic* (DSRV 2)

The Purple Heart to Mac and Ski (their second award)

At this awards ceremony, there were no reporters, no photos, no recordings, because as far as the outside world was concerned, Operation Ice Breaker and official recognition for the team's accomplishments never happened. The citations consisted of generic language and lacked specific dates that only hinted at what had happened, and that was how it would be for the next twenty-five years or more.

Following the ceremony, SecNav approached Captain Roken and shook his hand. "I want to commend you, Captain Roken. Your message reached my desk two days after you sent it from the waters off Point Barrow. Your eloquence—in a navy message no less—caused me to accelerate the entire award process so this ceremony could take place here today, and it convinced me to arrange for family members to share in this ceremony. I salute you, Sir!"

Then he turned to Mac, who stood to the side with his good arm around a beaming Kate. "You broke the mold, Commander. I'm damn proud to have met you!"

With practiced political savvy, SecNav quickly shook the hands of the other awardees, making sure he had missed no one. Then he left quietly with his escorts by a side door into the driving snow.

Master Chief Davis dismissed the *Teuthis* crew, and they mixed with the guests as they exited through the main door to the rear of the auditorium into the mess outside.

Mac approached Commander Roken with Kate. "Captain Roken, may I present Katherine Perry, widow of Lieutenant Josh Perry, who gave his life rescuing Captain Jack Petrikoff?"

"Miss Perry," Roken said. "You have my heartfelt sympathy. It was a brave and selfless sacrifice."

"Call me Kate, please. I've accepted the loss and made a life for myself here in Kodiak." She squeezed Mac's arm. "I'm finally moving on."

"I admire that, Kate. I wish you the very best."

Commander Roken turned to Mac. "We leave on the ten hundred tide tomorrow morning, Mac. I'll see you then."

"Where are you going?" Kate asked Mac, a quick shadow flitting across her eyes.

He held her tight. "I can't say, but I can tell you it will be a place both much colder—and possibly much hotter—than here."

CBC News article from November 2, 2016

—byline Jimmy Thomson[14]

Hunters in a remote community in Nunavut are concerned about a mysterious sound that appears to be coming from the seafloor. The "pinging" sound, sometimes also described as a "hum" or "beep," has been heard in Fury and Hecla Strait—roughly 120 kilometers northwest of the hamlet of Igloolik—throughout the summer.

Paul Quassa, a member of the legislative assembly, says whatever the cause, it's scaring the animals away.

The sound appears to come from the seafloor in Hecla and Fury Strait.

Boaters aboard a private yacht passing through the area also say they heard the mysterious sound. The noise can apparently be heard through the hulls of boats.

"The Department of National Defense has been informed of the strange noises emanating in the Fury and Hecla Strait area, and the Canadian Armed Forces are taking the appropriate steps to actively investigate the situation," a spokesperson wrote in a statement.

"As of today, we're still working on it," he said. "We don't have a single clue."

---

14 Actual news article from CBC, dated November 2, 2016

A Note about Saturation Diving

The air you breathe is about twenty-one percent oxygen and seventy-nine percent nitrogen. When you dive on SCUBA, your equipment supplies you with compressed air that matches the pressure of the water around you, and this increases by about one atmosphere every thirty-three feet. So, at a thousand feet, air enters your lungs at about thirty atmospheres or 450 pounds per square inch (psi).

Normal air becomes toxic under too much pressure. When you inhale more oxygen than about twice the amount you would when breathing pure oxygen at the surface, the oxygen becomes toxic. This happens at about two-hundred feet when breathing compressed air. Furthermore, nitrogen becomes narcotic at about the same depth. This is a lethal combination: You're breathing toxic gas and are so narked by nitrogen that you don't know what to do about it.

We solved this problem by reducing the total amount of oxygen in the breathing gas mix so that the actual amount in each breath is about the equivalent of the twenty-one percent we breathe on the surface. We replaced the nitrogen with helium that does not become narcotic. It made us talk funny, but we didn't get narked.

The formula for the resulting oxygen percentage at any depth is

$$\%O_{2\,(at\ depth)} = \frac{.21}{\left(\dfrac{depth_{feet}}{33}\right) + 1}$$

Consequently, at 1,000 feet, oxygen in the gas mix is 0.7 percent. At 470 feet, oxygen in the gas mix is 1.4 percent.

Right now, your body is saturated with all the nitrogen it can hold. Your cells, bones, organs, everything, have absorbed all the nitrogen possible. If you dive to thirty-three feet (one atmosphere) and stay there long enough, you will become saturated at thirty-three feet. If you stay at a hundred feet, five-hundred feet, same thing—stay long enough, and you saturate; you can't take up any more nitrogen or helium if you are breathing a mixed gas.

If you are saturated to thirty-three feet, you can come right to the surface without suffering any consequences. But if you saturate at forty feet, you cannot come shallower than about seven feet without suffering the bends, when the dissolved nitrogen or helium in your body comes out of solution to form bubbles. The bends are very painful and can be fatal. A body can tolerate a one-atmosphere difference between its saturation level and the ambient pressure. That's the background information. In practice, we have discovered that there is increasing leeway as the saturation depth is deeper.

An Upward Excursion Limits Table in the Navy Diving Manual lists the excursion limits for any saturation depth.

Please post a review for
Operation Ice Breaker

Authors rely on reviews, so I really appreciate your posting a review on Amazon and Goodreads. To post a review, scan the pertinent QR code below and follow the prompts. You will be prompted to log onto the platform. If you are not a member, you will need to sign up. It's free. Amazon will require a minimum $50 purchase volume during the past twelve months. Goodreads has no requirement. Thank you very much for going through this effort!

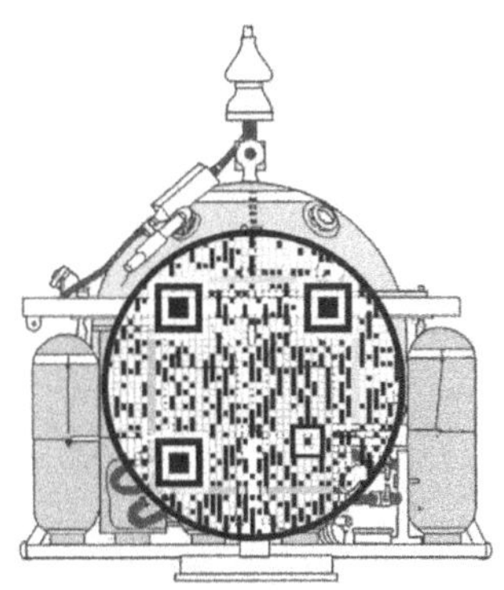

Scan to review on Amazon

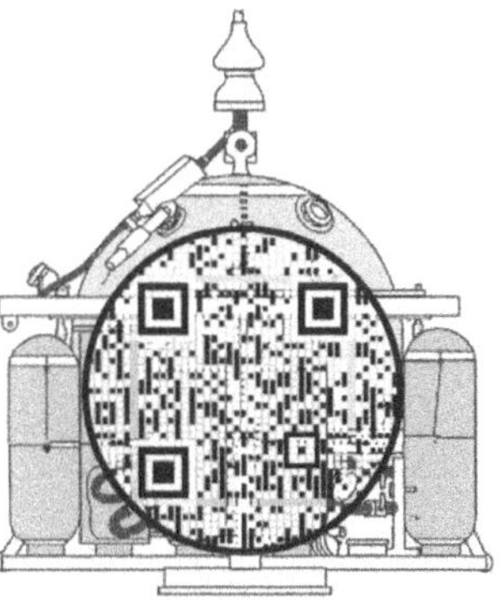

Scan to review on Goodreads

Excerpt from *Operation Arctic Sting*

by

Robert G. Williscroft

CHAPTER ONE

Kodiak, Alaska

KATE PERRY'S COTTAGE—KODIAK, ALASKA

I opened my eyes just enough to see Kate's golden hair spread across the pillow, her head resting on my chest, a sweet, contented smile on her lips. I felt overwhelmed by her presence. My heartbeat quickened. This cannot be happening, I told myself. Kate brushed her left arm across my stomach and pulled herself closer to my body. But it is…

The phone rang. I started at the sound, but Kate just snuggled closer and moaned softly. I picked up the Princess handset and brought it to my right ear, wincing a bit at the pain in my left shoulder. That was a wound I received from a Soviet dart underwater off Pt. Barrow shortly before we transited to Kodiak, and I still had my left arm in a sling. The bedroom window across the room was dark, but this was Kodiak in the winter. It would remain dark for several hours still. Outside was bitter cold; even the room air was more than chilly.

"Yeah, it's Mac."

"Mac, it's Jack…Petrikoff. Jack Petrikoff," his Russian accent heavy. "Wake up, Buddy!"

Kate stirred and sat up, rubbing her eyes, the sheet slipping from her pert nipples. "Wha…?" she started to ask, but I put a finger to her lips and shook my head.

"No time explain, Mac. You and Kate get out of there right now…I mean RIGHT NOW!"

"Jack…"

"RIGHT NOW, Buddy…house gonna blow…you and Kate gonna die!"

That got my attention.

Kate looked at me through sleepy eyes, her tongue moistening her lips. She reached under the covers, a coy smile creeping over her face.

"Mac, you hear me? RIGHT NOW!"

I grabbed Kate's wrist, interrupting her ministrations.

"Kate, we got a problem. Don't know what it is, but Jack says we need to get out of here now!"

Kate looked at me in shock.

"He means it…says we're in mortal danger."

Kate pulled the sheet up around her chin, her eyes like saucers. I grabbed her arms and pulled her to her feet.

"Get dressed warm, Girl…now!" I said sharply. "We're leaving ASAP!"

"We'll be out of here in a minute, Jack. We'll take Kate's Datsun. Shit…where do we go?"

Operation Arctic Sting 5

"Don't take her car. It's gonna blow too!"

I heard some yelling from his end and then, "Jesus, Fuck!" apparently not directed at me.

"One of my guys will meet you out back on Poplar. He take you to my boat. Grab what you can to stay warm."

I heard a shot.

"Go, go, GO!" Jack yelled, and the phone connection went dead.

SOVIET SLEEPER CELL—KODIAK, ALASKA

We rushed out Kate's back door to Poplar, I in hastily donned uniform with my peacoat tossed over my sling, and Kate in a long skirt, sweater, and fur-lined topcoat. We both wore unlaced mukluks on our feet. The bitter cold stung my nostrils.

One of Jack's crew was at the back gate in a beat-up pickup with the passenger door open.

"Get in quick!" the driver said. "We gotta get the hell outa here!"

Kate clambered into the cab, and I followed. The driver peeled away before I could shut the door. As we reached the curve where Poplar turned to end at Maple, a loud explosion ripped through the nighttime air, the low overcast reflecting a bright flash. I looked over my right shoulder in time to see pieces of Kate's cottage tumbling through the air, reflecting flickering flames from the twisted mess below.

As we turned right to approach Maple, a second explosion shattered the night air. In the reflected flames from what was left of Kate's cottage, I saw her Datsun roadster flip on its side, gasoline-fed fire engulfing it.

Our driver knew Kodiak well. We ripped down side streets, through alleys, across a couple of empty parking lots, and finally down East Rezanof Drive toward Alimaq and the bridge across the bay. At the end of the bridge, he turned hard right, and after about a minute, pulled into a parking lot overlooking St. Herman's Harbor.

"Hurry," he urged as we tumbled out of his rig and ran across a road to the outermost floating dock.

We ran down the walkway to an illuminated floating causeway that linked two brightly lit floating docks stretching into the harbor. The right one was filled with boat slips for smaller commercial boats. The left one, our destination, had six slips berthing larger vessels. Jack's boat, the St. Kate, was moored to the outer dockside away from the slips, starboard side to. A crew member stood on the brow, urging us forward. A shot rang out behind us. We ran faster. I could see that the lines were already cast off. Another shot ricocheted off St. Kate's steel side. The crew member pulled us across and then retrieved the brow.

Up in the pilothouse, Jack revved the engines and pulled away from the dock, pushing chunks of ice aside. As quickly as possible, he maneuvered past the breakwater and out to ice-pad-filled open water. Three more shots followed, one shattering a pilothouse window.

Our driver took us to the pilothouse where we met Jack standing at the helm—all five feet, eight inches of him. He gripped the large mahogany ten-spoked wheel with practiced ease. A Russian-style ushanka without a red star covered his salt and pepper hair, and his full beard was trimmed short. He reached out an arm to wrap around Kate's shoulders and kissed her cheeks. He shook my hand warmly and gave me a quick hug.

"That close call," he said. "I explain. My parents recruited in 1935 as members of Soviet sleeper cell in Kodiak. They die in 1950s. I never part of cell, but Soviets not agree. Last night, Soviets activate all ten members of cell with orders to kill Kate, blow up home and business, kill you, and destroy Teuthis. I call Coast Guard—they barricade front gate and notify Teuthis. I say I bring you and Kate by boat to Woman's Bay. Later, we talk more, but first, you call Teuthis. Say you and Kate safe. Say we be there in thirty minutes. Tie up behind Teuthis." He handed me a mike and set the hailing frequency on his overhead unit.

That was a lot to digest, but Jack was right. First, I had to call Teuthis.

"USS Teuthis, this is fishing vessel Saint Kate, over."

"Saint Kate, this is Teuthis. Switch to channel forty-three, over." Jack changed the channel.

"Teuthis, this is Saint Kate…"

I asked to speak directly with the captain. When he came on, I briefly told him that Kate and I were okay and that we would arrive in Woman's Bay shortly. I asked him to set up a meeting in his cabin for the four of us.

I glanced at my watch. It was 0530.

Forty minutes later, Kate and I were sitting on the red Naugahyde couch in the skipper's cabin, and Jack was in the easy chair. Commander (Cmdr.) Roken sat in his desk chair with his back to a fold-down desk. Jack had just finished explaining the background to his involvement.

"So, when I get activation order, I send my guy to Kate. I quickly call Kate, and Mac answers. I tell them to get out. A cell member tries to shoot me. I nail him, but cell blows up Kate's home, car, and shop. Mac and Kate escape to my boat, and we come to here." Jack's face was filled with worry. "Now, what to do?"

"Why do you think they are after Mac and Kate?" the skipper asked.

"After Kate, no reason," Jack said, "except she's with Mac." He sighed. "Sometimes the Soviets seek revenge for a serious wrong. Revenge often kill entire family, close friends, even pets. Must be something Mac did." He stopped talking and shut his eyes. "I introduce Mac and Kate when I take Mac to Kate's This & That?"

The skipper lifted his eyebrows.

"That the shop Kate set up after Josh killed. It was a beautiful little shop, but all gone now." He put his head in his hands, "My fault, all my fault."

Kate stood and put her arm around him. "Jack, I'm a big girl. I chose to be with Mac. You made that possible, and I love you for it."

The skipper's phone rang. He answered, and his face dropped. He looked at Kate. "I don't have time to explain, Kate. Please stay in my cabin, no matter what you hear or feel." Then he addressed Jack and me. "The Coast Guard Station has been attacked, and the front gate breached. The combatants are on their way here." He looked at Jack. "Jack, get your vessel out into Woman's Bay. Arm your crew to hold

off boarders from small craft." Then he turned to me. "Mac, get us underway from the wharf in the shortest time possible—two to three minutes. I'll be in Radio."

Jack sprinted topside to take care of St. Kate. I ran to Control and grabbed the 1MC mike.

"This is Lieutenant Commander McDowell. We have an all-hands emergency. We're getting underway and moving away from the wharf as rapidly as possible. Chief-of-the-Boat, take men topside and cast off all lines by the quickest means possible."

I turned to the Chief-of-the-Watch. "Sound the general alarm. Prepare to repel boarders. Get someone on the helm or take it yourself."

I still wore my peacoat, so I headed for the Bridge.

"Send two lookouts with rifles to the Bridge ASAP, and send up a sidearm for me," I told the Chief-of-the-Watch.

When I got to the Bridge, the COB had just cast off the final line, letting the lines fall into the frigid water. I grabbed the squawk box mike. "Port full on both thrusters," I ordered. St. Kate had already pulled away from the wharf and was standing by in the south end of Woman's Bay.

"Stop the rear thruster. Ahead slow, right full rudder."

We developed a good angle to the wharf and moved slowly toward the middle of Woman's Bay, cracking the thin ice layer. I brought the sub to a standstill about a hundred yards from the wharf, with the wharf broad on the port bow.

Just then, an old pickup screeched to a halt on the wharf, several men jumping out, waving rifles. One climbed onto the hood, rifle pointed toward us.

"Billy-Bob," I said to Seaman Yokum, who was with me on the Bridge, "how's your aim?"

"Never better, Sir."

"Okay, take out the guy standing on the pickup hood."

"Yes, Sir!" His rifle cracked, and the man pitched forward, a hole between his eyes.

A second vehicle drove up—an older model, dark-green something-or-other, driven by one guy. One of the three remaining men did something to the pickup load, and then all three sprinted to the waiting vehicle.

"Can you take out the driver, Billy-Bob?"

"Yes, Sir." His rifle cracked, and the driver slumped over.

The three runners pushed his body out of the car and drove away in a hurry.

About five seconds later, the entire wharf erupted in flames as the pickup load exploded. The percussion hit the sub's sail and rocked the boat slightly but otherwise caused no harm. I examined the concrete wharf through my binocs. I saw a large, blackened area and pickup pieces scattered across the wharf but no significant damage otherwise.

"Radio," I called on the squawk box, "immediately inform the Coast Guard that an older model dark-green sedan with three occupants just exploded a pickup on the cargo wharf. They are headed toward the front gate. Stop them at all costs!"

You have just been reading from Chapter One of Operation Arctic Sting. *the next book in Robert Williscroft's* Mac McDowell Missions. *Purchase this book from your favorite online bookseller.*

Other Books by this Author

Please visit RobertWilliscroft.com to discover other books by Robert Williscroft. Scan for more information.

Current Events:

The Chicken Little Agenda: Debunking "Experts'" Lies

Children's Books:

The Starman Jones Series:

Starman Jones: A Relativity Birthday Present

Starman Jones Goes to the Dogs (2026)

Biographies:

Mission Possible (by Gladys L. Williscroft)

Sŭbmarine-ër (by Jerry Pait; compiled by Robert G. Williscroft)

Short Stories:

Reality Hack

First Contact

The Cold Spot

The Virus

Novels:

Mac McDowell Missions

Operation Ivy Bells

Operation Ice Breaker

Operation Arctic Sting

Operation White Out

Operation Vela Redux

Operation Alfa Rogue (2026)

The Starchild Saga:

Slingshot

The Daedalus Files

The Starchild Compact

The Iapetus Federation

The Oort Chronicles:

Icicle: A Tensor Matrix

The Oort Federation: To the Stars

RAN: A Civilization in Hiding

KEID: A Lost Civilization

Beyond the Beyond (2025)

Connect with Robert G. Williscroft

I really appreciate you reading my book! Here are my social media coordinates:

Facebook: *https://www.facebook.com/robert.williscroft*
X/Twitter: *@RGWilliscroft*
Amazon author page: *https://buff.ly/2N5ZnlG*
Blog: *https://ThrawnRickle.com*
LinkedIn: *https://www.linkedin.com/in/argee/*
Book website: *https://RobertWilliscroft.com*
Newsletter: *https://eepurl.com/guZ5uv*

About the Author

Dr. Robert G. Williscroft is a retired submarine officer, deep-sea and saturation diver, scientist, author, and a lifelong adventurer. He spent 22 months underwater, a year in the equatorial Pacific, three years in the Arctic ice pack, and a year at the Geographic South Pole. He holds degrees in Marine Physics and Meteorology and a doctorate for developing a system to protect SCUBA divers in contaminated water. A prolific author of both non-fiction, Cold War thrillers, and hard science fiction, he lives in Centennial, Colorado.

Dr. Williscroft is a member of Colorado Author's League, Independent Association of Science Fiction & Fantasy Authors, Science Fiction Writers of America, Libertarian Futurist Society, Los Angeles Adventurers' Club, Mensa, Military Officers Association, U.S. Sub Vets, American Legion, and the NRA, and now spends most of his time writing his next book, speaking to various regional groups, and hanging out with the girl of his dreams, Jill, and her two cats.

Scan for more information

Glossary

1MC—Ship's announcing system.

ASR - Submarine Rescue Ship (Auxiliary Submarine Rescue)—Ships specially designed to rescue crews from downed submarines. They originally carried McCann Rescue Bells, later, two catamaran ASRs (the *USS Ortolan* and *USS Pigeon*) carried the DSRVs.

ASW—Anti-submarine Warfare

Baffles—The baffles is the area in the water directly behind a submarine or ship through which a hull-mounted sonar cannot hear. This blind spot is caused by the noise of the vessel's machinery, propulsion system, and propellers.

Basketball—A basketball-size, camera-carrying remotely operated vehicle (ROV) on a tether.

BCP—Ballast Control Panel; the console from which water is pumped into and out of a sub, and distributed fore and aft in the sub. The Chief of the Watch occupies this position, under the control of the Diving Officer or the OOD.

Belay that—Countermands an order just given.

Bird—A helicopter.

Boomer—Ballistic Missile Submarine.

BOQ—Bachelor Officers' Quarters; hotel-like quarters for bachelor officers.

Bottom—Bottom of the ocean, the seafloor. As a verb as in "to bottom," putting the submarine on the sea floor.

Bow—Front of a ship or sub

Bridge—The place on a ship from which it is driven. On a sub, it is the conning station at the top of the sail, (See Conn.)

Brow—Gangway onto a vessel from the pier or another vessel.

Bubblehead—Submariner

Can—Slang term for the fake DSRV (Deep Submergence Rescue Vehicle) that was really the saturation DDC on the stern of *Halibut*.

Capstan—A revolving cylinder with a vertical axis used for hauling in a rope or cable.

Captain—The officer in command of the ship or sub. He is an absolute dictator, subject only to the Uniform Code of Military Justice, and the orders of his superiors in the chain-of-command.

Chopper—Helicopter.

Clear the baffles—A submarine tracking another submarine can take advantage of its quarry's baffles to follow at a close distance without being detected. Periodically, a submarine will perform a maneuver called clearing the baffles, in which the boat will turn left or right far enough to listen with the sonar for a few minutes in the area that was previously blocked by the baffles.

Cleat—A T-shaped piece of metal or wood, esp. on a boat or ship, to which ropes are attached.

COB—Chief of the Boat; the senior enlisted man on a submarine.

Column—(water column) All the water above and below.

Come-home bottle—A small gas bottle that gets a diver back to the PTC/DDC in an emergency.

COMSUBPAC—Commander, Submarine Force Pacific; the commander of all submarine forces in the Pacific.

Conn—The location from which the sub is controlled by the OOD (Officer of the Deck)—also called Control. The Conning Officer (Conn), the watch position for the person who controls the sub's direction, speed, and depth. The OOD usually has both the Deck and Conn, but can pass off the Conn to another qualified officer. Sometimes the Captain will assume the Deck, leaving the Conn with the officer watchstander.

COW—Chief of the Watch; the enlisted watchstander (usually a Chief) who sits at the BCP and controls the ship's load of ballast water and its distribution throughout the submarine.

DDC—Deck Decompression Chamber; a pressure chamber on a ship's deck or just below the deck that contains a side lock for entrance and egress, a top lock to mate with the PTC, a small lock for passing in food or medical supplies, emergency equipment, and depending on how it is being used, bunks, lavatory facilities, etc.

Deck—The watch position of OOD (Officer of the Deck); the person in charge of the sub when the Captain is not in the Control Room, or has not assumed the Deck while in the Control Room.

Dive Locker—A place where divers congregate and stow their gear.

Dive Manifold Complex—A console with gauges, valves and indicators from where a saturation dive is controlled.

Diving Officer—The officer or specially qualified Chief controlling the submarine depth. Works directly under the OOD. The COW works directly for the Diving Officer.

DIW—dead in the water; a ship that is not moving through the water.

Dolphins—The insignia worn by qualified submariners, silver for enlisted and gold for officers. It represents about a year of hard study to gain complete, detailed knowledge of the submarine.

Dry dock—A narrow basin or vessel that can be flooded to allow a ship to be floated in, then drained to allow that load to come to rest on a dry platform. Dry docks are used for the construction, maintenance, and repair of ships, boats, and other watercraft.

DSRV—Deep Submergence Rescue Vehicle; a specially designed minisub for rescuing crews from downed submarines. The DSRVs replaced the McCann Bells, and now, both DSRVs have been decommissioned. They have been replaced by the Submarine Rescue Diving and Recompression System.

Executive Officer (XO)—Second in command of a ship or sub. Responsible for ship's administration and personnel.

Fast-attack—See "Nuke fast-attack."

Fast cruise—A one to two day period alongside the pier where all sub's systems are checked out just prior to deployment.

Fish—A towed, high resolution, sidescan sonar device that produces detailed images of the sea floor.

Fish—A torpedo.

Hawser—Heavy line used to moor subs and other vessels.

Helm—Ship's wheel and steering mechanisms. The person manning the helm.

Humboldt Squid—A large (5ft to 20+ft) squid found in the central Pacific and along the Southwest coast of North America.

LOFAR—Low Frequency Analysis and Recording

Maneuvering Room—That part of a sub where the engines are directly controlled.

Maneuvering Watch—The special set of watch assignments for a sub or ship that is getting underway.

Mark 2 Mod 0 Deep Diving System—The original second version of the Deep Diving Saturation System.

McCann Rescue Bell—An old-fashioned type of submarine rescue system deployed from old ASRs; a bell-type of chamber that must be lowered directly to the sub's rescue hatch.

Messenger line—A light line, often with a monkey fist at one end, used to haul or support a larger cable.

Monkey fist—A monkey fist (or monkey paw) is a type of knot, so named because it looks somewhat like a small bunched fist/paw. It is tied at the end of a rope to serve as a weight, making it easier to throw, and also as an ornamental knot.

Nav—Depending on context, the ship's/sub's Navigator; or the navigation stand—typically near the Conn.

Nuke fast-attack—A nuclear fast-attack submarine; a hunter-killer submarine.

OIC—Officer-in-Charge; the Officer-in-Charge of a unit or operation. A lesser command responsibility than a Commanding Officer.

OOD—Officer of the Deck; the individual in charge of the ship or submarine at any given moment. The OOD is responsible only to the Captain.

Operation Ivy Bells—A Top Secret Cold War plan to retrieve Soviet missile parts and tap into their underwater communication cables.

Ops—The Operations Officer

Port—Left.

PTC—Personnel Transfer Capsule; a spherical bell that mates to the shipboard DDC and can transfer a maximum of four divers to the underwater working site.

PUC—Presidential Unit Citation; a presidential award given to a ship or unit for exceptional performance (very rare).

ROV—Remotely Operated Vehicle, an unmanned underwater vehicle that is remotely piloted either by wire or untethered, using sound.

Secure—Stop or finish a process, such as "Secure from Maneuvering Watch," or when used as a verb, to make something safe, as in "secure the lines in the locker."

Secure the hover—Stop hover operations.

Secure the sidescan—Shut down the sidescan sonar.

Sidescan sonar—A towed-fish sonar that looks to both sides to produce a high-definition of the ocean bottom.

Sonar Shack—That part of a sub or surface ship that houses the sonar display equipment, where the Sonar Techs stand their watches. Usually close to the Bridge/Conn

SOSUS—Sound Surveillance System; a chain of underwater listening posts located around the world in places such as the Atlantic Ocean near Greenland, Iceland and the United Kingdom—the GIUK gap, and at various locations in the Pacific Ocean. The system was designed to track Soviet submarines.

Sound-powered phone—A shipboard communication system powered only by the sound of the speaker's voice.

SPCC—Strength-Power-Communications Cable; the umbilical that supports the PTC and supplies power and communications.

Starboard—Right.

Stern—Back of a ship or sub

SUBDEVGRUONE—Submarine Development Group One; the Navy command in charge of Operation Ivy Bells, where Mac had trained as a saturation diver.

T-bar—A piece of metal that has a T-shape in cross-section. Used as a strength member.

TOG—Test Operations Group; a code name for the team that operated from the *Halibut* and *Seawolf*.

Topside—The outside deck of a submarine. Can also refer to the watch station at the top of the sail when a sub is underway.

Variable depth sonar—A shipboard sonar system on a telescoping shaft that can lower the sonar sensors to variable depths to get under shallow layers.

WRT—Water Round Torpedo Tank; a water tank used to flood a torpedo tube to allow a torpedo to swim out of the torpedo tube instead of being shot out with a burst of pressurized air.

XO—Executive Officer (See Executive Officer).

www.ingramcontent.com/pod-product-compliance
Lightning Source LLC
Chambersburg PA
CBHW041751310726
48978CB00011BB/390